EMERGENCE

By Tyler Brand

DEDICATION & INSPIRATION

I dedicate this novel to my wife, my two boys and a SAR tech named Rob.

St. John's airport was known for long waits between snow storms. I sat in the loading gate area across from a tall fit man who was trying to make the most out of a short visit with his young son. He was a search and rescue technician stationed in Gander, Newfoundland. We sat on the plane together as he flew his little boy back across the country to Victoria where he lived with his mother. So many miles and so many hours on the plane for a few days with his son. Rob and I —we both worked in SAR—agreed that the death defying search and rescue stuff was far easier than navigating the challenges of being a great dad. A while after that trip I had a chance to read a Canadian forces news article where Rob had been lowered out of a cormorant helicopter into the freezing north Atlantic ocean, where he rescued a stricken crew member of a container ship. Why would Rob, or any of us, risk our lives like that?

So that others may live

CONTENTS

"It is not the strongest of the species that survives, nor the most intelligent that survives. It is the one that is the most adaptable to change."—Charles Darwin

ISBN: 1503137783
ISBN 13: 978-1503137783
Library of Congress Control Number: 2014920086
LCCN Imprint Name: Victoria, BC

1 Visiting Hours

George Dummigan's life went from bleak to horrible with the squeak of a hinge. The Bellevue mental health facility, built in the 1950s, was worse than any prison. The redbrick towers and stained-glass windows hid the cruelty of the place. George was locked in the basement. His was a musty subterranean restraint cell; here he suffered an unspeakable torture. His screams were soon to echo through the halls again.

Most patients who suffer from dermatillomania pica, an uncontrollable urge to claw and pick at oneself, respond to medication. Unfortunately, George was not responding to any treatment. The nurses had given George a nickname, "Houdini," because for the past three nights, he had mysteriously escaped from his restraints. Each morning he was found loose in his room, self-mutilated. George's recent dramatic episodes intrigued his psychiatrist, Dr. Baron. Who was preparing a case study on George. These attacks were extreme, sporadic, and always un-witnessed. The severity of George's self mutilation and subsequent tissue damage was rare; so rare, in fact, that three research assistants had yet to find another case like it in the data banks of bizarre psychiatric phenomena, hence the research paper.

The nurse wagged her finger at George, who was amazed at her unyielding triteness. She was unsympathetic to his pain; his last injury had involved ripping out his entire radial nerve, tendon, and the lateral fascia of his left forearm. The nurse had determined that four tissue strips were missing from the wound. George stood accused of eating his own flesh.

"You're a bad little camper," the nurse said to him yesterday as he lay, blood-soaked, in the corner. His wounds didn't even have a chance to start healing before the dark would set in again.

The nurse patted George's forehead after taping the leather buckles on his wrists. The tape constricted the blood flow to his fingers; he could feel tingling.

"Now, Mr. Houdini, we won't be up to our regular trickery tonight, will we?"

"Yeah, only truly naughty boys rip out their own muscles and eat their own body parts." George's sarcasm was desperate; there was no preventing his evening visit. The last morsels of organized thought will have evaporated from his consciousness by morning.

The hospital was scheduled to be demolished, and its sixty-two patients transferred to outpatient care homes. The main building was an impressive brick structure backed onto Seymour Mountain in Burnaby, a wooded suburb of Vancouver. The many acres around the building sat landscaped to perfection by the local blue-haired gardening society. Oak trees lined the long cobbled driveway that wound from Forty-Second Avenue up to the broad granite steps. The grounds behind the building were protected from the wild rainforest by a wall where mossy cliffs marked the beginning of the mountain. Above the brick compound wall, tall red cedars reached over with long green branches, as if to grab at the sodium courtyard lights.

Near the top of George's subterranean room were the ground-level windows that cast moonlight down onto the iron trusses. George's eye kept darting up to the window at the end of the middle truss. The lights flickered through the boughs of the trees casting shadows through the dirty glass. Every hint of movement at the window would cause him to gasp; the straps constricted his chest. He begged for a few more moments of twilight before the darkness set in.

Caracin's spines brushed the wrought-iron spikes cemented into the wall top. He dropped onto the shed roof with spiderlike stealth and stopped to scan the manicured lawns and shrubs for movement. This was a shorter route onto the property. He caressed his teeth with his black tongue. He was anticipating the taste of skin and muscle; maybe he would treat himself to a fresh tongue or a juicy eyeball tonight. Then his attention was caught by the rotating security camera. It whirred and then stopped. The reflection of the lens and the little flashing red light told him that he had been spotted. He should have stuck to his old route.

Miles sat in the guard shack staring at the screen. The new security system had been only half complete when the Liberal government announced the massive cuts to the health-care system. Miles was the only guard who had figured out the camera controls. His lip quivered when the black shadow on the shed became a figure. At first, it looked like the shadow of a tree branch in the sodium light, but then it stood up and stretched.

Miles squeezed the trigger on the radio mike. "Len, there's some guy on the roof of the boat shed, behind the video camera but in front of the light."

The radio crackled as the golf cart screeched to a halt. Len's eighty-year-old frame was not up for much excitement these days. He was patrolling the far side of the grounds and hated Miles's constant jabbering on the radio.

He lifted the radio and yelled into the mike. "Miles, what the fuck are you on about?"

"Len, there is a guy standing on the boat shed roof."

"What?"

Miles sighed. "I'll go check it out, but I'm not kidding. I think there is someone up there."

Miles exited the guard shack and lumbered along the rock path towards the boathouse. He reached down to check that his pepper spray and his telescopic asp were accessible. He wheezed with every step. *Stupid asthma*, he thought. The part of the cedar-shake roof illuminated by the floodlight was empty. Miles pulled out his aluminium flashlight and panned it across the shadowed portion of the roof. The light revealed the peak of the roof and an odd shadow with a spiky outline. The shadow had no visible source. Miles held his beam on the area as he walked closer to the eaves. He could see that the silver-grey shingles extended into an area with different textures. It was as if someone had spray-painted a giant porcupine with roof-shingle camouflage. Miles moved sideways and put his beam across this strange lump. Two large white eyes flashed open in the middle of the beam. A luminescent green reflected back from the pupils.

The primitive gaze peeled Miles's lips back over his teeth. He squawked like a startled goose and backed up as the hunched creature uncurled on the roof.

Caracin's spiny coat flashed colours for a moment and then turned to black. This chubby little guard was not on the evening's menu, but he was willing to try an appetizer. Miles turned and ran, sprinting down the path. His wheezing increased into high-pitched whistles as he lumbered towards the guard shack; his utility belt jingled. He felt movement ahead of him, then to his right. He stopped and turned to face the figure that crouched between two tall Japanese shrubs. He jerked his arm up to grab his asp, but Caracin was upon him before his fingers reached its handle.

Sweat stung George's eyes as he watched the shadows at the peak of the ceiling. *Not long now*, he thought. He tried to hold his breath until he passed out, and then he tried to tense his chest and neck muscles hard enough to blow a blood vessel in his brain. To his despair, his blood vessels held fast. George was still waiting for the squeak. The little voices that used to babble into his thoughts were silent. That strong notion that someone was listening to him through the TV and his computer screen had long ceased. No one was listening, and no one cared about his suffering. Miraculously, the adrenaline involved in his impending death had offered him a cure from his schizophrenia. George would gladly return to his delusional state. At least when he was feeling ill, there was an ongoing debate in his mind concerning what was real and what was delusion. Now there was no debate. His eyes darted at the shadow. The long darkness at the window frame made George cry out, his shoulders bobbing with the shallow breathing.

"No, no…no more, please go away." He whimpered.

The hinge squeak was real, and the darkened window framed a visitor that was there for him. The window creaked again as it swung up and clicked. A black arm reached in and grasped the truss. Caracin slid in and stretched across the beam. He popped his head down to gaze into George's dilated pupils. Caracin's round black face and bulging white eyes made George's breathing increase with his heart rate; his chest pushed against the restraints in heaves. Caracin smiled at George, revealing a wide row of jagged white incisors. But George did not register it as a smile.

EMERGENCE

Caracin was disappointed at the inconvenience of the guard, whose carcass had to be dressed and hung before he could visit his favourite friend. Caracin adored George; it was the adoration that a cat has for a bird trapped in its claws. Hanging upside down from the truss directly above, he stretched out his claws to slice the tape bindings. George grunted as he twisted his head side to side.

"No, no, please!"

Holding George's forehead down, Caracin paused a few inches from George's mouth. Tiny pupils darted up and down as he examined his prey's facial features. He pulled George's lower lip down and out. He extended his rough tongue into George's mouth. George tried to turn his head away. Caracin stretched George's tongue out until he could bite into it. As his flesh tore, George let out a guttural hiss followed by a howl.

This ward had no duty nurse, and the orderly at the top of the stairway was listening to his headphones. The hydrocephalic boy in the next room could hear the screaming but took no notice. Caracin gazed into the human's eyes as they rolled into insanity. He undid the buckles; he might as well let his pet run around for a while.

The next morning, the nurse stopped crunching her corn nuts upon entering the room. George was free from his restraints again. She followed the drag marks over to the corner where he lay prone on the floor, covered in blood and barely conscious. Gelatinous clotted clumps of blood shivered across gaping holes in his cheeks. A large pool of blood had drained and then dried from the hole where his scrotum used to be.

"There you are. How did you get loose? You're going to have to stop this, Mr. Dummigan; you're starting to really hurt yourself."

5

2 Rotten

Vancouver is dark green and wet. Pacific weather systems roll in from mid-ocean and stop at the foot of the coastal mountain range, bringing rainstorms that hang over the city like a porch roof. Occasionally the heavy systems dump enough moisture to rise over the forested mountains, leaving blue sky to shine sunlight into the modern glass downtown. The north shore lies on these slopes, and many backyards open up straight into the rugged British Columbian coastal rainforest. Douglas fir, Sitka spruce, and red cedar trees rise, some more than two hundred feet, above an emerald shag carpet of salal and fern. Only a few miles from the shopping centres and museums stand the lions, two huge pillars of black jagged continental shelf that gaze over the city from more than a mile in the air. If the lions had eyes, then their gaze would surely fall through the wilderness, landing on the city. As the city pushes into the forest, the forest pushes back.

The lights from the lecture hall at the University of British Columbia were dimmed. "When two competing species are both subjected to extreme environmental pressure, a few things can happen." The speaker looked up to the projection screen and pointed to the satellite photo of a forested area in Oregon. "Ten years ago, *Mycelium Omistithicus* was the dominant species in this area, then logging and warmer temperatures changed the rules. *Omistithicus* did not respond well to the pressure, but its distant cousin *ZygoSporus* did. This fungus responded both on a behavioural level—if you can call it that—and subsequently a genetic level. Now this entire forest floor is coated with one organism, one massive fungus, and it is organising itself to adapt further to the deforestation and changes in climate. This fungus is thriving and changing its properties as we speak. However, *Mycelium Omistithicus*, one of the other species of fungi listed here, did not adapt and is now gone. The species that can adapt in behaviour can precipitate a change on the genetic level, and therefore survive. This is a principle of both evolution and self-organizing biological systems."

Alan's snores caught the attention of the scientist sitting in the next row of seats. A louder snort reverberated through his skull and jarred him awake, or maybe it was the burning on the side of his head from Karen's emerald stare. His eyes darted to meet hers for a second; he sat up, licking the spittle from his lips. She was angry. The photo on the screen above the stage showed a petri dish full of green furry stuff. *Fungi Mycelium ZygoSporus,* the caption read. The audience was excited by some recent revelation on a slide that Alan had missed. He was an engineer, a decorated soldier, and having trouble getting excited about fungus.

Karen turned back to the screen. Her mouth was open a little and her eyes fixed on the screen; yes, this was exciting, whatever it was. The presenter clicked his remote and looked up again.

"Here is the viral load graph for H1N9 virus. Viral cultures were exposed to the mycelium for forty-eight hours; the VL number on the bottom is nine hundred eighty; that is a hundred times more effective at reducing the viral load as common anti-viral treatments such as Tormaflu. My little *Mycelium ZygoSporus* is only ten percent less effective at killing the virus than denaturing or cooking the virus with heat. Yes, this organism can kick some viral ass."

The speaker went on as Karen whispered to her colleague on the opposite side of Alan. The lights brightened, and many hands went up. Most of the questions were very specific to what this famous mycologist had done in his lab over the past three years.

"What's the big whoop about these mushrooms?" Alan asked as he and Karen walked down the aisle to the back of the theatre.

Karen snapped her head around. "Are you really asking such a ridiculous question? Yes, yes, of course you are." She was speaking to herself more than Alan as she exhaled and finished her answer. "These mushrooms apparently kill the world's deadliest viruses. The results are preliminary but important." She sped up towards the end of her sentence.

"Oh, well, that's a good thing, I guess. Why do you care when you're a geneticist?" They walked out of the lobby and down the steps. Karen didn't speak; she just shook her head as her heels made hollow clops on the pavement. Her strawberry-blond hair bounced in time with her long-legged stride; Alan almost had to jog beside her. He had noticed that she wasn't wearing her wedding ring that night, yet he didn't bring it up. He had never taken his off; even when he was lying wounded in the wreckage of a twisted truck in Afghanistan, he wouldn't let the medic take his ring off. "Did you want to go over to Zambris for a glass of red wine?"

Karen's eyes flashed up at him again and then down. Her face darkened. "Just take me home, Alan."

"OK," Alan replied. Both were silent for a while as Alan drove the car.

Karen looked up. It appeared as though she was carefully assembling her thoughts. Everything she did was careful and well planned. "I asked you to accompany me to this presentation because I thought that you could show some interest in me; some interest in what I do for a living, and you slept through it." She paused to let her words penetrate. "You obviously couldn't give two shits about me or my work." Karen's eyes were welling with tears.

"Sorry." Alan's mouth stayed open for a moment, but nothing worth saying was available.

"Just drop me off."

The drop off was brief and icy, as the door slammed Alan felt the sudden urge for a drink. Three hours later, something tugged his foot; it was a gentle, steady pull on the top of his boot. He opened his eyes, and the rusty fire escape above him slowly came into focus. The stench of rotten grease and urine from the downtown Vancouver alley made him blink as he coughed. He lifted his head and looked towards his feet to find a scrawny figure

trying to work his boots off. He snapped the steel toe straight up and caught the culprit under his chin. With a howl the skinny man recoiled and dropped to the black slippery cement.
He groaned. "What did you kick me for, dude?"
"Stealing my boots!" Alan got to his feet.
"I thought you were a dead guy. Sorry, man."
"I am not dead. I don't die easy."
Alan examined the boot thief as he swayed back and forth nervously; he was clad in a dark, stained button-up shirt and ratty jeans that were bunched up around his waist with a burlap belt. The soles of his shoes were flapping open when he lifted his feet. His socks were stained with dried blood. Alan sighed as he reached into his pocket. He pulled out two twenty-dollar bills and handed them to the alley dweller.
"Go buy some shoes."
It was a long walk home at three in the morning. He had just donated his cab fare to some homeless guy. It's difficult to sleep when the light fixture keeps spinning. After the last heave into the bucket on his lap, Alan stood up from the toilet. He winced at the smell, not the vomit, the shit. It didn't smell like shit; it smelt like rotting meat; it smelt as if he were sick. Maybe it was the flat little egg salad sandwich from the lobby table at the theatre last night. That sandwich could kill a virus. Maybe he was coming down with the flu, or was it the painkillers…the vodka? His face sagged in the mirror; his skin was grey and his eye sockets scalloped and sunken. He lay back down in his apartment and watched the ceiling spin, concentrating on slowing the rotation. He didn't feel especially different. This was most nights lately, yet his shit never smelt like that before.
Friday night turned to a rainy Saturday. The split-level two-bedroom condo was sparse; a few pictures of his para-rescue squadron days, hung on the walls above the furniture. Slanted stacks of books spanned every topic from biology to theoretical physics on the shelves. In the hall were boxes full of the material remains of his twenty-one-year marriage to Karen. His *Order of Distinguished Service* medal lay under his army boots and camping gear; dusty tread marks smudged its felt case. His bed was a metal-barred futon. A damp duck-down comforter twisted up in a roll around him. He watched the sunlight peek through the curtains and

then stretch across the ceiling. *How did I get myself here, in this shitty little apartment?*

The door swung open and Alan's fifteen-year-old son, Teddy; stood in the doorway. "Hey Dad...phew, this place reeks! Mom said you should buy me some new shoes today, and you can pay half of my kayaking trip from August." The tall, thin boy shuffled up the stairs to his awaiting video game console. "I'll be in my room."

While he brushed his teeth, Alan's mind cycled through his morning affirmations: *You need to get fit, stop drinking, spend time with Teddy, and do something nice for Karen. Alan, come on, you have the whole day—go for a run on the trail, and you will feel great.* Then the other voice spoke, sucking away his will and energy. *You'll never do it, Alan; even if you try, you'll give up halfway, you lazy shit.* These last three words repeated across the back of his mind like a ticker tape.

After finding a parking spot, Alan and Teddy approached the entrance of the mall. Alan stopped for a moment and yanked his cigarette case out of his jacket. Teddy shook his head and kept walking. After a couple of puffs, Alan threw the cigarette down on the pavement outside of the mall doors and walked inside towards the surf shop. He hated shopping malls—the noise, the unsecured spaces. His heart began to pound. His head snapped around at the clank of the children's train ride that rolled by him in the courtyard. Children giggled and waved, but Alan didn't see the fun. His neck was killing him. The racket in the mall made him feel as though his head was filling up with fluid. Teddy was trying on a hundred-dollar pair of overstuffed green runners with floppy red laces braided into decorative knots.

"You don't do up the laces, Dad," he explained. "You just let them flop; they're cool, hey?"

Alan stared. "What good are laces if you don't do them up?"

"Dad, don't be an ass for once in your life."

"What? Now I'm an ass for telling you the truth? Sure, go ahead and wear those shoes with those baggy pants that hang off your ass. When the wind blows, it will blow both your shoes and your pants off!" Alan regretted these words immediately.

Teddy threw down the shoes and walked out. "Forget it!"

Alan swallowed hard and walked after his son. He struggled to push his mind past his circular thoughts, the shallow ones that justified all of his brutish moves. Teddy was quickly losing interest in his father, and Alan could see why. He was a lazy, shitty father—that voice again.

"Hey, Teddy; I'm sorry, Bud. Let's go back and look at those shoes!"

Teddy flipped him a middle finger, glaring at him with an ancient teenage rage. Alan drew his breath; he couldn't find any words to defuse the standoff. He shook his head, muttering to himself, "The damned mall."

Monday morning was a school day but Teddy had a special assignment. Karen swung the car around and stopped in front of Alan's condo. Teddy marched down the stairs and opened the door.

"Where is he?" She asked

"Off being an ass somewhere; I don't know." Teddy opened the back door and threw his packsack on the back seat.

"Did you bring the stuffies?" Karen asked as she pulled away from the curb. Teddy rolled his eyes.

" I sent Mrs. Keller a reminder e-mail that you were doing this presentation today."

"You don't have to do that Mom; she knows."

"I know, I am just being your Mom. Do you have any last minute questions about your presentation?"

"Yeah what does reverse transcriptase do again?"

"It allows a retrovirus –aka *retroviridea*- to encode its RNA sequence into DNA and then that virus' DNA gets clipped into the cell's genome." Karen moved her fingers in a scissor motion.

"Ok that's what I thought. Herpes and HIV are retroviruses right?" Teddy reviewed his speaking notes while his mom drove him to the recreation centre.

"Yes they are." Karen explained further. "The virus brings its own special brand of reverse transcriptase into the cell so it can make the DNA copy and slip it into the genome. The DNA strand can lay dormant for years until one-day boom! A virus is made from the code, and the cell is infected again."

"That's why HIV positive patients can live for years before they get AIDS." Teddy added

"Yes and now the most effective treatments all block one key enzyme, and can you guess what that enzyme is?"

"Reverse transcriptase?"

"Correct, here's your bag and a bottle of water. Just take little sips and it will keep your voice from cracking." Karen flipped her fingers through his curly hair sorting the curls to one side or another. "You've got my eyes and your Dad's broad shoulders." Karen explored her son's sharp features.

"Mom, you are not allowed to watch, because I might say something wrong." Teddy opened the door and put one leg out.

"No deal, I am coming in but I will stand at the very back."

"Mom, do you have to?"

"Yes, I have to. I am so proud of you!" She squeezed his knee as he got up and out of the car. She was secretly glad that Alan had forgotten about Teddy's presentation–his loss.

The community centre library had tall windows that showered the big room with twinkling sunlight filtered by branches of leaves. Teddy stood in front of the excited children; the class was a grade one and two split and the audience of six and seven-year -olds filled the hall with excited chatter.

The young teacher put her hand in the air for a moment and then projected her voice.

"Class, class, be quiet please. I would like to introduce Mr. Theodore Wickey who is going to speak to us about viruses." Teddy stepped forward,

"Who knows what a virus is?" Teddy's breaking teenage voice silenced the voices; all of eyes in the room were transfixed on his hands. He was holding a bright yellow stuffed toy that had big eyes and a body shaped roughly like a star.

An excited little boy waved his hand and Teddy pointed to him "It turns you into a Zombie!"

Karen was watching from the foyer and chuckled at the answer.

"Well not exactly. How big do you think a virus is?"

"Small as a dot!" Yelled a little girl in a blue sweater.

Teddy continued "Imagine that I could shrink down the whole city of Vancouver to fit inside your big toe. This whole big building would be about the size of one of your cells. This little guy I have here would be his real size if this building was just one cell."

"Whoa, that's really small" One of the boys in the front row added.

Teddy continued, "Who knows where viruses come from?"

One little girl held hand up sheepishly. Teddy pointed to her

"My mom says they come from boys."

Teddy laughed with the crowd "Well, they don't originate from boys. We get them from animals like birds or farm animals." One little boy held his hand up and then blurted out

"Aids came from Monkeys!"

Teddy replied," Yes when we cut down trees and ruin animal habitat then sometimes the animals are forced to live close to us in the cities or towns. This is when these wild animals can transfer viruses to us. Sometimes a virus that gives a simple cold to a monkey could give us a deadly disease." Teddy walked out into the groups of kids all cross-legged on the carpet. "Who has had a cold sore on their lip before?" The girl with the blue sweater put up her hand and Teddy walked up and handed her the yellow stuffy. "This guy is called *Herpes simplex* number two, and he causes cold sores." The little girl hugged the stuffy and smiled as some of the other children chuckled. Teddy furled his brow and looked at the little girl. "Hey are you a Zombie?"

She giggled "Noooo I'm not a Zombie, silly"

Teddy smiled and wiped his hand across his brow "Sheeww! I'm glad you're not a Zombie, because that boy told me that viruses turn you into Zombies. Do you guys think that is true?"

"Noooooo!" The answer reverberated across the great hall.

He pointed to the yellow stuffy. "This little guy, Herpes Simplex, is a retrovirus, and he is a very sneaky little virus. If this building were one of your nerve cells, in your toe, this guy would sneak into through one of the vents in the ceiling. He would come right down here to the library, and pull out a secret key." Teddy reached into his pack and pulled out a plastic gold key. "The key is called reverse transcriptase, and it allows the little virus to make a secret code hidden in the cell's library. That secret code would be hidden in one of these books. No one knows which book; until one day someone opens the book and guess what happens?"

"The virus pops out!" The little girl shouted and threw the yellow virus in the air and all the children laughed and cheered.

"That's right and then you will get a sore on your lip!" Teddy pulled out a brown filo virus that looked like a snake and the children leapt up to grab it. He then explained how viruses made copies of themselves using the cells own mechanisms. After twenty minutes the children became restless. Teddy reached into his bag again and pulled out glittery purple ring that resembled a jelly doughnut. This is the corona virus, isn't it pretty? "Who wants to catch a cold?" He bellowed.

A tiny little girl in a purple dress leapt to her feet waving franticly. Teddy threw the purple virus up into the air and the little girl snatched it before any competitors could get close. She threw back her head and made a coughing and gagging motion. Then she flopped down to the carpet and stuck out her tongue in a dramatic death throw.

"It's ok its just a common cold, it can't kill you." Teddy announced

"You said they could change and become meaner or nicer viruses." She spoke with her eyes closed as she lay on the floor."

"Yes that is true." Teddy answered.

"Well this one turned mean, and now, I am dead."

3 Shrinking Your Brain

Alan sat across the desk from Dr. Callum, the Department of National Defence psychologist; his long-term disability benefits entitled him to a few sessions per month.

"Dirt roads?"

"Yes, and fruit stands," Alan answered the question.

"Fruit stands—why fruit stands?"

"I don't know, but they terrify me. When I see one, I drop to my knees."

"Your report says that the roadside bomb went off while you were passing through a street market in Khowst. Was there a fruit stand there?"

"I don't remember; maybe…There are lots of fruit stands in Afghanistan."

"Mr. Wickey, you are suffering from post-traumatic stress disorder, PTSD, along with some residual effects from your traumatic brain injury. These feelings of anxiety and the exaggerated startle response are all normal symptoms."

"Normal—there's that word again." Alan replied

The tall, thin therapist stood up. He was an army major and had done some time in Bosnia. He knew exactly what Alan meant. He had watched many good soldiers slide downhill with drugs and alcohol due to these types of injuries.

"That was the shrink blah blah blah—here's what I really want to tell you." Major Callum looked directly at Alan. "It's a choice that you have to make every day. You can choose to use your injuries as an excuse to do shitty things or as a motivation to do great things." The psychologist got up and walked across the office and leaned against the desk. "You are not an average guy. I am sure you play a legendary junkie and a champion drunk just as well as you did a world-class soldier. What's important is that with every new day, you have a chance to start afresh."

Alan nodded; he wasn't listening. His head was chattering with jumbled garbage. "Yeah, thanks, Doc. I just wish I had an hour a day when I didn't feel so foggy."

Dr. Callum looked at Alan's face for a while. Alan's eyes searched the room for something to stare at other than the doctor. Trying to avoid the awkward silence, he asked, "Can I go?"

Callum looked down for a moment, trying to conceal his impatience. "You can't get there from here."

"What?" Alan's eyes finally met the doctor's.

"Where you are at right now—denial, compensation, and avoidance—these are your tools. And with those tools you can't get there from here. It will only get worse, Alan."

"Get where? Where am I getting to?"

"You want to get to a peaceful place…yes?"

"I'll get over it, Doc. I just need a clean run, and then I can put this shit behind me."

"You won't get a clean run."

"You're supposed to be encouraging me."

"You'll be dead if you carry on like this; believe me, I know about it. I've lost three patients and two good friends, one from Bosnia and the other from the damn Somalian thing. You're next, Alan."

"What kind of doctor are you?"

"How many times have you had your pistol in your mouth?" The doctor's voice sounded more like a Major.

Alan was quiet; his eyes flashed up for a second, and then cast down. He wasn't going to answer that question, but he sensed that Callum already knew the answer. "Ok, what then?"

"There is an experimental program, run by a friend of mine here in town. It uses QEEG; that's the thing with electrodes on your head. This therapy, along with computer simulation, may to help you get control of the PTSD."

"What the hell is that? Can you just explain to me why I can't just put this shit behind me?"

"How do I explain this? You can't put these events behind you because they stay with you forever." The doctor thought for a moment. "OK, just imagine your mind is an old freight ship that

16

steams up and down all of the little communities on the coast delivering packages and picking them up." Alan glared at him; he hated academic metaphors.

The doctor continued. "The events that happen during the day are wrapped up like little packages and put up on the memory shelves in the brain's cargo hold."

Alan winced. "OK."

"Certain things that happen to you are so traumatic and massive that your brain cannot package them and stow them away. These events just tumble around in the middle of the cargo bay, creating havoc. Your little brain slash ship cannot function until you stow these massive things away properly; nothing you do will work out."

"Doomed ship, eh? OK, how do I stow these nasty packages?" Alan sighed with impatience.

Dr. Callum read Alan's scepticism. "Look, maybe things have not gotten weird enough for you yet. Maybe you should come back when you are ready."

Alan paused and thought about it, then he shook his head. "Sorry...I, ah, think I'm willing to give this a try."

"This fellow, Dr. Axel Heath, will set you up. Patient spots on this program are limited, so don't fuck around. Take it, or just leave it. Axel likes to take the mild cases for his data set, but you're not a mild case. He may send you back anyway."

Two days later, Alan walked into the posh clinic in West Vancouver. The sign above the desk read *Hunt & Heath Mind Management Team*. The words were embossed in the gold leaf usually reserved for corporate lawyers. He sat beside some kids playing with the toy box. A tall man clad in military green relish fatigues walked out from the treatment room; he was a big chief warrant officer, and he had tears running down his cheeks. He hurried past Alan and out the door. Alan gulped. *What have I gotten myself into?*

Soon after, Alan was brought into to a teak and mahogany office and given a chai tea to sip while he waited. A short, stalky man in an awkward sweater vest came in and sat down across from Alan. "My name is Axel Heath, and I'm here to shrink your head."

Alan looked up at his outstretched hand and stood up to shake it. "I can hardly wait."

The doctor's grip was reluctant.

"We are using some new technologies, both in the neuro-feedback field and battlefield simulation."

"Video games?" Alan had read some articles about the use of simulation in battlefield training.

"Yes, sort of a game, only it's not going to feel like a game to you. If your son played it, then he would think it was a boring and cheap version of an Xbox game, but to you it will be a bit of a nightmare."

"What's the strategy here?" Alan asked.

"Well, we use the simulation to induce a stressor and trigger a traumatic event in your brain. Then we will identify the nature of it, or should I say that you will identify the nature of it. And then we teach you get a handle on those feelings of panic and what not."

"Package them up and stow them away in the cargo hold?"

"Ha, I see you got the 'little ship' analogy from Jason Callum."

"Yes; when do we start?"

"Walk this way."

Alan walked into the dimly lit lab, which contained a large leather chair. On the table was a round flight helmet hooked up to a harness of tiny coloured wires. On the outside of the helmet were a whole bunch of steel rods sticking out from the top. Each one had a wire on it. Alan baulked at the sight of the apparatus. "Holy shit, this is real sci-fi stuff, eh? Do you really want to put that thing on my head?"

The lab assistant laughed. "Yeah, it looks like we are going to suck your brains out, doesn't it? Let me explain it to you. The rods just push up into your hair and make connections to your scalp, then the visor plays a movie and sounds into your visual field and ears. The QEEG machine monitors what's going on in your brain and when it gets to be a little freaky for you, then we stop the show. This monitors your brain activity and when you start to calm yourself down, it rewards you with some peaceful music. The idea is that you practice calming yourself down with music; when the music plays, it means you are getting calmer, and if it stops, then you are not getting calmer. After a few sessions, you teach yourself how to keep your panic levels under control.

Soon it will not be long until you get the calming music playing steady." The lab assistant motioned for Alan to sit down in the chair. He looked through the thick medical questionnaire. "OK, Mr. Wickey, from your file you have quite a few trigger events: IED scenario, mountain combat, and some open ocean stuff. We only have media for city combat and the IED, so you can pick."

Alan was definitely nervous; this helmet looked like something from a horror movie. "I can pick, can I? Have you got anything from the aperitif menu, because the dinner menu sucks."

Dr. Heath began to type into the computer. The helmet slid easily down over Alan's eyes. The lab assistant pushed in the rods one by one; Alan felt a gel goo squirt out of each rod into his hair. It made a squishing sound. The visor dropped, and a bunch of red lights surrounded his visual field. After a couple of computer clicks, the red lights appeared as if they were alternating near and far. "Cool 3-D," Alan mumbled as the chair started to rumble. "Whoa there."

"OK, Alan, we need a baseline, so we're going to drive you through the streets of Paris, and hopefully that will not trigger a response." Alan was now completely immersed in a 3-D movie from the point of view of a passenger in a car. The car was driving through Paris; Alan turned his head and could see the pretty girls on the sidewalk. One of them waved at him, so he raised his hand to wave back. He could see the girl waving as his head turned to the side.

After about twenty minutes, the doctor announced, "Alright, we have a good baseline, now we are going to Afghanistan. This is an area just outside of Baraki. You might recognize it." The red lights flashed, and now he was in a Humvee barrelling down the dusty road at night, the streetlamps and headlights flashing by as the vehicle rattled. He looked out at the deserted sidewalks and the heaps of cans and garbage piled along the side of the road. The sun was slowly rising, and golden light reflected off the dust on the bulletproof glass. Yes, this was Baraki all right; he knew this drive well. He usually didn't travel in a Hummer, but fair enough it was realistic. He looked over at the driver and then back to the street. Instinctually he started his spotting routine, calling out the points of note on the road ahead into the boom mike on his helmet. The virtual gunner's voice started to chime in with his calls, and the team was now rolling along in transit-ops mode. Alan's brain centres became active with the scenario. Alan was now immersed and engaged.

The two scientists studied his brain activity closely. Dr. Heath started to point to the red and yellow regions on the screen. "He's in for sure. Look at those numbers—his temporal lobe is lighting up, and here his frontal lobe is processing the visuals. He's got a classic coup–counter-coup signature in his frontal and occipital concurrence. That's the head injury, see that there'?" He pointed at a shimmering yellow zone at the back of Alan's brain.

The truck's gears rumbled down as the convoy slowed to let a group of cattle cross the road. Alan looked at the vending stands along the side of the road. One was a DVD video stand with a bunch of pants and jackets hanging from racks. The racks swayed in the wind, and Alan's heart leapt. "Video stand nine o'clock!" he barked into his coms.

The driver sped up, and the gunner replied, "Nine Clear!" The lab assistant was playing the gunner and replying to Alan's orders in the microphone.

Dr. Heath watched the brain activity levels. "He's triggering," He said softly as Alan's temporal and limbic systems lit up in yellow and red tones. "OK, shut it down."

"Eleven o'…fruit stand, fruit stand!" Alan screamed at the top of his lungs. The lab assistant paused in confusion. He looked at the video feed, but there was no fruit stand; in fact they were now moving through grass fields. He hit the pause button, and the video feed stopped.

"Fruit stand! Amundsen, fruit stand on your left! Amundsen, Amundsen!" Alan was howling at the top of his lungs. The fruit stand was empty; the small oranges were stacked high on the stand, but the chair was tipped over. Alan couldn't get Amundsen to stop; he kept going. The acid rose into his mouth as he clenched his jaw in anticipation. *Boom!* The whole vehicle spun into a wild, twisting corkscrew; the dust rolled into the cab as the grunting steel ground to halt. Amundsen was now draped on top of him, pressing down on his sternum. "I can't breathe!" Alan looked into Amundsen's eyes. The twenty-two-year-old corporal was gasping, trying to pull air into his lungs. Alan lurched and twisted as Amundsen slid off him. His body below his stomach was shredded into strings of meat. Amundsen stopped grunting after a moment and closed his eyes.

Alan looked down to his own legs. His ankles were shattered, and blood was rolling out of his vest. He shook his head. Axel Heath and his assistant pulled Alan's helmet off as he twisted and struggled. He was yelling, "Amundsen, I'm sorry, buddy; I am sorry!" Alan's eyes were darting back and forth rapidly; the colours on the monitor showing Alan's brain scans were bright red. He leapt up from the chair and dropped, then rolled onto his back, writhing.

The lab assistant held Alan down as Dr. Heath grabbed his chin and yelled into his face, "Alan, Alan, Alan!" Alan slowly came around and looked up at the two. He looked confused, whimpering. The two practitioners looked over Alan at each other, as if silently saying, "I don't know about this guy."

The next two nights were a torturous mix of daytime and night terrors. Alan was having trouble separating out the flashbacks and hallucinations from the normal day. He was thinking about the bombing at the firebase in the K Valley. The biggest fuck-up of his life—the day he killed two of his own men and won a medal for it.

4 The War of 1812

Six years earlier Alan had been posted in Kandahar. The canteen was truly Canadian: hockey jerseys signed by the great players hung from the walls, and flat-screen TVs showed the sports from all four sides. The floor crunched with peanut shells that soaked up two years of spilled beer. Yet the dust was Afghan, and the coloured tapestries behind the bar and the old mahogany wood pillars gave it away. This was not really Canada, but the Americans liked it just fine; there were real girls and real beer in this bar. None of that four percent alcohol piss-water here; nope, Kokanee and Canadian draft. This was real beer.

Captain Alan Wickey sat at the stool, sipping his vodka and coke, when one of the marines approached his corporal. The American private was drunk and looking for a fight. "What are you Canadian guys even here for? You seem to just piss around doing errands for the Hodgis."

Corporal Amundsen looked up. "Hey, why don't you sit down? You don't look well." Amundsen looked the tall man up and down as he swayed slightly.

"You fucking Canadians, what's your problem?" His words were slurred.

French Canadian Corporal François Dufour stepped in with his thick French accent, "Hey, you leave my guy alone; ee iz not hurting no one."

"You're a fucking French guy, where are you from? France?" The American turned to face Corporal Dufour.

"Yeah, sure…from France, whatever, eh. Where are you from, dah swamp?" The wiry little Frenchman looked back at his mates and made a questioning gesture.

"You know, the French never went into Iraq with us; they just sat and watched us fight, yeah French pussies!" François was starting to get angry now as Corporal Amundsen stood up to face the American. Alan waved over his sergeant and whispered into his ear. The Sergeant nodded and went through the back door. The American was being watched by half of his platoon when a US Army colonel walked in. He could see the troops were getting ready to square off. One of the big gunners in the American platoon spoke up: "Good thing these pussies aren't on the other side of the front lines, or we would kick their asses."

Amundsen spoke up: "Are you sure? I seem to recall that the last war we fought, the Canadians kicked your asses all the way down to Georgia."

"Fuck that, that's a damn lie! We kicked your limey asses out of our country!"

"No, no. I am talking about the war of 1812. We won it, and we were nice enough to give you your country back. And now look how you repay us." Amundsen grinned as he took a sip of beer.

The gunner spoke up again. "Bullshit! The US of A has won every war that we ever fought!"

"Let me see—you came in late in the First World War and finished weakly, you waited a whole two years to get into the Second World War, you stalemated the Korean War, lost the Vietnam War, and you got off the bus in the wrong country for this war. What were you guys doing in Iraq, anyway?"

The colonel approached Alan at his barstool. "Captain, do we really need this to get out of hand?"

Alan pulled out the stool beside him. "Evening, sir. I have a plan for these guys; not to worry."

The colonel looked Alan square in the eye for a moment, as if charging himself for a possible standoff. Alan's big, confident smile disarmed him, and he was exhausted, so he drew a deep breath and pulled up a stool beside Alan.

The silver-haired American raised his hand. "Carl Harris."

Alan grasped his hand and shook it firmly. "Alan Wickey, pleased to meet you, sir."

The Sergeant arrived with a box full of sports gear, sparring gloves and padded helmets. He projected his voice like only a sergeant could. "OK, gents, if you drink our Canadian beer, then you play by Canadian rules. Gloves and head gear on; all bets in the hat. Who's going first?'

The colonel cracked a broad smile and put his hand on Alan's shoulder. "I like your style, Captain Wickey." He stood up. "I have ten bucks on my gunner against the little French guy."

"I am in on that action." Wickey dropped a Canadian ten-dollar bill in the hat, and the whole room jumped up and made a circle. The hat filled up with bills, which Amundsen took up as the bet taker. François put on the gear and began to jump around the big, tall gunner. The gunner jabbed, and François ducked.

"Is dat all you got, Yankee boy?" He danced around and then spun a roundhouse kick that landed square in the American's jaw, who didn't seem fazed by the blow. François jabbed with his left into the big guy's ribs. Now the American swung with his right, and this punch landed squarely on the little man's jaw. François spun around, recoiling from the heavy punch. He shook his head for a moment and then got back into the fight.

"He's a tough little sucker, isn't he?" the colonel commented. He was truly enjoying the spectacle.

Alan chuckled. "Yes, you have to be tough when you're that annoying." Just as Alan finished his sentence, François landed a combination punch and kick that rang the gunner's bell. The American wiped away the dribbles of blood and started swinging. François was backing up while dodging the punches; he was making little grunts as he poked the big man in the stomach and ribs.

"What are they fighting about again?" the colonel asked.

"War of 1812," Alan replied wryly.

"Really. I mean, well, I guess that's as good a reason as any." The older man paused for a moment. "Yeah, I studied that war at West Point. The American books all say that we won it, but when you look at the history of the battles, it does seem a little sketchy on who actually came out ahead. I do recall that the Canadians and some Indians burnt down the White House." The colonel's thick Alabama accent carried across the noise of the fight.

"Yes, sorry about that. Your new one looks very nice, though; I like what you did with the curtains," Alan replied. He then signalled to the girl behind the bar, and she nodded. "Bartender, bring the colonel a Scotch to make up for burning down his house!"

At this comment the colonel broke into a thick laugh. "You guys crack me up." He turned his head. "Look at this little Frenchman." They looked over to see the gunner lifting the little man above his head while François punched down onto the top of his head. He was swearing in French as he was launched across the room, coming to rest on a table occupied by a group of nurses who were not at all amused when their drinks flew into the air.

Alan nodded at the sergeant, and he stepped in. The stalky Canadian walked up to the gunner and pulled up his hand. "I declare, the winner is the United States of America!"

"I protest this!" François hollered from under the table as he jumped to his feet. One of the ladies helped him up. His focus quickly shifted from the fight to the brunette, and all quieted down.

The next time Alan and Col. Harris spoke was over the radio.

"Foxtrot Oscar Bravo Monaco, this is Mako, SITREP on your FOB please." The radio crackled in Alan's headset. He was lying on his belly in the dirt, peering through the corrugated tin and dirt bag walls in a forward operating base in the Karengaal Valley.

Alan squeezed the trigger mike on his chest. "Mako, Monaco. FOB Gonzales hooch is taking fire from the Northwest grid U26.234 and V42.5. Seven to ten hostiles, light arms."

"U26.234 by V42.5, Mako checks that spot; are you requesting fire support?"

"Mako, Foxtrot Oscar Bravo, confirm; need fire support for U26.234 by V42.5."

"Fire support ordered, ETA one minute."

"Mako, one minute, roger." Alan pulled out his sighting scope and watched the dark patch of trees. He could see three Taliban clearly now. The ordinates whistled over the FOB, and the impact was impressive. The trees and the figures disappeared in the cloud. Alan waited until the dust cleared and surveyed the crater and debris around it.

"Mako, this FOB Monaco, confirmed four KIA, and all fire has ceased on Firebase Gonzales," Alan spoke into his radio.

"Monaco, this is Mako. We got that, congrats. Nice work." The colonel had been working with Alan on and off for a while and was impressed by his professionalism and his cheery disposition. He liked to play cards with Wickey and chat about history and trade the latest books they had read. The marines teased them by calling them the Oprah book club. Anything to pass the time in the valley of death. The marines had lost four men in the hillsides over the past two days. Alan's full squad was due to join them soon, and Alan dreaded this. His guys would be in extreme danger, and there was no guarantee that all of his boys would make it out alive. He was waiting for word about his friend Kelly, who was embedded with the US Navy DEVGRU, or SEAL Team Four. Kelly George was Alan's best friend. He knew that Kelly's company was overdue, and he had not heard any updates on the situation.

Alan worked his way across the dark and rocky valley. He was with two gunners and a medic as they moved up the rock face to the small firebase, home to a mix of a couple of his own men and American marines. The firebase had been under sniper attack during the afternoons for the last week, and Alan was going over to check on his guys, see how they were holding up. He was also to drop off some new night-vision goggles and cans of ammo. The climb up was steep, and their footing was precarious. The dust would coat the rocks, making the thin, brown film act almost like a lubricant. Alan slipped and slid down into the tall Yankee soldier behind him.

"Whoa there, Captain," the marine exclaimed as he blocked Alan's fall.

"Thanks."

They made it up to the hooch. It was a cold and dusty little medieval fortress. The walls were made of stacked bags of loose rock; the lower walls were made from wire cages filled with small boulders. The bunks were shaped out of loose dirt topped with plastic sheets. The little roof was made from two sheets of corrugated tin that was riddled with bullet holes.

The first Canadian greeted Alan with a handshake. "Hey Captain Wickey, welcome to the fart castle. Can I pour you a hot cup of Afghan dust roast? It's guaranteed to be twenty minutes fresh, or the cook will be shot."

Alan chuckled and shook hands with the dusty corpsman. "Kim, how are you doing?" He handed over the NVGs and some food while the tall American brought in the ammo case. "Hello gents, how's the war?" Alan asked the room in general.

"Well, the neighbours are loud and a little rude, but other than that, perfectly enjoyable." Kim smiled as he held up the cup of coffee for his friend. "We heard the spec ops team on the radio about twenty minutes ago. They're coming down the far side of the valley and will work along the ridge to us later tonight."

"Is that Kelly's JF squad?" Alan asked.

"Yeah, pretty sure it is; they have one prisoner, no casualties."

"That's good news. I will report that up to the colonel when I get back over. Which reminds me, I would love to stay up here in your little vacation spot, but I really have to get back to work."

Kim nodded and took Alan's cup. Alan and the gunner went back down the narrow trail for about a half mile. *Psst, psst.* A couple of bullets whizzed by Alan and the American, and they ducked down out of the way.

The radio crackled in Alan's earphone; it was the firebase. "Hey Cap, stay put for a moment while we take out this little bastard across the valley that's shooting at you." The marine in the lookout took careful aim and put four rounds across the valley into a pile of rocks.

"Looks like we distracted him."

Alan stood up, and the two started walking again. They made it back to the forward operating base without any further excitement.

5 Scope Ghosts

One week earlier and forty miles away, high in the Tarir Mountains, Kelly George sat in a small camp with eleven Navy SEALs and three other Canadian JTF2 members. Kelly was a Tsimshian native from the coastal mountains and one of the legendary Canadian Rangers. The Rangers are an elite force that patrols the wilds of the Canadian North, a mysterious group of highly trained soldiers from mixed aboriginal cultures across Canada. Their motto is Vigilance, "The Watchers," and the Rangers are without a doubt the best trackers in the world.

The team, led by the American Lieutenant Cyr, was a mixed-force strike team. The small group of fourteen men had made its way quietly up on the high mountain ridges and penetrated deep behind two Taliban strongholds. They were to establish a position behind a Taliban fort and hunt, capture, or kill one particular mullah. The men were exhausted from the thin air in the high mountains. They had covered only about seven miles that day: seven jagged, dusty miles.

"Those Taliban guys who shot at us today were assholes," Kit said in his thick Carolina accent. He swigged his water while squinting into the sun. The shadows were getting longer; the little gas cooker smoked away in the middle of the group.

Kelly spoke up. "Yeah, I haven't been shot at by any nice ones yet, but there's always tomorrow."

"Maybe the nice Taliban will see me and just decide not to shoot," Kit said.

"They might spot you guys, but they won't spot me," Kelly replied in his misty Indian voice.

"What are you talking about?" Kit protested.

Kelly smiled as the rest of the group leaned in to check out this potential bit of drama. "Well, white boy, I am invisible to scopes."

Kit was hooked in now. "Fuck you, Indian, what are you talking about?"

The Canadian Special Forces soldier leaned in. "He's right—he's a Canadian Ranger Indian; they are completely invisible to scopes, both normal and NVGs."

Kelly picked up the NVG scope, discreetly spinning down the gain with his pinky finger. He tossed it across the stove pit to Kit. "Here, whitey, have a look."

The SEAL team corporal caught the NVG and looked through it. "Fuck me…I can barely see him; he's right."

Michaels grabbed it out of his hand and looked through it at Kelly. "No shit, he's right. You can't see him very well."

Connor, the Canadian JTF2, leaned in and whispered to his partner, "Here we go. Watch this routine; it's fucking hilarious."

Kit was staring at Kelly through the scope on his rifle. "Shit. How does that work?"

Kelly answered, "It's nothing special about me; it's the salmon candy."

"Salmon, like the fish?" one of the other spec ops guys asked.

Kelly continued, "My mother is a very powerful medicine woman in my home village, and she makes this special salmon candy that makes you a scope ghost."

"Scope ghost?" Kit repeated as Kelly reached into his pocket and pulled out a tinfoil packet of maple candied salmon bits.

"I will share some with you guys; it will make us all invisible for the op."

Everyone leant in and took a piece from the deep-red pile of salmon nuggets.

"Shit, these are good. Thanks, Kelly."

They all started to look at each other through the detuned scope, convinced that the candied salmon had started to work immediately. Connor shook his head while he ate his caramel pudding from a pack. He had seen Kelly pull this gag before, and he couldn't believe how they fell for it every time. He was waiting for the famous punch line, but Kelly kept it up right until bedtime.

The next morning they got up and started out across the jagged rock cliffs dotted with green spiny scrubs and small pine trees. The sun was up yet the air was still crisp; their breath steamed out of their mouths. They had to make another ten miles to set up at their destination point. Walking to the X, as it was called. When they spotted villagers traversing the trails, they kept out of sight. They had to cross an open pass, so they chose to work up the ridgeline and go across as high up as they could. This way they would be up above anyone using the road in the small valley. Kelly's mission was to teach the DEVGRU/SEAL Team guys how to track on dirt or gravel—Canadian style. He pointed out the tracks that led up ahead of the team. Definitely some traffic up here.

Kelly looked across at the far side. "Shit!" He waved them down. They dropped and assembled into a defensive stance. Kelly pointed across the small valley, and on the other side, about three hundred yards away, there was a machine-gun nest. The Taliban gunner was using binoculars to scan the hills. The team was in the open and would be spotted for sure. They would have to make it up across the ridge top and down the other side without getting hit by the large-calibre machine gun. Kit had the gunner in his scope and was ready to fire, but this was a long shot, and the Taliban had a small rock wall as cover. He watched the binoculars swing over to him and stop. Kit's finger rested on the trigger as he controlled his breathing—*just be calm; don't fire until he makes a move.* The man with the long beard stopped with his binoculars pointed directly at Kit. Kit inhaled through his nose and exhaled through his mouth, for one, then two breaths. The Taliban dropped the glasses and pulled out a cigarette.

"Holy shit, I am a scope ghost. He was looking right at me, and he couldn't see me at all—we are fucking invisible!"

Connor was crouched below Kit. He chuckled and whispered to his mate, "How does he do this? Kelly did it to the Vandoos last year, and it fucked them up for a whole week, but this is awesome; it's going to be a new record."

The Americans were very fit and even Kelly was having trouble keeping the pace as they crossed the jagged snow-topped mountains. After seven hours of hustling, they reached a lookout where they could see smoke from a compound just over the next berm. They set up a camp and then started up the ridge to the observation point. There the soldiers dug into the hillside, their shovel blades bouncing off the rocks. The heat of the three stoves in the camp pushed back the icy thin air.

Kit rubbed his hands. "So, Kelly, have you got any more of those Indian salmon candies? That guy looked right through me today."

"Sure, you guys like being scope ghosts, eh?" Kelly reached into his pocket as the team gathered around him. He unwrapped the tinfoil carefully and said a few words in his native tongue and waved his hand over the small bundle of salmon nuggets. It felt as though they were eating something magic as they each took a piece.

"Hey, did you guys notice any of the side effects?" Kelly asked.

Connor leant over and whispered into the other Canadian's ear. "Oh shit, here it comes. Hold on and keep your cool; you will never see anything like this again."

Kit's eyes narrowed. "What side effects? You didn't mention any side effects yesterday."

"Yeah, I guess I forgot. They're no big deal...unless..." Kelly's voice faded off.

"What side effects? Unless what?" Kit's voice was getting louder.

"Well, a dry mouth and sometimes a little tummy trouble, and your cock shrinks a little." Kelly whispered the last bit.

Kit spat out the bits of salmon left in his mouth. *"What the faauck did you just say? What did he just say to me?"* Kit's voice boomed in an excited, steady tone as he stood up pointing at Kelly and waving his head back and forth.

"Yeah, well, your cock will shrink a little, but you see, that's no big deal because my cock is too huge; it hurts my wife's pussy when I put it in. So a little shrinkage is a good thing." Kelly stood up and moved over to grab some more crackers as he watched Kit and his team. Some of them realized that he was teasing, but Kit's eyes were darting back and forth. "You Indian bastard, what did you feed me?"

31

"Don't worry. It's better to have a small dick and be alive than have a big dick and be dead," Kelly added with his face was as steady as granite. Kit paced for a moment, and then he pulled the waistband of his pants out and looked down at his penis. One of his troop mates chimed in. "Kit, let's have a look at that thing. Pull it right out and we'll see if it has shrunk."

Kit turned anxiously and flopped out his cock for inspection. "I think it is smaller."

They all looked at it. "Yup, it's smaller all right," Michaels commented. Kelly unzipped his pants and pulled out his penis. "Holy shit, look at the size of that thing—it's like the size of a small mammal," Michaels blurted out.

Kelly replied, "Yeah, it used to be even larger."

"What did you do to me!" Kit was starting to lose his patience as he approached Kelly. He lunged at him, but Kelly turned and swung the smaller man down to the ground. The laughter was rolling out of the two Canadians sitting on the sidelines. They were buckled over at the sight of the two men wrestling with their penises flopping around the camp. "Oh…oh my god, I'm going to piss my pants," Connor wailed.

Lieutenant Cyr walked down from his observation post and unwittingly beheld the sight of the two grown men fighting with their bits rotating in the chilly air.

"Holy shit…um, hello! Is this my fucking international top gun elite team? I'm confused, because it looks like a bunch of complete boot-camp chimpanzee morons. So what's the after-action report going to say? We have engaged the enemy with our cocks?"

"Whoo, whooaaa ha ha! Kelly's got a Bazooka, and Kit has a two-shot derringer!" Connor and some of the SEALs were now laughing hysterically.

The lieutenant turned his head. "You two shut up!" The Canadians stopped laughing. "We are down range and a thousand yards from fifty Taliban soldiers, and you clowns think this is funny?"

"No sir," they both answered uniformly.

"Now you guys have gotten me yelling, for Christ's sake." The lieutenant stood in front of the two panting soldiers. "I can't believe you have brought me down to this. You two drop and give me fifty *uhhp*...and leave your cocks out!" Kelly and Kit dropped and started in on the fifty push-ups. Lieutenant Cyr turned and shook his head. "Indian legends and chunks of salmon, really? I mean, really?"

The night was getting colder; the red light faded into the dust of the hills. Kit kept looking into his sleeping bag, checking his penis. He could not decide if it was really smaller, or he was just cold. At 0400 the two were roused for watch. The lieutenant had rearranged the schedule so that these two, stood the double watch together. Kit was convinced that this crazy Canadian Indian had shrunken his holy shaft of manliness. There was no forgiveness for this, so they did not speak. Kelly stood up and proclaimed, "Hey little white noodle, be back in a minute." Kit replied with his middle finger. The tall native moved quietly down into the valley and snuck up to the Taliban outpost. At the outskirts of the compound, he slipped through the wire. He entered the machine-gun nest and stepped over the sleeping Taliban soldiers. He held out a small foil pouch of syrup and poured it onto the ammo belts of the two large machine guns.

The lieutenant's eyes snapped open. Kit was leaning over him. "Lieutenant, I need to speak with you."

Cyr popped up and looked around urgently, grabbing his weapon. "What...do we have contact?"

"No sir, it's the Indian."

"What, where is he?"

"He went off for a piss or something and didn't come back."

"What is wrong with you? That big-cocked Indian is your cover, and now he's gone?"

"Yeah, he told me he would be right back, and that was about forty-five minutes ago."

The lieutenant woke up the rest of the team. As they all got up and readied their weapons, they heard a rustling just outside of the camp. Kelly walked into the camp dragging a bearded man dressed in a long shaggy gown; the man was clearly Taliban.

"Is this the guy?" Kelly asked the lieutenant.

"What? Is this the...I haven't even briefed you yet, what do you mean, is this the guy?"

"This is a spec-op mission, there's always a guy. Is this the guy?"

The lieutenant huffed as he shuffled through his backpack and opened the Ziploc bag with the documents. "Fucking Canadians, why couldn't I get the Polish GROM or some Germans?" He sorted through the briefing notes and pulled out a photo and a physical profile. It read *Alman Whahabi, leader of the El Tarira clan.* Lieutenant Cyr held the picture next to the prisoner's face. "Yeeah, it's him."

"My Indian spirits told me it was him." Kelly had a slight smile.

"Will you fuck off with the Indian spirits? How did you know that he was the guy?" the lieutenant demanded.

"OK, OK…He was the only guy with a big-ass sat phone." Kelly held up the satellite phone. "Do we still hit the camp this morning, or can we just go home?"

"We're supposed to wipe out the weapons and take this guy dead or alive. I guess we still need to take out the larger guns so we can get a bird in to give us a ride home," the lieutenant answered. "Kelly, when you were sneaking around in there, what was the count?"

"About thirty or so guys, only two women, and no kids. They have a few RPGs, a couple of big-calibre machine guns, and a lot of AKs. I took care of the two forward nests with syrup, so unless they notice the smell and change ammo, then they will get only a few shots out before the guns jam."

The lieutenant shook his head,. "I guess I should call in this one since we already have our target in hand." The officer walked up to a bluff with his phone and called into the base. He spoke into the handset. "Yeah, roger that; no, if we can avoid a firefight and just call in an airstrike, then we incur a lot less risk. Yeah, we don't want to end up losing this guy, or getting him killed now that we have him alive. By the way, Carl, is that Canadian guy Captain Wickey around?…Yeah, I want to talk to him about this Indian."

Back at the base, Alan was called to the communications centre. He entered the room.

Carl Harris motioned to the conference call speaker. "Alan, Lieutenant Cyr has a question about Kelly George."

The voice crackled through the speaker. "Captain Wickey, this is John Cyr, and I just wanted to ask you a question about Kelly George's mother. Is she a medicine woman?"

Alan chuckled. "Uh no, she is a Canadian Supreme Court judge in Ottawa. Is this concerning some Indian candy and scope ghosts?"

"Yes, it's causing a little bit of a ruckus with a couple of my men," the lieutenant replied.

Alan answered with a slight chuckle. "The candied salmon is not magic, and certain body parts are not really shrinking, if that helps, John."

"Yes, that will help. Sorry for having to ask such a ridiculous question."

"It's OK," Alan replied. "The last time he pulled this stunt was in the Rocky Mountains in 2004, and a Quebec soldier almost shot him."

"If he wasn't such a good soldier, I'd shoot him myself. He's a real pain in the ass."

Five days later, the SEAL team dropped down into the firebase. Kelly was the last to enter and greet the boys. The group had climbed along the jagged ridge above them for about three hours. Now they sat in the hooch on a narrow ledge perched about a thousand feet up on a two-thousand-foot cliff. It had been tough going with three skirmishes on the trek along the top of the mountain valley. So far there were no injuries, and the prisoner was still alive.

It was crowded in the hooch. They had been out in the open for many days and welcomed a roof over their heads. The mood was friendly due to the international mix. The whole team bunked down on the soft dirt floors in the base and slept well; they would cross to the FOB tomorrow and get a bird to Kandahar. The Canadians in the firebase had heard about Kelly's salmon candy gag, and there was a little teasing until the lookout yelled out.

"What day is it?" Kelly asked.

"Saturday." The reply came from one of the bunks.

"Shit, I hate Saturdays."

"Yeah, the day after prayer day, all the hodgis revved up with Allah ready to kick ass," the voice from the bunk confirmed.

Ironically, a few moments later, a report from the lookout echoed through the dirt fort. "We have eyes on some unfriendlies; it looks like they might be getting organized for something."

Lieutenant Cyr called up. "Yeah, no surprise, we were just talking about that. Well then...shoot the mofos." His orders were simple.

The US machine gunner opened fire and released a maelstrom of bullets, which were returned from down in the valley. A few ricocheted around the rocks and made the soldiers jump up and grab their weapons.

"How are they getting a line of fire in here?" The lieutenant moved up to the observation station and peered through the big spotting scope. "Where did all those guys come from?" He waved for the radio.

"FOB Monaco, this is Firebase Gonzales." The radio chirped as he let go of the mike key.

"Gonzales, go ahead," Alan's voice crackled.

"We have advancing force of twenty-plus moving up through grid U32 and V20 armed with arms, four or five RPGs and a few RPKs. They have us pinned down, and we are taking fire directly into the hooch. We are going to need some air."

Alan's heart leapt as he squeezed his microphone. "Gonzales, where do you want the package?"

Cyr came back on the channel. "U32.23 and V18.54, as soon as you can bring it. We'll try to keep them pinned in that spot."

"Roger. Uniform 32.23, Victor 18.54, ordered fire to prosecute two parcels; ETA five minutes."

The group of insurgents worked their way slowly up the steep, rocky cliffs on the west side of the mountain ridge. The tracers flew down the mountainside as the invading pack drew closer and closer. The insurgents were pressing in quickly, and they no longer were at the fire coordinates. The A-10 warthog jet screeched in low and released its payload. *Boom. Boom.* The atmosphere in the valley pulsed as the huge clouds of dry talc dust billowed into the air.

Alan was surprised at where the bombs hit. They had landed almost directly on the main group of insurgents, but that was not where he had ordered the strike. Did he screw up the coordinates? This hit was way too close to the firebase; it was almost directly on top of them. When the smoke and dust began to clear, he saw the crater only a few metres from the walls of the firebase. Rocks and boulders were tumbling from under the base wall into the mountainside hole. Soon the outside wall gave way and dropped down in a crash of wire and boulders. Now the west side of the base was ripped open and exposed to the enemy.

Alan gasped; what had he done? That bomb did not hit where it was supposed to hit. Now his men were in real danger.

The fire now poured out of the gaping hole out into the night. The US and Canadian soldiers knew that they had to keep up suppressive fire or else they could be overrun. The bomb had wiped out over half the insurgents, but now the other half had open access to the men on the hill.

Alan called the aircraft in to light up the hillside with the Gatling guns. The pilot realized what had happened and came around to rip up the earth between the two forces. Alan watched an RPG sail directly into the base and exploded. He leapt to his feet as Colonel Harris came out and met him.

"What are you doing, Wickey?"

"We need to get our boys out of there," Alan replied in a sounding out of breath.

"Yeah, we do, but let's wait for my boys to get their kit together, and we can call the shots," Harris said cautiously.

Alan shot back, "No time, we need to get them now!"

Harris did not want to order Wickey to keep his station because if he went anyway, then he would be in serious shit. Alan started by rounding up the light armoured vehicle crews on the radio, but he feared that his men on the hill were running out of time fast. He looked over to the LAV closest to him.

"I'm going to go and get them." Alan jumped into the hatch of the LAV.

The colonel shook his head. "Bad idea, Wickey, but you're going to need a gunner, and I don't see anyone standing around." And then, against his better judgment, he put on his helmet and climbed up onto the top turret. Harris pulled back the breach of the C6 sixty-calibre machine gun and dropped the lock down. "I sure as hell hope you can drive this thing, Wickey!" he yelled as the engine fired up.

Alan sped around the road and down into the valley where they immediately started to take fire. Harris wasn't conservative with the ammunition; a hail of heavy bullets flew by Alan's shoulder, and smoke filled the driver's compartment. Alan had the hatch open as he sped along the rough, rocky road. Harris's voice crackled on the comms set. "Wickey, close your damn hatch; these guys are getting ready to blast us!"

The other LAV crews were piling into their vehicles to follow them as the radio channel filled with communications. Alan closed the hatch and looked out the viewport to see a rocket-propelled grenade streaming right at them. He turned sharply, and the RPG impacted on the front corner of the vehicle. The whole machine shuddered with the impact. Harris didn't even miss a shot as the fire and smoke rolled over the turret. The shredded front tire flew up in thick rubber strips that slapped across the turret. Harris ducked to avoid them. The vehicle continued on with seven tires instead of eight, but this did not slow them down at all. Taliban fighters were running across the road in a panic as the LAV plundered through their firing lines. Alan held the throttle down as they bounced through some trees and accelerated towards the face of the cliff. One of the Taliban fighters was running in front of LAV as Alan sped up to the gravel and slate at the base of the hill. He disappeared underneath the front cowling, and the vehicle rolled right over top of him.

On the hilltop, the bullets ripped through the hole made by the fallen wall as the soldiers all found cover. Two of the Canadians had been hit and were being treated by an American medic in the bunks. The first RPG sailed up into the firebase and exploded in the middle of the lookout. Kelly and Kit lined up shoulder to shoulder and began to lay down fire into the hillside across the valley. Kelly took a wounded Canadian sniper's rifle and inspected it. Kit had an automatic. Kit stopped firing and pulled up the spotting scope. Kelly fired the huge grey rifle once for a test and then reloaded with another magazine. "Last mag in the bag; let's make it count," Kelly said as Kit dialed in the scope.

Kit pushed laser guide and read out the numbers "OK, I'm gonna talk in English, OK? That guy in the RPK nest, two hundred fifty-five, winds one five northwest."

"Two hundred fifty-five what?" Kelly replied.

"Two hundred fifty-five what…yards, you dumbass Canadian!"

"Yards, right. I can do the math to meters, I guess," Kelly replied.

"Shoot the fucking guy in the hat. The one with the big machine gun!"

"They all have hats." Kelly squeezed the trigger of the McMillan Tac-50. The big fifty-calibre round whistled across the gully and hit its mark. The white cap on the gunner's head blew apart with a spray of blood.

"You got him; now the next guy over there in the truck." Kit pointed and then beamed the laser over to the target. Kelly didn't wait for the data; he pulled the trigger, and the target dropped. "OK, now that guy at out twelve hundred fifty yards holding an RPG." Kelly dialed in his scope and made a one mark allowance for the wind and squeezed the trigger. The incoming bullets whizzed past their heads. "Missed…two to the right and lead him." *Bang!* The target dropped.

"Nice shot, Kelly," Kit said. Kelly wheeled the gun sight over to watch the LAV thunder through the enemy lines.

"Looks like Wickey is coming to get us in that LAV." Kelly pointed.

"He drives like my mom. Let's see if we can clear the way for him," Kit replied. "RPG guy in the nest over there at four hundred fifty yards." Kit lit him up with the laser. Kelly fired and dropped him. They watched the LAV hit the rocks at the base of the hill and bounce over the rough boulders.

"Holy shit, your guy is climbing the cliff with that Canadian Volkswagen, and he has a full-blooded US colonel as a gunner. That's something you don't see every day." Kit tracked the vehicle with the scope. "Kelly, let's get those guys on that rock outcropping—they're going to be trouble if we don't." Kit pointed the tiny spot on the cliff out. "Let's see how you are at eighteen hundred yards."

"See, they all have hats," Kelly said as he looked at them through the scope.

"They are not hats; they're called keffiyehs. Wind 5NW, eighteen hundred thirty yards, lighting up the guy right now." Kit relayed the data, and Kelly dialed his scope and gently squeezed the trigger. *Bang!* Kit watched the bullet spin as it flew over a full mile through two crosswinds. At this distance a sniper has to take into account the spin of the earth while the bullet is in flight. Three seconds later it hit the man in the center of his chest. "Hit him! That's a lucky-ass shot!"

"Big dick, big balls, big luck," Kelly said as he swung the barrel down. "I am out of ammo."

Kit dropped down to scrounge through the supplies for some sniper rounds. "Found some US rounds—will they fit?"

"Yeah, let's see." Kelly took a bullet out and inspected it. He slid it in the chamber. "I don't know, slides in OK, but let's give it try." He snapped in the magazine and aimed at the small group at the bottom of the hill. He pulled the trigger, and the bullet ripped through a bush and a wooden barricade in a shack. "Whoa, these fly hot." Kelly squeezed off another couple of shots into the woods at the bottom of the hill, and one man fell. "Yeah, these are nice."

Alan kept the throttle down as the injured vehicle bounced over the rough boulders and then climbed straight up the pitch. It kept climbing as Harris fired his gun across the valley. Harris looked over to the FOB to see two other LAVs and a G-Wagon following down the road about five minutes behind them. A group of insurgents were halfway up the cliff with the intention of overrunning the now-vulnerable base. They turned around in surprise to see a vehicle attempting to climb directly up the cliff face behind them. The machine gun raked through them, but now Harris had to be careful of his line of fire. The momentum finally stopped the big LAV as it began to slide backwards down the hill a few feet.

"OK, that's about as high as we are going to get," Alan chirped into his radio as the bullets bounced off the armour. Alan looked up as a bullet skipped off of Harris's carbon helmet and ricocheted onto the turret, sending out a loud ping.

"Nice place to park, Wickey," Harris called.

The team in the firebase didn't need prompting; they poured out of the gaping hole as the top gunners pounded the area with machine-gun fire. The air was a fog of lead and smoke as the smoke canisters rolled around the vehicle. The few Taliban on the hill were cut down, and the soldiers moved down the hill to the waiting LAV. Alan lowered the back door as Harris turned around to cover the entrance. If any Taliban were to get a shot at the back of the vehicle, the soldiers would be pinned inside, creating a fire trap until the door was closed. The troops filed around the vehicle and climbed in as Harris clipped in his last box of rounds. All of the soldiers and the wounded climbed in to one crowded dog pile. The remaining men, mostly gunners, ran alongside the vehicle as Alan backed down the hill to meet the other LAVs. The colonel didn't give up his gun post until the LAV was up the other hill and behind the compound walls. The A-10 flew back into the smoke-filled valley and ripped up the hillside with its cannons. Alan opened the back ramp and started to pull out the men. Three were walking wounded with blood on their uniforms from small shrapnel hits, and two men were still lying supine on the benches. The medic looked up and shook his head. "This one bled out, and the other guy was killed instantly with a headshot. Sorry, Captain."

Alan recognized the one who died in the vehicle. It was his man, François. Alan touched his face. "Thanks for doing what you could for him."

"Don't thank me. I'm sorry," the medic replied.

Harris walked up and looked at the two casualties. "Sorry, Alan."

"It was my fault; I dropped the ordinance on the wrong spot," Alan said.

Harris tilted his head to catch Alan's gaze. "You didn't drop any ordinance, and you didn't shoot these guys. So, get yourself off that ridiculous train of thought, Alan. It's easy to carry around the first men that you lose on your shoulders, but take it from me; they get too heavy." Harris kept his eyes locked with Alan's, but he was disappointed to see that his words did not penetrate Alan's fog of emotions.

6 Alive!

The late afternoon sun was lighting up the tops of the trees. Alan sat on the cement stairs outside of his Vancouver apartment. His battle against his Afghan ghosts was going on five years, and he was losing. He was losing his family, and losing his sanity to the whirlwinds of desert dust that clogged his soul and gummed up his mind. His weapon of the day was exercise. His psychological treatments were working a little, but his head still hurt. He strapped on his runners and headed up the steep alleyway. The cool fall air filled his lungs as he walked up the lane towards the British Properties. Alan's new runners skidded on the wet leaves; he pushed his way into a slow jog. His belly chafed against his waistband as he willed his way past the tightness in his chest. Just beyond the discomfort and breathlessness, there would be a better place for his mind and his soul. He knew the solution for his ills was as simple as a daily workout. He used to be a superhero, jumping out of aircraft into the Mid-Pacific Ocean and scaling the mountains of Afghanistan. Now he felt sick and exhausted from a drive to the mall. Alan moved onto the chip trail as the sun began to drop behind the trees. *Just five kilometres is all I need to get me started, nice and easy.*

Sentrous was hunting early, too early to kill. He pulled in his claws as he flew across the fifty-foot gap between trees. He sailed through the air and landed easily into the brush top of a seventy-foot Douglas fir tree. He was tracking some female hikers below him on the forest floor, just for fun. They smelt fresh, like roses; he was forbidden to take one. He was condemned to eat only bad meat. Humans were the most plentiful prey and very easy to hunt, but the laws of Kamptra required only rotten ones were to be taken, and only taken at night—no sound, no trace, no stories for humans to tell. There were so many rules lately. Sentrous hated the rules, almost as much as he hated rotten human junkies.

Alan appeared on the trail, and he didn't smell like roses. Sentrous watched him run; this was odd, because the rotten ones didn't run, they just wandered around and talked. Maybe this one would taste differently.

Alan was listening to a tune in his earphones as the large animal drifted through the twilight above him. The sunset lit up the leaves in small patches on the forest floor. As his target approached the turnoff from the trail back onto the street, Sentrous became impatient. It wasn't really dark enough yet, but who would know?

Alan jogged towards the opening in the trail, which ran along the street for a kilometre or two. He approached the yellow-lit circle in the leaves, only a few steps from the street. The blackness of the shadows made the trail tough to navigate. Movement from the heights flashed in his right periphery. Something dropped; he stopped and stared. It swayed quietly as the black changed to a green. It was tall, eight feet or so. The shadow shimmered and swayed slightly.

He couldn't make it out. *It's just a pine tree.* He let out a sigh, and then a laugh while trotting forward. Alan's nervous system fired a bolt of impulses through his adrenal gland as he touched the black shadowy figure. He had expected branches; this was not a tree.

The figure broke its stillness by swiping his prey on the top of the head, sending Alan straight to the ground with a thud. The air whistled out of Alan's lungs. He gasped; could not inhale. He leapt up from the forest floor and darted through the trees, pulling breath through his dirt-cached nostrils. Branches swayed behind him; he could feel the air moving, and then it was quiet. His Olympic pace slowed to a trot, and he looked back and saw nothing; he heard nothing. He exhaled with his hands on his knees. *What the hell was that?* Long claws gripped like hooks into the base of his skull and lifted him off his feet. The quill-coated beast flopped Alan onto his back. Like razors, the jagged teeth slid into his skin, pushing through the muscles towards his oesophagus and trachea. He gasped as one of the incisors deep in his throat, pushed up against his jugular veins, stretching the vessel walls. The monster cocked its head to look into Alan's eyes. Alan felt a calm peace, almost a feeling of euphoria. This was the last shot of hormones released by the pituitary gland.

Sentrous didn't like the colour of this one's eyes. They were yellowish, not white. The taste of Alan's blood washed over his tongue. It was rotten, really rotten! Sentrous relaxed his grip on Alan's neck. Recoiling from the taste and smell, he spat out blood and lymph, retched, and spat again. Appetite lost, Sentrous dragged his prey over to a patch of leaves. After a half-hearted attempt at burying Alan, he swung up into the trees and disappeared.

A wave of guilt hit stopped Sentrous at the power lines, sloppy and reckless. He should return to the kill and deal with it properly. Someone from the clan would enjoy it. Leaving a corpse behind was forbidden. Sentrous turned back and dropped down to the shallow grave. It was empty! Sentrous's heart jumped as he moved to the tree line and watched as Alan stumbled, in a trail of blood, up the stairs of one of the small brown houses on the row street just out of the forest. Sentrous quickly scanned the street, but there were cars and people walking. He could not get to Alan unnoticed. The door of the house swung open; a woman screamed as Alan collapsed into her doorway.

The doctors at Royal Columbian had never seen wounds like this, and neither had Ryder, BC's leading conservation officer. "Cougar attack, eh? Nasty business." Said the police constable.

"Yeah, a big one. Maybe a hundred and fifty pounds." Ryder looked at the photos of the gaping holes in Alan's neck. "Could be my ex-wife—she's around that weight, and she lurks around North Van looking for unsuspecting guys to claw up."

"He told me it was a eight-foot-tall hairy monster." Perry smiled.

"See, it was my ex all right. I'll give you her address; you should go over and pick her up," Ryder replied without cracking a smile. He stared intensely at the digital photo of Alan's neck. "It looks more like a tiger bite, but a tiger would have torn him into shreds."

"Yeah, the last I heard the West Coast Canadian Tiger was on the endangered list, but you're the wildlife conservation guy. You tell me where we could find a tiger," the RCMP officer quipped.

"Maybe one ran up from the San Diego Zoo. I'm not an expert at this stuff; I chase raccoons and seals for a living. We'll say it's a cougar for the paperwork, and the media," Ryder replied. Ryder was going into his tenth year as a conservation officer in the Vancouver and lower mainland. Contrary to his claim, he was an expert at this stuff. He had seen a few cougar and bear attacks, but this one looked like a very big cat. Another thing that was strange was Alan's claim that he had been buried under leaves—that was a bear thing to do, but these were not bear teeth marks.

The RCMP officer looked up from his statement form. "Can't you guys do a scan or something to determine exactly what size of cat did this?"

"Oh yeah, I'll take this photograph and have my lovely assistant scan it through the mass spectroscopy reconstitutor in our animal CSI lab. It will identify the animal and track it with satellites," Ryder retorted while looking over the RCMP officer's paperwork. "They just gave me a damn cell phone last month, and last year's technology upgrade was a fax machine that took real paper!"

Perry laughed. "Sounds familiar. OK, big cougar it is."

The curtains were drawn back, and the hulking RCMP officer sat down beside Alan. Perry looked at the woman who had not left Alan's side since he'd arrived four hours ago.

"Is there a chance that I may have a minute alone to speak with Mr. Wickey?" Karen Wickey nodded and walked out to the sitting room down the hall.

"For an ex-wife, she seems like she still cares about you."

"We're not divorced yet, just separated," Alan replied. His voice was crumbled and rough.

"Alan, you're an addict," Perry stated.

Alan turned his head to meet Perry's gaze and protested, "I take pain killers for my back."

"You're an addict, and you're the luckiest addict I have ever met. I think you have been given an opportunity here, why don't you take advantage of it?"

"I am not an addict. I am an engineer, and a veteran."

45

"Yeah, OK, you keep telling yourself that, and I'll see you when you hit the skids downtown." Perry rested his hand on Alan's shoulder and got up to leave.

"Aren't you going to take my statement, regarding that thing that tried to eat me?" Alan asked.

"Your statement's no good to me, Alan. Clean yourself up, and then maybe I will listen to you." He walked out.

Karen returned to the bedside, and Alan looked at her. "That guy is an asshole."

"Why—what did he say to you?"

"He said that my statement was no good to him, he's not going to do anything."

"That doesn't sound right," Karen replied. She could see that he was lying or leaving something out. Karen had always been able to tell when people were lying. It was the eyes, the tone of voice, the position of the head, or something else, but she always knew. To her, lying was so transparent that it was ridiculous to attempt it. She never lied. She had married a man who possessed a host of amazing skills, but skilled deceit was not one of them. For the first ten years of their marriage, he had rarely lied; maybe once or twice about the price of his new stereo or about leaving the garage door open. To Karen, it was as obvious as if a big red light flashed on his head, reading "Liar." Now he lied frequently. What was happening to him? She had no idea what had happened in the woods. Why was he behaving like this, and where did he get this crazy monster story? She wondered if it was his PTSD, or maybe it was the drinking and the pills.

Alan was sick all right. He had twelve holes in his neck the size of dimes, his back ached, he couldn't sleep, his head buzzed. His stomach clenched with constant fear and pain. He felt startled, all of the time; adrenaline burned through his arteries like gasoline. When he first returned from Kandahar, he had occasional dull combat-type of fear. He would shake it off, or it would fade. Then he started to drink vodka for the anxiety. The pills would dull the pain in his head, back, and neck. As the months went by, he needed more vodka and more pills to keep the edge off. Now, in the hospital, every moment felt as though he was going to be killed. There were no pills and no vodka.

EMERGENCE

The physician looked at his blood work and decided to take him off the painkillers. "This guy needs to dry up while he's here; if the pain starts to get the better of him, then you can give him some Tylenol 3s, but just one every four hours. We should try and keep him here for a couple of weeks; his oesophagus has been punctured so he will be on an IV. No food or liquids for a while." The nurse nodded as she wrote down the orders on Alan's chart.

Constable Perry spoke to the doctor on the way out. "What do you think of him? Why is he seeing monsters?"

The doctor replied, "I don't know. He is definitely addicted to the pain meds, and he's drinking too much, but he doesn't seem delusional. Maybe the combination of darkness and a big cougar trying to eat his ass kicked off some kind of psychological event. He was injured in Afghanistan by a roadside bomb; sometimes the blast can do funny things to your head. If he didn't have post-traumatic stress before, then this cougar definitely gave it to him."

"OK, thanks, doc." Constable Perry finished his report and headed out to his car.

The first week in the hospital was brutal; Karen and Teddy visited him daily but felt uncomfortable due to his nasty behaviour. Withdrawal had Alan lashing out at all who approached. He told the hospital pastor to go and fuck himself and was short with Teddy during his visits. Alan would sweat through the night with a fever due to a low-grade infection in his neck. His skin was yellowish due to his stressed-out liver; his blood was full of toxic ketones as a result of his system cleaning itself out. His breath stank, and his skin was clammy.

Alan stood six feet tall and had come into the hospital weighing 240 pounds, about forty pounds overweight. By the second week, his weight was falling due to the lack of food. His IV ration was only 1,400 calories per day; this was enough to keep him healthy, but the extra pounds were dropping. By day thirteen, he was back on fluids and his weight had stabilized at 195 pounds. This had been his weight when he was posted to Afghanistan in 2003.

At the end of the second week, he was feeling a little better and sleeping a few hours each night. The downside was that these hours were filled with nightmares. He didn't dream of the creature that had him pinned to the forest floor; he dreamt of the *Calico.*

The dream repeated the real story over and over. *Calico* was the name a sixty-foot, 140-ton small ship that had been spotted foundering fifty miles off of Cape Scott. A passing trawler reported her in distress, but no one had heard directly from the boat itself. The seas were thirty feet high, and the winds gusting to seventy knots. The Canadian Coast Guard cutter *Gordon Reid* was en route, but she was three hours away. Rescue 312, a yellow fixed-wing aircraft, dropped a line of parachute illumination flares to light up the listing hulk. The small ship's bridge lights were on, and her engine was running; she was making about three knots, dead slow, and rolling beam to the seas.

"MV *Calico,* what is the nature of your distress?" The coast guard radio operator repeated the message every five minutes, but there was no answer from the stricken vessel.

"Rescue 910, this is Prince Rupert Coast Guard radio; what is your ETA to MV *Calico?*"

"Prince Rupert Coast Guard Radio, this is Rescue 910; ETA one zero minutes, will have approximately five zero minutes of hang time on scene." Alan listened to the pilot of the Cormorant SAR helicopter reply over his headset as he went through his final checks for hoist.

The helo and the fixed-wing plane were going to be working together over top of the listing fishing boat. Alan hit the internal comms button. "What's the story, Richie?"

Richie, the pilot, replied coyly, "The story is that we are going to play my favourite game. It's called Wickey on a string."

"Nice…try not to spill your coffee while you're dropping me onto a heaving, sinking vessel."

"Nobody's going to drop you, Wickey; besides, if something happens, then I will take good care of Karen for you. I already bought a little nurses outfit that will fit her perfectly." Richie sighted the *Calico*'s lights in the darkness and pointed them out to the co-pilot. "Target sighted, three minutes."

"Roger three minutes, opening door," the hoist man called into the intercom. The wind howled through the aircraft as the door swung open, and the hoist man leant out to get a look at the boat. The big searchlight lit up the wallowing vessel as the helicopter held station over top. "Shit, the deck is a fucking horror show—

gear everywhere, the cargo boom is loose. This is not going to be a fun hoist. It's your call, Wickey; go or no go?"

The big yellow aircraft circled the small ship as she took a big wave across her stern. Her list was severe, about fifteen degrees over on her port side. There was no movement on the decks or on the bridge.

"Hey Richie, does it look like she's taking on water to you?" Alan asked.

"Can't tell for sure, but she seems buoyant and her pumps aren't running at all. The deck gear is all piled up on the port side; it looks like she took a big one, and her load shifted."

The *Calico*'s huge vacuum pump had broken loose on the deck and was pushed half over the port-side rail. The ship's life rafts were still on their racks, and that meant that the crew had not abandoned ship.

"Weirdness for sure. Just keep the line away from the rigging, OK?" Alan looked at the hoist man and poked at his helmet visor. He nodded his head in reply. "OK, Richie, if it's a go for you ladies up there in the palace of knobs, then I'm good to drop back here." Alan released the transmit button and started his final check.

"Prince Rupert Coast Guard Radio, this is Rescue 910. We are on scene and preparing for a hoist on MV *Calico*; we confirm info from 312: there are no signs of movement on board. SAR-Tech Wickey is standing by to hoist."

"Rescue 910, Prince Rupert, roger last. Victoria Rescue Centre says go with hoist if safe to do so."

As Alan leant out the open door, he looked down at the heaving deck below. It looked like a junkyard. He dropped out of the aircraft and descended slowly. The ship's mast whooshed by him as the vessel rolled violently.

"Left...left...left...ten feet...OK, down." Alan guided the hoist operator on every move. Just before Alan touched down on the heaving deck, a wave struck the starboard side and sent a crab trap careening towards him. Instinctively he released the hoist hook, but the cable flew from his hands and spun, tangling tightly around one of the rigging blocks. Now the helo was in jeopardy. *"Hooked up!"* Alan yelled the emergency signal as he leapt over top of the crab trap towards the fouled hoist line. The hoist man could give Alan a few seconds before he cut the line. Alan grabbed the hook and spun it around the steel rigging, but the line sliced through his glove as it snapped tight with a clang. Now the heaving vessel and the aircraft were directly connected. The 140-ton vessel tried to yank the huge helo out of the sky. Rescue 910 lurched under the load. The pilot swore over the intercom as the fishing vessel wrestled with the aircraft. This was too much excitement for the hoist man; he pulled the guillotine and cut the line. The helicopter spun around 180 degrees and dipped wildly as the pilot struggled to regain control. The cable fell down from the swirling mist and coiled in a pile on the deck. Alan braced himself for a large wave that swept across. The aircraft disappeared into the dark sky with a roar as the pilot hit the throttle and accelerated out of the spin. He gained altitude quickly up to five thousand feet and circled around.

Alan paid no attention to the blood pouring out of his glove, or the smashed radio on his vest.

The pilot called "OK guys, that was not funny. Wickey, are you there?"

There was no answer.

"Richie, the number one winch is screwed. I'll need to change the pinwheel before we are ready to go again on the number two," the hoist man cut in.

The pilot ignored the hoist report. "Nine-ten to Wickey, please acknowledge." There was only silence. The helicopter pilot barked out an order to the circling plane. "Rescue aircraft 312, please do a low pass to get eyes on Wickey." The fixed-wing was circling above at ten thousand feet.

"Rescue 910, this is rescue 312. We are descending through seven thousand now, passing north south; hold station while we get eyes on SAR tech."

The silence in the cockpit was profound as everyone's hearts pounded in anticipation of the next radio call. "Recue 910, this is 312, we have eyes on Wickey; he just flipped us the bird on the pass. His radio is out, and he is heading up to the bridge to regain contact."

The crew of 910 let out a sigh of relief at the news that Alan was OK. "Roger that, 312; thanks for the good news. Could you please let JRCC know that we are down to twenty-five minutes till bingo fuel and have damage to our hoist? We have one crewmember on board the *Calico* and will report soon."

"Nine-ten, roger, we will relay that message to RCC. Say again your hoist status please?" The circling airplane was busy with multiple communications.

Below Alan had worked his way up the side of the wheelhouse to the bridge wing. He closed the bridge door behind him and retched at the stench of the rotting dead. A high-pitched alarm was squealing from below the instrument panel. He moved slowly towards the wheel. The captain's remains were slumped in a heap between the wheel and the navigation station. He lifted the head, and the flesh fell off the captain's cheek. Alan moved to the alarm panel and checked the fire and bilge section. He did not see any lights flashing. What was that alarm? Alan moved down to the galley and noticed that the engine room door was wedged open with another dead and rotting body lying on the stoop. The same alarm was sounding down in the galley. Alan walked back up the steps into the wheelhouse.

"Break, break, 312 and 910, this is Wickey onboard MV *Calico*, VHF channel twenty-two alpha."

"Wickey, I was just breaking out that naughty nurse uniform for Karen. Sorry to hear you're OK, over," Richie replied from the circling helicopter.

Alan broke the humour with a serious tone. "Yeah, yeah. I got one code black on the bridge and one in the engine space so far, and not sure what happened yet. Any of you nautical types know what alarm this is, in the background? It's not from the main panel."

The co-pilot was an ex-fisherman and immediately pushed the transmit button. "Wickey, get the fuck out of that boat; that's the carbon monoxide alarm!" There was no answer. Once again the radio silence gripped the crew. The big yellow bird circled low and approached into the wind. With only minutes of fuel left, the helicopter hovered over the rolling vessel, searchlights panning around the vessel looking for signs of the rescue tech.

"Motor Vessel *Calico*, Motor Vessel *Calico*, this is Rescue 910; please respond." There was no response and no sign of Alan Wickey on the deck.

51

The pilot spoke into the microphone. "He won't have long to live in there if the boat was full of CO gas; we need to get him out as fast as possible."

"Shit, Rescue 910, this is 312. We can parachute a sartech in to swim over and climb aboard. I got Riley; he's ready to go." The crew circling in the airplane were frantic.

"Three-twelve, this is nine-ten; negative, that's too risky a swim. This boat is steaming along under power and there is no easy way to get on board, plus if Riley missed, we couldn't hoist him."

Richie was the on-scene commander, and the protocols were clear on this decision: it's twice the tragedy if two sartechs die as opposed to one. The MV *Calico* steamed into a very thick fog bank, and 910 reached bingo fuel level, barely enough to return to shore.

"Three-twelve, this is 910. We are now at bingo fuel and departing the scene for Port Hardy airport and repairs to the winch."

"Nine-ten, roger that. We don't have eyes on the *Calico* due to visibility, but we will stay up here at altitude and provide top cover."

Not far from the scene, the 150-foot coast guard cutter pounded into a goliath sea. The white spray shot up above the mast and shrouded her searchlights. The saltwater washed down the bridge windows in torrents to reveal a dirty, dark-grey sea. The ship's radios crackled again, and the coast guard officer released his tight grip on the grab rails by the radar to reach for the HF radio mike. He had been listening to the drama unfold and waiting for the radio traffic to pause for a moment.

"Rescue 312, this is the coast guard cutter *Gordon Reid*. We have launched our fast rescue craft, call sign Gordon Reid One, GR1—their ETA is twenty-five minutes, as long as they can stay upright."

"Roger *Gordon Reid,* your boat's ETA is twenty-five minutes, thank you." The fixed-wing pilot slowly circled the glowing fog patch below.

The twenty-six-foot orange Zodiac surged up the face of a steep frosty wave and bounced over the crest; the hull of the three-ton vessel became airborne. The twin two-hundred-horsepower outboard engines gave a scream as the propellers sprayed out of the water. These little boats were built for speed, but she was not speeding tonight. Flying foam whipped the coxswain's face as he looked down into the black canyon that appeared beneath the wave crest. The boat dropped into the open mouth; the engines stuttered as the coxswain tried to slow down. The hull careened down the slope like a surfer on a huge break.

"Hold on!" The coxswain spat out a mouth full of water as the craft pounded into the black ditch. The sea surged over the bow and smashed into the crew's chests. The orange boat tubes prevented the nose of the tiny open vessel from a terminal dive into the deep. The battered crew sighed as she rose up to meet the face of the next big wave. While on the wave's top, they spotted the lights of the stricken *Calico* in the distance.

The *Calico* was now listing badly; the load shift was threatening the vessel. "A few more hard hits, and she'll be tits up," the coast guardsman yelled. The GR1 approached the fishing boat. The first task of a coast guard crew's is always to stabilize the vessel, make her safe. Often the toughest part is just getting alongside and climbing aboard. The rescue vessel approached the fishing vessel from the downwind side, and one of the crew leapt on board. He pulled the holding pins on the side rails, and the steel gate blew open, allowing the pile of nets and machinery to slide into the sea. As the vessel dumped its cargo, she rolled back, dousing her port side deep into the ocean; then, like a dog fresh out of the bathtub, the lumbering ship shook itself free of excess water and jumped up proudly to meet the next set of waves. The GR1 rescue specialist collected his wits and headed for the deck door. The door was open and the smell of rotting bodies wafted through the opening.

"Sartech Wickey, are you all right?"

"Come on in, guys. Coffee's on."

The guardsman slowly climbed the stairs up into the galley where Alan Wickey sat at the table with a hand of cards and a smoking cigar. A corpse was sitting across from him with a pair of sixes. The coast guard guy stood grinning while shaking his head.

Wickey shrugged his shoulders. "What? This is the only way I can win at five-card stud. Don't look at me like that. I found him that way." The crewman was relieved to see that Alan was OK, black humour aside. Alan filled them in on what had happened to him during the last half hour.

Knocked out cold on the bridge floor by the exhaust gases and lack of oxygen, he was certain to suffocate until the unlatched bridge door flew open. A cold swirl of fresh air revived him. Alan crawled over the doorframe out onto the deck, gasping. He lay on his back for about ten minutes before he stood up. Rescue 910 was gone, and it was too foggy to see 312 circling high above. Alan opened all the vents on the top deck and then opened the lower deck doors. Once he was sure that the fresh air had circulated throughout the sealed vessel, he ducked into the engine room, stepping over the body on the stairs, and hit the emergency stop button. The *Calico* came to a wallowing halt in the high waves. A large wave then broke over the stern, washing over the deck and pushing more cargo up against the rail. The last shift made the *Calico's* list even worse.

Alan was feeling better now as briefed the coast guard guys. They slowly put the clues together. There was obviously an exhaust leak in the engine room. It was the engineer who realized what was happening and tried to make it up to the living spaces to warn the crew, but he was a large guy and his exertion accelerated his demise. He fell on the stairs and died; his body held the engine room door open long enough to flood the rest of the *Calico* with exhaust gas. The captain was probably trying to figure out which alarm was sounding when he fell. Alan could relate to that. Alan found one crew member sitting hunched over at the galley table and the other three crew dead in their bunks. By the level of decomposition, this boat had probably been way out at the black-cod banks a thousand miles offshore and been idling along slowly with its dead crew for days, maybe even a week.

Alan woke up in the hospital, gasping as the image of the captain's rotting face slowly faded from his mind. The doctor was pulling the feeding tube out of his throat; he felt it snake all the way up from his gut, burning as it dragged past the newly healed rips in the oesophageal lining. The doctor looked down his throat with a light.

"Well, Alan, we are going to start you back on solid food, but I would stick with the mushy stuff for now and just eat lightly for the next twenty-four hours. Don't pig out, or you will get sick and vomit. And that, I guarantee, you won't enjoy."

Alan stood up and stretched stiffly. He looked in the mirror and was shocked to see his face. "Whoa, hello there, skinny boy." He posed for the mirror, flexing his biceps until his ass popped out of the blue gown. "This is your big chance, Wickey boy," he said to himself. "You're sober, you're skinny, and now you can get back on the sky train and get that job that was posted at Vector Engineering. That job was made for you."

The first couple of weeks after getting out of the hospital were tough. Alan avoided the cougar story as much as possible. His friends didn't understand why. It was one of the most amazing stories ever, and Alan was usually happy to break out one of his rescue stories, but the cougar night had no details. Alan struggled with living a normal life. It seemed that a normal life was everything but normal for him. His normal was helicopters, explosions, manufactured meal packs, and saltwater dripping down the crack of his ass. Normal was supposed to be a mix of the perfect wife, the perfect house, and the perfect family, and maybe it would be, if it weren't for the constant fear. Fear caused by the whistle of lawn mower blades, or the sound of a slipping clutch. The shopping mall is the horror of all horrors—he could face storms, insurgents, and bullets, but the thought of a shopping mall would send him over the edge of oblivion. The pain was manageable but the fear; the fear bent him in half. The fear and the pain pushed him to take a pill or have a drink. And now he was afraid of everything.

"I guess he just jumped me" was about as far as he would go. Karen didn't ask, especially after listening to his crazy ramblings at the hospital. The encounter began to change in his mind. It moved from horrifying, unexplainable facts to a fanciful impression. A strange interpretation of what had to be a cougar now sat propped up in his memory like a cow painted up to look like a zebra. If you squinted your eyes and didn't look directly at it, maybe it could be a zebra. If the memory got fuzzy, the chest-pounding fear certainly didn't. Alan's adrenal glands pumped high-octane fuel into his vessels throughout the day, and he could not shake that feeling of imminent death.

7 A Familiar Face

Alan was on his way to a job interview at Vector Aviation. This was the job posting that he had been waiting for. Kyle, his old engineering buddy, worked there and had been keeping him apprised of the opportunities. The job opening was in the avionics repair and inspection branch; he had some experience working with aircraft in the military, and his engineering degree helped. He hopped on the sky train, arriving a half hour early at the headquarters in Richmond. The long, modern building was a showcase for minimalist design, and cement and stainless steel complemented the industrial hallway. The reception area had a fifteen-foot-high glass-etched mural that loomed above a porcelain-skinned receptionist. Alan stared at her horn-rimmed glasses and candy-red lips as he announced his name and mission. She asked him to take a seat, and he waited while she spoke on the phone. After a few minutes, she stood up with an uncomfortable expression. "Mr. Wickey, it seems that you may have gotten the wrong address. Mr. Lansky has rented a room downtown for these interviews. You've missed your appointment."

Alan's mouthed opened, and he struggled to find his words. "Uh, I assumed that the interviews were here. I'm sorry. Can I reschedule?"

The receptionist avoided his eyes. "I'm afraid that, when it comes to interviews, Mr. Lansky has a 'one strike you're out' policy."

Alan was flushed as left the office. "Shit, I can't believe that, you stupid idiot," he mumbled to himself under his breath. The station lights flashed through the windows of the sky train. Alan just sat, his shoulders swaying with the train's motion. The ticker tape was rolling in his head. *You idiot, you knew that you would screw this up; you're fucking broken, Alan! Idiot, idiot, idiot.*

Karen slowly opened the door of Alan's apartment and walked into the kitchen holding three loaded bags of groceries. She stopped to look at the two half-full vodka bottles on the counter. The infamous Mickey Mouse tumbler sat beside an ice tray full of melting cubes. She walked into the living room and noticed the smell of booze.

"How did the interview go?"

The closer she got to the couch, the sillier this question seemed. Her heart sank as she slid down on the couch. "Alan, you were doing so well." She spoke more to herself, not expecting an answer from the drunken heap beside her. The flutter of his eyelids showed some signs of consciousness. "What are we going to do with you, Alan Wickey?" She ran her fingers through his hair.

An hour or so later, Alan awoke. He grabbed at the pillow that had, miraculously, made it from his bedroom to his couch and tucked itself under his head. "Karen, are you here?" He got up and walked into the kitchen, wincing at the thought of the state she had seen him in. "Shit!" He opened up the fridge to see it full of groceries and a freshly made bowl of chili wrapped with plastic wrap. *You've blown it now, Wickey. Idiot.* The ticker tape ran and ran. He poured himself a glass of the whey powder and wheatgrass mix and gulped it down.

Alan dialled Karen's cell phone, but she did not answer. He finally noticed the note on the table:

> *Alan, stay away from Teddy and I*
> *until you are sober.*
> *I love you,*
> *Karen*

Alan paced around in a panic for a while. "Nice one, Wickey, you stupid shit, you shit!" The rage was more than his two-bedroom apartment could contain. Alan strapped on his runners and sprinted down the street for a block and then slowed to a lumbering canter. The sun ducked down and the dusk set in behind it as Alan moved along the street towards the brown house where he had dragged his bloody body up the front stairs just a month ago. As he passed the stoop, he couldn't tell if his pulse was racing from the run, the booze, or the shadows in the trees. These were the trees where he was attacked. The shadows were deep and dark. There was movement in the branches. The blackness was staring at him; it was hunting him. That thing was there watching him, he was sure of it. He stopped at the corner and glared into the woods. As his eyes darted at the shadows, bile washed across his tongue; fear filled his gut. Overwhelmed, he staggered. The creature was there in the shadows waiting for him, wanting him. He could smell its breath, the gamey reek of its saliva; it was right there. Alan was paralyzed; he could feel the teeth sliding into his neck. His thighs gave way, and he dropped to his knees, staring at the blackness in the trees. He continued to the ground, curled at the base of a telephone pole. Alan covered his eyes and sobbed, waiting to be taken, waiting to feel the teeth close into his arteries. A car drove by, and his eyes snapped open. Why hadn't the thing come yet? Was it teasing him, or playing with him maybe? Maybe it was too scared to come out. "Come here, you fucker!" Alan leapt to his feet and ran straight into the blackened hole. Grunting wildly with arms outstretched, his hands were clawed to grab at the monster's face and rip it to pieces. He dove at the dark shape and fell through the boughs of cedar into the brush. The quiet replaced the bounding in his veins. He lay calmly looking up at the branches and the stars above them. A minute or maybe ten drifted by. It was just the woods, the leaves, and the shadows. He was in the shadow now, looking out at flashing blue-and-red lights.

"Hey, you come out of there right now." The officer shouted.

For the second time in a month, Alan was in a blue gown with his ass sticking out, but this time there were no friends or relatives. The Royal Columbian psychiatric ward smelled like dry old underwear, and this was day two in the *loony bin* for Captain Wickey. The chubby psychiatrist stood across the tiny office from him and asked him the same questions. "Alan, how do you feel today? Apart from your episode in the woods on Tuesday, have you noticed any strange happenings today or yesterday?"

"Other than a large orderly stripping me naked and dressing me up like his play doll…no, nothing," Alan replied.

"Have you had the feeling of being watched before?"

"Only when someone was watching me." Alan knew that his smartass answers were not going to expedite his release, but he couldn't help himself.

"Alan, you need some treatment and you need to stay on your meds unless you want this sort of incident to become routine in your life."

"Yes sir. I understand."

"I am going to release you and suggest that you follow up with Major Callum's sessions twice a week."

"I will, doc; I promise." The orderly arrived with jeans and a toilet bag. Karen had dropped off some basics for him, but she did not visit. He got himself dressed and signed out of the hospital.

What a shitty week, just when I thought it couldn't get worse. He winced at the recollection of the RCMP officer who had extracted his delusional ass out of the trees. He was embarrassed by the scene he had made over an empty bush. Maybe it was a cougar attack after all; maybe the stress of things just added to my nasty little experience, and I imagined that thing. Alan's mind struggled to make sense of the senseless. His new medications were making things cloudy, but he did notice the constant feelings of dread were now dulled—perhaps a little. *If I tell myself over and over that it was a cougar, then it will become a cougar. Cougars are no big deal. He surprised me, that's all.*

Alan dialled Karen's number, but she didn't answer. A few moments later, a text message arrived on Alan's cell phone: "Stay away from us for now."

Vancouver was a big city in the shadow of the coastal mountains. In the winter it was one of the warmest places in Canada, and the homeless lived there by the thousands. The provincial government had cut back on community health and shelters in 2007. The mayor and premier were convinced that most of the indigent were visiting Vancouver on holidays like geese flying south for the winter, and they crossed their fingers, hoping they would all just go away. Obviously suffering from a lack of air miles, they didn't have anywhere to go. So tent cities sprung up in the parks and on the streets of the east end. The 2010 Olympics were only a few months away, so the city officials handed out two thousand Olympic track suits to anyone who looked dirty or down on their luck. Anyone who took a tracksuit had to sign affidavits to promise to wear the suits during the month of the Olympics. Sure, they signed them happily. The sight of the indigent and destitute dressed up like national athletes out for a jog was oddly absurd.

Alan was on a binge. His military disability cheques were spent at the liquor store and the local pub Sailor Hagars. Alan was running out of cash. It had been a month since he last saw Teddy or Karen, and the last few weeks were a drunken haze. He had gained ten pounds and stopped all therapy and contact with his friends or family. Karen heard only fleeting reports from one of his drinking buddies at the pub.

On Halloween night there was a huge protest rally in Stanley Park where hundreds of track suits were thrown into a massive bonfire lit by the protesters. The Vancouver police donned their hats and bats and beat a path to the fire to allow the fire department to drive up and douse the flames. The mayor stood before the cameras on BCTV News and said, "We won't let the actions of a few ungrateful thugs ruin the spirit of the 2010 Games." Alan looked up at the television above the pub fireplace. The reporter was commenting on the escalation of violence around the park; fires were being set, and the determined groups of protestors were growing braver. Alfred, a local pub ruffian, stood up and grabbed Alan by the shoulder. "I'm going down to the park to beat on that silly bastard right now. Come on, big Al, you can be my wingman. Let's go kick some mayoral ass!" Alan and three other guys climbed into the back of a red Suburban, and they headed across the bridge as the sun dipped below the trees. They parked on the backside of the park and walked a half mile along the trails to emerge at the bonfire.

The park was mayhem. People were running about being chased down and beaten by the riot squad. Alan was sober enough to stay out of the streams of pepper spray and to keep his face away from the TV cameras. One protestor accidentally fell into the fire and was taken to hospital by ambulance with some minor burns, but by 11:00 p.m. the fun was over. In the meantime, Alan and his buddies had had many more drinks. While stumbling back towards the car, they happened upon a small fire lit by a half dozen of the protestors who offered up some more beer. Alan and his crew joined the campfire party.

EMERGENCE

The Lions Gate Bridge was Western Canada's most impressive and historic iron icon. The design and style were of the same era as the Golden Gate Bridge, and the twin-tower span connected the North Shore with Stanley Park and the bustling city core. Sentrous leapt from girder to girder, soaring in fifty-foot bounds between the steel supports. He glanced down at the three-hundred-foot drop, the dark ocean swirling around the bridge supports below. The noise of the traffic on the bridge deck above them made it difficult to have his high-frequency conversation with his hunting partner ahead. Aelan loved the big bridge, and he was showing off by jumping across to the far spans and back. Sentrous gave him a shout: "Stop it."

Aelan was younger then Sentrous, and he did many things that Sentrous did not approve of. Aelan was wearing a backpack that Shaman had found for him. She had asked him to bring back some special bones from the kill. Sentrous did not like this dangerous business of wearing clothing. Backpacks got in the way; Aelan was noisy enough in the trees, and he didn't need a backpack to make him louder.

To make matters worse, Sentrous was in trouble due to his rebellious attitude. If the laws were broken, punishments by the elders were severe. A few months ago, Sentrous was almost killed by his mother, Sartra; her wrath had been tempered. She knew the moment he returned that he had broken the rules. The rules of Kamptra dictate the art of silence and the removal of any traces of hunting. Apec females were the experts at this craft of environmental invisibility.

The two sat perched high above the fire, watching the action in the park. They were quiet now, counting and categorizing the humans by their smell and appearance. Something smelled familiar to Sentrous, but he could not place the odour. The laws of Kamptra were very clear on which ones they could take and which ones were off-limits. They identified two that were optimal, and luckily they were sleeping side by side against a tree. Ideally they would be alone since the rules required silence and no witnesses, but this would be an easy take. Both Aelan and Sentrous held their grommets ready for throwing. Grommets were small chestnut-size rocks shaped like teardrops. When thrown by a skilled hunter, they could penetrate a car roof. The grommets flew straight down into the skulls of the two homeless forms sleeping at the base of the tree. One of them flinched at the sudden impact and death. Sentrous and Aelan hauled the bodies up into the tree.

Even drunk, Alan didn't sleep well. He opened his eyes slowly and peered through the smoke over the crackling fire. He squinted and rubbed his eyes at the strange sight. A set wiggling legs was being pulled up into the big tree across from him. He looked up into the canopy and directly into the pinprick black pupils that were so familiar to his nightmares. There was a look of instant recognition from something that could not, in any shape or form, be confused with a cougar. Alan's capillaries dilated and his heart sent a wave of blood to his muscles; his vision flashed white and then tunnelled in on his foe. All was silent, except the sound of the pulse pounding through his temples.

Sentrous was so shocked to stare at the face that brought him so much shame and agony that he almost dropped his prey. He pulled the corpse up and draped it across the tree limb and burst a message to Aelan, who had also seen the awakening human. "Please clean up the mess while I get this guy."

Alan was jolted out of his frozen state by the sudden movement in the trees. He leapt to his feet, running towards the road. He could hear the branches thrashing high up and behind him. He ran straight across the road, his clothes momentarily lit up by the headlights of an oncoming truck. A *whoosh* followed by a thud came from the tree above him. He could hear the trees move as this creature descended slowly, passing from tree to tree. He knew he had only a few seconds to act. The beach path lights were shining through the trees. As Alan ran through the thick brush, he felt something grab hold of his nylon jacket collar and tug, but the collar ripped away as he lunged over the small rock wall, landing with a thud onto the pavement. He popped up in front of a teenage couple out for a midnight skate on their boards. Alan wheeled his head around towards the trees. There was no movement; the shadows were silent.

"Whoa dude, are you OK?" the young skateboarder asked. Alan ignored the question, his eyes scanning the spot where he knew Sentrous was waiting for him. Alan's face was scratched and filthy. His jacket was torn, and his breath stank of booze. The couple tried to walk past him, but he paced them, staying uncomfortably close. He could hear Sentrous passing through the trees about fifteen feet up into the tree line. The couple, wary of Alan, jumped onto their skateboards and wheeled down the shoreline path. Alan backed away from the path onto the rocky beach. "Yeah, you bastard, you don't like to come out of the trees, do you!"

Alan stumbled over a rock as what felt like a bullet whizzed past his nose. The water behind him chirped as the projectile entered the smooth ocean surface. Alan's eyes widened as the tall, lanky creature leapt out of the bush across the path towards him. Alan ran straight down to the beach and dove into the black water. His pulse jumped again at the shock of the cold. The icy ocean covered his face, and he swam under the surface for as long as he could stand it. As he popped up, he spun around towards the beach; it was empty. The water in front of his face flew up as a grommet entered the water and pierced his skin above his collarbone. He turned and swam as fast as he could out to sea. He swam out to about two hundred feet from the shoreline. Another grommet whizzed past his head and splashed in the water. Alan kept swimming.

He turned to swim parallel to the shore for a while, and then he stopped. He stared at the trees above the pathway but couldn't detect any movement. He had swum with the current for around a half mile, following the path around the point, and he started to tire from the cold. He slowly paddled to one of the support cement caissons about a hundred feet from shore at the base of the bridge. Once out of the water, he lay on his back, panting. The current was strong here, and the water swirled around his little concrete-and-steel island.

"Cougar, my ass. I was right, that thing is real," Alan announced to the steel beams below the bridge. "Yeah, you spiny bastard, you missed me again!" Movement above him caught his eye. There were two of them, and they were practically flying under the bridge. The first one reached the top of the pillar and started to descend the columns towards him. As Sentrous grew closer, he picked up speed. His mouth stretched open as he let out an ultrasonic howl of rage. Alan couldn't hear the howl, but he could feel the high-frequency vibrations penetrate his skull. His ears and eyes burned from the screech. Clutching his ears, Alan leapt into the ocean once again, and the current swept him out into the harbour shipping lanes. Sentrous stopped at the bottom of the pillar and watched Alan float away. Alan waved at him, and he could see the anger in Sentrous' eyes.

Swept by the currents in First Narrows pass, he drifted into the middle of the harbour. Alan was fading in and out of consciousness. After an hour in the currents, the cold was seeping into his body core. He didn't feel cold or scared, just calm. His thoughts drifted back to his training at the navy dive school. There he'd endured days and days in the waters of Esquimalt Harbour and the frigid waters of the Juan de Fuca straights.

Seventeen years prior, on a dreary coastal day, Alan and his wet-suited troop mates sat in a grey Zodiac. They were exhausted after a two-hour dive in the ripping currents of race rocks. The instructor looked over to the nearby beach and announced, "OK, guys, you've had a hard day in those currents and you're all maxed out on your dive tables, so I just want one more little drill. Swim over to the beach, grab me a piece of driftwood, and bring it back to the boat, and you can take the rest of the night off."

The guys all cheered, and Alan didn't even bother to put on his wetsuit top as he dove over the side and raced to the beach. He grabbed the biggest piece of driftwood that he could carry and swam it back to the vessel as if it was a victim. His other teammates all had smaller pieces, and they caught up with Alan as he approached the boat. There was just one problem: when he got within ten feet of the Zodiac, he realized that the boat was idling in reverse away from him. The instructor had his fishing rod out, and the salmon flasher was spinning in the water just beyond Alan's reach. Eventually the whole troop joined Alan on his little log, paddling behind the Zodiac as it trolled slowly out into the straights of Juan de Fuca. After a few hours, the instructor berated the students for scaring off the fish and finally let them back into the boat. Alan had looked up across the water at the sparkling city lights and realized that they were only a few miles off the American coast and almost at the harbour entrance of Port Angeles. They had swum over twelve miles across the frigid straights.

His flashback ended. The alcohol in his blood dilated his vessels, speeding up the heat loss and altering his hormone levels.

Luckily the extra fat on his body acted as an insulator and prevented the last bit of heat from leaving his tissues. He could feel the strength in his arms waning as he stroked into the darkness. Alan's circulation was being slowed and the warm blood shunted protectively to his thorax. As his temperature dipped below thirty degrees Celsius, he could no longer pull himself out of the water, if he managed to reach shore. His blood pressure was being propped up by the squeeze of the ocean on his submerged body. Even if a rescuer plucked him from the water at this very moment, he could still go into a cardiac arrest and die. There were no rescuers in sight, only the shiny black sea and the city lights. He had survived so many tight situations over the years, but now he lay on his back and waited for the cold to spill into his lungs.

The rubber mask covered Alan's nose, and the heated oxygen valve was opened to let the warm air flow. The aluminum deck vibrated, as the coast guard hovercraft skidded around the corner and shot up the boat ramp to meet the waiting ambulance.

The coast guard rescue specialist spoke to the paramedic. "Hey Arnold, this one's not a bridge jumper. No obvious trauma, he's just really cold—core temp twenty-eight degrees Celsius."

"Twenty-eight Celsius, that's pretty cold; we'll get him to the hospital so they can start re-warming him."

The painting was old, maybe 1970s; a grey donkey ordained in a Mexican poncho stood attached to a two-wheeled cart. Alan pondered how many lunatics had gazed at this Donkey in the past forty years. It was the same room in the psych ward. Once again, Alan's ass hung out of the gap in a blue hospital gown. It was a dismal place, yet Alan was elated. He wasn't delusional, he wasn't crazy, and he didn't need antipsychotics. That thing that he was dancing with last night was no cougar. It was a real monster, a vicious, long-armed, yellow-toothed, big, black, and spiky monkey monster. He felt better than he had in a long time. Maybe it was the thrill of a big scare, mixed with the exertion from a long swim. It was as if the cold ocean had cleansed his brain, rinsed out the cobwebs. His mind was sharp, and although he was weak from the long hours spent in a hypothermic state, he felt energetic. It seemed as though depression and addiction had robbed him of his energy and enthusiasm for years. Now the creature had given him back his drive. He checked himself out of the hospital.

Alan checked his phone. It had been drowned, along with his wallet and credit cards. He looked up into the blue sky between the hospital towers and smiled. The colours looked sharper and the air was crisp and cold. Karen obviously had known that he was in the hospital; she had dropped off some dry clothes and fifty bucks. He started walking briskly down the hill towards Lonsdale Quay. Memories of the last month of pitiful, selfish behaviours flooded into his mind. The ticker tape of regret and self-loathing started again.

Whoa, what an idiot I've been. OK, buddy, don't talk yourself down—you just beat the pants off of a cold-blooded beast. You were one of the fittest, brightest officers in the military, and you still have all your limbs and your head still works...kinda. As Alan encouraged himself, the negative messages started to fade.

"There's a monster out there and...wait, two monsters, and they knew who I was." Alan would often talk to himself while walking or running, and he was talking excitedly as he turned down his street. "Jesus, that spiny bastard recognised me! He looked genuinely surprised, like, 'Holy shit, it's you!' Ha ha, you ugly fucker, it's me all right, and I'm not your regular homeless beef sandwich!" A woman walking on the other side of the street stared at Alan as he jabbered about monsters.

Don't act crazy, Alan, he thought as random questions began to race through his head. *Where did these things come from? Where were they living? I had better lose some weight and start working out. These things are like Alcoholics Anonymous from hell; every time I get pissed or high, they try to eat my ass.* As he approached his building, he noticed the police car parked in his parking lot. He walked up the small flight of stairs and opened the door to Karen. She embraced him tightly, squeezing for longer than the usual hug. He looked over her shoulder at the pile of coats and shoes.

"Hey babe, who's here?" Alan looked into the crowded living room and recognized all of his friends and family. The group of a dozen perched nervously around some bowls of nacho chips and pitchers of juice. "Holy shit, who died?" Alan said.

Constable Perry stood up from the kitchen table and walked into the living room. "You, Alan—you almost died." Karen held Alan's hand and walked him to the couch while all eyes looked upon him. Teddy was there, Kyle and Roger from the squadron, a couple of his Afghanistan buddies, Bryce and Mark, and his parents. They all looked intensely concerned.

"In case you didn't notice, I am not dead. I'm OK."

Karen answered, "Constable Perry has been good enough to keep me informed on what you have been doing in the last few weeks. He saw you drunk and stoned on the east side a couple of times. When he got the report that you had jumped off the bridge, he suggested that we do an intervention."

"Karen, I didn't jump off a bridge, and I don't need an intervention. I'm OK. I feel a lot better, actually." Constable Perry jumped in.

"Alan, you need to check yourself into a rehab program and get yourself some help. The alcohol and the drugs have to stop now, or you will lose this beautiful family."

Alan grasped his situation quickly and realised that argument or protest would not help. He had seen interventions on TV and understood what was up.

He loved these people, and they were all there out of concern and love for him. It was no use trying to explain that a huge spiny monster had chased him into the ocean—that story would only help ascertain what type of program he would have to check into. Maybe a little structure in his life would be good.

"You are right. I am ready to clean up and smarten up. Where do you suggest that I go?"

8 Twelve Steps and a Monster

Week three in the rehab facility, and Alan had come to the conclusion that his room was too small for both him and his roommate. The slim character in the next bed was snoring, but it wasn't the snoring that kept Alan awake; it was his taste buds. He was imagining the taste of a double vodka and coke, the look of condensation on the glass and the jingle of the ice cubes. Sobriety was sobering. He had been clean for only a couple of weeks, and this was his first real midnight craving. He was clean and sombre; no more fun, no more parties, just dark grey days sipping mint tea until he dropped dead of old age. He felt like he would never smile again. Everything was so damn serious.

The next morning Alan sat at a lounge table in this ten-bed facility; Scrabble boards and jigsaw puzzles surrounded him as he scratched away at his notepad. He needed to map out his situation on paper. He needed to define what was real and what was crazy. He needed a process that would guide him through a situational analysis. He couldn't find any monster metric worksheets on the web, so he stuck with the SWOT analysis (strengths, weaknesses, opportunities, and threats). SWOT was a common analytic tool taught in business schools, and he thought he'd give it a try. *Let's start with the cool stuff—monsters.*

EMERGENCE

SWOT/ BFH Monsters

Strengths/Positives:

1. I am alive. I didn't get killed by BFHM (Big Fucking Hairy Monster). Why wasn't I killed?
2. I am smart and a trained killer (looks good on paper, maybe not so smart and not so tough).
3. I am sober.
4. I stopped whining about all my shit.

Weaknesses/Negatives:

1. Being hunted by a BFHM. Is he hunting me? (maybe, maybe not).
2. I am an alcoholic and addict.
3. The fucker bit me.
4. Am now freaked out by BFHM. (As if I needed more things to freak me out.)

Opportunities;

1. Sort my life out and get in shape.
2. Get Karen back.
3. Get Teddy back.
4. Get organized and kill these mofos. (How do I do that? Who's going to believe me? My mom?) Can't do this by myself.
5. Forget about the BFHMs and get on with my life. Not bad!
6. Save the world! Not great.

Threats:

1. Monsters killing people in general (that's bad). How many? How long has this been going on?
2. PTSD ends up fucking me up beyond all repair.
3. If I start talking about monsters, then people will think that I am nuts. (Maybe I am nuts?)
4. Get locked up in the loony bin. Throw away key.
5. Could lose it and start drinking again, end up a hobo, get eaten by BFHM (again). Or spend the rest of my life in the street being a hobo that babbles on about big hairy monsters. (Rather be eaten.)

6. *Maybe the monsters are aliens taking over world...yeah OK, see Number 4.*

Alan sipped his coffee and scanned over his notes. He focussed in on the key questions:

Who are these guys?

He didn't have a clue. They looked like huge black monkeys with white eyes and nasty teeth. They acted like humans. Alan opened up his laptop and looked through pictures of different monkeys. They resembled a black howler monkey, only much bigger and meaner. The web search showed a host of photos of cute monkeys commonly found in Costa Rica and South America. *I should really ask Karen about this stuff, she's got the doctorate.* Alan wrestled with the idea but could not figure out a way to get into the subject without the BFHMs coming up.

Why didn't the creature kill me the first time?

He and his buddy had certainly killed those two homeless guys in the park. *He had me in his jaws, and he just released me. Maybe I'm not very tasty.* Alan laughed at his mental joke.

Was the one creature actually pursuing me?

He thought that the chances of him seeing the same monster twice were astronomical, but then there was the unmistakable expression of surprise on its face when they'd locked eyes. *Maybe he's looking for me now that I have pissed him off...maybe.* There was no mistaking the look on his face when Alan swam away the second time.

How many are there? How many people do they kill?

Now there was a question that he may be able to answer. Alan started a web search for missing people in BC. The first hit from the search was a master's thesis written by a woman from Simon

Fraser University in 2005. As of July 2005, 2,293 people were presently missing in BC alone, and over seven thousand Canada-wide. Alan could not believe this figure. He assumed a few dozen people maybe, but over two thousand people right here? The United States had over one hundred thousand missing people, a staggering number. How many of the missing were food stock for these creatures? They must have other animals or vegetables in their diet. *They can't just eat humans, or we would have known about it earlier.*

For Action

Priorities

1. *Bring Karen some flowers and apologize for being an asshole.*
2. *Call Teddy and take him to the movies.*
3. *Research the BFHMs.*
4. *Call Kelly George.*

Questions:

1. *Are the BFHMs out to get me? Am I done with them?*
2. *Do I forget about these guys and carry on with the higher priorities?*
3. *Can I just let them eat people?*

The West Coast natives must know these guys. Alan thought for a moment and then picked up the phone and punched a memorized number.

"Hello." The greeting was deep and prominent.

"Hello, Kelly. It's Alan Wickey."

"Wickey boy, I heard you lost your marbles after you got eaten by a cougar, and now you're locked up in the looney bin, licking the windows." Kelly's laugh rolled out like thunder. "I would have shown up to your intervention, but I was on a plane."

"Kelly, can I meet you for coffee?"

"As long as you don't have climb out the window, crazy Wickey." More chuckles rattled on the other end of the phone.

Kelly signed Alan out of the facility. Kelly parked behind the supermarket in Horseshoe Bay. The small harbour was bustling with ferry passengers mixed with the occasional local. The beachfront of marinas and green parks was in the shadow of the hulking ferry terminal. In amongst the trinket shops and art exhibits sat a cottage-style building topped by silver cedar shakes. It was a little greasy spoon called the Boathouse. This was a standard haunt for Alan and his buddies. Kelly had a permanent smile. Even in the midst of a firefight, Alan had never seen Kelly in any state other than calm and joking.

"Look at you, crazy Wickey. Looks like that cougar might have pulled that stick out of your ass. You look better than I've seen you look for years."

Alan laughed as he let out a sigh of relief. Kelly always had a way of making a serious situation seem like no big deal. "Kelly, what do you know about Sasquatch?"

Kelly shook his head, and the smile changed to a hint of disappointment. "Alan, the Sasquatch is an overweight American actor in a hairy suit. That suit is probably hanging in a dusty Hollywood storage room. Sit down and visit with me. How is Karen?"

"She's OK. We're separated, but working on getting back together."

"Wickey, if you're too crazy for her, then I will take her out for a few dates and take care of her for you until you figure your shit out." His teeth flashed again.

"Yeah, sometimes I wish she didn't love you so much."

"I know, Wickey; you know that all of the women love me," Kelly replied. "Since you are in such a hurry to get down to business, let me see the bite marks." Kelly's tone changed slightly. Alan pulled down his black turtleneck to expose the lines of red teardrop-shaped scars. Kelly leant over to have a closer look.

"It wasn't a cougar. It was some type of huge primate like a monkey. It flew in the trees and had porcupine quills."

"Stiyaha."

"The what?"

"The whistlers. They are creatures of the night that live in the treetops. They live with us in the woods." Alan dropped his fork and looked up. Kelly chewed his bagel as he spoke. "They are an old legend. Nobody has ever seen one. Supposed to be very respectful; they only take elders and sick that are ready to die."

Alan just stared at Kelly in disbelief. "You knew of these things, the whole time?"

Kelly raised his eyebrows and shrugged his shoulders. "Alan, in native folklore ravens run the wilderness and bears talk." Kelly frowned as he bit into his bagel again. "White men are like little kids, they only hear what they are ready to hear. I could tell you that I have the cure for cancer and the cure for your marriage, and you are just going to hear the part about the monster. It is OK, my friend, I will still be patient with you. I will tell you again when you are ready to hear it."

"What do they look like?"

"Alan, I just told you that I have the cure for your marriage, and you want to talk about monsters. I think that I should sleep with Karen. She probably needs some attention."

Alan blushed. "OK, what's the cure for my marriage?"

"Effort, Alan, effort; a marriage is like an old sailing ship, you have to work on her every day, sanding, polishing, fixing. If you just sail her around on sunny days and let the work pile up, eventually, the seams open up in the hull, and you just sink."

Kelly just looked at his friend's face for a long moment. "Here're some ship-fixing tools, Alan." Kelly held out two glossy tickets imprinted with colourful depictions of native art. "These are tickets to the Roy Henry Vickers and Friends exhibit at the UBC museum. Roy is my cousin, and he gives me these tickets. I have seen all his old Indian crap a million times. Take Karen out for a nice night on the town; some dinner, some culture. Hot white girls love Roy's stuff; why do you think he paints it?"

Alan took the tickets. "Thanks, Kelly, you do have a way of putting things into perspective."

"There are always monsters of some type to chase, but the harder thing is the loving. Once you have taken that girl out and she is smiling, then come back and we will talk about your friends in the trees." Alan paid for the coffee.

A week later, Alan had completed his stay in rehab. Karen sat in the passenger seat as the car glided between the lights that lined Marine Drive on the way to the Museum of Anthropology at UBC. "Did you thank Kelly for the tickets?" Karen asked. She was excited.

"How did you know the tickets were from Kelly?"

"Alan, you could have married a dumb little blonde, but you didn't, did you? You married a red-headed PhD." Karen took her gum out of her mouth and placed it back into its tiny wrapper, folding it precisely into a square. "It's OK, honey, you took the time to arrange this—we had a really nice dinner—and here we are, actually going. You get full marks for that."

Karen thought the exhibit was stunning, and even Alan—not a huge art fan—was impressed. Karen was the ultimate butterfly; her orange-flecked green eyes and her tall, striking figure made her an art attraction in her own right. Mr. Vickers and the other artists gravitated towards Karen, whose natural enthusiasm and engaging questions kept them tickled. Alan strolled into the back section of the exhibits, where some of Bill Reid's carvings were mixed with ancient totems from the 1700s. The really old pieces were sitting in glass cases. He was only mildly annoyed at the attention that his wife drew; he was used to it. He recalled the last official event they had both attended at the Orpheum theatre. After awarding Alan with his medal, the Order of Distinguished Service, both the governor general and the prime minister had introduced themselves to Karen and struck up a long chat with her that had to be interrupted by the first lady. Karen could speak elegantly on any subject under the sun. How Alan Wickey had ended up with a woman who had such an aura of royalty certainly baffled him. *Effort, Wickey, effort.* Kelly's words rang in his head.

Alan stopped dead at a tall three-hundred-year-old carving. The face on the carving looked back at him with a familiar gaze. *Stiyaha*, the engraving read. Alan's stomach rolled and sweat started to spill down his cheek. The long arms and sharp claws had Alan backing up until a hand touched his shoulder. He yelped.

"Mr. Wickey, I didn't mean to startle you. My name is Roy, and your wife told me you were here. I just wanted to say thank you."

Alan caught his breath and turned to meet the artist. "Hello, Mr. Vickers. What are you thanking me for?"

"Mr. Wickey, you saved my cousin, Billy Robinson, on the *Mariah II*." Roy held onto Alan's hand while searching his eyes.

Alan's mind immediately flashed back to the sad scene in the middle of the Queen Charlotte Straits. The *Mariah II*, a fishing boat, had rolled over in a storm so quickly that only half of the crew had time to escape, let alone don their survival suits. The survivors had clung to the overturned hull, waiting for rescue for many hours. Markus Robinson was the older of two brothers on the crew; both were able to climb up onto the overturned hull, but young Billy did not have a survival suit. He was dressed in his boxer shorts and a T-shirt. During this time, three of them slipped away into the water. Markus knew that his little brother would succumb in the freezing winds, so he took off his survival suit and wrestled Billy into it. The storm raged all night, pulling the heat from Markus's body. After the second hour, Billy was desperately trying to hold onto his older brother, but his frozen body slipped from his grip and sank into the sea. The 442's Buffalo aircraft had spotted the hull at first light, and Alan's helo crew made it to the scene shortly after. Billy and the other survivors had spent the better part of the night in the ocean, and all were close to death when Alan dropped down onto the swamped hull. He had treated Billy as he was flown to the hospital in the helicopter.

"I'm sorry about Markus." Alan spoke with his eyes down.

"Mr. Wickey, Billy is doing well now, and Markus's spirit has been watching over him. Billy was into the drugs there for a while, but now he is working in my shop with me and even going to school in Nanaimo. He is sober and has a little boy named Owen. He owes his life to you and your crew." Alan was quiet, and the two looked down for a moment.

"Kelly was saying that you may need some help." Roy reached out and gently pulled Alan's shirt collar down to reveal the bite marks. "The whistlers are very elusive. Few have seen them, and they don't leave witnesses. The legends say that even the people they take never see their faces."

"They are not very attractive, let me tell you."

Roy laughed. "They took my grandmother when I was little. We had a big party, and she said good-bye to the whole family and walked off into the woods. I followed her to the waiting place; I hid behind a tree until the sun went down. Nothing happened for a while; she just sat on the ground. She was singing a song, quietly. Then she yelled out to me, 'Little Roy, you have to leave or the Stiyaha will not come!' She had seen me hiding. Then I heard the wind whistle through the trees and then a real high-pitched squeal in my ears."

"What did you do?" Alan asked.

"I ran away; I was only nine. The next day I went up to the family resting place on the high ridge, and there she was, clean pink bones in a bundle, looking over the river in her hat and shawl. Her special things placed beside her, neatly. She's still up there."

"The elders say that only the children can hear the whistlers. I remember hearing the same squeal in the woods at night sometimes when I was in my bed." Roy smiled. "My mother used to threaten me when I was being bad. She caught me stealing change from her drawer. 'Little Roy, I will call the whistlers to come and get you if you steal my quarters again!' I didn't steal any more quarters." Roy laughed. "You've been stealing quarters, Alan?" Alan looked up to meet Roy's smile.

"Why did these guys pick me?" Alan asked.

Roy's mood sobered as he reflected on Alan's situation. "I don't know why they didn't take you when they had you the in the woods. I have never heard of anyone meeting them face to face and living to talk about it. Maybe they changed their mind, for some reason."

"What are we going to do about this? I mean, these guys are taking people right out of the city. Should I go to the police?"

"Yeah, the police are going to like your story about creatures living in the forest, swinging from the trees." Roy smiled again. Alan sighed as Roy continued. "I have never heard of them hunting humans, especially not white men; maybe there are too many of you. I mean, you are all so fat and pink and tasty; a meal that they couldn't resist." Roy laughed.

"Now you sound like Kelly."

"He's my cousin. Alan, if you're thinking about hunting the Stiyaha, then let me know. I will stay here and give your lovely wife Karen some painting lessons."

"Cousins, eh…figures." Alan chuckled.

"Painting lessons? Sign me up!" Karen startled Alan by joining the conversation. "What's this about hunting?" Karen asked.

"Hunting, uh, what do you mean?" Alan replied. Karen squinted her eyes with suspicion at Alan's obvious dodge.

During the drive home, Karen was quiet. Alan knew that she didn't like to be left out of the loop. She had a knack for analysing situations and solving problems. As a scientist, she was an aggressive pursuer of truth. To fill the silence, Alan decided to strike up a new topic, inadvertently wandering into an emotional trap.

"So, what can I do to improve our communications?" Alan asked in earnest. Karen gave him a look as her mind flashed through the various paths that this conversation would take. She was already annoyed at Alan's coyness and his obvious attempts at concealing something. Most of Alan's perplexing situations were neither complex nor unpredictable. Her biggest challenge was usually being patient while Alan figured out his own stuff.

"You probably don't want to go there right now," Karen replied as a fair warning.

"No, really. I want to learn how to communicate with you better."

Karen drew a deep breath. She opened up the carrying case between the car seats, pulled out a roll of tape, and cut out a small square with her nails. "If you really want to learn something, then try this for a minute." She leaned over and taped Alan's mouth. Alan's eyebrows lifted and he thought, *Hey, I'm not a big talker, I'm a quiet guy*. Karen started her lesson.

"One of my biggest frustrations with you is not that you talk too much, but that you say the wrong things at the wrong time. You are not describing your feelings; the things that you are saying when you reply to me are things meant to pacify me or make me understand something." Karen paused for a minute, letting her words sink in. Alan drove, quietly mumbling a little through the tape. Karen put her finger up to her mouth and continued. "Alan, when I talk to you about my feelings, they are my feelings, not a list of your shortcomings, or a list of a bunch of things that you have to run out and fix right away. No, honey, I am not looking for one of your brilliant solutions or promises to try harder or do better. I just want you to listen and let me know that you heard me!" She raised her voice. "You see, I just need to talk about my feelings to get them out in the air so that they can congeal and mature into something that you and I can deal with. That's the process, buddy boy, and you are not getting it; you miss it every fucking time. It's on page one of the girl's manual. I need you to listen to my feelings so that I can work with them and rearrange them. We have not yet made it through one of our conversations without it becoming about you: what you think, what you are going to do, or how it hurts your feelings and is not fair."

Alan drove on, his urges to interject, to react, and to fix suppressed by the tape. Karen let the silence emphasize her words as they danced around in Alan's head like ancient Greek characters. Alan tried to make sense of what she was saying; there was a startling realization in there somewhere. This could not be how women actually were. Karen leaned over to rip off the tape. "Alan, this is the part where you paraphrase my feelings and what I said without you talking about you." Alan nodded in compliance, and Karen ripped off the tape.

"How do you mean, paraphrase?"

Karen thought about it for a moment. "Give me a military situation report on our conversation."

"Right, OK. Uh…" Alan proceeded carefully. "You would like me to learn to listen to you while you vent your feelings without interjecting my own junk, reactions, and trying to fix it all. Tach 629er out." Alan couldn't help the wit.

"That's not too bad."

Unfortunately Alan continued. "So…girls don't have a clutch between their brains and their mouths—they actually have to talk in order to think things out? Weirdness."

Karen's smile dropped; she sighed with frustration, and then came the sparkling eyes reflecting the welling tears. Alan looked over and realized that he had done it again; for the thousandth time, he had missed the cue. Yes, that cue that told him it was important—not just important but vital—that he take her message seriously. He had just blown her off with his trademark brashness and sarcasm. He could play out the next four exchanges in his head like an old eight-track tape. Here it was, the ancient labyrinth of marital communication. This was a maze that he often wandered into and had no idea of the path out, yet Karen had provided him with a string and a way out.

Ten minutes left in the drive, time to completely screw it up or come out a hero. He thought to himself, *OK, no drugs or alcohol to cloud my judgement. What's my next move?* Here it was, a new five seconds of time and space opened up between choices. All of his old paths in the maze ended in frustration and despair. Alan knew them all well, for he was preconditioned to follow them with comments like, "Hey, I didn't mean to blow you off" or "Don't take me so seriously, babe, you know I love you," or just stoic manly silence. Now was the time to make the move, but what was the move? Oh wait, she'd just spent ten minutes telling him the move.

Alan pulled the car over to the side and stopped the clock.

"Karen, you're married to a guy who has trouble with this stuff, but here it goes. You need me to listen to your feelings, without interjecting, reacting, and being an asshole. You need me to help you work out your thoughts by letting you talk about them, and I am supposed to tell you that I hear you, and that I care about what you say. I do really care what you say and how you feel. I promise to carry this roll of duct tape around from now on, and hopefully over time and with some practise, I won't need it anymore."

She looked up into his eyes and searched them for a moment and then looked down again. "I never thought that I'd hear you say it...ever." Karen paused. "Of course I did just give you answers, laid out step by step." She laughed a little.

Alan started up the car and pulled out, grinning like a little boy who had scored a goal. He drove on; for the first time in his marriage, he had actually made it out of that damn maze. Alan smiled and thought, *If I'm going to pull this off again, I'd better write this shit down; it's like some crazy riddle.*

The car stopped in the driveway of their home, and Karen invited him in for a coffee. As soon as they entered the door, Karen pulled him up the stairs and started to undo his shirt buttons. He pulled her dress up over her head and unclasped her bra; her nipples brushed against the hair on his chest as he moved down her neck, pulling her panties down her long legs. It had been months since he had touched her soft skin, and the sight of her neatly shaved pubic hair made him take a deep breath. She lifted her feet one at a time as he flung the panties away. She threw her head back and gasped, grabbing his hair. Still standing, she pulled his face to her body. He reached up to grab her hips, tilting his head to push his tongue between the folds of her labia. She moaned and pulled with her hands, kneading his hair through her fingers, opening her stance a little to give him better access. After a few moments of caressing, her moans grew deeper and her hips moved to his tongue. She gasped again, thrusting her mound into Alan's mouth, her legs shuddering during her climax. Alan hoisted Karen onto the bed with her legs held back. She gasped as he her entered her. His thrusts were slow at first, but he increased his rhythm with her breathing. She started to moan when he pushed deep into her warmth. She arched her back and climaxed again..

.

9 The Lair

Cathedral Mountain looks over the city lights of Vancouver. Its peak sits 5,700 feet above the still waters of Indian Arm. The bottom of the mountain is frequented by hikers, but few venture up into the jagged cliffs that cover the top. The black rock penetrates the snowy pillars that stand one thousand feet above the alpine tree line. Mountain pines and spruce trees cling to the steep slopes, their branches weighted with snow.

Far down in the valley, a white university van pulled up to the water's edge at Rodgers Lake. When the doors open, a group of four young entomology students clamber out and walk towards the lake shore.

Professor Hamilton rolled down the driver's window. "Please don't urinate in the lake! Go and get your hiking gear ready because we have a full seven kilometres to go, and this trail is a tough one."

The reddish pine needles covered the path as they ascended the steep trail. Sun illuminated the long boughs of the evergreens that covered their trek like a thick green rooftop. The four students, two girls and two guys, were excited about the possibility of catching some rare green pine beetles; these beetles were once common, but a newly introduced invasive beetle was wiping out the green beetle. The voracious mountain pine beetle was also devouring thousands of acres of forests in western Canada.

The professor followed the young group, narrating over their heads, his gaze turned up. "Our field of awareness is restricted to a narrow vertical beam ranging from the ground just ahead of you to a spot about four feet above head height. Anything outside of this field is generally invisible to us. Occasionally you will ponder the skies to gaze at the stars or check the weather, but really, when was the last time you looked up into the canopy? Up is the realm of the insects, birds, and undiscovered creatures. It is the neglected mid space in the universe, forgotten or ignored until something drops out of it. You cannot track creatures that fly through the middle of the trees; you cannot see them from the air, and you cannot hear them coming. They can hear you, smell you, and prepare for you long before you arrive. This is why they are so elusive and why we have look up and pay special attention to the life just there in the canopy. We are so busy tearing down our forests, destroying whole habitats, so we can ship raw logs to Asia. Unless people like you and I stop and take a look at what's living just up there in the trees, a species may disappear and become extinct before they are even discovered." The professor finished his monologue with a deep sigh.

Because they were not really looking up, even after the lecture, the group was unaware of the upheaval in the canopy. A male sentry sent out a warning burst to the lair, a mile up the trail. The elders sent out warning signals and woke up the young ones and the rest of the clan. The young were loaded onto the backs of the hunters and sent to the cave. The woven treetop burrows were ripped apart to clear the trees of any visible structures. Now that the clan was ready for action, the fema members moved to reconnaissance positions high above the forest floor, waiting for the hikers to arrive. Only two male hunters were allowed to take forward positions and wait for direction from Sartra.

Sartra was larger than any of the males, and a very powerful leader. As she hung upside down in the top of an old-growth cedar, her quill coat took on a green-and-brown-flecked colour.

The Apec quills were full of a carotene-like protein that could change the quills' colours at will. This made them almost invisible in the woods or in the wilderness in general. Their culture of Kamptra had kept them hidden from Western human awareness. However, the native Indians in the area had always known of them. This clan had about thirty members. The fema was the senior group of five females that lead the clan in decisions and discipline. Sartra was the clan chief, and Shaman served as Sartra's advisor on most matters. She watched the students and professor approach.

The first student, Parker, looked up at the trees and said, "Hey guys, look at these old fir stands."

EMERGENCE

The professor corrected him. "They are red cedars, Parker." One of the girls chuckled at his mistake but stopped when she looked down and noticed parts of the woven branches on the forest floor.

"What are these? They look like they have been hand woven." She took some photos of the odd arrangements, then pointed the camera up at the trees. The lens was pointing right at Panshua. She was curled into a tight wrap around the tree about fifty feet above the group. The camera whizzed with an electronic shutter click. Sartra watched the human with the camera. Purely nocturnal, they rarely moved during the day. A daytime mission was dangerous, and Sartra had to balance the rules of Kamptra with the needs of the clan. The camera was going to be a problem. Sartra signalled Panshua, asking her to take care of the camera; she took one of the hunters with her. Panshua and Aelan slowly moved up towards the group of humans.

"Hey Lisa, what are you taking a picture of?" Parker asked.

"The pretty branches here and the treetops, just some artsy pics for my computer desktop."

"Do you get the feeling like we are being watched?" Parker asked.

"Shut up, Parker, don't be a loser; you're always trying to freak us out."

"Parker, I would appreciate you not making the girls crazy," Hamilton added.

The five walked along the path, all looking straight up at the small group of fema high above them. Round white eyes stared down at them. Panshua and Aelan followed them down the trail, waiting for an opportunity. The group of students stopped at a cliff face and looked down the steep gorge to the river. It dropped down into the misty turbulent swirl of white water. The Bear River roared through the valley and towards the sea. Panshua gave Aelan the signal to act.

Lisa held up the camera to take some shots of the rushing water below. There was a loud crack, and the camera flew out of her hands, tumbling through the misty canyon air.

"Oh my god, my camera!" Lisa looked down into the gorge. "What the hell was that? It was as if someone hit the camera out of my hand—did you hear that crack?"

Panshua was very pleased with Aelan's shot. She was relieved that she did not have to sneak into a tent or worse, into a house, to get the camera.

Panshua assigned Aelan to follow the hikers for the next few hours; they passed through this spot again on their way back without any further events. As they skipped down the path towards the parking lot, Panshua paused to breathe in the dreamy scent of the clean ones, the forbidden ones, the delicious ones. Panshua knew their taste because of the special offerings. Rarely, young and clean humans would happen upon a lair or sight a clan member, and they would have to be taken. This was only done upon the order of the chief and after careful consideration. Shaman would set loose the prey for chase by the younglings in hunting practice. Once the young ones had finished their kill, Shaman would prepare the remaining meat with specials scents and roots. She would hand out little treats to the young and then offer the rest to the clan at a special ceremony. Here Shaman would tell the stories of the old times and talk about the ancestors of the Salt Clan. These were specials nights of cheer and spirits.

Later that week, a special night came again. The telephone company had a powerful transmitter station near the mountain peak. These towers were connected to a small generator shed that had to be refuelled and maintained a few times per year. A jet ranger helicopter sailed above the treetops near the peak of the mountain. The pilot was trying to stay under the cloud cover. It popped up above the tree line and circled the wooden landing pad perched on the ridge. At this altitude, the air was thin, so the pilot had to keep on the pitch and throttle to bring the bird gently down onto the pad. Two men stepped down from the helicopter and hiked the short trail over to the transmission tower and shed. The small generator shack perched on a snow-covered peak at five thousand feet. Garnished with a veranda around the front and two windows, the little shed had an unintentional gingerbread look to it. Inside were a TV, a fridge, a couch, and two beds in the event that the work crews were weathered in for a few days.

The two men did not realize that the mountaintop transmitter facility had an unwelcome squatter. The two generators in the shed ran continuously, making it impossible for Shaman to hear their approach. The male sentry that she had assigned as a lookout had gotten distracted and had left his post. This was Shaman's second home; here she could watch the TV news and study the humans. She was also working on her human skeleton project. She would ask the hunters for a particular bone or pair of bones. She was using these various bones to rebuild a whole skeleton with bits from all the kills over the past two years. The door swung open, and Shaman leapt up to the ceiling as the two technicians walked in and turned on the lights. They dropped their bags and rubbed their shoulders at the chilled sub-zero air outside. The shed was warm because of the constantly running generators. The ceiling of the shed was open with crossbeams supporting the weight of the steep, snow-covered roof. Shaman lay on top of the beam and waited for the moment to strike. She cursed herself for leaving her prized bone puzzle out for discovery, and she knew that they would soon discover it and then she would have to kill them. The clan would be delighted to eat the clean meat and enjoy the special night, but Shaman was the keeper of the rules of Kamptra, and she knew that taking clean ones had dire consequences. As much as she looked forward to the taste of the kill, this was a bad situation and she should have known better than to allow herself to get into it.

The two men walked over to the generators and set up their tools and laptops, not noticing the gruesome bone puzzle laid out meticulously beside the couch. Once the laptop was plugged into the running generator, one of the two techs walked by, inches away from Shaman's protruding quills. Thomas strolled over towards the TV and sofa. Shaman now knew there was no chance to keep Kamptra, and she reached down and around to grab the light bulb.

"Hey Ned, what the hell is this?" The lights went out, and she swiped down with her claws and knocked Thomas out cold. He fell with a grunt that was imperceptible against the loud roar of the generators. Ned hunted around in the darkness looking for his flashlight. Locating it, he turned it on. It lit up the face of the predator hanging upside down a few inches from him. Before he could scream, Shaman clasped his head with one hand and poked her other claws into his larynx. She held his head as he struggled to pull back. She could feel the sinewy texture of his vocal cords, so she grasped them and pulled them out of the hole. He began to shudder as the breath and blood shot out of and then was sucked back into the foamy gash. Shaman leant forward and licked up the trickle of blood oozing from his skin. She kept her eyes on the unconscious one as she controlled the big six-foot technician. Shaman rarely hunted these days, and today she would have to be clever enough to keep these two alive long enough to let them be used in the hunting games. She gave the tall one a last lick to keep too much blood from staining the floor. Holding his head against the wooden support post, she then reached down and grabbed his knee. She twisted his patella out of place to dislocate it. He writhed in pain, breathing in spurts through the hole in his neck. Shaman threw him over her shoulder and carried him down the mountain and into the trees where she lashed him, upside down, at the top of a large pine. Now that she was clear of the generator noise, she sounded an alert to rouse the clan.

While waiting, Shaman worked the tech's knee cap back into place, hoping that he would heal enough to allow him to run well in the hunting games. Sartra arrived first and surveyed the catch. Shaman told Sartra that she had to leave and retrieve the other prey. She dashed back up to the cabin. The other one was gone.

Thomas had woken up from his blow to the head. He had tried the cabin phone, but Shaman had pulled out the wires long ago. Shaman stared at the snow and found his tracks; this was going to be glorious, a real hunt with clean, healthy prey.

Thomas worked his way down the ridge past the helipad. The helicopter wasn't due back till late afternoon, and it was only two o'clock now. He couldn't figure out what had happened. Did Ned hit him? And what was that pile of bones on the floor? Was he being stalked by some psycho murderer? He ran down a rockslide and crossed the steep cliff. He was still confused, from the blow. He stopped at the base of a pine tree and caught his breath. He reached into his jacket pocket and pulled out his cell phone.

"Police, fire, or ambulance?" Thomas paused at the question.

"Police, please." The phone clicked, and he was transferred.

"RCMP call centre; what is your emergency?"

"I've been attacked by someone."

"What is your location?"

"I'm on a mountainside just south of..." Thomas stopped speaking as he spotted the large creature sailing through the trees, coming lower and lower right at him. The ghoulish white eyes locked on his. Thomas stood paralyzed in fear, his breath rapid and shallow; the adrenaline was taking blood from his brain and pouring it into the large muscles in his legs and arms. This animal was coming for him. He jabbered into the phone as Shaman glided towards him, the pine trees bending and swaying from her weight. Her long arms framed her round, ghoulish face. His voice pitched into a higher tone as his words all ran together. He realized that his phone conversation was not going to have any impact on his chances of surviving. He snapped the phone closed and leapt down the steep grade through the trees.

The adrenaline affected his vision; his field of view was only clear in the middle with a white halo in his periphery. The cliff was steep. The shale under his feet began to slide under his long bounds down the hill. Thomas tumbled and then somersaulted across a patch of slag and ice. Lying semi-prone, he turned his head to see Shaman. She knelt down and plucked the phone out of his hand. She twisted it until it crunched and the pieces dropped. She used one claw to grip his hair, holding his head down on the rock. She ran her claw down Thomas's back to open the skin. She then ripped open his pockets, emptying them of any possessions or weapons. Thomas wept uncontrollably as Shaman licked the wounds in his back clean.

Soon Sentrous arrived, grinning arrogantly, as if to say, "See, you screw up too sometimes." Shaman snarled at him. She instructed Sentrous to hang this one beside the other one and watch them until dusk. She warned him not to touch the prey; this kill was to be saved for the young ones.

Sentrous slung the tall man over his shoulder and swung through the trees towards the hanging tree. He yearned for the taste of clean food; he went over many different ideas on how he could steal a taste for himself before the young ones ripped into him. He could take an eyeball, but that would impair his running, and the little ones loved the eyeballs. He could strip the meat off of a finger or two. He reconsidered his plan, due to the fact that Shaman was very suspicious of him lately. They had never gotten on well, and she resented any special treatment Sentrous got due to his mother, Sartra. So far, Aelan had kept the secret of the one that got away, but Shaman definitely suspected something. When the two had returned late with only two kills, Shaman knew that something had happened.

Shaman and Sentrous were not close; even seventy years ago when Sentrous was a young one, Shaman had been hard on him during his training. Yet that did not stop him from being a champion hunter, the fastest and the strongest. Now at the age of a hundred he was a young adult in his prime. Not old like his mother or Shaman, both were over two hundred years old.

Two painful hours passed when the helicopter returned to the mountain worksite to retrieve the two techs, but they were gone. The cabin was empty. The phone not working, the pilot and engineer used their voices to search, walking up and down the rock face, looking for some sign of their lost crew. They stood at the place where Shaman had caught up to Thomas. There they found some of tiny parts of Thomas's cell phone. The green plastic was mixed with the gravel and shale. The pilot looked across the ridge at the curling dark clouds. "Something has definitely gone wrong. We can't stay here long; we'll have to call down and start a ground search."

As the jet ranger lifted off, they did a slow circle just above tree height. The helicopter slowly passed directly above Ned and Thomas as they hung upside down in the treetop, easily visible from the cockpit of the aircraft. They screamed, but the eyes in helicopter were scouring the forest floor, not the forest canopy. They flailed and fought to get loose of their bindings. The helicopter faded into the dark mountain clouds, and the fog rolled in behind the rotor swirls. Their hopes and prayers faded with the sound of the helicopter.

Five young ones gathered around the hanging prey. Shaman gave them an anatomy lesson, pointing out different body parts. She stated a human's maximum speed through the forest and the typical range before exhaustion. She spoke to the little ones about the cameras and the cell phones. She passed the bag of cameras and phones around for them to explore and touch. She spoke a little about guns, explaining that handguns were rarely deadly, but the bullets hit hard and hurt. She passed around a hunting rifle and explained that this weapon could penetrate the coat at close range and that a gunshot in the face could be fatal. She quizzed them on the technique for avoiding rifle shots when in the trees, and they all answered enthusiastically, "Swing right, swing right, then left when the gun is pointed at you; keep moving to the side."

The young hunters, bubbling in anticipation, could not keep their hands away from the rare clean meat. One of the young ones hung close to Ned. Ned couldn't stop shaking as he locked eyes with the creature. The juvenile was about the same height as Ned, but his arms and legs were much longer and leaner. Spittle dropped from its coffee-coloured flaring nostrils as it sniffed at the human's forehead. It ducked down to look at each of Ned's eyes, as if to size them up as future treats. The creature's eyes were perfectly round and white, bulging out of its flat face. The pupils were tiny and back without any iris. The eyes darted down to Ned's neck and chest. Ned was struggling to breathe, and air escaped from the hole in his throat on its way up to his mouth and nose. Blood foamed out of the hole on his exhales.

Shaman and Sartra both explained the rules of the hunting game. Two teams assigned to the rundown, and the others would perform a silent attack and kill. The fema would guard the boundaries to prevent an unlikely escape. The wining team would get to eat some meat at the kill site and they would also win the biggest rib strips during the feast.

The men were lowered to the forest floor; both scrambled to their feet and started to run through the woods together. Ned's knee was slowing him down. The young ones were very quietly watching from high above, planning. One team dropped down to split the Y and get them running in different directions. The young male glided right towards them, and Ned bolted out to the right while Thomas ran to the left. Ned tried to move back towards Thomas, but Thomas was running faster than Ned could manage, and he dropped back. He looked up into the trees and all seemed quiet; there was no movement. He knew the creatures were hunting him, but a part of Ned's mind wanted to believe that they were letting him go. He slowed to a walk while he scanned the forest for danger. If he could just make it out to a clearing, then he would have a better chance.

A hundred meters west, Thomas ran through a thicket and then tumbled down a depression. The fear sparked him forward as he struggled out of the bushes. Pulling himself up, he tried to pace himself. The lack of a moon made the forest black. A branch slashed at his face and startled him. He yelped and froze. The only sound was his breath; the breeze quietly moved the trees above him. Maybe they were gone. He started walking quickly towards a lighter patch of trees. The young male dropped from a height of twenty feet onto Thomas's back, sending him forward, making a few steps until he succumbed to the weight of the creature. As a former high school wrestler, he stayed on all fours, protecting his neck and stomach. The creature sat on his back and shoulders, its face pushed up to Thomas's ear. Thomas felt the breath on his skin. The cloud of skunkish breath and spittle swirled in his face. The creature gripped his earlobe with its incisors and held Thomas's shoulders securely as he slowly tore the top of his ear, tugging gingerly until the sinewy lobe came off.

Thomas redirected his energy into screaming. The weight lifted from his back as he sprang up to run. His pituitary gland now dumped a rare mix of primordial hormones into his bloodstream. This cocktail was different from your standard fight-or-flight stuff; these were dying hormones. His decisions were now controlled by his brain stem, and the finely tuned neurological structures took over. There was no reasoning or analysis, only the stimulus from a predator and the response of its prey.

The young hunters, finally practising what they had learned, herded him towards the kill zone. Thomas jumped over a small pine and crossed a stream. While screaming for help, he stumbled through the icy rocks. Two hunters dropped down, one in front and the other on his back, biting deep into the cervical vertebrae at the base of his skull. Thomas saw bright-white lights shooting across his visual field and then nothing. It was as though his lights had been switched off, and he dropped with a crunch. His pain was over.

The youngsters tore some pieces from his twitching corpse as he grunted and jerked, but this was just a reflex. The young males sat triumphantly on Thomas's chest, catching the spurting blood in their mouths. His heart kept beating for a while.

Ned was not far behind. His knee burned; his knee cap kept sliding sideways, sending shooting pains up his legs. He would sit down to catch his breath and then wrench his knee back in place. He had listened to the change in Thomas's screams; they started as the screams of a man and ended as the screams of a desperate animal. Running for another five minutes, he made it to a small clearing and fell to the ground, coughing and gurgling. He could hear the movement in the trees around the clearing; he was surrounded. He sat up on a rock and tried to catch his breath. Bile rose in his mouth, followed by vomit shooting out of the hole in his throat like a yellow geyser. High above him, the two hunters aimed their grommets carefully. *Whap, whap* Ned jerked as the blood shot out of the hole in his head. He lurched forward and staggered around, his arms waving wildly, the blood pouring down his face. He dropped, and the young ones closed in and tore his chest open. The celebration began.

10 The Search

Alan lay in his marriage bed. The reflection from blue Christmas lights flashed in sequence along the ceiling. The light came in from the balcony, where an hour before he had had an unfortunate tangle with the stepladder. The aluminium slide had hit his forehead while he wrestled it up into position to set up the roof lights. A small lump and bruise on his brow was normally no big deal, but since the bomb blast in Afghanistan, every bump on the head sent shimmering stars through his brain that left him with nausea and an awful humming in his ears., He dared not move and disturb Karen, who had grown accustomed to sleeping alone. Invited to stay the whole night, he was determined to be a quiet husband. It was the end of a normal family day; the kind that he had missed terribly over the past six months. He had worked in the yard for a bit and then tackled the lights with Teddy.

Karen had slept with her cheek on his chest for a while, and then rolled over to her side of the bed. The sounds of the house came back to him, the ticking of the radiator in the hall and dripping of the rain down the spout outside the bedroom window. Sleep was a rare thing in Alan's life. Like found gold nuggets in a riverbed, he rejoiced at a gift of a few solid hours. Most nights he spent listening to his stress, crackling like static in his skull. Along the back of his mind, the ticker messages ran in a repeating reel. *You will screw this up; it's a façade. She can't deal with the real you. Give it up, Wickey.* Alan closed his eyes again, trying to recall some of the meditation exercises he had learnt in head injury school. Maybe sleep was too much to ask for; sleep was more or less just gaps between nightmares. It was in his nightmares, where one ship sailed almost nightly.

EMERGENCE

The *Ocean Huntress* was a dying ship. The green seawater swirled around her deck; the white-and-orange net cord tightened around his thigh. It twisted, cutting into Alan's suit and then through his skin. He was tethered, and helpless. Saltwater churned around his face, stinging his eyes; thick wooden deck boards popped up and creaked as the ship heeled into the oncoming seas. Then she settled quickly, bowing below the violent surface. His lips opened to suck in a last gasp of air before going under. The cords pulled at him; he struggled to get loose. The sun penetrated the ocean waves above and lit up his orange flight suit. He gazed down to see the ship dropping away from him into the green. The big reel of netting was uncoiling from the drum like a leash, with enough slack to allow him to float closer to the surface. Looking up through the sea into the blue sky, he kicked and spun, trying to unwind himself. The grip loosened but did not let go. He looked down again into the depths. The red and green sidelights from the ship's wheelhouse winked at him from the pitch. Alan's lungs burned; he reached up with his hand and pierced the surface with his fingers. The long, twisted roll reached its end. The cabled umbilicus held its grip on him. Mouth open, water pouring into his lungs, he was snapped back down into the darkness.

Alan sat up; his eyes opened with his gasps. Karen's hand caressed his shoulder blade as his breathing slowed.

"You and your nightmares," she whispered.

Alan was still breathing heavily. "Yeah, they're the highlight of my evening."

The next morning he managed the energy to go for a run. Alan was now running five kilometres per day, and today was the first time he dared venture back onto the old path. With his feet rolling along underneath him, his mind drifted along with the sounds of the birds. He passed underneath the Upper Levels Highway; the snow crunched under his shoes as he leaned into the uphill climb. The midday sun was dodging the silver-lined stratus clouds that rolled along in the sweeps of the winter winds. Alan no longer listened to his iPod while running; his eyes and ears were carefully scanning the forest canopy. As Alan reached the spot of his attack, his heart raced. He stopped and looked at the ground where he had fought for his life months before. There was no trace of anything familiar, no hair on the trees, no mysterious tracks. It was just a patch of bush in the forest. He finished the five kilometre trail and turned around to lap it once again. As he ran, his thoughts fell upon the creatures. What was he going to do? Get on with his life, his marriage, and pretend that this had never happened? What about the homeless victims in the park; were they being eaten every day? Did he owe it to society to convince the authorities that these creatures existed? Maybe it was his job to go and find one of these things and kill it for proof. He knew that he needed to continue his workout routine before heading out to hunt monsters; he also knew that the exercise was making it easier for him to think clearly. Maybe hunting monsters was not in the category of clear thinking. Alan's phone startled him, and he stopped on the sidewalk to answer it.

"Alan, it's Mark Pollen from Northshore Search and Rescue. I see that you're back on the active list. Are you available for a search? We have some missing telephone techs up on Cathedral Mountain."

"What's the altitude?"

"The search will start at the top, around six thousand feet, and work down the slopes. We need some of the old pros for this one, because of the weather. I hoped that you would be good to go."

"Flattery will get you nowhere, Pollen. Where's the staging?"

"Grouse Mountain parking lot trailer at 1230 hours. The chopper will pull you and your team out at 1630 in a clearing above Bear Lake."

"OK. I will meet you at the trailer on Grouse Mountain in forty minutes." Alan jogged home and collected his climbing gear. He had been off the active list at Northshore Search and Rescue team since his return from Afghanistan. When he first left the SAR squadron, he'd missed the excitement, and he joined the volunteer team. He enjoyed the camaraderie of the weekend training trips into the bush.

The white aluminium trailer was a small portable perched by the gondola base low on Grouse Mountain. Alan had checked over his gear twice before the other team members arrived. Kelly drove up in his big burgundy dual-wheeled truck. He smiled at Wickey as he analyzed his face and eyes. "Looks like Wickey boy is finally getting some." Kelly whacked Alan on the shoulder. They walked across the ice and gravel into the trailer.

Mark laughed at the sight of the two in the doorway as he rolled out the topographic chart. "Look at you two, like a couple of little old ladies. The other five guys are kinda young and green, so keep them close to you. Have a look at the map." The aroma of stale coffee filled the little room; the painted-over wood-paneled siding was now peeling. The rest of the team sauntered in and gathered around the table. Some of them walked over to the coffeepot and poured out a cup. Alan made a yuck face, and Kelly smiled. Pollen could not make a pot of coffee to save his life, and that pot was probably a week old.

Mark cleared his throat. "OK, Rescue 910 will on the pad in twenty minutes so I will be brief. Yesterday two telephone technicians went missing from the generator shack on Cathedral Mountain. The RCMP requested our assistance with the search this morning after their teams came up with nothing. Ned Pringle and Thomas Caswell are both in their forties and experienced bushmen. You guys are the hasty team, assigned to do a quick trail sweep from the peak to the extraction site along this ridge. You will use all means to attract attention: whistles, calls, and names. With two lost subjects, the chances are that at least one of them will be responsive. There are other trails at the base of the mountain, but they'll be covered in a general search at first light tomorrow."

Kelly spoke up. "In order to make that distance, we will have to keep the pace up. This means a quick track search on either side of the trail. I assume we're to maintain a sixty-minute reporting schedule?"

"Yes, that is correct, Kelly, but not so quick as to miss them. The weather is getting worse, so don't cry if you have to spend a night on the mountain. We can always pick you up in the morning."

Wickey smiled and leant over the table to point at a road junction in the valley. "Mark, if you leave us up there overnight, then you can pick us up at the alternate extraction site here." The whole pack laughed as Alan's finger pointed to the well-known Waterwheel Pub below the mountain.

Mark shook his head and chuckled. The *whump whump* of the huge Cormorant helicopter began to vibrate the trailer. "OK, goof balls, get going. Channels 4A and 7C for backup. Kelly has the sat phone. Check in after you're dropped off and then on the hour after that."

The Cormorant flared on approach. All but Kelly and Alan ran out to watch the landing. Some of the gear was blown around the parking lot in the downdraft. A tall SAR tech jumped down from the open door and pulled his helmet off. The blades slowed as the crew walked out and greeted their old comrade. Woody Metcalf pointed his finger at Alan.

"Wickey buddy! I heard that you got blown up in a Hummer and then eaten by a cougar. That sucks; I'd rather get a hummer from a cougar myself." Woody grinned and hugged Alan. The pilots greeted Alan with handshakes as they gathered around the table for a quick flight plan review.

The huge yellow aircraft pulled its wheels up above the tree line, and Alan dialled in his headphones and checked his gear once again. The conversation was reminiscent of some very happy times spent in the same helicopter. This was Alan's old crew, except for the new pilots. Woody was one of his closest teammates, and the other two SAR techs were both prior students of Alan's. Kelly sat across from Alan, smiling at the lively chatter on the intercom.

"So I heard that Karen dumped your sorry ass," Woody's voice squawked through the earphones. Alan stuck up his middle finger at both Woody and Kelly as they smiled.

"She let me back in the house and we're working on it. You guys are big pricks."

"Yes, we are big, and Mr. Wickey, you are a little prick and maybe that's the problem—too much Indian candy," Woody replied as the laughter broke out on the intercom. The yellow bird circled around the valley and climbed up through an overpass. Ears popped as they climbed up four thousand feet. The clouds cast dark shadows that scurried across the gleaming white snowpack. The big bird was now above the cloud level where the trees were shorter and the peaks lined with fresh snow speckled with long, jagged runs of ice. The snow swirled in the aircraft's shadow as it crossed the wooden landing pad. The wheels touched down gently.

The pilot announced to the search team, "I can't shut down on this pad so you will have to unload quickly and get clear. Keep hold of all your shit; I don't want it flying around!" The door slid open as the search team climbed down the stairs.

EMERGENCE

The peak was sunny at negative five degrees Celsius, with a brisk breeze bringing the wind chill down to about negative ten. The first stop was the generator shed—definitely the warmest spot on the mountaintop. A tall bearded man opened the door and waved the team in. The small shed was now a makeshift headquarters with radios and laptop computers. There was an intercom system due to the constant roar of the generators. An unlucky RCMP corporal and the telephone company line manager were bedmates in the shed until the search was over. The Mountie handed out photos of the missing men, paper-clipped to the info cards. Meanwhile, Kelly checked into base camp on the radio and then tested the sat phone as the team did a final gear inspection. They all tested the batteries on their locator beacons and had a final look at the map.

Both Alan and Kelly walked around the cabin looking for some indicators of the search subjects' last known position. Kelly asked the linesmen a bunch of questions regarding the normal routine for these two, what gear they had on, and what they had found in the cabin. Kelly knelt down on the reed mat by the TV. He wiped at a smeared stain and rubbed the whitish-yellow substance between his fingers, smelling it.

"Do some of your guys use this cabin for hunting?" Kelly asked.

"Not supposed to, why?"

"Smells like tallow or marrow, and it looks like some blood stains on the mat." Kelly's gaze turned to the beams that stretched across the open ceiling. He ran his hands along the tops of the beams, looking a place where hunters would have hung their kill. "The top of this beam had no dust, but the other one is covered."

"What does that mean?" the linesman asked.

Kelly shrugged his shoulders. "Means your cleaning lady sucks, I guess."

The wind hit them square in the face as Alan and Kelly walked down the stairs and stopped. The team all strolled out to the bluff, marching single file along the ridge.

"Where are those guys going?" Alan asked Kelly as the wind frosted his goggles.

"Heck if I know. Hey, you donkeys! Get your asses back this way—the search starts here!" The five turned and sauntered back up the ridgeline. Kelly pointed at the bottom step of the cabin porch and bellowed in his low sergeant's voice. "This is the LKP, last known position, and it's the commencing search point. The farther we get from this point, the less chance we have of finding them, or the probability of detection goes down. Spread out in a line and sweep the ridge on both sides. Search every snowflake on this peak. We can speed up a little when we get on the trails below the tree line. Don't lose sight of the search line." Kelly waved his hands in the direction of the ridge. Clearly the five were not impressed as they formed up in a line that stretched over both sides of the peak.

Shivering from the strengthening wind, they waded through the waist-deep snow. Sweeping down the ridge, at a distance of six feet apart, the team called out for Ned and Thomas. They pierced the snow pack systematically with their hiking poles on both sides at every step to search the layers of snow around them for any sign of a body underneath. The sun ducked behind a dark storm front as the team descended into the shadow of the glacier. After an hour, one of the five approached Alan and tapped him on the shoulder with a gloved mitt. "It's getting kind of cold out here, and some of the guys are feeling dizzy. Should we call in the helicopter?"

Alan's eyebrows rose. "Sorry, Bubaloo, but the ceiling is too low now. We are sleeping on the mountain tonight. We might as well keep moving; the sooner we get down to the treeline, the nicer it will be." Alvin looked at Alan in bewilderment and turned back into the wind.

Kelly looked up and strolled over to Alan. "What was that all about?"

"Oh, the princess over here wanted to call in his private helo for a ride home. The lads are feeling woozy and cold."

"They are young, aren't they?"

"Wee babies." Alan smiled. "Wee two-hundred-pound babies."

The swirling snow blew off the cornices and disappeared into the thick clouds. The temperature dropped, and the cold wind was blowing directly up from the ocean, which glittered in the distance four thousand feet below. Alan Wickey was exhilarated. Up here, all challenges were self-evident, all the dangers were real and manageable—usually, and all consequences were predictable.

What more could a man ask for? This was the primordial environment in which humans were supposed to exist. The wilderness was full of life and death; these situations could create real pleasure and real pain, and sometimes both simultaneously. In the wilderness, Alan was alive, he was breathing, he was cold, his feet were stiff, his back was sore—ecstasy!

"Kelly, this is awesome!"

Kelly laughed and shook his head. "A guy…finally pulls his head out of his ass and then can't stop talking about how nice the air smells. Wickey, maybe you shouldn't stick your head up there in the first place."

Alan laughed again, his voice booming out into the slopes. The slope was covered in pine and alpine spruce trees. The spruces were short and had a distinct blue tinge, yet the blue was barely discernable in the snowy air. The team closed in as the ridge steepened on both sides. The thin ribbon of ice and snow split their stride with every step. Little rocks rolled like marbles underneath their feet, making it a struggle to stay upright. As the trees got taller, the shadows deepened and the grey haze turned to fog. The clouds hung low in the tall cedars, the wind muffled by the branches. The forest floor was soft, and the thin layer of snow crunched with every step. Many eyes were on the search party now. Those eyes were waiting for the sun to set and the cold winter darkness to set in.

Both Aelan and Sentrous sat up in the canopy. They had watched the helicopter set down and then leave. Hours earlier, the whole clan had moved out to the caves, and the two sentries shadowed the search team. Sentrous was badgering Aelan about clean meat and clear minds. He was obsessed with breaking the rules, and this talk made Aelan nervous; it was treasonous and foolhardy. Apec males who willingly betray Kamptra always pay for their crimes, usually meaning a public execution at the hands of the fema. Sentrous had somehow forgotten this. Aelan also hated the taste of the city meat; he felt listless and sometimes dizzy after consuming flesh from the rotten ones in the park. He often had trouble sleeping after hunting in the city; the fumes, the noise, and the lights were sickening. Sentrous's words made sense, but he knew that the ideas of treachery often made sense; they would make perfect sense right up until you were caught and killed.

Now Sentrous was going on about the whistle cross. This was a rarely used hunting technique; it supposedly stunned and blinded prey. Sentrous had been practicing the whistles and finally had convinced Aelan into trying the two-hunter technique on a robin's egg the day before. The two hunters sat in separate trees a few hundred metres from a robin's nest. They focussed their loudest whistles onto the nest. Once the two whistles reached harmony, the eggs cracked and broke open, the yolk reduced to a yellow soup.

Sentrous left his post and flew across the treetops circling the search team and positioning himself downwind; Aelan followed reluctantly. Sartra had forbidden contact with the humans. This group was too big and had communications, yet Aelan knew that Sentrous would not be able to resist some type of indiscretion. Sentrous called over to Aelan excitedly. When Aelan caught up, Sentrous explained that one of the searchers smelt familiar. He smelt like the one that had gotten away. Sentrous was sure of it; he had never forgotten a scent. Now the hard part was going to be determining which searcher he was. Even Sentrous was not brazen enough to disobey the fema directly. Sentrous needed Aelan to cooperate for his plan to succeed.

Alan was walking beside Alvin. Alvin was busy explaining the difference between two computer programming languages. Alvin was a UBC software engineering student. He and Alan were comparing their experiences at the UBC when Alvin stopped and shook his head.

"Do you hear that squealing?"

"What squealing?" Alan replied.

"There it is again, a real high-pitched squeal, like a chipmunk singing soprano."

"Nope." Alan scanned the woods carefully and looked back towards Kelly. Kelly had stopped and was looking up at the trees. Kelly walked slowly over to Alan.

"Got that feeling again, like we're being tracked," Kelly whispered. Alan's heart began to pound as he looked deep into the layers of mist that wound around the trees. The light was starting to fade.

Kelly waved over the rest of the searchers into a huddle. "OK, guys, listen up; because of the fog, we will not be flying out tonight. We will carry on searching the hillside and cross the river before dark. We can camp on the other side of the ravine. Stay in sight of the whole group and continue your calls and whistles. Look for boot tracks, wrappers, anything. We are losing the light, so let's make tracks!" The seven searchers slowly walked through the salal bushes on either side of the trail, their feet gliding through the powdery snow in the quiet woods.

Two deadly shadows followed along high in the trees above, their spiny fur coats changing from a green leafy texture to brown bark to grey rock as they moved silently. Sentrous had the scent narrowed down to two searchers, but he could not get close enough to determine which was which. His vision was terrible in the daylight.

The men reached the cliff face and looked down into the ravine. The river rushed along almost a hundred feet below them, and the water vapour mixed with the fog swirling up the canyon. Kelly reached the cable crossing. This three-cable bridge was a very primitive method of getting across the canyon. The main one-inch steel cable was strung bar tight across the expanse. A few feet above it were the two hand lines that provided the cable walker something to hold on to and balance with. The search team donned their harnesses and rigged up their safety lines and snap hooks. Kelly snapped on to the hand line and crossed first, almost slipping on the wet green algae that covered the thick old logging wire. Alan crossed next and was about three-quarters across when Alvin started across. Aelan and Sentrous sat in rocky crevasses situated on either side of the ravine. Sentrous started the harmonic ultrasonic whistle and aimed at his target. Aelan started his whistle; he also focussed on the red jacket high on the wire.

Alan shook his head at the piercing pain in his skull. What a lousy time for one of his brain attacks. That familiar sharp lightning shot through his eyes. Stress or a crowded place, like the shopping mall, normally triggered these attacks. A few feet from the other side, he dropped to his knees on the wire and began to wobble.

Alvin, now halfway across, screeched and clawed at his head. "I can't see; my eyes are all grey! Help me!"

His feet slipped off the cable, and he dropped until his safety line arrested his fall. Now all of his weight hung from the short lifeline fastened to the hand rope. The hand rope stretched down in a V as Alvin hung helplessly, his red jacket wrapped around his head.

Alan steadied his stance and started out onto the cable. He unclipped his second lifeline so he could use it as a rescue line for Alvin. The left-side hand rope dipped well below the main cable, and it groaned under the weight. Alan was still clipped on to the lower left rope and slid carefully out to Alvin, getting low on the cable. Kelly moved to the cliff edge and pulled out the radio, calling base. Alan reached the spot above Alvin and dropped to a squat. He began to wobble but steadied himself. He slung his right lifeline and dangled it in front of Alvin's head.

"Alvin, I have a pull line dangling just above your head—grab it and clip on!" Alvin reached around, groping blindly. The left guy wire let out a groan as it wound out slowly. The wire was only meant to be a handhold, not support the weight of a man. The strands started to twist and groan. Alvin's cry was muffled by the crack emanating from the rock anchor. The line dropped quickly with Alvin's weight. Alan was yanked into the air and fell, towed down by his own lifeline. He held firm to the flailing guy wire. The two swung across the canyon, but Alvin's carabiner slid down the length of the hanging wire, and he dropped off the end. The young man's body spun twice in the freefall before bouncing violently off the rocky shelf below. He landed with a muffled thud on a large exposed rock in the middle of the river. The blood ran out of his split skull into the waters.

Alan swung across the ravine and glanced off a mossy bluff, hanging only by his grip. His feet bicycled in a desperate search for a foothold.

"Wickey, are you there?" Kelly called with panic in his voice.

"Yeah, but not for long, Kelly!"

Kelly already had a belay point set up on a huge tree. He checked his harness and descender. Alan hung inverted onto the wire with both hands and his legs wrapped around a small broken tree trunk that stuck out from the rock face. He felt an impact and heard a loud crack on the side of his helmet. He assumed that some rock had dropped from the cliff face above until his eyes focussed on the dark shape hanging upside down in a crevasse on the opposite cliff. Sentrous's eyes were covered by the sunglasses, and his elbow was stretching back to find enough room to throw again. Alan swung around as the grommet flew; it ripped through the fabric of his pack and deep into the bone of his shoulder blade. Alan swung around again, and Sentrous was gone. Kelly's rappel line dropped down beside him, shortly followed by Kelly.

"Wickey, are you OK? Hang on buddy, I got ya." Kelly secured Alan's harness and hooked it to the third line dropped by the other four on the cliff top. The two slowly dropped sixty feet down the emerald green cliff to the rocks below. Alvin's body lay bent backwards in the swift current, fresh water washing the blood and spinal fluid out from around his exposed brain tissue.

Sartra and Shaman, accompanied by four other fema, charged through the treetops towards the canyon. The ultrasonic whistle-cross had given both Sentrous and Aelan away. The clan was in immediate danger; both the hunters were out of control. Sartra assigned a fema member to watch over the search party while the rest hunted Sentrous and Aelan. Shaman chirped instructions in short bursts of the fema hunting language, which was unknown by the males. The females were systematic as they wove out farther and farther down the valley. Aelan stood up from his hiding place, and Shaman tackled him viciously. Aelan groaned as woven ropes tightened around his arms and neck. He was taken back to the cave.

Sentrous had eluded the search party by hiding inside a tree trunk on the cliff face. He knew that his mother would be angry. The fema had killed males in the past for disobedient acts like this. Sentrous was unsure if his mother would order his death or spare his life, but he knew that his life would not be the same after his failure. He had failed on all measures: he attacked the searchers (this was specifically forbidden), he had killed a clean human, and he had missed his mark. The human whom he meant to kill was still alive and had spotted Sentrous again. Sentrous's fear slowly turned to rage as he waited patiently for the dusk to turn to night. This human had made a fool of him three times now. He had to finish the kill.

Rescue 910 slowly circled the ravine looking for a clear path through the fog. The searchlights lit up the skies above the party, but the beams could not penetrate the thick cloud cover. The crew bagged up Alvin's body and packed snow around it just outside the campsite.

"Shore party, this is 910. Sorry, guys, no visibility, no hoist." The radio crackled as the four searchers shook their heads and sighed heavily. Both Alan and Kelly were busy making a fire and setting up their tents. The fire crackled as the flames engulfed the damp kindling and took hold. The smoke filled the failing light as the search party finished getting their camp organized. As the fire gained intensity, the crew sat down on the logs surrounding the pit. The four young searchers stared blankly. Three lights hung from the top of the tent. Kelly dug into Alan's shoulder with the hot collapsible pliers.

"Ahhg!...It was that black hairy guy that killed Alvin, you know, your stiyahooe whistler dudes."

"Wickey, I didn't see any back hairy guys, and I was right there the whole time."

"I'm telling you, it was him."

"Alvin got dizzy and fell, you tried to pull him out, and the guy wire snapped. Wickey, it sucks, but it was an accident." Kelly swabbed out the wound as he looked at the bullet-shaped rock he had extracted from Alan's shoulder.

"Have you ever seen a rock that looked like that?"

"It's a rock; what's it supposed to be shaped like?" Kelly replied.

Alan sighed. If Kelly didn't believe him, then who would?

Kelly paused. "OK, Wickey, how did you see it go down?"

"It went down the same way for me as it did for you. Alvin was clawing at his ears and then apparently went blind and fell. It was not until I was hanging upside down on the cliff face that I looked over and saw the creature on the other cliff chucking rocks at me. One bounced off my helmet, and the other is in your hand. I'm not crazy!"

"Allan, the Stiyaha are a legend. I have neither seen one nor seen a trace of one. I can't understand why they would be chasing you." Kelly sighed "Ok, maybe we should do watches tonight just in case there is something out there. You do the first watch, and I will do the second shift."

Alan could tell that Kelly was humouring him. He poked at his bandage and reached for his shirt and jacket. "Thanks, Kelly." He said.

"I will organize the kids for the morning watches, and then I'm going to sleep. Wake me up at 0100 hours" Kelly replied.

Alan sat close to the fire with the other guys. One of them pulled a whiskey flask out of his pocket.

"You were in Afghanistan? You must have lost guys before?" the tall lanky searcher asked.

Alan looked down to the fire "Yeah, losing a guy is not a regular thing, certainly not something you get used to."

"Here, have some Jack Daniels. You look like you could use some."

Alan took the flask and stared down the spout for a moment, then he drank. His head swam from the buzz; jumbled thoughts drifted along with the time. Kelly came out to pee in the snow. He twisted his head around to look at Wickey. "What the fuck are you doing? You are trying to quit drinking, and since when have you ever gotten drunk on a mission?"

Alan looked down again "Yeah…"

Kelly had zipped up his fly and now stood facing his friend. They looked at each other for one long minute. The other searchers, feeling awkward, got up and went to bed. "I guess it just hasn't gotten weird enough for you yet." Kelly touched Alan's shoulder as he walked to his tent.

Time passed; Alan was alone, with the empty flask in his lap. The fading fire cast shadows that flicked in the orange glow through the snow-covered trees. Furious eyes fixed on Alan in his stupor. Sentrous had been evading the fema for hours and knew that he had only a few moments to act. The trees above the fire swayed as Sentrous jumped into a freefall. Alan looked up as the shadows above him transformed into the shape of his attacker. Sentrous hit him, claws extended out in front. The two forms bounced off the log from the impact and Alan landed pinned to the ground. Sentrous opened his jaws to tear out Alan's throat. Alan gasped and closed his eyes to wait for his death. He hoped that this time it would be less painful. Before the long teeth touched Alan's freshly healed neck, another beast ripped Sentrous from his kill. Alan, holding his neck, looked up to see two creatures tumbling through the snow; then three, then four. The new creatures were larger and stockier then the first one. The fight rolled through the camp again, bouncing over the corner of Kelly's tent. Alan recognised Sentrous as he fought for control. The females quickly subdued him without a grunt or growl. They lifted his body up into the trees. Kelly leapt out of his tent, holding his hunting knife out in a defensive stance. He looked up as the shadows swallowed the beastly shapes again.

The fire crackled. Kelly looked at Alan for a second. Alan stood panting and swaying, his shirt ripped, his mouth open, his pupils wide. Kelly's eyes tracked around the disturbed ground where the fight had rolled through. He knelt and touched the snow, his gaze following the path of the ruckus.

"Some people shouldn't drink, Wickey."

Alan replied in a shrill, cracked voice. "Yeah, fuh...no shit!"

Kelly looked up into the trees and then looked back at his friend. "I'll make you some green tea, get you calmed down a little."

Alan sat and sipped the tea quietly while Kelly watched the forest canopy. The others slept soundly in their sleeping bags. Alan reached down and pulled some of the quill-like fur from his shoulder.

Kelly broke the silence with a smile. "Well, Alan, I think you've been having unprotected sex with a grizzly bear and not telling me." Alan let out a short laugh. Kelly reached over and took the quills from Alan. He pulled his flashlight out of his pocket and examined them. Kelly squeezed the thin spines, and a clear liquid oozed out from the root. The four-inch colourless quills were made of a clear fingernail-like protein. They were sharp but also flexible.

"Have you ever seen those before?" Alan asked.

"Nope, it's definitely not grizzly fur. It looks a little like polar bear fur, but porcupine-ish. I doubt a ten-foot porcupine raped you. Of course that would explain a lot of things about you, Wickey." Alan finally smiled and shook his head.

The sun pierced the trees as the rotor wash of Rescue 910 filled the air. The group had packed up the tents, and they all started out towards the open field. The tall lanky guy took his whiskey flask back from Alan.

"How did you sleep?" Alan asked.

"Like a baby. It was my first time camping in the snow. It's kind of fun."

"Yeah, kind of fun," Alan replied, exchanging eye rolls with Kelly. A second search crew was climbing out of the helicopter as they opened the door to take Alvin's body.

Sentrous hung upside down. His calls out to his mother went unanswered for a while until the young ones arrived telling him to shut up. They pelted him with grommets; the ones that hit him in the face stung and welted. He was sure that he would die soon. The sun was rising, and the little ones went up to the cave for bedtime.

Sartra and Shaman had agonized all morning over who would execute him. Shaman volunteered, but Sartra knew that it was her job. She announced that it would happen at sunset. The clan was sombre; many did not sleep that day.

Sentrous was weeping with fear and sorrow. He would feel calm for a while, and then his anger would rise. He struggled to get free but could not loosen the ropes. His legs and arms were burning with pain, and his head was pounding. The wind whispered through the treetops, and he felt a presence above him in the tree. Maybe the fema had arrived to do their nasty task. The line recoiled, and Sentrous fell to the forest floor with a thud. He looked up into the trees to see blue sky. When Shaman went to check on him at midday, he was gone.

Alan and Kelly sat at their regular table in the coffee shop, sipping dark roast out of large, bowl-shaped cups. Alan looked at Kelly nervously. Kelly was staring at Alan with a comfortable half smile.

"So, do you believe me now?"

"Wickey, there was never a time when I didn't believe you."

"Now that you know that they are out there, what are you going to do?"

"It's not what I am going to do that matters."

Alan squinted at Kelly's words. "What do you mean?"

"The Stiyaha exist, they live in the forest, so what?"

Alan stuttered, his voice pitching up. "Wha…what do ya mean, so what? They're eating people!"

Kelly smiled. "They're just eating white people." He turned up his palms and chuckled.

Alan did not think this joke was funny.

Kelly continued. "We live in a natural world filled with life other than ourselves. Maybe you are not on the top of the food chain anymore."

"Why do you keep referring to me? You're in the same bag, dude."

"Us Indians haven't been on the top of the food chain since you guys sailed up in your big boats. This is your crisis, Wickey, not mine. Why don't you focus on more important things?"

Alan's mouth opened in disbelief. "Like what's more important than this?"

"Teddy, for one thing. I think that Xbox is bad for his brain." Kelly could see that Alan was not pleased with his answers. "Wickey, I am your friend, and if you want to run around in the woods with automatic weapons killing monsters, I will help you out. I just want you to know that it wouldn't be my first choice of things to do with my weekend." Kelly was quiet, stirring his cup.

The two were silent in the truck as Kelly drove up the driveway. Karen stood at the side of the drive silhouetted by the sunshine, her hands on her hips. Alan hopped out, grabbed his gear out of the back, and walked around to the driver's window. "Thanks for the ride, buddy." Karen walked up to the truck and hugged Alan.

"It's all over the news—you could have called me to tell me that you were OK."

"Sorry."

Karen turned to Kelly. "Thanks for the text, Kelly; at least someone has a brain!" She punched Alan on the shoulder. "Did he drink?" she asked Kelly directly as Alan's mouth opened in objection.

"Alan Wickey's drinking days are over, believe me." Kelly flashed a look at Alan.

"That doesn't answer my question," Karen replied.

Kelly leaned over, kissed Karen on the cheek, and backed out of the driveway. Alan carried his bags up the driveway. "Why didn't you ask me?" Alan protested.

"Kelly always tells the truth, and I didn't want to give you the opportunity to lie."

Alan's silence was annoying. Karen should be used to it by now, but it still annoyed her. She punched his arm twice in the same place and glared at him.

"Ow!"

"Tell me what happened."

Alan's thoughts raced through the events as he tried to come up with a story that was truthful yet not crazy-sounding. "This young guy, Alvin, was crossing the wire bridge a few steps behind me when his head started to hurt; he got dizzy and fell. He was hanging from the guy wire. I went out to get him, and it snapped. We both fell. Luckily, I was holding onto the wire with gloves, but he wasn't, so he fell to the bottom of the canyon. Kelly came down and rescued me, but Alvin didn't make it."

"Are you hurt?"

"No."

"Why did he get dizzy?" Alan's mind raced, she always asked the zinger questions.

"I'm not sure."

"What did he say?"

"He said that he couldn't see; he went blind."

"That doesn't make sense. Why would he go blind?"

"I don't know; I'm not a neurologist?"

She stared at his face for moment, scanning his mouth, eyes, and forehead. "Hmm." She punched him again in the same spot.

"Ow!"

"Get your shit off my floor, and come help me with dinner."

Alan walked behind her. *Jeez, she should get a job as a CIA interrogator*, he thought.

Saturday, Alan took Teddy out kayaking in English Bay. An old SAR tech buddy was running a kayak rental place in False Creek, and he and Teddy got to pick out the best of the kayaks. Alan was reviewing his action plan in his head. *Don't get excited, don't yell, he is just a little boy.* These words ran through his mind as they both stroked away underneath the Granville Street Bridge. Harbour ferries criss-crossed around them as Teddy struggled to get the hang of paddling. The weather was cold and wet but the paddle was enjoyable as Alan made efforts to break through the teenage fog. Teddy was quiet for the first hour and then he started to talk.

"How come you don't talk about Afghanistan?"

"There's not much to talk about. I was an operations officer; for most of my second tour, my days were spent staring into laptop screens and looking at satellite photos. I saw some action up in the mountains, and then I got blown up."

"Did you ever shoot anybody?"

"Yeah...uh, can we talk about the Xbox? I really think that you are spending too much time on that thing. I think it's hurting your brain."

"What, are you afraid I'll grow up to be like you?" Teddy was a very quick thinker and lethal in an argument. Like his mother, he had a way of getting his mind through all the permutations of a conversation before Alan had finished his second word. "You haven't earned your dad stripes back yet, so...back off the Xbox. If you were so worried about my brain, then you shouldn't have left Mom and me like you did."

Here he was, back in the old stimulus response trap. His first impulse was to start yelling. He inhaled slowly. "OK, big boy, how do I earn my dad stripes?"

Teddy kept paddling, the tears welling up in his eyes. "You shouldn't have to ask." He sped ahead in his boat as if to escape.

"Yes," Alan said.

"Yes what?" Teddy replied.

"Yes, I shot some people."

"Why, what were they doing?"

"I accompanied a US force recon team in Helmand province. I was there to provide intelligence on the local insurgency. We were up in the hills watching a section of the road when some bad guys came out of the bush to bury an IED. We called for a helicopter, but it was too far away, so we had to engage. I shot one of the guys."

"Cool, I mean that's good, right? He was going to kill the good guys, right?"

"Yeah, he was a bad guy for sure."

"It was guys like him that blew you up."

"Yeah, for sure."

"Tell me about the bomb day."

Alan sighed. "Teddy, I am not ready to talk about that yet, buddy. I will tell you about it one day, OK?"

"OK, Dad."

Teddy ran up the stairs to take a shower as Alan walked into the kitchen. Karen had been surprised at Teddy's glowing report of the day spent with his dad.

"You're his hero, you know that, right?"

"He snapped at me pretty hard. It seems like he hates me some days."

"He's only fifteen. His legs are too long, and his voice is squeaky, and he is struggling with pubic hair and zits. It's not about you."

"Yes, I have a vague recollection of the whole ordeal."

"I suggest that you get better acquainted with those memories, because I can't get him through some of this stuff. He needs a dad that is here, present, around, *ici, comprendez vous*? I don't just mean your physical presence; he needs your attention, your effort."

"I am here."

"Yeah, we'll see how you do."

"Being dropped onto a glacier in the middle of the Rockies and hiking fifty miles out with just a lighter and a pen knife is easier than this fatherhood stuff!"

"Stop being a pussy."

11 Little Shoes

The clan was in turmoil over Sentrous. The fema were out at night hunting for him, and the males were resentful about the added suspicion and scrutiny. The fema were even hunting for prey in the city; this had not happened for years. The children complained about the meat being worse than usual. It seemed that the males made better choices for kills, tastier, leaner meat. Some of the prey was toxic with drugs. The young ones got dizzy and confused after the meals.

After supper, the young ones picked the bones clean and handed them to Aelan. It was Aelan's job to collect the water beetles and wrap them tightly in with the woven bundle before disposal in the bone pool. Aelan weighted the wrapping down with rocks. He enjoyed the waterfalls, the mist rolling around in swirls by the cool wind. The fish and the birds were busy in the bustle of the natural ecological intersection. Freshwater prawns were teaming, fed from the remains lying at the bottom of the great rock cauldron.

He stood on the rocky outcropping and threw the bundled remains into the middle of the pond. He watched the bundle sink. As the bubbles diminished, Aelan turned back to the canopy but then spun around to look. A flash of blue and white, just under the water, rose to the surface with a pop. The tennis shoe floated heavily, bottom up, in a slow swirl. He was shocked as he realized what this was. Aelan leapt for the branches that extended over the pool. As he clambered out onto the narrowing limb, it dipped closer to the water. Aelan hung inches above the dark-green pool and reached out for the shoe. The branch splintered under Aelan's weight, and he fell. He splashed through the deep icy cold, thrashing and throwing his long arms and legs out desperately. He had never been in water over his head, and now he was struggling to breathe. The shoe touched his forehead, and he grabbed it as he struggled back towards the sandy bank, his arms flailing awkwardly. His foot touched the mud, and he slowly climbed back up the slippery rocks where he lay, panting. Apecs did not swim well. He thought that Sentrous was crazy for trying to learn how to swim. Sentrous was obsessed by the rotten one that had swum away. The rotten one was rotting Sentrous, and he would pay with his life. He must bring this shoe to Shaman.

Back at the Lair Shaman examined the running shoe; with each rotation her mind raced through different scenarios and possibilities. There was no way that any clan member would sink a body into the bone pool with its shoes still on; they would kill any male for that blatant stupidity. She recalled news stories about shoed feet washing up on the beaches around Vancouver and Vancouver Island.

The news report had highlighted the investigations by the Vancouver Police and the Royal Canadian Mounted Police of seven running shoes with feet attached, all from different individuals. A forensics lab identified one of the feet as belonging to a missing West Vancouver hiker. The theory mostly invoked was that a serial killer was at work in the lower mainland. It was almost impossible to track the origin of the shoes, though; therefore the two-year investigation had stalled. Shaman did not understand all of the English but generally understood what the story was about. Shaman wondered if their bone pool was the source of the shoes and the feet. She knew that if the hunters left the shoes on the bodies, then the feet would eventually float off the body when the joint decayed. They would regret such a blatant act of negligence. Who else could be dumping bodies into their pool? It could be that humans were dumping their own bodies upstream, but that was not likely.

Shaman had a nagging suspicion that it was Caracin's pack. She had seen some other Vancouver news stories of missing people that had the trademarks of Apec kills. Was Caracin hunting nearby? Were they using the pool? Shaman had recently met with the Attla, chief of the Moss Clan. Caracin, one of their stronger males, had broken away with four of his friends about a year ago, and they still had not been found. Caracin was a reckless fool, and Attla was at the point of desperation. Her hunting parties had been attacked twice, and two more of her hunters, along with one young female, had either been taken or had left by their own choice. Attla was asking for help, and both Shaman and Sartra were going to respond by assembling a fema posse with the Moss and the Whiteline clans and tracking down Caracin and his band of thugs. That was before Sentrous escaped.

Breakaway packs were dangerous enough, but a pack run by males was outright subversion. Males did not possess the natural abilities for planning and care, especially in regard to Kamptra. They gave into temptation and took risks. These risks would bring the city humans closer to awareness. City humans offered no harmony. They were either unaware or at war. After discussing the situation, Sartra and Shaman assigned round-the-clock watches to the pool and asked the fema members to supervise the males when they dumped the bones.

Sentrous sat high in a red cedar at the bottom of the valley. He was far enough away from the home territory that he could rest for a while. The fema had been tracking him, but he had evaded them easily. He had heard of Caracin and his vagabond lifestyle. Hunting all the sweet meat he could find, chasing the quick ones through the trees and killing in the city streets. Sentrous thought about freedom. The freedom to do whatever one pleased: no chores, no hunting the rotten ones every night. Yes, this freedom was no longer a fantasy—he could be in charge of his life and kill the sweet humans at will. Maybe it had been Caracin that had freed him.

Sentrous watched the valley and then out over the hills to the city lights. Behind him, Cathedral Mountain stood more than six thousand feet into the heavens. Here was where he was raised, his home. He already missed his family, but returning would mean death. He could hunt and live around here, on his own.

There was a strange high-pitched squeal up towards the bridge. The river wound down out of the mountains with a winter rush. On the peak of Olsen's hill, a smaller shoulder peak adjacent to Cathedral, was a small lodge with a logging road that lead up to it. The road crossed the river about a mile up the hill from the bone pool. Sentrous started up the slopes to investigate the noises. As he approached the bridge, he discovered the source of the sounds. A vehicle sat at the north side of the bridge. The headlights illuminated a rock slide that was blocking the road. The squeal had been the driver hitting the brakes to avoid running into the boulders. A young family had assembled around the headlight beams to look at the obstruction.

Sentrous had moved up to a treetop down the slope from the road base; he was almost eye level with the humans. Two children walked back towards the bridge as the father started to shovel away the loose debris from the base of the larger rocks. The biggest rock was about the size of a barrel, movable with some effort and leverage. The mother was chatting on her cell phone, craning her neck to locate her ten-year-old son and his six-year-old sister. The little ones slipped under the bridge railing and crept up to the edge of the old wood trestle to look down upon the three-hundred-foot drop. The little boy held the little girl's hand as she leant over to see the black swirling water rushing under the bridge and then tumbling over the geyser of a waterfall. The little humans fascinated Sentrous. He moved up closer to the bridge to listen to their voices and to smell their delicious scent. He hung upside down and focussed on the milky skin of the little girl's arm as she leant over the bridge deck.

"Katie, be careful; it's really high." The little boy raised his voice over the rushing water. The mother was now making her way over to the bridge, calling the children by name. Sentrous sat motionless, watching from his tree and looking up at the bridge. He focussed on the girl but then, looking past the little fingers beneath the little hand, he saw movement in the shadows under the bridge deck. A shape nestled in the huge cross beams. The shape was Caracin. He turned his head and met Sentrous's eyes. Sentrous shuddered with surprise, his eyes locked in a trance. Caracin smiled and reached out, tickling the little girl's fingers from below. The child recoiled. "Something touched me, Paul," she told the boy.

Caracin kept his eyes locked on Sentrous as he licked his fingers and smiled. He pursed his lips and called out a meowing sound. The little girl turned back to the deck. Katie turned to face her brother. "Paul, there is a lost kitty down there! I can hear meowing!" The mother had located her children now and was climbing over the rail to retrieve them. Katie was sure that the lost kitty had brushed her hand, and now she was climbing to the rescue. As she bent down and looked over the edge, Caracin was there, waiting. She saw Caracin's face and screamed. She tried to pull back up just as her mother was reaching for her feet. Caracin pushed his claw up into the soft under part of her chin and then flung her down into the swirling water. The mother screamed as the little shoes came off in her hands and her daughter splashed into the black current; she had enough time for only one short cry before rolling through the rocky surge and over the falls. The mother screamed wildly as she ran across the bridge deck towards the gravel slopes on the side of the bridge.

Sentrous was both horrified and mesmerized by the sheer reckless disregard for Kamptra and the rules of society. Caracin looked at Sentrous and extended his hand towards the river, as if to say, "There you go; I have left a present for you." The mother ran directly under him as he looked back to find Caracin, but Caracin had disappeared. Sentrous started down the cliff, bounding from treetop to treetop. Sentrous caught the scent of a little girl's body in the river. He floated from tree to tree with ease and ended up at the bone pool. She was there, floating facedown, her tiny body broken from the horrendous fall. She drifted towards his perch; she was only a short reach away. She would be the sweetest thing he had ever tasted, and she was clearly a gift. Maybe a life of freedom was not looking so bad.

Alan answered his cell phone. "Alan, it's Mark. I hate to ask you to go out again after that last incident, but I need a dive master. It's kind of a weird request and please feel free to say no, because it falls outside of the normal volunteer role."

"What's the call?"

"Little girl fell off the bridge last night and went over Bear Falls."

"Ouch, that doesn't sound like a rescue. It sounds like a recovery."

"That's where you come in. The RCMP and 442 are flying divers in to search the basin at the bottom of the falls, and they are short a dive safety officer. Woody asked for you specifically."

"For an unemployed guy, I'm getting more work than I used to get when they paid me for it."

"Alan, I feel bad about the accident in the canyon, and I almost didn't call you, but"

"It's OK. Can you arrange a ride up to the falls for me?"

"Sure, I'll have a truck pick you up at your place in twenty minutes. They have all the gear in the bird, so just bring yourself and a warm jacket. Oh, and thank you."

The truck drove up the logging road and stopped at the burn pile. The sound of the rushing water filled the small canyon. The fir branches swayed slowly with the breeze created by the lower falls. The skies were dark with rolling clouds, and humidity from the roiling rivers filled the air with mist. Alan stepped out of the truck and walked past a group of police officers. There was a lot of work to do, and far too many chiefs standing around looking to give orders. Alan had seen enough incident scenes where the authorities wasted time trying to assume control. A tall RCMP officer, Staff Sergeant Mullens, announced his rank and name, followed by the claim he was in charge of the search. He then got busy fighting with the military liaison officer over the coveted green vest. Alan ignored the silliness and got to work setting up the dive sites. The dive team was two men short, and the gear bag lay open at the water's edge. In the bag was the standard equipment for a river search. There were three sets of falls to worry about. The divers were set to search the pool below the big falls first and then the second pool below a smaller falls. Alan's first concern was to set up catch lines to prevent the divers from getting too far downstream and being swept over the next set of falls. Sergeant Mullens approached Alan.

"Hey you, you don't need all these lines. You can't tether our divers if that's what you're up to."

"The military divers will want to be tethered. I would suggest that your guys do the same because we don't have a boat."

"Who are you?"

"Name's Alan Wickey; who are you?"

The Mountie did not like this reply; he turned and marched over to the military liaison. Alan could see from the gestures and the finger-pointing in his direction that the conversation was not going well. The air force captain walked over to Alan and spoke with a less confrontational tone.

"Who are you?"

"Retired Captain Alan Wickey." Alan sighed at this needless delay.

"Brian Chelsea, pleased to meet you. Can you hold on a second?" The officer pulled out his cell phone and called Rescue Centre, who in turn called the inbound helicopter. The whole conversation reverberated across the VHF radio that was set up at the command post. Alan recognised Woody's voice booming in from the approaching helicopter.

"You tell that fucking Mountie that there will be no dive unless Wickey is our safety officer, over."

The military officer chuckled as his phone rang.

"Nope, I don't have to tell him; he heard you guys on the radio loud and clear."

The red-faced Mountie pointed at Wickey and bellowed, "You will not tether our divers, you hear me? Do what you want to your own divers. I couldn't give a shit!"

Alan looked across the mossy rocks. "That guy sucks balls."

"Yeah, I was just thinking that," Brian replied with a quiet chuckle as Alan waved and nodded. "Tethering one diver and not the other is going to be stupid."

"Situation normal," Alan replied.

Alan went back to work setting up the multiple barrier lines as the big helicopter passed over on its way to the parking lot. An hour later, all of the divers were ready to go. The police dive team was swimming free, and the military dive team had a tether line rigged. They searched the top pool for an hour and found nothing but mud and rocks.

Alan followed Woody along with the tether while the RCMP diver covered the far shore alone. Woody was swimming ahead of Alan's spot on the shore of the bone pool. Woody was around a rocky outcrop. The tether stretched across the trees as Alan walked up the shore to keep pace with his diver. Woody swam at a depth of twenty feet, slowly floating with the current until he passed over a rocky shelf. The underwater canyon was deep. He dropped over the edge where he could barely see the bottom of the cauldron; it sank past fifty feet. The pool was milky green in the top thirty feet and then the water cleared at the thermal line. The current disappeared at this depth. Woody's halogen dive light reflected white shimmers in the blackness. White sticks stood out from the murky mud. Woody couldn't understand what he was looking at first, but as he sank into the clear layer, his light revealed a horrendous sight. Bones, thousands of human bones, filled the huge basin. It was impossible to judge the height of the pile without seeing the bottom. Woody gasped and pulled a small gulp of water past his regulator. He couldn't believe the underwater mountain; there must be a thousand bodies down here. He ascended quickly up towards the shore. He felt two sharp tugs on his line, which indicated something urgent was going on above.

Alan stepped cautiously along the small ledge. He could not see Woody or where the line was leading. It was caught up on something on shore around the bluff. The line went taut, and Alan was yanked off the ledge. He plunged into the water.

Woody broke the surface. Shaman had the rope in her hand; her thorny claws ripped off his mask. Their eyes met for a few seconds before she savagely grabbed his head and tore his neck open. Her claws opened the buoyancy vest, and the air bubbled out as Woody slipped back under the surface, his blood gushing into the swirling water.

Alan surfaced with a gasp to see Woody floating just under the surface. "OK, Woody, stop fucking around." He spit water out of his mouth and swam over to his friend, who sank slowly. He reached down and pulled on Woody's vest. Blood filled the water around him as Woody surfaced, his eyes blinking and his body twisting as the last pint of blood left his carotid artery. Alan gasped and grabbed Woody's neck, squeezing the pulsing vessel closed. The line came tight again. Alan swam hard, pulling Woody.

"Help! Hey, you guys, help me!" he yelled towards the beach, and the line pulled him quickly. As his foot touched the sandy bottom, he turned towards the shore to face Shaman. She clutched his jacket and pulled him up the beach like he was a stuffed toy. She lowered her face to sniff at his quivering lips. Sartra dropped from the heights and took over control of Alan. She pulled back her lips and opened her jaws. She tasted Alan's skin, glaring into his eyes. He could see her anger, her rage. Shaman looked across at the approaching crowd and pulled Sartra back. Alan dropped to the sand with a thud.

The search team found Alan on the shore a few seconds later. The line had run out into the water as Woody's body slipped over the falls. The tether line was entangled in one of the large logs jammed at the top of the falls, and Woody's lifeless body tossed and tumbled in the furious foam at the base of the falls, hanging like a condemned man on the gallows. The lower search team struggled to reach him but finally turned away from the ghoulish spectacle. After a few long minutes, the line snapped to end the horrific display.

Alan sat in the SUV and stared out at the trees. He could hear the conversation between Sergeant Mullen and Captain Chelsea.

"I told you about the fucking tether line. Your guy here killed him sure as I am sitting here. I'll press fucking negligence charges, you mark my words."

The following police interview did not go well because the investigator could tell Alan was leaving things out of the story, but he could not come up with an alternate scenario other than Woody getting entangled in the tether line and going over the falls. Dark clouds rolled through the skies. Alan could feel the thunderheads closing around the mountains; this would be a long storm. The rain rolled across the hill in sheets, and the rising muddy waters made any further searching of the pools impossible. The little girl's case file dropped into the cabinet with the thousands of other missing persons files in the basement of the detachment office.

Somehow, Alan managed not to drink in the days that followed the death of his good friend. The fact that he'd lost his wallet in the confusion probably assisted his sobriety effort. The only people who spoke to him were his family and Kelly. Alan knew that the accident investigation may take years and that the RCMP could charge him at any time during the process. He felt responsible for Woody's death. It was obvious that the creatures were there for him and that they killed Woody to make some kind of point. What point would they be trying to make? Why were they attacking the people around him and not him?

The muddy wallet dropped from the tree down to the sidewalk near the north shore trail. The rain bounced off the brown leather. A woman walking her golden retriever leant down to pick it up. Her dog startled away from the trees with a yelp, pulling wildly at the leash. She skipped behind the retreating animal, which leapt up the house steps in fear.

She spoke into the phone. "May I speak to Alan Wickey, please? Yes, I have found your wallet. Yes, I just live over above the Quay…Oh, you're very welcome, yeah, I lost mine last year; it was a huge pain. Would you like to pick it up? All right, yes, I live at 1027 Pickerton. OK, great; see you in ten minutes."

Soon after, with the wallet on the dash, Alan drove back home with the music turned up. He did not notice the trees swaying high above his vehicle. Shaman and Aelan jumped up to a hundred feet across the roads in the daylight to keep up with the car. They found a perfect perch as he pulled into the family driveway. The big cedars hung high above the small backyard as the sun dipped below the ridge. Shaman watched through the darkness into Alan and Karen's kitchen.

Coincidently, Caracin had seen Shaman fly across the road way from high up the valley. He tracked the two Salt clan members across the West Vancouver neighbourhood until they came to rest in the trees above Alan's house. Caracin realized whose house this was, and he was very careful not to alert Shaman. He sat in a higher tree a few hundred yards from Shaman, quietly watching the stakeout. Was this a trap for the human, or was it a trap for Sentrous and himself? He left to tell the others in the Free clan.

Caracin returned and sat quietly looking over Shaman and the house; Tehna was due to relieve him soon. Tehna slipped into the treetop and sat beside him. Caracin pointed down to Shaman's tree, and Tehna nodded. They were downwind and could smell Shaman; if the wind didn't shift, this would be a good spot for the night. They were both afraid of her, but that did not deter them from their watch.

Alan stepped out onto the back porch and stretched his arms out. The moonlight peered through the rainclouds. Alan looked up into the trees, directly up at the black patch of trees where Caracin and Tehna sat. Tehna looked at Caracin with a surprise. Caracin shook his head; there was no way Alan could see them; the humans had terrible vision. Alan's hair stood up on his back as looked in the blackness. He couldn't shake the feeling that they were up there. Shaman was surprised to see Alan standing so close and staring into the woods. She followed Alan's gaze up to the higher trees. Tehna and Caracin watched Shaman's head turn slowly around, and to their horror, she met Caracin's eyes. Tehna drew a sharp breath as Shaman flashed across the one-hundred-foot span. Caracin leapt up and out over the house beside them, but Tehna had no chance to gain any speed. Shaman tore him from the heights. The two tumbled down into the forest, but Tehna was dead before he touched the earth. Alan watched the trees sway wildly with the ruckus. The big shadows flashed across the night sky, and he heard the sound of the struggle as Shaman snapped Tehna's neck.

"Fuck me, I knew it. They are right there!" His heart pounded at the violent upheaval in the darkness. They had found his home and his family.

Caracin flew across the power lines at full speed; he could hear his pursuer gaining ground. He darted across a house roof and then to another. The pursuer stopped at the tree line and hesitated. Caracin looked back and recognised the smiling face. It was not Shaman. "Waiting for someone?" Sentrous called.

"Come with me before Shaman, or worse, your mother, catches up to us." Caracin lead Sentrous down the valley.

12 The Whistler Owl

Conner Whalin smiled at the recording. The frequency shift transformed the dancing oscillations on the graph into an eerie, warbling squeal. "Whoa, look at the complexity of that song; that's not a bat, that's for sure." He spoke to himself often. This could be an owl; their songs were complex like this, but he had never heard of an owl calling in ultrasonic frequencies. He had been out walking in the park at night. His dog had been reacting strangely, barking into the wind and whining. He had turned on his recorder on a hunch, and when he transferred the file back to the computer, there was something there. It was in the higher frequencies, but the sound was quite loud, a very strong signal. Now that he was listening to it, he thought it very strange. He e-mailed the file to his ornithology colleague at UBC.

To: Labtech38@ubc.ca
From: kingcon@studiomain.ca
Check this weird recording I got in the 21 KHz range from the forest. It came from aboveground so looking at bats or bugs.

The reply came back.

From: Labtech38@ubc.ca
To: kingcon@studiomain.ca
Weirdness, what was the exact frequency? Not bats, owl maybe.

Conner could not wait for the darkness to come. He decided to share the file with his friend Curtis, who worked in the defense field.

"Hey Conner, long time no chat."

Conner stared at his friend's face on the LCD screen. "Curtis, are you still doing secret defence stuff for the gov?"

"No, they fired me. Besides, it was just data conversion, not so secret."

"Oh, sorry to hear that—what are you doing now?"

"If I tell you, I'll have to kill you. Ha ha, just kidding, Conner. I'm doing web design for a dotcom."

"Oh yeah, cool."

"So what's up dude? Why did you call me? It's not like you're my best friend or anything."

"Uh, yeah, I wanted to ask you about ultrasonic weapons."

"The Yankees are using them for all kinds of stuff; apparently they can hit you with a sound gun and turn your eyes and brain to clam chowder. I think it's ultrasonic."

"Here, listen to this file and tell me what you think." Conner transferred the file to his friend.

Conner watched the screen camera as his friend placed headphones on his head and modulated the high frequency file down to an audible range. His face showed confusion. "That's freaky. It doesn't sound like a weapon, though; it sounds more like a language. It could be a new way to transmit messages without radio signals. Sometimes the special forces use different communication tools like lasers and stuff; maybe this is new? Here, look at this file I just sent you and compare the two patterns when I extend yours out."

Conner opened the file and looked at the sound wave patterns. "Oh, yeah, looks similar. What file is this?"

"Play it. Its George Bush's 'smoke 'em out of their holes' speech."

Conner laughed as he played it. "So, George Bush is hiding in the bushes behind my house and squeaking like a bat?"

"I'm not saying that. This may be a bird or cricket; it just looks similar to a language pattern. Look at the lexicon and the repeating patterns; it's like an encrypted alien language, dude."

"Little green men are behind my house quoting George W.? Great, thanks for the help."

"Hey, Conner, it could be lots of things, but it is a little odd. Good luck; you had better go buy a can of alien repellent. Ha ha!"

"Cheers, dude." Conner clicked the end call button.

EMERGENCE

An e-mail arrived from UBC.

From: Labtech38@ubc.ca
To: kingcon@studiomain.ca
Conner dude: It's not a bug, maybe a bird, but very very weird. You've got the whole department mulling on this one.

Conner strapped on his raincoat and headed out to the park. It was raining and he knew that this would probably make a good recording impossible, but he could not wait. He strolled down the walkway watching the dog carefully. The flashlight lit up the trail, and his dog suddenly stopped and let out a low growl. He was looking up into the forest.

Caracin and Sentrous had been hunting near the city; they sat and watched the hiker. "Why is he pointing at us?" Sentrous asked as Conner unveiled his sonic dish and donned his headphones. He adjusted the frequency, and then he jumped up and walked towards the tree with the dish pointed upwards at the duo.

"Do you think he can hear us with that thing?" Caracin whistled loudly to test his theory, and Conner jumped with surprise. Conner walked into the bushes, ignoring his dog's panic. He adjusted his dials and raised the flashlight beam. Caracin looked at Sentrous and shrugged his shoulders; they just sat and watched as Conner approached the tree. "He's coming right towards us, wow. I wonder if we can get him to climb up here and lie in my lap?" The beam flashed high up through the branches with silver blazes.

"Come out, come out, wherever you are, my little owl," Conner called and shone the flashlight until the beam lit up the two creatures. Caracin looked into the light and waved as Sentrous dropped off the tree trunk above him.

"What the...oohmph!"

A few minutes later the dog paced at the bottom of the trees, whimpering and barking, while Conner hung high in the canopy, his warm body still twitching. "He is very tasty." Sentrous licked his lips. "I think this one wanted to be eaten." Caracin tapped Sentrous on the shoulder, and when Sentrous turned around, Caracin flashed his lips open to reveal an eyeball; he rolled the eyeball with his tongue to make it appear as if it was looking up out of his mouth. They both broke into howls of laughter. *What a grand life*, Sentrous thought to himself. "We had better bring the kill back to our clan." Sentrous said this with pride; his new little clan was set up right in the middle of Capilano Park. At any time, the food was walking around at the base of the trees. Stupid humans never looked up, and even when they did, they could not see the camouflaged quill coats of the Free clan. When the two arrived with the kill, the other members were only partially interested. Many carcasses hung from the trees around the camp.

The customs of Kamptra were abandoned, now replaced with unrestricted indulgence. The Free clan ran wild: hunting, killing, feasting. The time of awareness advanced across the sky like a line of black storm clouds. Sentrous sat, torn between the thoughts of sense and caution that flickered between the powerful euphoria that accompanied anarchy. Caracin seemed to live without regret or regard for consequence. He existed in the moment and could just barely see across into the next moment. Sentrous was worried about the future, yet he desperately tried to let his anxiety fall away. Caracin possessed a childlike wisdom, he thought; wisdom built in the ways very opposite to his mother's teachings. Was it wisdom or reckless abandon? Sentrous had chosen his path already and therefore had to stick to his newfound doctrine. But who cared about the time of awareness? *If we are the chosen and superior race, then the Apecs will prevail over the humans.* Caracin's words rang like a song in Sentrous's mind and almost extinguished the flickers.

13 Crypto Hunters

"I am Dr. Joe Beam, and I am a crypto-zoologist on a mission to expose the real story behind the legends and lore of both modern and ancient monsters. The Crypto Hunters are a crack team of scientific investigators that travel around the world in search of evidence to prove or disprove the existence of monsters." Infrared camera shots of the investigators wandering around in the forest and digitized flashes of spider webs and greenish eyes filled the screen. *Crypto Joe* was a very popular program in a new genre of reality thrillers. The Crypto Hunters announced that they were coming to British Columbia to investigate a rash of Bigfoot sightings in the forests around Vancouver.

YouTube and Twitter buzzed with reports and a series of grainy videos that depicted figures moving in snowy clearings. There were some photos of large footprints in the snow along with many reports of noises and sounds in the bushes at night. A growling in the bushes startled a family camping in nearby Lynn Canyon. Their video camera recorded the sounds, but they failed to catch the mysterious animal on film. The Crypto Hunters' research team combed over all of the web evidence; they contacted the family and arranged an interview with Dr. Beam and his lovely assistant, Anna.

The Crypto team arrived at Vancouver International and checked into a hotel in West Van. They brought night-vision cameras, motion sensors, and still cameras along with a huge film crew. Anna and Dr. Beam walked through the trails of Capilano Park facing the camera crew. Anna was wearing very short khaki shorts and her long blond hair up in a bun under her Crypto Hunters ball cap. Dr. Beam wore a camel skin jacket and tall mirrored aviator sunglasses. His grey-streaked ponytail hung below his safari hat.

"Our Crypto Hunter research team has led us to Vancouver, British Columbia, a beautiful, majestic city set in the West Coast rainforests of Canada. The Pacific Northwest wilderness is the home of the Bigfoot. Bigfoot sightings are common in Canada due to its millions of square kilometres of unexplored, rugged wilderness. Recently there has been a series of sightings right here near the city of Vancouver."

The crew approached a family standing beside a picnic table. "Mrs. Cellios, is this where you had your encounter with the Bigfoot creature?" Anna asked.

"Yes, we were at this campsite last month. Our tent was over there by that big tree. At around two in the morning, we were awoken by rustling in the bushes, right outside our tent. It was so loud that we all jumped out and shone the flashlight into the woods. That's when we saw the eyes and heard the growling. The eyes were green, and the creature was in the form of a dark shadow. Sean, my son, grabbed the video camera and started to record the growling as the creature backed off into the trees."

The camera tilted down to focus on the boy. "Sean, can you walk us through the footage?"

Sean answered as they played back the fuzzy green image from the handheld camera. "Here is the spot where I saw its eyes looking out at me, and when I held up the camera, it dashed back into the bush and growled. It was big, and it made a real loud thrash in the bushes." The growling in the woods rang out from the tiny camera speaker. The sound was muffled and indistinctive, but certainly the growl of some type of animal.

Dr. Beam pulled his sunglasses down to the end of his nose and knelt down to face both the boy and the camera. He spoke in a sympathetic, condescending tone. "Sean, don't be afraid, son, I need you to be very clear with me." He paused for a dramatic moment. "Did you actually see the face of the creature?"

The young camper replied, "No, sir. I could only see the dark shape in the trees."

Dr. Beam turned to the second camera and looked over to his right to make an announcement. "All right, team, let's get set up before dark; we have a job to do!" He spoke towards an empty park bench for the outtake. They would cut in footage of the team later.

Later that day in the hotel room, Beam's eyes winced in the smoke; his short cough shot the marijuana joint across the table into Anna's silky blouse. She bounced up from the table, slapping and squealing in the swirl of sweet-smelling smoke. Dr. Beam cracked out a bellowing laugh as Anna found the smouldering ember and pulled it out. "It burnt a hole in my new blouse!" She reached over her head and pulled the blouse off. Anna's perky, bare silicone breasts pointed straight out on her way over to the sink. She lathered up the garment and scrubbed the spot. "It's ruined!" The other members of the film crew always enjoyed it when Anna dropped her gear. The grip craned his neck to get a better look at the weeping starlet wobbling at the sink.

The setup crew worked well into the frosty night. Caracin and Sentrous were at an impasse. Caracin preferred the challenge of clean meat and wanted to take one of the film crew now. Sentrous did not like this plan; he pointed out how the team worked together and used phones and radios for communications. Hunting would bring police and aircraft. Although Caracin was fascinated with the group, he told the clan to pack up and move up the valley to the knoll. They were reluctant and resentful. The whole idea of the Free clan was that the days of pack-ups were over. Caracin had said they would stand and feast on the clean ones. Apecs were stronger, faster, and smarter than the humans. Why were they running up the hill like all of the other clans? Caracin knew that he had to appease Sentrous for a while. Sentrous was clearly struggling with the bohemian approach. Once the clan move was complete, Caracin returned down the valley to watch the film crew set up the camera sites. He was surprised to see them work up the valley with battery packs and small generators at different sites. The team set up infrared video cameras on tripods deep in the trees; they also set up trap cameras that flashed when the sensors detected movement on the forest floor. The closest cameras were only a half mile from the new clan camp at the knoll. Caracin sat above one of the cameras and dropped a branch down. The flash startled him. Sentrous startled him again as his hand touched his shoulder.

The camera crews circled Dr. Beam and his bubbly, safari-clad assistant. She knelt down and smelt the earth, rubbing the soil in her fingers for a close-up on her inquisitive lips. Beam switched on the small fan motor as a plastic black hairy ape slowly inflated into a bobbing hulk. "The Bigfoot decoy is designed to provoke the lone creature into a mating frenzy. We will play the sounds captured from the howls of a brother creature in the Ohio wilderness. In fact, I have practised the savage call myself, and I will call out tonight during our explorations in order to attract the creature to the area." Beam stood up, looked into the sky, and howled, "Haooooooagh! Haooooooagh!" The call echoed through the woods.

Caracin's eyes twinkled. The two stood directly above the decoy inflatable ape, their heads moving in time with the bobbing. "Look at that thing!" Sentrous was stupefied. "Sartra always told me that the humans were very clever and dangerous. This is clearly evidence to the contrary."

Caracin couldn't resist. "It kind of looks like your mother."

Sentrous' face darkened. "Don't talk about my mother, or else those cameras will be taking pictures of you dying." Sentrous then cracked a smile; his reluctance was giving in to curiosity. He moved around the film site. Sentrous was the visionary; Caracin sat quietly and waited for his friend to make the proposal, and when Sentrous looked up and started to dictate the plan, it was worth the wait. Sentrous's plan was fantastic.

The fog rolled off the water and tumbled over the buildings. The thin blanket of mist rolled up the valley to the film site. Everything below the treetops was shrouded in the mist. The makeup girl swabbed Dr. Beam's cheeks with a copper swirl of foundation. His eyes were rimmed thickly with black mascara lines to highlight the whites of the eyes in the green glow of the infrared cameras. Anna popped a green pill to wake her up from her long afternoon nap as the wardrobe staff stitched and tucked her safari shirt. This was the second season of the show that criss-crossed the globe looking for mythical monsters. The Bigfoot hunt was the going to be the season finale, and the scriptwriters had been working right up to the shoot night on different permutations of spooky "reality sequences," but reality was about to take the show away from the writers.

As the sun began to set, the Crypto Hunters team shot some hiking sequences to make it appear as if they packed their gear far up into the mountains. The lens focussed in on Anna's lips again as she pretended to adjust the lens of one of the trip cameras. They had hired a local native theatre actor to play their Indian guide. He knelt down and smelt the leaves, and pointed forebodingly up the valley. "The Bigfoot lives in these hills; he is watching us now!" Teddy Two-Feathers did not know that his lines were true. Dr. Beam pushed his way forward up the trail as the sun dropped behind the peaks. The base camp was in sight of the Free clan lair; all of the members were out on assigned tasks. Dr. Beam stood up and pronounced, "OK, team, let's go. Lights out!"

Beam smiled at the camera and began his narrative. "We have set up base camp here in the wild and dangerous Canadian coastal mountains of British Columbia, the home of the dreaded Bigfoot. Teddy Two-Feathers our Indian guide, has led us through many miles of coastal rainforest to this remote valley where there have been recent sightings reported by the local Indian hunters. Teddy has fled back down the valley in fear. Hopefully he will survive the long mountain hike." Actually, Teddy had been paid for only two hours of acting, and now he was eating chips and dip in the catering tent.

The glow of infrared lights lit up the faces of the Crypto Hunters. Beam spoke again, "Sharon and Sonny, you go out to the north trail and investigate this canyon. Anna and I will head out to look into the cave on the ridge. Harold and Benjamin, you stay at base camp and monitor the cameras." Dr. Beam and Anna wore backpacks with periscope cameras pointing in their faces. They started up the trail surrounded by cameras. The star duo traipsed through the thick fog. They spoke loudly so that the cameramen ahead and behind could hear them. The whole crew was spooked by the strange mist swirling around the big trees. It actually felt as though they were deep in the wilderness. Beam stopped with his hands outstretched in a halting motion while he squatted down to the dirt. "Anna, look at this huge footprint! Here in the mud—this print must be at least eighteen inches long. This beast must be over ten feet tall. His physical features must be massive!"

"Hmmm, he sounds like a good date." Anna giggled after her comment.

"We will have to edit that comment out, Anna; this is a G-rated show." Beam reached into his pack to pull out his casting kit. After sweeping the twigs and needles out of the print, he poured the powder into a little mixing bowl and began to stir. The plan was to cut filming after the pour, and then he would get out the Bigfoot cast that had been made back at the studio and pull it out of the dirt.

"Listen to that wind whistle in the treetops." The cameraman pointed up into the thick mist. Just above the mist, the treetops were in clear air. A soft sunset gave way to a dark-blue sky, the small wispy clouds revealing one star after another. The cold air made the stars twinkle more brightly.

Clan members looked down through the blanket of fog where they could track the camera crews and action. The fog made the hunting plan even more effective. The Free clan was out of breath because the plan had required some furry help recruited from the high mountains. It had taken a few hours to get the talent in place and ready to perform. Caracin called out the signal, and Sentrous began the chase.

"I just heard a sound." Anna looked out into the forest. "It sounded like branches."

Harold chirped in with a radio announcement. "Dr. Beam, we have movement and a heat signature in the bushes about four hundred metres ahead of you."

Beam hesitated for a moment because this part of the script was out of order. "Anna, let's go and investigate!" Beam ran out ahead of Anna and lumbered through the bush.

"Uh, guys, this movement is real, and there are two figures racing down the valley towards you. The trip cameras are all going off, and we are officially off script."

Beam and Anna stopped and looked at each other. "What do you mean?"

Harold and Benjamin, along with about twenty film staff, stared into the trip camera screen. The photo showed something huge and hairy racing by. Deep in the fog, the distant sound of trees thrashing grew. Beam and Anna listened to the approaching maelstrom. The two infrared cameras both tracked the recognizable yellow-and-red shapes. "It looks like two large bears running full tilt down the clearing directly towards you." Harold's breath made the radios pop. The safety team grabbed their hunting rifles and started up the hill. Anna looked ahead and saw the two huge animals coming towards her. She screeched. Beam turned and ran back towards the base camp, leaving Anna frozen with fear, screaming. The female grizzly ran past her down the path. Beam sprinted down the path, stumbling on roots as the pine branches slapped across his face. His pulse raced up above 180 beats per minute as his cardiovascular system switched to an anaerobic state. The blood taste in his mouth was due to the extreme buildup of lactic acid in his system. Beam started to scream as the big bear's paws reached out and pushed into his middle back. The force easily took him to the ground, and he landed facedown, pounded by the weight of the bear as she trampled over his back. Beam's backpack crunched as the camera and transmitting gear was shattered. Beam groaned as the big bear disappeared into the bushes. He struggled to his feet as Anna's screams changed. They became shriller and more violent as the sound moved across and up into the trees.

Beam looked across at the other bear as it ran down another trail just a few metres away. It lumbered in a rocking gallop until something dropped into its path. The bear stopped in its tracks, then reared up on its his hind legs. It growled as it attacked, but what was it attacking? Beam could not quite distinguish it. The large black figure dropped onto the bear's back and reached forward, steering the big head. The snorting fourteen-hundred-pound grizzly bucked and spun around and then ran by him again. The black figure flipped backwards off its mount and landed in front of Beam. Beam held his breath as looked into the eyes of the creature before him. He never imagined that he would come face to face with a real monster. The great monster hunter had never seen a monster and had never harboured any real ambitions to meet one. Caracin stood partially crouched but stood up and widened his shoulders, revealing his full size. He peeled back his lips into a curled smile and directed Beam with his long arm pointing to his right. Beam turned and ran in the opposite direction through the wilderness. He grunted and then yelled for help, soon meeting one of the female Free clan members, who was hanging upside down from a tree. She flashed her teeth, and Beam turned again, stumbling backwards where he turned back into Caracin. Caracin shook his head and gestured to the right again, and Beam ran off down the directed path. He was gasping between screams while he chased the grizzly running ahead of him. The big bear stopped, blocked by something again. It turned and reared up. It snorted at the doctor as he stopped within a few feet. Their eyes met. The grizzly's interest in him was fleeting as it scanned the forest for its predator. Its snout waved back and forth to catch Caracin's scent, but the human's stench drowned all other smells.

The safety hunters were running up the trail towards the mayhem. The going was tough due to the encroaching darkness and fog, but the sound of the screaming from ahead was guiding them. The front hunter stopped and held his hand up at his shoulder. He dove to the right as the grizzly charged down the trail. The second hunter had no chance to react as a huge claw tossed him into the bush. He curled up in the foliage with a broken arm. His gaze fixed into the canopy where a dark figure stopped directly above him and looked down. Sentrous descended towards the sweet-smelling prey. The hunter swung the rifle swung up and aimed. Sentrous waited for the muscle movements that telegraphed the trigger pull and then dashed left. The bullet whistled by as he landed on his meal. The hunter started a yelp but went quiet as razor-sharp teeth tore through his trachea. Silently, Sentrous lifted him into a nearby tree.

The first hunter walked directly below the hanging body. He swiped his hand at the drips of blood landing on his hair, then continued cautiously on up the path, his gun aimed from his shoulder. Sentrous watched and waited for the next sequence. After his bellowing signal, he leapt across the canopy sailing from giant tree to giant tree. The fog below was lit in beautiful yellow and green quilted patches of light. Sentrous loved the echoes of the screaming and shouting as his plan spun along perfectly. Yes, his quiet life in the mountains was over, and now he would be his own master. He was master of the clean flesh, master of the human hunt.

Caracin wanted to play with Beam for a little while before the humans organized and closed in. Beam noticed the bear's attention drawn into the trees above at the same time he felt the hot breath cross the back of his neck. Caracin was hanging above Beam. He grabbed Beam's ponytail and lifted his two-hundred-fifty-pound frame with one arm. Caracin used his long claw to pluck out Beam's eyeball; he popped it into his mouth. Caracin could taste the drugs and alcohol in Beam, but he did not care. He was having too much fun. Blood squirted out of the socket as Beam fell to the forest floor. He got up and screamed for help again as he ran, zigzagging through the trees. He could hear his hunter moving just above him as he traipsed, blood still pouring from the gaping socket.

"Help!" he managed to cry between wheezing breaths. He fell to the forest floor and rolled over. Caracin swung down to land on him. Holding Beam's forehead down, he gingerly encircled his remaining eye with his lips. Beam was quietly panting until Caracin applied suction, and out came the remaining eyeball. The weight came off as Beam screeched and wailed. He scrambled to his feet again and ran into a huge cedar tree. "Help!" Caracin was getting bored.

It was now time let the bears out of the hunting grounds. Sentrous felt sorry for them as they bounded back up into the mountains. He remembered as a child when they occasionally hunted and ate bears. They had started to disappear, along with the deer. The humans were the only real food source now; there were so many of them. Sartra thought humans were so smart, but they were stupid, and they were here for harvesting. Sentrous could hear the police cars and ambulances rolling up the winding road, and he knew that the hunt was over. He let out the call to end the hunt and to pack the prey out to the ridge. Sentrous stopped at a curious sound hidden amongst the yelling and the sirens; it was the sound of a tiny motor whirring below him. He caught the smell of the breath of an overlooked camera operator. He dropped into the fog. *Here you are.* The red light of the camera twinkled in the mist as the lens twisted to focus on Sentrous's white eyes, but the show was over.

When the fog lifted, four of the crew were missing, including the two stars of the show. Only a few drops of blood were found, and mysteriously all of the individual gear was gone. The RCMP crime scene investigation team worked through the site over the next week. They found very little trace of anything but bears and blood. A hunting team was sent out with helicopters to track down the two grizzlies, but after thirty kilometres of tracks they lost the trail. The news crews flew in from around the world as the infrared footage of the bears was shown over and over. The RCMP spokesperson was intentionally vague about the conclusions of the investigation, saying only, "This was a very rare wild animal attack." This was the only statement that was certain. The CSI team remained stumped, for nothing in this case made sense. It was clear that it was not a simple bear attack.

14 Damn Prowlers

Alan stood open-mouthed in front the TV. The newscaster started with the standard literal quip, "Did the monster eat the monster hunters? Sounds like a tabloid headline, but no, folks—it is real. This B-rated reality show just jumped off the charts as its stars were attacked on camera by two rogue grizzly bears. Four are missing after the taping of the reality-based TV show *Crypto Hunters* took a bizarre turn on Thursday night. Apparently, two grizzly bears attacked the film crew while they were searching for the mythical Sasquatch. Now the famous Dr. Joe Beam, his trusty sidekick Anna Sparks, and two film staff are missing. And things do not look good for them—the police reported that blood was found in the forest at the film site." The colourful infrared footage of the two grizzlies ran throughout the story. "We will have a crew on site soon to give you the latest updates. I am Paula Zoom reporting for CNN."

"Holy shit, it's them!" Alan said.

Karen looked at him. "Who?"

Alan's eyes flashed towards her and then back to the TV.

"Alan…who is *them*?" Karen was frustrated with the only thing left unresolved in their relationship. Alan had stopped drinking, and stopped acting like an idiot, but he was concealing this forest stuff. The series of horrible accidents that had been surrounding him for the past few months seemed to be random accidents, yet Alan was not acting as though these were just bad luck. He was acting as if he was being hunted. Karen briefly considered Hell's Angels or maybe Asian gangs, but this didn't make sense considering the nature of these bizarre accidents, all in the wilderness. It had all started with that stupid cougar attack. Karen's mind raced to make sense of it, but she couldn't. She didn't want to press him into lying, for he was doing so well. *Kelly knows about this*, she thought. Maybe her husband was losing his mind—he could be having paranoid delusions? The pictures on the TV didn't look like a delusion. Clearly the story excited Alan. He could feel Karen's penetrating gaze. Alan knew that Karen could figure out any puzzle if given enough time. The phone rang.

"Hello, Kelly," Karen answered.

"My number is blocked; how did you know it was me?"

"I'm psychic…Here," she said tersely and handed the phone to Alan.

"She's pissed, eh? What did you do?" Kelly asked.

"Nothing…Did you see?"

"Yeah, the spiky bastards are getting bold!"

"No shit—wanna go for coffee?"

"Yeah, meet you in twenty."

Karen watched as he left the driveway. Their relationship was far from fixed.

The tiny mountaintop shed was full of the fema and some of the males. They all stared at the fifteen-inch TV screen. They didn't need Shaman to translate; they could see what Sentrous and Caracin had done. The whole world could see the Apecs' work, thinly veiled behind a grizzly attack.

Sartra shook her head and looked over to Shaman. "The humans are not that stupid; this is not going to go well at all. The mountains will be crawling with soldiers and hunters soon. We will need to retreat to the slope ledges. We cannot even hide in the caves, because they are looking for bears in the caves. Idiots!" she said.

In the diner, Alan sipped his coffee. "What are we going to do with these guys?"

Kelly crumpled his brow. "What guys, and who is we? Wickey, you are still not getting this. You do not have to engage these animals. They ate Crypto Joe and his tasty little sidekick. This is not your problem."

"Kelly, don't give me this nature's balance shit—they are eating people right here in the city! They are on CNN; these guys are changing. They are not just eating tired old native grannies. Plus, they are staking out my house at night."

Kelly's eyes narrowed. "Why was Karen pissed off?"

"Don't you change the subject, you sneaky bastard."

"Wickey, did I ever tell you the story of Kahyla the whale hunter?"

"You're doing this to me again."

"Why not; it works." Kelly spoke while Alan listened impatiently.

A hundred years ago, a little boy from the Squamish village disappeared while swimming in the bay. The village hunters searched the waters for him, but he was gone. During the search, the hunters spotted a pod of orca in the waters surrounding the bay. Some of the villagers shouted, "The child was eaten by the whales!"

Kahyla, a young brave who was trying to prove his strength and cleverness, declared that he was going to paddle out in his canoe and kill the whales. The chief said, "Kahyla, don't be a fool. The whales did not take the child, but they will take you if you are foolish."

Kahyla was furious. He called the chief an old fool and then climbed into his canoe. When he arrived at the pod of orcas, he drew his spear at the big dorsal fin that was gliding gently in front of him. Before he could throw the spear, his canoe lurched up and he fell into the sea. The whales took his spear, and they then tore off his clothes. The big bull orca swam up to the naked young brave and said to him, "Human boy, look at how small your cock and balls are." The huge whale swam away and left Kahyla for a moment while the smaller cows swam in circles laughing at him. The big bull swam back with his huge penis hanging out. "Come back and fight when your little cock grows up." The boy returned to the village in shame.

"Nice. I suppose this story has a moral to it," Alan replied impatiently.

"Yeah, don't go hunting orcas unless you are hung like a whale." Karen's voice boomed over Alan's shoulder. She sat down in the booth and scanned their faces; they looked like two little boys hiding a bullfrog from their mother. "Alan, if you were hung like a whale, then I never would have kicked you out of the house." Kelly snorted as Alan elbowed him.

"Seriously, what is going on with you two? Do not lie to me."

Alan and Kelly looked at each other. It was clear that Kelly was not going to say a word. "Uh…I can't tell you all of the details, but there is a gang going around and murdering people. They are well organised, and the police don't believe they exist." Alan watched Karen's face as she absorbed his words.

"You have a big red light on your forehead that flashes when you're lying. Did you know that, Alan?"

Alan's eyes flashed up for a second as if to see if he could spot this mysterious light. And then he looked back at Karen sheepishly. "You two are big cowardly babies." She pointed her finger at Kelly. "You too, you are just as gutless. No problem running around in the bush playing Rescue Ricky, but when it comes to dealing with your shit…gutless, both of you." Karen stood up and threw Alan's coffee into his lap. The two watched her spin gravel from the tires as she drove out of the parking lot.

"She's Irish."

"Thought you said she was Ukrainian."

"Irish-Ukrainian."

"That explains it."

"What do I do?" Alan was serious now.

"She's your wife; tell her the truth. She's smarter than you, so she will figure it out. She's on the warpath now, so it's only a matter of time."

"About the monsters."

"You say they are staking you out? How do you know?"

"They were hanging in the trees above my house. They could be anywhere, in any tree. Maybe they're in that tree right there."

"Why do you think they're after you specifically?"

"I think I pissed off one of them by living. I don't think they are used to having witnesses."

Kelly thought for a moment. "Did you actually see them, or did you just have a feeling that they were there?"

"I was watching the trees out behind my yard, and then there was a huge ruckus in the tops of the big cedars. I saw some movement," Alan said.

Back in the trees above the house, the moon lit the cedar boughs and made them look silvery grey. The stratus clouds rolled through the treetops in swirls.

"I will not take him," Sartra said.

Shaman's eyes followed her leader's tortured movements, her laboured breath and tensed neck muscles. "Just take him! He smells like he has been rotten," Shaman said.

"If I can prove that he is rotten, then I will kill him immediately. I will strip his flesh and eat his eyes in front of the clan. As long as he is clean, I cannot touch him."

"The whole clan understands and would encourage you to take him clean or rotten. He is the only live human witness to our clan, and he is the one responsible for Sentrous's betrayal. You are allowed by Kamptra to kill witnesses."

"Sentrous betrayed the laws of Kamptra of his own will, knowing well of the consequences. I cannot break the laws that keep us safe. Kamptra is the only thing that holds off the storm of awareness. Humans have no principles, and if we abandon ours, then we will become like them. They will overrun us with their weapons and aircraft."

"Principles are not supposed to put us in a situation where we are forced to kill the ones we love and spare the ones we hate." Shaman spoke quietly.

"Turning us around from vicious impulse? That's exactly what they are supposed to do."

Sartra swept through the river valley and past the recreation centre. She leapt across the five lanes of the Upper Levels Highway and down Capilano Drive. She sat down beside Panshua in the tall cedar and looked into the Wickey household. Panshua had been watching Teddy; he was jumping up and down in front the Xbox 360, yelling at his virtual partners. Panshua could feel the anger radiating from Sartra as she licked her lips at the thought of the teenager's blood running over her tongue. She would make Alan watch his son being eaten, before killing him slowly and painfully. One drink of alcohol or the pills would make him rotten, allowing her to take him. She would know the smell; it was only a matter of time. They never stayed clean; they were a dirty race.

Alan was getting sick of these AA meetings. He pulled out onto Marine Drive and started homewards. There were too many sad stories and tears for his liking. He didn't have any urges to fight. Maybe he was not an alcoholic after all, and the fuss was about nothing. He could probably just go back to having a nice glass of red wine in the evening with Karen, and that would be it.

That was what everyone else did, just not the druggy whiners at the meeting. He was stronger and smarter than the average bear, so why couldn't he drink responsibly? He walked into the kitchen, picked up the bottle of red wine, and spun it slowly in his hands.

Sartra watched as he moved to the open back door and stepped out into the night air. He looked deep into the trees, analyzing the shadows. Was he paranoid? Every time he looked into the trees, he got the feeling that they were out there, watching him. Yet he had not seen them, only a rustle in the trees that could have been raccoons or an eagle.

The Xbox was cackling as Teddy shouted again. Alan leaned into the open bedroom door. "Teddy...Teddy! Time to go to bed, buddy."

"Fascist oppressor," Teddy replied with a short sideways glance from the flashing screen. Alan's eyebrows furled, and he shook his head. He walked down the hall and slipped into the bedroom quietly. Karen was sleeping, or maybe just turned away from him. She was still angry, and the silent treatment was agonizing. He leant over and kissed her cheek; she blinked her eyes but didn't move. He slid into bed beside her. His mind was racing until he drifted off to sleep. His sleep was anything but peaceful.

The dust rose over the small dirt hills at the side of the road as the convoy drove towards the small town. Alan and another observer sat in their foxhole and looked through his scope and watched the market stalls. The sniper was taking a piss, and Alan was anxious. So far there was nothing to be anxious about; the last four convoys had gone through just fine. The Canadian grizzlies rolled past the petrol station and the causeway. They slowed to a crawl as the radio chirped twice and then crackled. "Steadman four five one, this is Oprah nine two east; are we clear for pass?"

"Oprah, this is Steadman, good to go, nothing to report," Alan replied as the convoy accelerated back up to speed. Alan looked back into the lens and focussed on the row of shacks. He saw a shadow move in the back of one of the empty shacks. He focussed his scope and noticed the thin blue wires running out of the dirt and along the plank floor. The wire end that wrapped around a stack of plastic crates wiggled as Alan's heart leapt. "Oprah, Oprah, IED on your right! Sniper, where are you?" The red flash and blast wave travelled up the little hill and pushed dust and branches over Alan's head. The air swirled around his helmet, and he could smell the mixture of C-4 and dust along with another smell. This was a musty animal smell that blew up into his face; he felt the hands of his sniper gripping into his shoulders and exerting a constant pressure.

Alan opened his eyes, and the mixed images swirled as they faded. The smell of the creature's breath still lingered; yes, the smell still lingered. Alan sat up in the early light. Pine needles slid down the sheets to his waist. His eyes cleared of sleep, and he looked around the bed. Pine needles and four large round mud smudges covered the yellow sheets. Alan's eyes darted around his bedroom to rest on a smudge on the wall and ceiling above his bed. Karen's rhythmic breathing matched the rise and fall of her sides. Alan stood up and rolled out from under the sheets. He could see a few sparse needles in the hall as he walked towards Teddy's room. Alan's pace quickened as his mind raced through the possibilities; he pushed open Teddy's door and walked in.

Teddy lay on his back, snoring. On his face were two mustard-coloured stripes stroked down his cheeks. Alan could see the mud prints and pine needles on the floor around his bed. He could smell the rotten stink of the creature's body. They had marked his son. Alan walked backwards into the doorway, his pulse bounding as a hand touched his shoulder.

"Good morning, honey." Karen stood behind him. He turned to speak but stopped silent; a mustard-coloured stripe adorned her forehead as she passed on the way to the bathroom. He walked into the bathroom and grabbed a facecloth as Karen sat on the toilet. He wiped her forehead, much to her confusion, and then went into Teddy's room. Teddy groaned as he wiped the twin stripes off his face. This stuff smelt disgusting. Alan did his best to wipe up the mess as Karen strolled back towards the bedroom. "Where the hell did all those pine needles come from? What were you doing last night?"

"Uh, I had a little problem with a raccoon in the crawlspace. I guess I didn't clean myself up very well." Karen scanned his face and apparently was not sure if he was lying or not. Maybe the red light wasn't flashing.

"What's that smell? At least it's not vodka and Coke." She pulled the covers back up over her shoulders. Alan sat up in bed and looked up at the huge grey handprints on the ceiling above his bed.

15 Red Flashes

Sentrous stroked the girl's hair and waited. The city lights sparkled from the rooftop of the Orpheum Theatre. The horns and sirens wailing in the background almost drowned out the sounds of the girl's panicked breathing. He gripped her cheeks, and she twisted her head in an attempt to recoil from his touch. His black hide chaffed her white skin like sticky sandpaper. The girl was drunk and a recreational drug user; she smoked pot and snorted cocaine only occasionally. She was perfect for tonight's plan. Kamptra outlined a few other indicators, such as social status, clothing, and cleanliness. This girl was certainly not on the outskirts of society. She was a party girl, dressed well, too clean to take by Sartra's standards, but Kamptra was up to interpretation. This young lady was on the borderline between being eligible and forbidden, and she was irresistibly tasty!

He had parked himself in the middle of his old hunting route. Luckily, his wait was short. Sentrous looked up over the railing to see the shadow approach. As Aelan soared over the theatre, a grommet smacked his back, between his shoulder blades. Surprised, he almost missed his landing. He swung around but could see nothing. Wait, what was that smell? It smelt delicious. Aelan turned and swung across to the theatre roof. There she was, hanging upside down, blood dripping down her face into her eyes. The hole in her throat prevented her from screaming as she looked into Aelan's eyes. Aelan walked over and sniffed her breath. Her face was smudged with mud. She wasn't rotten, but she wasn't clean either. Aelan turned to the night sky, trying to see who had left him this little gift. It was no mystery; this was Sentrous's work. Aelan recollected the many times when he'd begged Sentrous to kill one like this, not rotten but not clean. It was Sentrous who had forbade him; he would go on and on about Kamptra! A forbidden gift from a forbidden friend. Aelan touched her thigh with his claw, and she began to writhe. All this wasted time, he thought; watching the man's house, waiting for Sentrous to appear; meanwhile he was dancing on the roof of the city eating treats like this, or even tastier. Aelan paced the roof and walked back to her. He could leave and let Sentrous eat her, but what if he was gone? She would be discovered, and that would not be acceptable. Aelan did not have to think about it for long. He licked her neck to get a taste, but then turned away. *Sartra would forbid this*, he thought. Then he swung around and bit deeply into her neck, letting the blood pour across his tongue. She was fantastic! This unexpected surprise put Aelan behind schedule. He would need to find a suitable kill to bring back to the camp.

In the Alley below, Carl was shaking from the cold. His blanket was full of holes, and the campfire was out. Crumpled beer cans clinked as he curled up his legs. Dew dripped from the tree branches onto Carl's hat. It was too cold to sleep. It sounded like some ravens were fighting in the building top. Carl shouted, "Hey, you stupid birds, shut up!"

Aelan was surprised and looked down. Maybe he would not have far to look for tonight's catch? Aelan leapt over to another tree and dropped down to see who was talking to him. Carl followed the shadows as the figure descended towards him. Aelan stopped on a branch about fifteen feet off the ground. Carl squinted to make out the dark shape until Aelan peeled his lips back in a smile and opened his eyes to meet Carl's. Carl stayed perfectly still, but his pulse jumped and the blood vessels in his limbs dilated to redistribute blood to his major muscle groups. Adrenaline poured through his arteries like fuel. Aelan raised his hand and waved at Carl. Carl, breathing in short puffs, slowly waved back. Aelan thought this guy was funny, waving back at him. Carl leapt up and turned to run, but he made it only a few steps before the yellow ivory teeth sank into the back of his neck, pulling the top of his spine out of its home in the base of his skull. Aelan did not have time to waste; he had to get some meat back to the clan quickly or Shaman was sure to suspect something. He smiled at the thought of Sentrous.

Shaman's penetrating glare disrupted Aelan's stumbling explanation of the slow night. She leaned in and smelled his breath while their eyes met. She had been waiting for Sentrous to contact Aelan. Now it had happened.

"Did you see him?"

"See who?" Aelan replied. Shaman drove Aelan's body across the stand and pinned him up again a thick bough. At two hundred years old, she was as fast and deadly as any. Her grip was twice that of Aelan, and he struggled as the last wisp of air escaped from his throat.

"Sentrous and Caracin will be my clean meal soon. I would rather not have you for dessert, but if it turns out that way, then I will serve your heart with acorns and salt." She swung his body out into the air and dropped him, where he reached half consciously out to a branch, halting his fall just before he hit the forest floor. He pulled himself back up into the canopy where he huddled quietly on the trunk, bobbing back and forth. His thoughts were repetitive and vengeful.

Staff Sergeant Mullens walked up the steps and pounded on Alan's door. "I just thought I would stop by and let you know that the RCMP is investigating the accident. I personally think that you were negligent in your actions, and I will do everything that I can to make sure that you go to jail for your carelessness."

Alan's blood rushed into his temples. "Listen here, you pencil-neck prick, I will be the one testifying at the inquiry about what a completely fucked-up search you were running. Woody was my friend, and I don't appreciate you using his death to cover up your incompetence."

"You've got a lot of nerve, Wickey. I will make sure that you do time for this."

"Hey, stay the fuck away from my house. If you are going to actually charge me, then send one of your monkeys to do it, because I don't want to see your face here again."

"I'll be back, Alan." Mullens walked down the driveway and got into his patrol car. Alan walked back into the house and started to pace back and forth, talking to himself.

"What a fucking moron that guy is; he can't just charge me without opening the whole can of worms. He would be cooking himself, not just me." He opened up the liquor cabinet. Australian

Shiraz 2006—that would be a nice bottle of wine. His eyes traced the label and scanned the cork. Hmm…Where was the corkscrew? What time would Karen be home?

"Don't be an idiot, Alan!" His breath bounced off the bottle; he dropped it back on the shelf and closed the cupboard door. Alan's thoughts were spinning in circles; the more upset he became, the tighter the thought circles. His iPhone chimed, and he picked it up and glanced at the small screen. It was a reminder to pick up Teddy from school.

As Alan waited in the school's outer parking lot, he started to organize his thoughts. A dimwitted RCMP staff sergeant was the least of his problems. These creatures had crept into his house while he slept and marked his wife and his son. How was he going to protect his family? What were his next actions?

Helplessness was like acid in your veins. Alan had to get control, because the situation was controlling him. *If you don't have control over the situation, then you your coping mechanisms will eventually fail.* These monkey bastards had control over his life. If he didn't change that, then he would either end up dead or crazy.

Alan watched as Teddy walked towards the car. He was growing up too quickly. The look in his big green eyes was so serious and solemn. What was going on in his mind? Grades, girls, and video game scores, Alan hoped, but the look on his face was too morose. He was worried about something.

Teddy opened the door, and the vehicle suspension bounced as he landed on the seat.

"Hey Teddy, what's up?"

"Just drive."

"OK, no problem." Alan swung the car out of the parking lot and drove down the steep drive as Teddy looked out over the view of the city.

"Are you guys going to be able to stay together, or are you getting a divorce?"

"Whoa, dude, that's quite a question. What's on your mind?"

"What are you, a politician? Just answer the flipping question, for once."

148

"Uh, OK…Mom and I are struggling through lots of issues, but I think that we'll be able to work things out. I hope so, anyway."

Teddy liked this answer better than the last one. "What did you do to piss her off—did you lie to her?"

Alan took a deep breath. "Yeah, I sort of didn't tell her all of the details of something I should have."

"Mom is all about the details; don't you know that? Are you going to continue to lie to her? If you are, then she's gonna divorce your ass. You know that, don't you?"

Alan was quiet as they drove along Marine Drive. Teddy continued, "This is what you always tell me: 'Teddy, you have a choice, it's your choice, blah blah blah.' So, Dad, are you going to be a loser or not? It's your choice." Teddy stopped and looked down at his feet. "Yeah, well, I hope that you get to stay my dad. Your apartment sucks, by the way. If you do decide to be a deadbeat loser, then I don't want to stay at that shithole of yours."

Alan's mind was racing. "Uh…OK. I will give that some thought." Teddy was clearly aware of more than he had thought.

"Don't think about it too long," Teddy said as they pulled up into the driveway.

As they walked into the front door, Karen greeted them from the kitchen. "Dinner's going to be pizza because I have to go back to the university for some stuff."

"Karen, can we have a chat before you go?" Alan looked at her intensely.

"Yeah, sure, honey, just do me a favour and go through Teddy's bag and make his lunch up for tomorrow. Don't give him those fruit jellies because he just throws them out."

Alan started to assemble Teddy's lunch as Karen climbed the stairs to interrogate Teddy on his homework assignment. Teddy was right; maybe he should just tell Karen the truth. Even if she thought he was nuts, then at least he wouldn't be a liar. She would just insist that he go back to the shrink for another session to deal with his delusions. That's not so bad.

"Hey, can I take you out for a coffee tonight?"

Karen looked at him with a quick sideways glance. "Yeah, sure. I'm heading out to the lab—why don't you come with me?"

"Yeah, OK. Will we have time to stop on the way out for coffee?"

"I think so." Karen managed to produce a half smile.

Karen Wickey—formerly Karen Cutter—was a geneticist. The third of four girls, she was happy to fill in as the tomboy that Daddy never had. By the age of twelve, she was an expert shot, a good boat handler, and a fantastic angler. At fourteen the gangly long-legged teenage girl was chosen to represent the Canadian Army Cadets in the world championship marksmanship competition in Chichester, England. Her father took a leave of absence—almost losing his job at the paper mill—to escort her team. She started off from well back in the pack and then shot a perfect round in the final to win the world youth silver medal. Her bedroom wall was a stark contrast to those of her three other sisters: countless shooting, fishing, and hunting trophies hung in place of frilly needlework and dolls.

It was Karen's toughness and gritty attitude that had enchanted Alan when he met her. After her undergrad degree— biology at University of Victoria—she had worked as a hunting and fishing guide at the world-famous Painter's fishing lodge in Campbell River. Staying in her parents' basement, she worked off her student loans by taking tourists out into the rapids and facilitating the capture of some rather large salmon. Her charm was legendary among the rich Californian senators and businessmen who flew a thousand miles to spend a weekend watching her give a casting lesson or jump the guide boat over a ten-foot stand wave. Karen was one of the few high rollers. She had a knack for finding the monster spring salmon, and most of the pictures that hung in the cedar log lounge at the lodge were shots of Karen and her clients holding up springs that weighed in at up to seventy pounds. Karen Cutter was a rarity. Although there were a handful of high rollers on the coast, she was the only one that stood five foot, ten inches tall with river-water green eyes and a bushel of long golden strawberry hair. This rough-and-tumble fishing guide averaged a marriage proposal per week. Her (genuine) little-girl innocence and square white smile paid off in large US dollar tips. Karen managed to pay off her thirty-five-thousand-dollar student loans in just two summers.

EMERGENCE

Karen had little time for boys until she met a young search and rescue technician during an unfortunate incident in the rapids. She had taken some of her regulars out to Aaron Rapids early in the morning. Two Wisconsin lawyers were busily trying to convince Karen to fly to the Bahamas with them and be their charter-boat skipper for a three-week island tour. She had heard this offer before; the last guy had already picked out what bikini she was going to wear during the trip. She was pleased to see their mouths snapped shut by the scream of their Shimano reels. Two big Coho salmon ran off in different directions, almost pulling the chubby middle-aged warriors out of the boat. Lawyers squealed like little girls when they had fish on. Karen looked over at her new trainee in the other boat and saw something that worried her immediately. Carter had followed her out with his client, an older senator. Karen had noticed that the old guy was not looking well at the breakfast table, but she had attributed that to a hangover. Carter was young, nineteen or so; he had enough trouble dressing himself in the morning. It was too much to assume he was aware of other people. The senator looked a little greener then he should have.

"Senator Payne, are you all right? You look a little pale to me." Karen called over the short span of water.

The senator was having trouble speaking. "I'm fine, sweetie. I'm just feeling a little tired." He then clutched his chest and dropped to the bottom of the boat.

Carter's eyes bugged out. "Karen! Help me out here, girl; he's doing the funky chicken."

Karen turned to her clients. "Wendell, can I ask you to take over as skipper? You know the way back to the lodge from here, don't you?"

"Yes ma'am, certainly do. I will take over for sure." Karen backed her boat over to Carter's and jumped in. The old man was lying very still and not moving. Karen had the advanced first aid kit with oxygen and airway tools, so she went to work on the lifeless form.

"Mayday, Mayday, Mayday—Comox Coast Guard radio, this is Painter 301. We have a medical emergency in Aaron rapids; request help."

Karen finished her assessment and stood up. "Carter, you do CPR while I drive. His pulse is very weak and he's not breathing; he doesn't have long to get to the hospital."

"Why do I have to do the CPR?"

"Carter, do even know where the evacuation dock is in Campbell River?"

Carter hesitated for a moment and then dropped to his knees to listen for breathing. Karen spun the boat around and gunned the engines; she knew that he needed advanced care quickly and she could not delay his evacuation at all. The radio squawked. "Painter 301, Painter 301—we have one helo and two fast-rescue boats heading your way; please stand by at the rapids."

"Comox, Painter 301; negative, negative. We are evacuating the patient to the north jetty in Campbell River; please have advanced life support waiting. Our ETA is twenty minutes." Karen would have to take a shortcut through the dreaded boat passage. The tiny narrows had ferocious tidal currents and very shallow waters. If Karen made even a small navigational error, they would end up piling onto one of the many reefs in the channel. Yet Karen had run this route a hundred times and driven through the tight turns at full speed.

Carter looked up over the rail at the trees and rocks whizzing by and whimpered. He decided that he was better off keeping his head down and concentrating on the CPR. The first coast guard boat arrived at the entrance to the passage but was not brave enough to follow her through.

"Comox, CCG 509. Yeah...uh, Painter 301 just went through the boat passage on a low tide; we will not be following her, so it's up to 442 Squadron to meet her somewhere on the other side."

Alan hung out the helo door and looked down at the small boat turning through the small clusters of islands at breakneck speed.

"Painter 301, this is Rescue 310. Please alter course to Heriot Bay, and we will transfer the patient there."

Karen's voice came in, buffeted by the wind. "Negative, negative, Helo 310. Please have an ALS ambulance waiting at the north jetty; my ETA is ten minutes!" Alan had to laugh. He shook his head as he squeezed his microphone and spoke to the pilot. "Scoop, she's not turning, and she's not slowing down."

The pilot replied, "I am going to order her to pull over and give us the patient!"

"Scoop, you can do that, but I would make sure that there is an ambulance waiting for her just in case she tells you to suck rocks again. Besides, she's right—if we transfer now, it will add fifteen minutes onto this poor sod's ride. It will be faster if she just keeps going."

The big yellow bird now thumped the air above the speeding launch. The radio crackled again. "Painter 301, this is Rescue 310; please turn and dock at Heriot Bay." Karen looked up and flipped her hand at them as if she were waving off a wasp. Laughter filled the intercom. "Well, Scoop, you told her. You do have a way with women, don't you?"

The whole crew chuckled as Scoop pulled up to five thousand feet and accelerated to the north jetty. "Alan, I will drop you down in the parking lot, and you can help with the transfer. It looks like the ALS unit is on the way."

"Okey dokey, Scoop baby, beginning pre-hoist checklist," Alan replied, knowing how annoyed Scoop was at this whole ordeal. Alan swung out and dropped down from the bird. By the time he hit the pavement, the patient was being carried up the dock ramp at the marina and heading towards the ambulance. Alan walked over to the ambulance, and said hello. "Hey Wickey do you want package of aspirin?"

Alan's voice dropped in tone "No..why would I need an Aspirin?"

"Maybe you guys are sore from the ass whoppin' that that one-hundred-thirty-pound fishing princess gave you." The ambulance door shut with cackles of laughter; even the barely conscious senator managed a weak laugh as the ambulance sped up the hill with its sirens wailing. Alan walked down the ramp and approached the Painter's Lodge boat. The coast guard vessel had arrived a few moments earlier, and now the three-man crew was asking Karen questions and filling out the paperwork. They all looked up at Alan with wily grins.

"Hey, why didn't you pull into Heriot Bay and transfer the patient to us?"

Karen looked him up and down with a mild flash of annoyance. "You were too slow, GI Joe!" She reached out and playfully poked him in the shoulder.

Alan was now annoyed. "Well, that's debatable. You are supposed to let the professionals figure these things out and follow the instructions we give you."

"You are wearing a bright-orange jumpsuit with a giant pumpkin on your head, and I am supposed to take you seriously as professionals?" By this time the sixty-five-foot coast guard cutter had pulled alongside, and the entire crew erupted into catcalls.

Karen and Alan locked eyes as Karen tried not to smile. Alan just stared back; he had met his match. He turned to glare at the coast guard guys, who all looked up and whistled quietly, pretending to ignore him. Using his two fingers, he made the "I'm watching you" sign by pointing to his eyes and then at them. He walked over to the big red boat.

"OK, what's her name?"

"Not telling you, Wickey; you should have been here faster." There was more laughter.

"You guys are all bum lickers." Wickey stormed up the ramp and met the helicopter as it touched down in the dusty parking lot. One of the junior coast guard cadets ran up to the chopper and handed Alan the incident report. "Here is the paperwork; the mate just told her that you were a gay man with herpes."

"Thanks for that, Skippy. We will get you guys back; you know that, don't you? We know where you eat, and we know where you sleep."

As the bird lifted off, pushing a blast of swirling dust directly into the face of the cadet, the winch man leaned over. "So, Wickey, how did it go? Was she hot?"

"I don't find your comments appropriate, and I do not wish to discuss it." The cabin crew laughed as Alan looked over the paperwork. Karen Cutter, hmm.

Alan did not see her again until two weeks later. She was sitting at the pub with four girlfriends. Alan approached her from behind. She could tell from her girlfriends' reactions that something was up.

"Hello, my name is Alan. We met the other day out on the water. You may not remember me."

Karen turned to meet his eyes and smiled. "How is your rash, Mr. Wickey?"

The girls giggled quietly as Alan stuttered on his reply. "Uh...I don't have a rash." Alan had forgotten about the coast guard comment. He had thought that they were kidding about actually telling her that stuff—the bastards!

"I'm glad to see that it's all better." Now Karen's big square smile flashed and took Alan's breath away. He was normally quite clever and witty with the ladies, yet today his head spun in a swirl and his brain ground to a complete halt. He just stood there with his mouth open.

"Are you going to stand there and catch flies with your big mouth or are you going to buy us all a drink?" He stared for a second and then took her cue. He turned and walked off to the bar to get a round for the girls. He walked back over with the tray of drinks and sat down beside Karen. She immediately got up and walked over to the other side of the bar.

"So, Karen told us that you are gay and that you just started working here at the pub as a waiter. Is it a good place to work? Does your boyfriend live in Comox too?"

For the fourth time Alan stammered, clawing for an answer. His voice oscillated. "I'm...uh, a search and rescue technician, and I'm not...I don't have a boyfriend. I'm not gay!"

"That's what all the boys say," Karen announced over Alan's shoulder upon her return, and the girls giggled loudly now. Karen looked into Alan's eyes and saw that she had pushed him a little too far. She reached over, put her hand on his knee, and whispered into his ear. "It's OK, silly Mr. Wickey; I am just teasing you." Alan was never the same after that light touch on the knee.

The next morning the door swung open, and Alan sat down at the crew briefing. The seven men stopped talking and fell silent; all were staring intensely at Alan. Scoop lifted his arm and pointed at Alan's face. "Look at that, yes! I told you guys two weeks max! Pay up, you suckers." Scoop held out his hand, and four crumpled twenties landed in his open palm. There were moans of disgust.

The co-pilot, Dustin, was a Newfoundlander who had just sworn to the boys that the great Wickey would never succumb.

"I'm not paying until I get confirmation!" Dustin announced. "OK, Wickey, did you sleep with her yet?"

"Don't be so crude," Alan replied with a disgusted look.

"Oh my good Lord tunderin thunderin' Jesus. Wickey, you are in love." The co-pilot pulled his twenty out and slapped it onto the table in front of a smiling Scoop. "I never thought I'd see the day that the great dirt dog Wickey fell with shame, like a Great Dane puppy."

Her doctorate had been a tortured affair. She endured three years of hell with an advisor that was constantly hitting on her because her husband was in Afghanistan. Once her genetic thesis advisor realised that he was not going to get into her pants, he abandoned any interest in supporting her thesis work. She submitted the two-hundred-page document ("Gene sets that mark vulnerability in pancreatic cancers") eight times before the department head took over and scheduled her doctoral defence. On the day of her four-hour defence, she scheduled tea with her advisor's wife. The little coward almost had a heart attack when he walked through the cafeteria and saw them talking. Karen had raised her teacup and met his eyes over the middle-aged woman's shoulder. She knew that there would be no surprises at the defence, and she was right. After three years of sixteen-hour days split between studying, mothering, and working a lousy part-time laboratory job, she graduated. Teddy was no stranger to playing in the hall or under a lab bench by the time his dad returned from Afghanistan.

Karen now lived in his every thought and his every breath. Alan smiled as he recalled that first touch on the knee. Karen's hand was on his knee now as they drove up towards the lab. Yes, it was time to buck up and be a man; his son was right, he had no choice. Karen had warned him that it would not be easy to be married to her. She expected a lot. "More than the average bear could deliver," she had said many years ago. Well, Wickey had been a pretty average husband and a pretty mediocre father in the past few years. He knew that Karen was OK putting up with an average husband, but the mediocre father bit was not acceptable. That's why she had thrown him out six months ago. "If you can't find the energy for me, then find it for your boy. If you can't find it for your boy, then go have a drink and feel sorry for yourself. Just don't do it here." The words had stung, because they were true. He was feeling sorry for himself; he didn't know how to stop it, then. *One move at a time, Wickey; one move at a time.*

Alan parked at the faculty coffee shop, and they walked in together holding hands. They sat a quiet table overlooking the campus, and he ordered his wife a soy latte and himself a black coffee.

"OK, I have something to tell you that you probably won't believe because it sounds crazy." She was quiet, her face completely neutral. He could never read her thoughts by reading her face, and to his frustration, she could always read his.

"Remember when I told you that there were some gangs that were after me?"

"Yes."

"Well, I sort of lied."

"Yes, you lied; you didn't sort of lie."

"Yes, well, …there are these creatures that live in the trees, and they attacked me that day. And somehow I pissed them off, and now they are after us."

Karen's eyes scanned Alan's eyes and then his mouth. Her expression did not change; there was no reaction at all to his proclamation.

She replied in a very casual, calm voice, "See, that wasn't so bad, was it?"

Alan's mouth dropped, and he stammered, "You believe me?"

"I can tell when you're lying and you are not lying."

"How long have you known about them?"

She started a half smile and then stopped. "A little while. I mean, they broke into my house, for Christ's sake, and they painted some slimy shit on my forehead. You didn't think I would notice that?"

"Why didn't you say something?"

"You were too busy lying, so I didn't discuss it with you. I have a policy; I never work with liars."

"So do you have some kind of a plan?" He realised what a stupid question that was because Karen always had a plan. "I mean, what's your plan?"

"I am not telling you. I said I don't work with liars. I am not sure how I ended up married to one, but I definitely will not work with one. You can do your plan and Teddy and I will do ours, and then we will see who gets eaten." Karen was dead serious.

"Wait a minute; I am not—"

Karen's finger met his lips before he said it.

"Don't do it, Alan. If you are promising to stop lying, then that's another sentence." As he began to speak, Karen scanned his face like a pit boss at a casino.

Alan measured each word. "I will…uh, it is my intention to stop lying to you and Teddy. I do not want to be a liar." Alan let out a long, nervous sigh.

"Good, I hate liars," Karen replied, and then changed the subject. "I think that we are dealing with some kind of descendent of Homo cercopithecidae. We will find out pretty quickly, because Kevin Mallsner at the lab ran the samples that I gave him last month and he says that the zoology guys are all pretty excited at the find. They will have lots of questions, and I don't think that we can answer them."

Alan was dumbfounded. "Last month? What do you mean, last month? What samples?"

"Who does your laundry, Alan?" Karen was getting impatient.

"The porcupine spines in my pocket, of course. I was wondering where those went."

"I am considering setting a minimum IQ for my team, so smarten up, Wickey."

"What's a circopithaguy?"

"Cercopithecidae, it's a distant cousin to Brazilian howler monkeys, only there is some significant genetic drift. I ran the first strip from the sample, but I realised that I was in over my head so I sent it to Vermont. Vermont guys are threatening to fly out here, so I need to convince them not to come."

"We can tell them that it was a sample from a museum." Karen glared at him. "Oh, uh, right—no lying. Shit, this is going to be hard. What do we say?"

"OK, you're annoying me again. I want to ask you some questions, and I want you to be careful with your answers."

"OK, shoot."

"Describe them to me."

"Well, they are big and really ugly, and they've got spiky spiny thingies instead of normal hair, and they have a face sort of like this." Alan made his eyes bulge out and peeled back his lips. Karen got angrier and angrier.

"What did I just say to you?"

Alan realised that his description wasn't very scientific. "OK, OK, let's start again. What's the first aspect I should describe?" Karen grabbed Alan's iPhone and searched the browser for a minute. "Here's a picture of a howler monkey. Now I will start drawing it, and you can tell me how these guys are different."

"OK, good; this will be good."

"Height and weight."

"I would say that when they are standing fully erect, they are about eight or nine feet high." Karen was surprised by this. "I figure they weigh about two hundred pounds; they are pretty skinny. There are two different types. The second type is bigger and meaner than the skinny ones. The skinny ones have longer arms. The bigger ones are heavier, maybe two-fifty to three hundred pounds." Karen drew as he spoke.

"Did they screech or howl at all?"

"No, they were dead quiet, but I did notice this extremely weird hissing in my head when Alvin went blind on the bridge. It hurt my skull. I had a headache for a day or two."

"Ultrasonic calls." Karen was speaking quietly, almost to herself.

"What do you mean?"

"You know, bats and bugs can use ultrasonic frequencies to communicate, long-range calls that cannot be heard by the prey. Hmm, I have an idea for that. We will have to call Sebastien tomorrow." Karen paused for a minute. "OK, do they have tails, and if so, how long are they?"

"No tails."

"Tell me about these quills."

"They are long and very sharp like a porcupine, and they are full of this liquid that changes colour really quickly. Most of the time when I have seen them, they have been black, but I noticed that the one that pinned me down by the campfire changed colour to white when he hit the snow."

"Facial features?"

"Really ugly. I mean, this little monkey in the picture is kind of cute, but these guys are really fucking scary-looking."

"You're yapping like a little schoolgirl, stop it. Eyes, ears, mouth, nose—you know, facial features."

"Eyeballs were white."

"Sclera, the whites of the eyes are sclera."

"Yeah, OK, whatever that is. These were really white with blackish-red pupils. The pupils had orange flecks in them."

"Shape of pupils?"

"Roundish oval. The nose was a flat snout, not as flat as a bull dog's, but flat. It had big-ass nostrils the size of loonies."

"Teeth?"

"Oh yeah, I know all about those babies. They were like a combination of shark teeth and tiger teeth. They were really sharp and tore into your flesh easily." Alan paled and looked down for a moment.

"Sorry, sweetie, let's talk about something else for a bit." Karen placed a hand on his knee.

Alan got up and walked into the bathroom for a minute to catch his breath. He looked into the mirror. He took a long, deep breath and gathered his composure. *She actually believes me, she isn't just playing along, she actually believes me.* Alan walked back out and looked over Karen's shoulder at her notebook. Karen was working furiously on one of her legendary lists.

"Alan contractors are installing a security system in the house today while we are here. If you behave I will give you the door code."

Karen continued writing for a moment, and then she got up and walked to the truck as Alan followed. He opened the door for her and went around to the driver's side door. As they pulled out and drove down the wide boulevard, the huge oak trees pulsed by the window. Alan stole a few sideways glances at Karen; she was staring at him, analysing him. "Alan, when you were in Afghanistan doing recon and intelligence in the mountains, what was the most important thing to you—the mission?"

Alan thought about the question for a moment. "Uh, well, the missions were important for sure, but the most important thing was getting home to you and Teddy."

"Yeah, that's what you are supposed to say. I want you to focus on telling me the truth, though."

His first thoughts were full of defensive denials, but before he spoke he took another slow breath in and then let it out. Karen didn't mind a little silence, she was actually happy not to hear the standard "Oh, but you have me all wrong, honey." Alan gathered his thoughts and started slowly. "OK, well, when out on patrol or holed up in an observation post, the most important thing to me was keeping my squad safe and alive, not letting them down. Even the slightest mistake could put everyone in danger, and sometimes I could be forgetful, so I was always really worried that I would screw something up and get someone hurt."

"When you got intelligence reports on the radio, did you share them with your men or keep them secret?"

"Oh, I would share everything right away; I mean, these guys were my squad. I trusted them with every part of my life. There are no secrets inside a ten-foot plywood hooch; their pastime was to track the progress of MRE Chicken Kiev through each other's bowels."

"How do you feel towards those guys now?"

"I would walk across the Rocky Mountains to help any one of them, anytime."

"Even the ones that pissed you off, or guys you had arguments with?"

"Yup."

"Hey, Mr. War Hero, if I were to tell you that Teddy and I were your new squad, back here in Canada, then how would you rate your leadership in the last few months compared to the military standard?"

What a question! Alan almost swerved off the road as his mind weeded through some defensive rhetoric and settled down to the glaring truth. Shit, she was right; his leadership sucked. He had committed all of the worst offenses: keeping secrets, drinking, taking off on unannounced trips, soloing, and not checking in with the squad. His recent actions with Teddy and Karen would have had his beloved Cougar squad cornering him in the latrine and

161

beating the shit out him. His conduct would have been close to mutinous. Karen watched his face as a new reality took hold of him.

"Shit...I, um, don't know what to say."

"Shit is right, Captain Wickey. Shit is the right word for it."

Alan drove along in silence until they reached the lab parking lot. They walked into the tall glass lobby of the UBC Centre for Genetics research, and Karen scanned her ID card into the reader. Alan filled out the security registry, and the guard handed him a badge. They started up the stairs to the cafeteria. Outside of the rows of tables, there was a sitting lounge with some leather chairs and a coffee table. At one end of the sofa was a short little man with a grey tweed hat accompanied by a tall thin fellow dressed in khaki slacks and a polyester red sweater. They both jumped up to meet Karen. "Dr. Wickey, how glad to see you."

"Dr. Malsner, Dr. Atkins, this is my husband, Alan Wickey." They shook hands and sat down. The two academics were noticeably excited as Dr. Atkins began. "Karen, we have done some analysis of the materials that you sent to the DNA lab and the results were shocking, to say the least. There has been much interest in the past few days, and the board would like...Well, we need to know where you found those samples."

"I am sorry, gentlemen, but I will not tell you at this time," Karen replied.

They balked at her reply. "Dr. Wickey, we cannot imagine why this would be a secret. This is a whole new species that has run parallel to the Homo sapiens lineage. There is a significant drift from its original branch off from early hominids. We have not been able to identify physical traits other than the fact that this is a new species of primate and that on many chromosomes the genes are very different. Can you give us some regional information, or even a physical description of the animal—size, weight, characteristics?"

"No, I am not going to divulge any more information right now. Gentlemen, you took my sample without asking; you did not consult with me after analysing it, and now you are running around like a pair of dumbstruck little boys."

Alan looked across the thick airspace above the coffee table, from the pair of deep frowns over to Karen's stunning green eyes, shining bright above a quiet, neutral expression. The duct fan above them whistled in its sheet metal housing. It was clear that she was not to be swayed.

"Dr. Wickey, you are one of the foremost telomerase specialists in the world, and it would interest you that the telomeres on the specimen's chromosomes are more than twice as long as homo sapiens chromosomes. Are you sure that you don't want to look at the strips? It would be a shame if the real discoverer of this new find did not get the proper recognition she deserves." Karen smiled as her eyes locked onto his. Dr. Malsner continued, "You know as well as I do as a scientist that discovering something new and radical can be as much of a curse as it is a blessing."

"Are you readying yourself to relieve me of that burden, Doctor?" Karen replied. Atkins knew Karen well enough to realize that Malsner did not have a chance of winning a mental melee. Great chess players can think up to four or five moves ahead in game, but Karen had a reputation for thinking about ten moves ahead in the game of life and science.

Atkins didn't know her reasons, but he did know that she had a damn good one for not sharing. "Karen, we were not aware that you were working on anything other than the telomerase and TA 65 proteins. This find is quite exciting to us, as you probably know already. Let's work together on it if we can. May I ask, exactly, where you found the genetic materials, and if you would be willing to share another sample with us?"

"I found it in my husband's pocket while doing laundry. Alan, do you have any more of that stuff in your pocket?" Karen spun around with a half smile.

Alan's eyes widened as he looked up at the trio; he pulled his hand out of his pocket and produced a ball of lint, then shrugged while they all stared at him.

Malsner's face darkened. "I don't appreciate you playing games with us." He stood up and moved towards the hallway. Atkins followed behind him and turned. "Good day, Karen."

Karen explained. "It should be easy for them but it's not, because they don't get it either. Malsner hates me because I caught him cheating on his baseline data for a joint lineage project. I forced him to start over on a whole series. It put him back months. Liars can only see liars; they project their lies onto everyone else."

TYLER BRAND

Karen took a left turn at the bottom of the stairs, and Alan followed her. They travelled down the hall where she swiped her card at the reader. The light turned green, and she opened the door. They walked into the genetics laboratory and down along the benches of computers and machines. Karen walked into the glass-walled office and turned on the lights. Alan looked around the stylish corner office. The last time he had been at Karen's workplace, she was out in the bullpens with the rest. When did she get this office?

Karen sat down at her dual screens and moved her mouse to light up the displays. She typed in her password and called up some electron micrographs. A brilliant colour picture of a long tube rolled down the screen. The scan was enlarged five hundred times; it showed the hair-like shaft as a cylinder lined with scales. Karen started, "See these scales on the hair shaft? They're characteristic of many primates. This hollow hair shaft is much like a polar bear, but the weird thing about this sample is that it is filled with a keratin pigment. I've never seen anything like it before. It could be a contaminant from your pocket or even the rain, but if it was, I should be able to isolate some common markers in it. The proteins that we got out of this sample were new to the databanks."

Alan stared at the screen. "They blend into the forest, the grass, and the night. They change colour—green, black, brown, or whatever—depending on where they are. I'm not sure if they have to think about it, or it just happens, but it happens quickly."

Karen uploaded her file to her online account and then deleted all of her data on the local computer. "The department will be after these files soon, once they get permission to break into my account. I've left traps so I'll get an e-mail when they break in."

Alan walked around the office looking at the magazine covers framed on the walls. The journal *Nature* actually had a picture of Karen on the cover with the tagline "The Eternal Life of Cells?" Alan walked to the next article and read it silently as Karen typed on her keyboard. "What's telomerase?" he asked.

Karen smiled; Alan had never showed any real interest in her career before. "Well, telomeres are the end cap for chromosomes. They are burned up a little each time a cell divides, and these structures can define the lifespan of cells along with the

164

lifespan of an organism. When telomeres run out of length, the cell stops dividing. Cell division is regeneration, no regeneration means no healing. Telomerase is a fairly rare protein that can lengthen telomeres."

"Eternal life?" Alan asked.

"Yeah, that's not such a novel concept in biology. Cancer cells live eternally, and lobsters live forever, until you cook them. In fact, I have cancer cells in the fridge that come from a woman by the name of Henrietta Lacks."

"Are you helping her with the cancer?" Alan turned to face Karen.

Karen chuckled. "Uh, not really; she died of her cancer in 1951."

"Oh, no kidding, eh? What did that little guy mean when he said that the sample had very long telomeres?"

Karen replied, "He was just baiting me. Long telomeres can mean a long lifespan, but it's a little more complicated than that."

"So you are working on making cells live forever, by using telomerase?"

"It's not something that you can just drink and live forever. It's kind of like saying you can create farming in Africa by dropping ten thousand tractors out of airplanes. I am working out the mysteries behind how the cells use telomerase and when they use it."

"Cool, that's amazing. I didn't know what you did, or that you were so well known."

"You haven't asked me about my work since you got back from Afghanistan."

"Yeah, I guess I have been a little distracted."

"Yeah, I guess you have."

Alan closed Karen's door and walked around to the driver's side. They drove down the wide boulevard; traffic was quiet. The sunlight flickered through the treetops across the black leather dashboard as Karen started talking.

"We will have to move out of the house if they are watching us."

"Yeah, we can stay at my apartment; it will be tight. We will have to stay at the house tonight though."

Karen replied, "The alarm system should be installed soon, and I can get Shannon to take Teddy for a sleepover with his buddy Austin. I also called Kelly. He's going to come over and stay with us."

Alan looked at Karen, realizing that she was carrying out a very complex plan. Just like the many that she had made for things like family vacations, birthday parties, and renovations. They had all been planned out to the smallest detail with assigned roles to all involved. "I pulled out all of your army gear and charged up the batteries for your night-vision goggles and stuff. I figure we can put Kelly on the roof with his sniper rifle for the late shift. I'll take the first watch."

"You'll take the first watch?" Alan replied.

"Alan, don't get all macho on me; I can outshoot you on the range one handed with a baby in my arms. If you think you are going to be bossing me around because you are a guy, then forget it; you can go back to your apartment."

Alan laughed. "OK, boss. What's my job? Cooking and lunches?"

"Yes, exactly!" Karen shook her fist at him with a half smile. "You are on a need-to-know basis, buddy boy." The car pulled up the driveway just as Kelly was talking to the alarm guy.

Alan walked around and opened the door for Karen. "Is it OK if Kelly and I discuss the actual tactical plan?"

. Kelly was waiting in the driveway smiling at them.

"So what did the scientists say?"

"The sample is from some new species of monkey no one has ever seen before," Alan replied.

"It's real, hey?"

"What do you mean, it's real hey? You mean you didn't believe me?"

"Yeah, I sort of believed you, I guess. I mean, you are a recovering addict and all; maybe you were hallucinating." Kelly smiled, and Karen laughed.

"What do you mean, an addict? I, uh…" Alan took a deep breath with the realization that he was being teased. "Very funny." He opened the door, and the alarm system began a steady signal. Karen punched in a six-digit code and silenced it. The new system showed a floor plan of the house, and the zones were lit in red or green. All of the windows and doors were alarmed, and each room had night-vision video cameras with motion sensors. The system had a web interface that allowed the homeowner to log into the cameras and the house's status page to see the video feed. Alan downloaded the app onto his iPhone. Kelly and Karen sat out on the porch as the sun dropped behind the mountains. Alan walked out onto the porch and handed out hot chocolate. The mountain air was crisp, and the mugs warmed their hands.

"OK, Alan, tell us the whole story and don't leave anything out," Kelly said.

Alan started with the encounter on the running path and traced his every thought and move since that day almost four months ago. He recounted his drug and alcohol abuse, his face-to-face meeting with Sentrous in Stanley Park, his narrow escape into the sea, and the close call on the bridge footing. Then he covered the search for the lost Telus technicians on the mountain and Alvin's fall from the bridge. Both Karen and Kelly were listening intently. Karen asked, "When this guy on the wire bridge said that he couldn't see, did you hear anything?"

Alan answered carefully. "Not exactly, but it was like there was a vibration running through my head, sort of like when you are around high-power lines and you can feel something in the air. It was an intense almost squealing, but not a real sound that you could hear. Yet the birds sure heard it, or felt it—they all took off in a huge flock just before Alvin started to freak out. He looked like he was in severe pain. He was holding his eyes before he fell."

Karen looked at Kelly. "I think they may be communicating ultrasonically; there are many frequencies of sound that are not detectable by the human ear." Karen pulled out her cell phone and punched in some buttons. She dialled her own number, and the phone began to flash. "It's ringing," she said.

"It's not ringing—you've got the ringer off," Kelly replied.

"No, it's a ringtone that is in the ultrasonic range; dogs and teenagers can hear it, but we can't because we are old. Our ears have lost the ability to detect sounds in these ranges."

"That is why the legends say that only children in the village can sometimes hear the whistlers in the forest, but the parents can't." Kelly added excitedly, "That makes sense."

"So they communicate using ultrasonic frequencies—would that mean they can talk over a greater distance?" Alan asked.

"I'm not sure, maybe...I will have to look into it," Karen replied.

"I wonder if we can detect the high-frequency sounds using some help?"

"Most recording devices can detect sounds in the fifteen to twenty kilohertz range," Karen said.

Alan pulled out his iPhone and waved his finger as he sorted through the application listings. "Hey, here it is: ultrasonic ring or whistle detector. It only costs two dollars." Alan chuckled. He watched the tiny screen for a moment and touched the screen a few more times. "It installed quickly. Let's give it a try." Alan sipped his hot chocolate. "It is supposed to make the screen flash red and tweet when it detects the ring. Karen, try your ringer—"

Alan's jaw dropped. The small screen was flickering red, and the signal was twittering away in time with the flickers. "That's not your phone, is it?"

"No." Karen stared at the screen in shock as it continued to flicker.

"Maybe its bats?" Alan proposed.

"Yeah, maybe." Her heart leapt with the realization that something was close enough to be plainly heard by the phone.

"Shit!" Kelly rose to his feet, picked up his rifle, and looked through the scope into the blackness of the trees. He flicked the night vision on and scanned the forest behind the house.

"Higher, Kelly, they live in the tops of the big ones."

Aelan froze as the rifle swung over to his direction and stopped. Kelly pointed it directly at him. Aelan could feel his pulse bound as he concentrated on his colour change. His quills tightened, letting out less heat through the dense thicket of needles in his coat. Rifles made him nervous because he had heard stories of the longer bullets being able to penetrate the thick Apec hides. Aelan's mind raced while the gun sights rested on him, but he kept still. Kelly looked through the blackness in the trees trying to make out shapes.

"Now if I were a big ugly monkey, I would pick a nice spot like that one to hang out in." Kelly squeezed the trigger. *Crack!*

The bullet whistled between Aelan's legs and tore off into the trees behind him. He jumped up into the canopy above and flew through the air to another tree in retreat. The giant red cedar lurched with the sudden shift of weight and movement. The shot echoed against the dark mountainside.

"Holy shit, I...uh...Did you see him! Did you see that? He was right there; I almost took his head off. Holy shit, holy shit! Alan...He was a big mother too, eh?" Kelly proclaimed.

Alan just shook his head and calmly stated, "I hate those fucking things." He turned and strolled into the kitchen and opened the cupboard to stare at the wine bottle on the shelf. Both Karen and Kelly stood quietly staring through their rifle sights. They both were in a state of complete disbelief and shock. The iPhone continued to flicker red and tweet actively on the table behind them. "This is real, Kelly," Karen said.

"Yup, seems real all right," Kelly answered as the neighbours looked out their windows trying to locate the source of the shot.

Alan looked up and down the long sleek bottle and sighed. He closed the cupboard door as he addressed the bottle. "Bye-bye, darling; guess I have to stay sober for a while if we are going deal with these guys in the trees." He licked his lips as he sat at the table and sipped from a bottle of water.

Karen walked in and sat down. "We have to get out of here."

"Yup, we do."

"Kelly's out looking for blood drops."

"He didn't hit it; I heard the round head out into the woods."

"He scared the shit out of it, though."

"Yeah, they don't scare easily. They'll be back before first light."

"Let's go to your apartment. They don't know where your apartment is, do they?"

"Don't think so, but I don't know what they know. For all I know, they have Internet. They don't act like animals; they're really smart. The second one on the bridge was wearing a backpack, and the one in the canyon—my little buddy—was wearing sunglasses."

"Sunglasses?" Karen was surprised; her eyes darted back and forth as her mind raced with this new information. "This changes everything, you know."

"Doesn't change anything. These guys are smart, fast, and ruthless."

"I mean scientifically speaking—the use of human tools makes them adaptive, extremely adaptive. It means that they could have weapons."

"What, like missiles?"

"No...more like bows and arrows, or clubs maybe," Karen replied.

"I forgot to tell you, they throw rocks, like marble-sized ones, shaped like pointy eggs. They are really good shots and they throw them hard, like almost bullet velocity. I saved one." Alan packed up all his stuff into a duffel bag. He dropped it beside Karen's bag; hers had been packed for hours. Kelly went home, and Alan and Karen drove over to his apartment. Karen was more excited than frightened. She continued to ask Alan questions, for most of which he did not have answers. Karen pulled out her iPhone and activated the tracking software for Teddy. His location flashed on Google Maps.

"Is he at Austin's?" Alan asked as he drove.

"Yeah. We should tell him what's going on tomorrow," Karen replied, showing him the symbol on the map.

Alan was quiet. She hated his glum silences. Her eyes were burning into him as he focussed on the road.

"This is the part where you say, 'Yes dear'!" Karen exclaimed.

"Yes, dear," he replied as she punched his shoulder. She was right. He needed to buck up and engage that boy before he became someone he didn't even know. He needed to get over his self-pity and become a real dad. For the first time in five years, he actually felt like he was making progress and getting his life in order, bit by bit. Then these stupid creatures had to jump on him and screw everything up. It could be worse—at least he wasn't drunk, divorced, and soon to be monster meat.

As they topped the stairs at his apartment, the wind whistled, twisting around the leaves in the small brick courtyard.

16 Shopping Cart Blues

Sentrous was getting tired; he was staying up late during the day, then hunting prey at night. He went back to the site of his first big mistake, on the wooded chip trail. He then sat in the top of a 150-foot tree that overlooked the neighbourhood, his sore eyes barely open as he struggled to shake off the sleep. He couldn't go to Alan's house because Sartra and Shaman were there, waiting for him. This was a trap that he would not be able to escape.

Sentrous was enjoying his freedom and the chance to be a leader and a great hunter. He was looking forward to his foray into the middle of the city with Caracin this night. Every hunting trip was something new, a new taste of prey; a new adventure. Caracin was addicted to the thrill of killing the clean ones, but he was starting to take risks. They walked the fine line between reckless abandon and an organized plan as they took more and more normal people from the street.

As much as he had enjoyed hunting the television stars, he knew that the Free clan was headed down a road to possible ruin. Shaman's words hung in his mind. She had said that when the humans started to actively look for the missing healthy ones, then it could lead to the time of awareness. She often described how the humans would hunt them relentlessly with aircraft and heavy weapons. She predicted that most in the clans would be killed and the survivors would have to run back up into the high mountains and stay there. Caracin's reply to this was, "Let them come; their weapons don't penetrate our hides. We will kill them all and pile up their bodies in the valley. We will have a huge feast."

In the wake of the highly televised disappearance of Crypto Joe and his monster hunters, local authorities fought bitterly over the investigation. Because the prime suspects were two grizzly bears, Ryder, the conservation officer, was technically in charge of this high-profile investigation. The RCMP was asked by the attorney general to assist the conservation and protection officers in the missing persons case of the four television crew. Staff Sergeant Mullens and Ryder had had a screaming match every day since the trailer was set up. The RCMP detachment inspector had to come down to the site to sort out the pecking order: "Mullens, what the fuck do you know about animal attacks? Just let these guys do their jobs here at the scene, and you support them."

Where the hell are the bodies? Ryder wrote on the whiteboard. He turned to look at the other four conservation officers. "Bears ate 'em!" one officer replied.

"Don't be stupid; we are not talking about Smarties. Joe Beam weighted two hundred and forty pounds. You think that a big male grizzly just gobbled him up and coughed out his keys and his camera?" The conservation officer shrugged his shoulders sheepishly. "This is the middle of hibernation season; where did these bears come from? This doesn't make any sense at all. It's almost like someone planned a circus stunt for publicity."

"You idiot—you saw the videos, those were no circus bears. There is a flipping video of them hunting down these actors and camera guys. The bears dragged them away and buried them farther up the valley. It's not a conspiracy!" Mullens replied, spit flying from his lips.

Ryder looked squarely at Mullens. "There are four missing people and there were two bears—what you think, the bears carted the bodies away in homemade wheelbarrows? I am telling you, something very strange went down in that park last week. The rangers have covered every inch of the upper and lower valley with search dogs, and there are no bodies." Ryder locked eyes with Mullens.

Constable Perry was tired of listening to the two fight, so he had volunteered on one of the search crews. He filed through the woods slowly. He was abreast of another twenty-five RCMP members and volunteers. He liked Ryder but thought that Mullens was an asshole. He just rolled his eyes when Mullens would confide in him: "These CO guys are all losers; we should be running this investigation, you and me, heh?" He was too stupid to see that Constable Perry did not like him. Ironically an RCMP corporal was actually running the missing persons case from the office, but the chief inspector had assigned Staff Sgt. Mullens to work under the conservation service while processing the scene. Mullens was so angry at this virtual slap in the face that his face had been beet red for the whole week. Occasionally Ryder would tempt Constable Perry around the back of the trailer for a cigarette. Perry would coach him through the steps of crime-scene processing. Mullens hated the fact that this Ryder was not missing a single step in processing the scene of this incident. Just to rile Mullens, Ryder had assigned a few of the RCMP officers with the task of collecting the animal evidence, mainly picking up bear scat (of which there was a lot). One of the searchers called Perry over to look at something stuck to a tree branch.

A few moments later, Perry swung open the trailer door. "Hey, Ryder look at this—one of the boys found this on the trail." Perry held out a Ziploc bag. Ryder held it up and examined the long quills. "Is that a porcupine?"

"There are no porcupine around here." Ryder continued to examine the long quills. "Remember that cougar attack guy, Alan Wickey? He had one of these stuck in the ass of his jogging shorts. I thought it was from a plant so I threw it away, but this one has a big follicle root on it. It looks like it's from an animal."

Mullens had walked in quietly and decided to interrupt. "How do you two know each other? Is that Alan Wickey the ex-army guy? I hate that guy. He's on my special list. He's responsible for that diver getting killed during the search in the river."

Ignoring Mullens, Ryder looked at the quill under the light. "Yeah, last time I saw him he looked pretty good; lost some weight, was back with his wife. His kid Teddy and my kid both go to Hansworth together. I didn't recognize them in the hospital until I saw Karen the next week at the high school. She's a tall drink of water."

"Yeah, Wickey has a nice family. I hope he can keep his act together," Perry replied.

Mullens's face went crimson. "OK, Perry, get your ass back out on that search. That's enough dog fucking." Mullens opened the door and motioned for Perry to leave. He flashed a look of disgust at Ryder. "You'd better find those bodies, or there will be hell to pay." The two left the trailer.

"What is wrong with those guys?" One of the CO officers got up from his desk and looked at the bag of quills.

With his attention back on the sample, the officer scratched his chin. "I have six years of microbiology and three years of conservation training, and I have no idea what this is. It's definitely from an animal, though—maybe something exotic like a Komodo dragon or a rock cod or something?"

Ryder laughed as he replied. "Well, that explains the missing bodies then. A giant Komodo rock cod jumped down from the cliff, ate the blonde, and then chased the bears up the mountain."

"Betcha that blonde was tasty, num num."

Sentrous looked down upon the city from the thirtieth floor. He and Caracin had moved through the city swinging from flag poles and jumping from rooftop to rooftop. Some jumps were over one hundred feet across. The landings were hard because the cement surfaces were not giving like the swaying treetops. Caracin rolled like a car crash across the roof after his last jump. He popped up and brushed himself off, smiling. Sentrous laughed and laughed. "Let's go over and check out the bridge deck; it's a little darker over there." They started across the city towards Stanley Park and the great Lions Gate Bridge. As they came out of the trees and crossed over to the span wires, Sentrous made a quiet signal. He could hear Aelan and Taran below the span. He gave Caracin the signal, and they dropped to the walkway and then slowly crept over underneath the bridge deck. They stayed up high in the stringers and looked down upon the two Salt clan hunters perched on the tower.

Taran was a young Apec of only fifty years. Aelan was very impatient with him during hunting. He was not too smart, so Aelan thought. Tawny Biggly pushed her shopping cart full of pop bottles along the causeway and then directly under the bridge. It was quiet but she was nervous; she had had a bad few weeks on the east side. She'd decided to walk over to the park where some said it was warmer. There was nothing warm about the park tonight. It was wet, cold, and damp. The mist blew across the pathway as the huge iron tower of the bridge rose up above her. The massive rusty stations disappeared into the foggy shadow beneath the bridge. Taran was working his way down the tower leg towards the ambling bag lady. She hummed to herself loudly as she looked up often. This had Taran uneasy; he was still learning to hunt stealthily in the city and move on manmade structures. He would freeze and hold his colour when she looked his way, but the last time she caught his movement and stared right at him. He was close, only about twenty feet above her. She squinted her eyes as she tried to make out his camouflaged shape. Tawny let out a wild, warbling scream and began to run forward with her shopping cart swaying. "Help, help, help me!"

Both Caracin and Sentrous had tracked the two and were watching from above as Aelan bobbed his head back and forth, trying to assess this unfolding hunting disaster. Sentrous shook his head. *Terrible! Taran was terrible! What is wrong with this kid? Aelan, have you not taught him anything?* Taran leapt off the tower base and landed on the Tawny's back but was not expecting to end up in the shopping cart with her; it swung around 360 degrees and then toppled over. Tawny shook him off and ran. Taran gave chase, but he was now free from any top cover. This was an Apec nightmare. He leapt on her again and bit into her neck, snapping her spine. But she was still screaming. Taran was trying to bite through a thick scarf to crush her larynx. He spat out bits of material and held her as he bit again. Her screams finally stopped. He sank his teeth deep into her throat as she jerked and recoiled from the impulses running through her nervous system. The blood flow to her brain stem slowed, and her heart flopped into a useless, shivering rhythm. He started to drag her back to the span, but her clothes were tangled in the cart. And the cart was clanking along behind him as he dragged them both. Sentrous and Caracin laughed with astonishment as Aelan came down to assist. He was at the bottom of the span when a man jumped out of the bushes and ran up behind Taran. He yelled, "Get off of her, you bad dog." He kicked at Taran repeatedly and began a tug-of-war with Tawny's limp body. This went on for a few seconds like a macabre Three Stooges skit. It ended when Taran stood up and swung his claw and slashed across the man's face. The man looked up at Taran and began to back up as the blood poured from his open wound. "Holy shit, help, help!" he screamed.

Aelan had leapt off the tower and into the trees to intercept the man. He shot a grommet down towards the trail where the man was running and hit him in the back of the head. Aelan dropped down to finish him off.

Sentrous was thoroughly amused until he saw the flashing lights and heard the noise of a car engine coming around the point. He looked across at Caracin, and they both knew that they may have to intervene in this mess in order to keep things from getting out of control. Taran was now struggling to lift Tawny's body up the tower leg. She wasn't too heavy, but he was having trouble keeping hold of the many layers of clothing she was wrapped in. The Vancouver City police car approached with lights flashing and stopped at the foot of the tower where the shopping cart rested, turned over sideways and covered in blood. The lone police officer stepped out and walked up to the cart. She flashed her flashlight up the tower but did not see Taran, who was now directly above them. The flashlight scanned over the overturned cart and the droplets of dark-red blood. The officer turned the light to the bushes. The light shimmered through the branches and lit up Aelan as he stripped the guts and fat from the man's body. The beam illuminated the scene, but the branches and shadows hid the details necessary for the officer to comprehend what she was looking at. Aelan sat completely still as the beam moved on to the other bushes. The police officer got back into her car. She squeezed the microphone. "This is Charlie Monaco, I am 10-59 at the base of the bridge tower; something is wrong here. Can I get a supervisor? I think someone might be injured. I've got some fresh blood at the caisson base." The radio squelched and squawked with other traffic. There was a fight at a local bar on Nanaimo Street, a stabbing downtown, and a gas leak at the Granville Street Bridge.

The radio squawked again. "Charlie 259, you are on your own. All the bravo units are tied up. The platoon says go ahead and do your own investigation."

She released the mike. "Yeah, sure, F you too. No resources, my ass; I know where you are, you bastards. I passed you all having coffee at Jack's Emporium. Just 'cause I actually like my job!" She was talking to herself more and more these days. Sentrous's eyes went wide as he pointed up to Taran. Caracin looked and his mouth opened in amused shock.

Taran's claws extended in a frenzied attempt to clench the rolling bundle as it suddenly unravelled in his arms. A quiet *whoosh* was followed by a thud as the police car's windshield collapsed under the impact of Tawny's body. The glass exploded as the falling mass bounced from the dash into the officer's chest. The officer gasped and struggled free from underneath the bloody carnage. The impact had shifted the car into drive, and she rolled out from the open driver's door. The rear wheel slowly bumped up over her ankle. She yelped as her metatarsal bones snapped under the weight. The car rolled on as she drew her weapon. Now lying on her back, she met Taran's eyes fifty feet above her. Even she could read the "Oh shit!" expression on his mammalian face. *Crack, crack, crack;* the nine-millimetre bullets puffed into Taran's chest. The pistol was lifted from her hands as she looked up at Sentrous; her life ended quickly.

Taran dropped down beside him; he reached into his quills and dug around for the bullets. He shook from back to front, and the bullets dropped out onto the pavement.

"Pick those up, you fool!" Sentrous had never in his life seen a worse mess. Taran was Sartra's newest hunter, and he had made enough mistakes in ten minutes to earn him death ten times over. Sentrous swatted his head and told him to take cover in the woods and wait. Taran hesitated for a moment, trying to comprehend this situation he was in. He jumped up into the trees and moved up a fir tree. Aelan jumped down beside Sentrous, and they worked quickly, cleaning up the blood and teeth. Sentrous prepared the body of the police officer for transport. The guts came out very quickly along with some of the heavier clothing items. He tied the body up in a small bundle and swung it over his shoulder. Caracin was in the driver's seat looking at the controls of the squad car. It had bumped up against the pole and stopped. Caracin played with the shifter but couldn't get it to work. The radio was quiet as Caracin found the accelerator.

"What are you doing in the car—you can't drive!"

"Driving can't be that hard; humans can do it. I'm going to try and move it into the ocean. You go and make sure that those two morons don't take off." Caracin smiled with his tongue half out of his mouth as he depressed the gas pedal. The police car revved up and jumped sideways across a small patch of grass and onto the pebble beach. Caracin let out a yelp of excitement as the car lurched and heaved in the soft round pebbles. The hood splashed into the sea as the car stalled with the influx of seawater. The back of the car was still sticking up out of the water as Caracin struggled to get out of the vehicle. Looking like a drowned rat, he joined the trio in the fir trees. Taran sat slumped on the branch, clearly moping.

Caracin pronounced, "I can drive a car!"

"That wasn't driving, that was a spaz attack with an engine involved," Sentrous replied, keeping his eyes locked on Taran.

"I thought it was great—did you see how fast I went?" Caracin bragged.

"You left the back half of the car sticking out!" Sentrous replied.

Caracin was quick to change the subject. He looked at Taran. "You…You hunt like a retarded beaver!" Taran's eyes were still downcast. "You are carrying the police woman, beaver boy." Aelan was sullen also. He had let his trainee down by putting him in a situation that was clearly beyond his ability. Now they could never return to the clan. Sartra would kill them both immediately. Sentrous and Aelan knew that this situation had the makings of an awareness incident. Sartra had warned against a major screwup that would prompt the human authorities to investigate an Apec killing and discover something definitive. This incident was clearly a high risk. A missing police officer, a wrecked car, and a bloody killing scene would definitely fall into that category. Caracin was not as worried; he seemed to think that awareness was not going to be much of a problem. The humans were not very smart, and they couldn't fight very well. Caracin had always thought that Kamptra was a waste of time.

The three moved across the city to the Free clan lair. The clan was growing in numbers; the idea of freedom from the harsh rule and class system of the fema was growing popular with the males from other clans. Sentrous had been surprised to find out that Caracin had been visiting all the clans on the coast and in the valley. He was whispering ideas of freedom and adventure, tempting members to trade in the rigours of Kamptra for a free-for-all cornucopia of feasting. He was giving gifts of clean meat and equipment. In many clans equipment, such as sunglasses, backpacks, tape, and twine, was forbidden.

One by one they would show up with Caracin; it was if he never rested. He could change his demeanor to fit the needs of whomever he was with: the older brother that you always longed for, the nurturing father figure, the scheming and mischievous pal. Caracin had a gift for identifying and exploiting weaknesses and staying on his message. Sentrous knew on some level that he was being manipulated, but he did not care. He was a great leader, revered as a pioneer of the new age for Apec culture. Defecting females were reluctant to buy into the power differential. They were drawn in by the promise of clean meat and freedom but still clung to the idea of female superiority. They reluctantly yielded to a male-dominated clan. At one point some of them tried to assume control of the clan upon arrival. Caracin would sit close and listen to them, nurturing their fears and worries. "We live in a free clan where both males and females have equal rights to all prosperity. We work together to make the right decisions." The females listened and agreed; meanwhile, Caracin had set up a group of five males ready to attack from below if the females did not buy into the deal. Caracin seemed almost whimsical at times, but that was an illusion. He was always calculating and reassessing his situation and position, playing his chess pieces carefully, all with a master plan in mind. Hey would say that there was no plan, only freedom and bounty. Sentrous was no fool. He could see the pieces line up one by one; for what overall reason, he did not know.

All of the females in the clan got pregnant shortly after arriving in the camp. Sentrous thought this odd. Apec females did not get pregnant often; maybe once every fifteen or twenty years. It could have been because the free members were having more sex, feeling uninhibited. Sentrous thought that it may be due to something else, possibly the change in diet: clean meat and the increased consumption of the fat, healthy humans. For the past fifty years, the lost humans had been laced with many substances: prescription drugs, crack cocaine, crystal meth, and alcohol. Clan members usually became addicted and therefore went through withdrawal during their first few weeks at the Free clan. Caracin would take care of them while they shook and vomited. He would announce, "Look, the sun has come out for you!" when the withdrawal symptoms subsided. He was everything for everybody. And the Free clan grew in numbers as well as in the strength of their ideology.

17 Sobriety Is Overrated

Alan's tiny apartment was not built for a family. Rain pelted the windows like blasting sand. Behind the drops that rolled down the glass, dark-green cedars flailed in the winds. The pressure waves came through the crack under the door. The rattling windows would announce the whistling winds. Alan sat on the couch with the remote control, surfing through the channels and muttering, "Boring, boring, boring." Karen was at the computer typing away at a genetics paper.

Teddy walked in. "Hey Dad, do you want to play Call of Duty with me? I bet that you would rock at it. Seeing as you are a combat vet and all."

"I don't shoot people for fun, and I'm not crazy about you doing it all the time either. You should be working on your homework," Alan replied.

"It's just a game, Dad; it doesn't hurt anybody. And I get all As at school, so don't make it sound like I'm a slacker."

"Well, I'm sure that there's something that you need to work on at school, so get working on it."

"You know what I'm working on at school, Dad?" Karen was watching this conversation unfold with growing anger. Her green Irish eyes were focussed on Alan's face, but he took no notice. Teddy continued, "*Animal Farm,* the novel by George Orwell. The story symbolizes the Russian revolution. Stalin was a fascist oppressor." Teddy emphasized these last two words by saying them slowly while holding up his fingers in a quote gesture. "Much like yourself."

"That's correct, Teddy; this is a dictatorship and I am the dictator, and you will obey my command. Or you will meet the fate of the little Trotsky guy...What was that pig's name again?"

Alan's tone was bordering on childish. Karen was now fuming. She reached back and let a spatula fly across the counter and bounce off Alan's head.

"Teddy, go to your room," she said calmly.

"Whoa...I guess we know who is really Napoleon in this family, hey Dad?" Teddy quickly retreated up the small flight of stairs.

Alan drew a breath to speak, but Karen's hand was outstretched to halt his words; her eyes were focussed beams. He closed his mouth.

"Alan, your boy, your son, just approached you asking for your time and attention. It's not about the game, you idiot! You just lectured him, putting him down, ordering him around. If you were paying attention, you would have noticed that he did his homework over an hour ago, yet you didn't notice, did you? You ask about connecting with him, getting close to him, yet you're handling this like a moron. Stop feeling so sorry for yourself and smarten up, Wickey! I swear if you spend another minute lying on that couch feeling sorry for yourself, I will stab you through the heart with this bread knife!" She wielded the knife in a repeated stabbing demonstration for Alan's benefit.

"Oh, you're taking his side, of course. Did you see how he spoke to me? He gets that from you and your tone, your disrespect!" The bread knife flew, and Alan dodged it. He sat up and walked to the door. "You are a crazy chick!" The door slammed behind him.

He walked for hours out in the storm as tiny tree branches flew by. He walked out onto Marine Drive and looked through the darkened shop windows for a few hours. He felt more comfortable in a storm than he did dealing with his own family. He kept walking until he finally arrived at the house. As he opened the door, a series of alarms went off. Oh yeah, you were supposed to disarm this one before you entered, like a car. What was the damn code? After disarming the alarm, he went into the kitchen and opened the wine cupboard. He felt a cool puff of air rushing down the hall. "Karen, are you home?"

He looked back at the bottle; both the cameras in the house were waiting to see what he would do. He looked at the cork; it was lodged half in and half out. He opened the bottle and inhaled the vapours emanating from the top. *Hmmm, that's odd.* He tasted the liquid. "Spuhh! Water! Damn it, Karen." After pacing around for a few minutes, Alan walked into the dark bedroom and collapsed on the bed. He noticed a slight musky odour and looked over at the laundry basket.

His head was spinning with a cocktail of urges and emotions. How was that woman always one step ahead of him? The bedroom door swung open, and his wife's silhouette filled the doorway. He looked at her shape; shit, she looked like she did when she was twenty. There was a plastic bottle of water in Karen's hand. She raised her arm, and the bottle whizzed across the room and impacted into Alan's belly button.

"Ooof! Hey, be nice!"

"You are not nice—why should I be nice?"

"How do you always know what I am going to do?"

"There are some very bright scientists at the lab, and I can usually figure out their next move. You...you big moron, I know your next five moves!"

"Oh yeah, well, one day I might surprise you with something new."

"Doubt it."

"If I never surprise you, then why do you love me?"

"I'm not big on surprises. You have a big heart, Alan, and I like your big heart."

"Hmm, I thought it was because I was so good in bed."

"You're OK, I guess." She smiled as she climbed onto the bed.

"I am better than OK."

She crawled up and lay on top of him, tapping his forehead with her index finger. "You need to work on being a better father; it takes lots of effort and energy. Teddy needs you to be on duty full time right now. Don't you dare run off into the bush hunting monkeys and not come back. This family already watched you fly away and come back broken. Now you need to be a dad. Do you hear me, Alan Wickey?"

Alan drew a deep breath. "Yeah, I hear you."

"Good. It would be a shame to have to cut off this nice little scrotum of yours." She reached down and undid his belt. She didn't have to touch him for long before he was hard and ready. As they kissed he pulled her jogging top up over her head. She stood up beside the bed and slowly pulled her yoga pants and panties down to her ankles. Gracefully she climbed on top and slid down on him. He gasped with anticipation as she started a slow and tantric pace with her hips.

Something lifted Alan from the depths of his deep sleep. His eyes fluttered into the pitch darkness, opening and then closing as the warm, weighty sleep filled in again. Then, the strong odour drifted into his sleepy consciousness. That smell. He felt the bed move underneath him as the air around his nose swirled for a second. He struggled to open his eyes and pull himself up from the sleep. Another swirl of acrid hot air entered his nostrils, and now his eyelids flashed open. He looked up into Sartra's round white eyes; her tiny black-and-red pupils were fixed on Alan's. Her face was only inches from his; he was frozen in the dead space between fight and flight. He could not move, look away, or make a sound. The tiny nerve centre in the base of his brain that paralyses the muscles during REM sleep had not yet handed over control of Alan's physical will. The adrenaline would rush up across his blood brain barrier and fix this little wiring problem soon, but right now the seconds ticked by. Sartra calmly examined his face. He could read her ghastly expression. Her hate and frustration crossed the species barrier. Nerve impulses finally broke away from the synapses and ran down the axons to reach his large muscles. The blood pulled away from the periphery and channelled towards the legs and arms. Sartra felt him start to struggle and retracted her left claw from its anchor in the drywall. She transferred her weight by shifting her grip to Alan's forehead. As he pushed up with his chest, she rose and flipped up and away from him. He let out a deep groan.

Bang, bang! The muzzle flash was only a foot from his face as he rolled off the mattress into the narrow space between the wall and the bed. The spidery black shape plunged down the hall. He recovered his wits and popped up to witness the next series of muzzle flashes. *Bang, bang, bang, bang...bang!* Karen was crouched into the shooter's position and had fired the seven shots in semi-auto mode. The gunpowder smoke wafted over the bed as Alan turned on the lights and looked down the hallway. The house alarm siren began to squeal. Karen kept the gun aimed past Alan's shoulder.

Alan walked down the hall and looked into Teddy's room. He turned and looked at his wife. Her lips were trembling as a drop of spittle stretched across them; her pupils were dilated so wide that they obscured almost all of her emerald irises.

"Can you please not point that gun at me?" Alan walked in and closed the window.

"Sorry." Her voice cracked a little as she dropped her arms.

"Hey, I thought that that Mountie took my gun."

"He did, and then he gave it back to me to hold on to." She sobbed.

Alan hit the alarm code to silence the wailing and then he yelped at something burning hot under his feet. He reached down and picked up the nine-millimetre mushroomed bullet. It smoked a little as he popped it from palm to palm. He looked down and saw a few more smoking lead balls in the carpet. He managed to collect six of the seven slugs, two on the bed and four in the hall. The seventh one was missing.

"I think you hit that thing."

"I know I did."

"It looks like some of the rounds bounced off its fur, like rubber."

Karen put her hand on her chest; her breathing had been thrown off rhythm by the long breath holds during her trigger squeezes. She now wheezed and coughed as the tears welled up in her eyes.

"Alan, that thing really scared me." She was sobbing now.

Alan moved to cradle her, taking the pistol from her. "Scared you? I was the one smooching with it on the bed."

"That's first time I have ever fired a gun in an emergency."

"Honey, you hit that thing seven times in four seconds."

"Alan, I know how to shoot."

"Yeah, let's just say that I have a better appreciation for your close-quarter skills." She laughed weakly and began to wipe her tears.

"What are we going to do about these things, Alan?"

"I think we are going to have to kill them. They are trying to kill us."

"I don't think she was trying to kill you."

"She? How do you know it was a she?"

"I don't know. I just got the feeling it was a she; only a woman could be that pissed at you."

"Yeah, I think you are right. She was different from the other one that tried to eat me. He was skinnier and had longer arms, a little lighter, maybe two twenty. This one tonight was fucking big—did you see her shoulders?

The phone rang, and Karen picked it up. "Yes, this is Karen Wickey; the number is W4567. Yes, we left a window open, and the alarm went off." Alan walked around the house and checked all the doors and windows.

"Do you think the neighbours heard the shots?" Karen asked.

"Doubt it. It's still blowing like hell out there. But if they did, we will know about it soon enough." Both Alex and Karen looked out the window for a police car, but none came.

"We've got her on video," Karen pointed at the camera in the top corner of the ceiling.

"No way."

Their spare laptop was slow to log into the security system. When Karen got the video running, the entry log showed Alan disarming the system and then Karen coming in and re-arming it. They watched carefully through the whole conversation and then the sex. They watched the recording at double speed for an hour. The image showed them tossing and turning quickly in their beds. The alarm was silent as the black shape appeared from a corner of the bedroom. The shape was hard to distinguish, almost ghostlike, until she took position beside Alan's side of the bed. They both gasped as Sartra leant directly above Alan's face inhaling his breath, as if to catch a scent. She was there for a long time before Alan finally woke up.

"Holy shit, where did she come from?" Karen watched the footage of the shadowy figure over and over. "I can't figure out how she could sneak in past the alarm while we slept, unless she was there the whole time." Karen rewound the video to when Alan first arrived and advanced the frames ahead slowly. "She was there waiting for you." She pointed to a shadowy shape camouflaged between the dresser and the closet door. "There, see that right there?" They both looked over across the room to the wall, and that space was empty. "Jesus, she was right there the whole time." Karen ran the tape back to the time just after she had arrived. While Karen was on top of Alan, her hips swaying rhythmically, there was the fuzzy dark shape. Sartra had been right there, within a few feet, sitting quietly crouched down beside the furniture. Karen wound the video back even further. The digital readout said *Alarm disabled 21:32*. Karen clicked through the other two camera angles; they both watched Alan arrive, stroll into the kitchen, and open the cupboard. The grainy screen flickered green as the blurred figure flashed in front of the camera. The shape moved down the hall into the bedroom. She had snuck in after Alan had disabled the alarm and waited patiently for over four hours.

"She could have killed us both at any time. Why didn't she?" Alan asked.

Karen added, "She didn't seem to be interested in me at all; she was definitely after you, she was sniffing your face. Maybe she liked your aftershave?" she joked to break the tension.

"Joint Operations Desk," Constable Perry answered the phone. "Stupid" was his answer to the standard "how's it going" question that followed. "Yeah, OK, OK, this monster TV show, bear attack thing is getting to be too much. Yes, they are all paralyzed from the neck up, especially Mullens. He is really starting to piss me off…Yeah, I finally escaped, and now I'm catching up. I heard about this new task force." The voice on the phone chattered. Perry replied, "No shit, I own about ten of those files. Yeah…I have them right here. No, there is no such thing as cold files on my desk, dude; they are piled up like pillars, messy but not cold." Perry looked up at the towering stack of files. The voice on the phone chattered again. Perry started to make some notes. "Listen, Owen, I will see if the boss will assign me over to you guys for a few days. No promises." Perry listened. "Yes I do, yes, yes—I do think that they are linked to this missing female officer in the park." The detective on the line continued to speak. Perry answered his question. "Yeah, Owen, I agree it may be a serial killer or maybe more than one. There are more than fifty files between our two offices, and we haven't even gone through Surrey's pile yet. Yeah, more like a bunch of guys screwed this one up! Both departments are on the hook, especially after the

Willie Pickton thing and all. OK, I will get down to the bridge and check it out." The detective on the other line explained his theory to Perry. "No, I don't think you're crazy; I think you may be right. Someone is using dogs or some type of animal to hunt people. Owen, I am going to bring Ryder, my conservation animal tracker guy, down to the crime scene and let him have a look. Yeah, no shit. Yeah, I have a conservation guy, get over it. OK, I will see you down there at the south bridge tower in an hour. No, no, now it's your turn to buy; you're the big-city detective with the Rolex and a silk tie; yeah, grande low-fat please."

Constable Perry chuckled and put down the phone. His mind kept going back to Alan Wickey. The war hero with a big bite in his neck; something was weird there. *Sometimes I feel like I'm living that* X-Files *show*, he thought to himself.

Ryder and Perry arrived at the base of the huge bridge tower. The traffic division was using a laser to create a three-dimensional map of the scene. The patrol car had been pulled out of the water and was up in the parking lot being combed over for evidence. Detective Owen Smithers brushed the muffin guts off his silk tie and got out of his black Dodge Charger. He handed the low-fat latte to Perry.

"Thanks, slick," Perry said. "This is Ryder; he's a conservation officer officer, specialist in animal attacks." Owen extended his hand for the shake. Ryder smiled and shook his hand.

Owen started the tour by pointing to the shopping cart and the blood-stained cement block. "OK, I got the scoop from the CID guy. Here's a standard-issue bag lady shopping cart and evidence of horribleness over here. The GPS puts the car stopped here, when she called in and asked for another officer. This blood on the ground is not hers, type AB positive; she is O. There is more blood over here in the bushes, type A. Someone else, I guess."

"What about the camera in the car?" Perry asked.

"Yeah, apparently saltwater and electronics don't mix well, so no footage so far, but the computer geeks in the lab are working on it," Owen finished.

"What makes you think there was an animal involved?" Ryder asked.

"Have a look at the car." They approached the car, and Owen pointed to the roof above the driver's seat. "Look at these scratch

EMERGENCE

marks in the metal of the doorframe and on the dashboard, and look at this scarf." Owen held up the remnants of a navy-blue scarf; it was shredded into strips and soaked with blood. One of the CID guys leaned over and pointed at the seat with his pen. "Hey, guys, have a look at the seat, but don't touch because we aren't done there yet." Perry knelt down at the driver's door and looked at the seat. The back and bottom of the vinyl upholstery was covered in little punctures.

Owen commented, "Yeah, I saw that. I was thinking it might be one of those punk rock dudes with the steel spiky jackets."

"Have you ever seen one with spikes on his ass?" Perry pointed to the seat. "It would make it a little hard to sit on the shitter with big silver spikes tickling your nuts." Owen laughed as Perry popped his theory balloon.

"Yeah, I thought that he might have lain down on the seat during the struggle, I don't know! You let me know when you have a theory on this whole fucking mess. The deputy chief just assigned twenty officers to this taskforce, and now he is pacing circles around my desk. So any suggestions would be welcome." Owen's voice travelled up an octave.

"Yeah, I gotcha on this, Owen. Don't worry; there is lots to do on this baby. I am just worried about how big it's going get." Perry's eyes scanned the ground for traces or prints.

"The media hasn't really picked up on this story yet because they haven't been down here. But as soon as they see this mess, all hell is going to break lose. What's pissing me off is that we have a missing VPD constable, and so far none of this making any sense," Owen said. Ryder took pictures of the faint footprints in the dirt and the scratch marks on the car.

"Can you tell us what kind of dog it could be?" Perry asked. Ryder scrunched up his face and rubbed his chin.

"Yeah, it's a Tasmanian sabre-toothed Chihuahua. I can tell by the angular bite marks, and here I have fibres from his tiny little Mexican poncho." Ryder rubbed his thumb and index fingers, pretending to hold up some tiny little fibres. He continued in more serious tone. "I don't know what did this. It could be a dog or a...dog or, I don't know. I might have to send these pictures to some experts. Just let me take some measurements."

"What a fucking mess, and it just keeps getting weirder," Owen said.

"Yeah, there is no shortage of weirdness this week," Perry answered.

18 What a Girl!

Teddy slammed the car door as he got in. His brow was furrowed and his eyes cast down at his lap. "Hey, Dad," he mumbled. Alan drove down the lane away from the movie theatre.

"How was the movie?"

"Boring." Teddy sighed and looked out the passenger window. "Dad, are you and Mom fighting again?"

"No, actually, for once we are getting along."

"What do you guys fight about?"

"Sex, drugs, and rock and roll, Teddy." Alan smiled at his little joke. His headlights illuminated a tall girl clad in capris pants and a thick duck-down vest. Her brunette ponytail swayed as she walked briskly along the sidewalk. Teddy looked past the rolling wipers at her. "Hey, that's Wendy Mercer."

Alan's eyes looked over the young, athletic figure and then over to his son's expression. He knew that look. "She's a cutie, Ted. I am going to pull over, and you are going to get out and open the car door and offer her a ride home."

"Dad, no, don't! Oh my god, Dad." Teddy's hand reached up frantically as Alan stopped the car.

"Get out and open the damn door! Yah big wimp." Alan's military bark managed to startle the youngster into opening the door. Wendy hesitantly looked at the opening door. Her pursed lips opened into a broad smile as she recognized Teddy.

"Hi, Teddy," she offered. Teddy's light-green eyes gave him a puppy-dog gaze. His shoulders were broad and his arms and legs lanky. Teddy's long bangs hung over his cheeks, now flushed crimson with the panic instilled by the words of a girl.

"Uh, hello, Wendy. Would you like a ride home? My dad, he said he could drive you, I mean us, or you, to your house, I mean," Teddy stammered as he swung the back door open for her. She laughed a little and nodded.

"Yes, thank you, Teddy; that would be nice of you." She climbed into the backseat as Teddy closed the door. He moved to get back into the passenger side, but Alan quickly clicked the lock closed as Teddy pulled at the handle. Alan rolled his eyes, motioning Teddy to go around and sit in the back with the girl. Teddy pulled at the handle once more and finally got the hint. He climbed into the backseat with Wendy, and Alan pulled out into the traffic.

"I live over on Glenford Drive at the top of the hill; I hope that's not too far."

"Not at all, Wendy."

"Thank you, Mr. Wickey."

"So how's it going?" Teddy's voice was unsteady as he spat out the words. Wendy held up the conversation enthusiastically. Alan smiled empathetically, watching his son's nervous expressions as he spoke. It was obvious to him that this young lady was fond of Teddy. This was far beyond Teddy's perception; the poor boy was concentrating on keeping his sentences together.

After a bit more prompting, he followed her up the path to her door and bade her good night.

Then he climbed back in the car. "Jeez, Dad, did you have to?"

"What, you don't like her?"

"Yeah, she's only the hottest girl in the whole school."

"She seems to like you. And she's not snobby or anything."

Teddy looked over at his father. "Do you still get nervous around girls, or does that go away?"

Alan laughed. "Jumping out of an airplane and landing on a sinking ship doesn't scare me half as much as talking to girls."

"Were you nervous when you met Mom?"

"Oh, your mom was ruthless; she teased me so badly. I couldn't put a sentence together around her for the first year that we dated!"

"Yeah, she's brutal; she still makes you stutter like a baby," Teddy added, smiling. "So why don't you ever talk about the time that you won the medal in Afghanistan?"

Alan had avoided this question for years, but he knew that his son deserved an answer, an honest answer. "Uh, well, I got the award for driving a Grizzly up a hill while we were under fire. I got our guys out of a bad spot. At least that's what the CBC News said happened."

"What's so bad about that? Why don't you tell people about it?"

Alan drew a deep breath. "Well, the part that the news didn't say was that it was my fault that these guys were getting shot at in the first place. I called in an airstrike to the wrong spot and almost killed them all. The bomb took out their barricade and allowed the Taliban guys to move in close and shoot at their position. I opened the door for the enemy, and some of the guys got killed."

Teddy sat quietly. "But you fixed it, you jumped in a Grizzly and drove up a cliff! You and Kelly held off like fifty Taliban fighters long enough to get all of your guys out of there, right?"

"Yeah, but you shouldn't get medals for fixing problems that you made in the first place."

"Well, I think you deserved it. How many people have you saved in your life, a hundred, maybe two hundred?" Alan didn't answer Teddy right away.

"Teddy, war does damage to your soul. Afghanistan is a place where nothing makes sense and people all around you do awful things. The lines between good and bad get lost, and you get to the point where you only care about two things: your ass and your squad mates. Once you have been over there for a while, you just want to stay alive and go home. When you get home, the damage to your soul makes it hard to love the things you missed. It makes everything hard. Getting an award in Canada and trying to get people here to understand what happened over there is like trying to explain life on Mars."

"They gave you that award because you went over there to keep the world safe and you tried your best. The medal is Canada's way of saying thank you. You should be gracious and accept it. I want to feel proud of you without you screwing that up."

Alan looked at his son. These words struck him directly. "I, uh, I guess I never quite looked at it from your perspective." His eyes stayed with Teddy's. Alan reached out and rubbed the back of Teddy's neck. "I love you, big guy."

"Love you too, Dad." They'd been sitting parked in front of the apartment for a few minutes now. Teddy opened the door and looked at his cell phone for moment and smiled. "Wendy just texted me—never thought that would happen. She says to thank you for the ride."

"Nice! Text her back, and ask her out."

"I'm not taking girl advice from you; you suck at that."

"Hey, what do mean? I got your mom to marry me."

"Yeah, you got lucky, and you almost blew it. Jury is still out."

"Teddy, you are on your own for a few hours. I am going over to the house to meet Kelly. Tell your mom I will be back later." Alan drove over to his house where there were four or five vehicles parked at the base of his driveway.

Alan yelled as he entered his house, "Hello, Kelly, is that you?" The living room was busy as the group of military men sorted through their gear. Eight men sat around the little coffee table. "Wickey buddy, how the hell are yah? Your nacho chips are stale," a low voice called out.

"What the…This isn't another intervention, is it? I am sober, I swear."

Kelly laughed. "I called the old team together for a hunting trip."

Alan looked around, bewildered. "I thought you told me to focus on my family?"

"That was when I thought you were imagining things, but now I know these fuckers are real and they are staking out your home. I called the team in to help," Kelly proclaimed. Alan could tell by the hesitation on the others' faces that they were not sure what Kelly was talking about.

"Wow, are you guys sure?"

"Anything for you, Wickey. Now what the hell is Kelly on about, Stiyhahaahwho?" Roger quipped but ended the sentence with a serious expression. Faces lined the couches and the kitchen stools as Alan met all of their eyes. The loss of his best friend Woody struck him as he gazed on the flight team minus one. He could see the loss in their eyes, but he didn't see what he'd expected to see: blame.

Roger spoke up. "OK, Wickey, all evidence points to the fact that you are nuts, so let's hear your crazy-ass story, and if it makes you feel better, we will all go camping with you and entertain your delusions about monsters. I will even shoot at imaginary monsters for you, if that's what you need to get over your craziness. You've saved all of our asses more than once, and in my opinion you deserve our time and attention. Besides, if it's furry and lives in the forest, I can kill it."

Alan laughed. "Well, Kelly, it looks like you've done a great job in convincing them." He opened up his MacBook and double-clicked the security camera footage from the night of the break-in. They watched while sipping their drinks until the dark figure slipped down the hall and into the bedroom. Roger dropped his water in his lap. "What the fuck is that? That's a bear in your house." He leant forward into the green glow of the footage. Now all four necks craned for a clear look at the figure as it changed colour in the bedroom and sat quietly waiting for Alan. "That's no bear. What the hell is that?"

On the video, Alan walked in and lay down on the bed; the faded figure was there watching. Karen came in. Then Alan fast-forwarded past the sex and the sleeping. His friends, eager to catch a glimpse of his wife taking off her clothes, were disappointed as Alan caught up to the scary bits. The creature darkened and slowly climbed over Karen to get on top of Alan. Long spider-length legs straddled across the corner of the room as the creature used the walls and the headboard to stay suspended just inches above Alan's face. She sat there inhaling Alan's breath for twenty-two minutes. Karen woke and rolled over; it was clear in the video that it took her a few seconds to comprehend what she was looking at. She slowly rolled over to reach into the bedside table and pull out Alan's handgun. It was this movement that Sartra noticed, and she turned to meet Karen's gaze. The screen was a green blur of movement and gunfire. Karen assumed a firing position and managed to empty the whole clip as the black figure bolted out of the room.

"Holy shit! I can't believe this is real—what is that thing?" Roger said.

195

"Karen hit it, center mass, like more than once," Kelly remarked.

"Seven times—six bullets were all lying on the carpet in almost-perfect shape; they bounced right off this thing."

"Shit, remind me never to piss off Karen." Roger shook his head in disbelief. After watching the video, Ken Coleman walked to the back of the room and made a call from his phone.

"Who's he calling?" Kelly asked

"Kitigawa," Roger answered. Kelly looked at him inquisitively. "You wouldn't know him; he was a co-pilot in 442 Squadron when Rescue 318 crashed in Squamish. Three guys died, including the pilot. He was discharged on medical after the crash. Everyone thought he was crazy because he claimed that a creature hanging in the top of the trees threw a big branch into the tail rotor and caused the crash."

"Are you kidding?" Kelly asked.

Alan broke in. "Yeah, the first day I woke up in the hospital, I realized that I had seen what Shawn had described from the crash. Ten years ago we all thought that he had lost his marbles."

"Wickey, you could have brought this up earlier."

"Yeah, Roger, I was going to call you up and invite you to coffee to discuss big hairy monsters that hang from the trees and eat people. That would have been a short coffee date."

Roger chuckled. "You're right."

Kim put down the phone. "He's coming over right away. I didn't fill him in at all."

Alan began to tell the story of what he had been through over the past six months. The room was silent as he spoke with emotion. The group asked no questions as Alan finished. "How many do you think are out there in the woods?"

"They live in the trees, I think, and I don't know how many. They communicate in ultra-high-frequency squeals; you can't hear them," Alan replied.

"You can detect them with the iPhone though; they got an app for that," Kelly added with a grin. He held up his phone, and the screen flashed green. "I've been watching this ever since I downloaded it, and it was lighting up in Lynn Valley Canyon and over in Lion's Bay. There must be a few small groups of them around." Kelly fiddled with the phone and waved it around; the screen stayed green. After about a half an hour, the door opened, and the forty-something Japanese Canadian entered the room and looked around suspiciously. He exchanged nods to greet his old comrades, some of whom he hadn't seen in ten years.

Roger pointed to the couch in front of the MacBook. "Shawn, do you want a beer?"

"Don't drink, thanks. What am I looking at?"

"It's security video footage from this house, last week." Roger clicked the play button. Shawn watched until the creature appeared. His eyes went wide and his mouth opened. "What are you guys doing? Is this some kind of cruel fucking joke?" He stood up and looked into the faces of all those around him.

"It's real, Shawn. It was real the whole time, and we just didn't know it. We all owe you an apology."

"No, no. It's not real. I was just seeing things in the night; it was a raccoon, I swear!"

"I saw your drawing, the one that got you fired, or whatever happened to you. It was no raccoon. You were right, this guy took you down. They live in the treetops. It all makes sense." Roger completed his sentence as Shawn Kitagawa put his hand over his mouth and darted for the bathroom. Kim Casic followed him in as he began to vomit. He slumped back on the wall beside the toilet, breathing heavily.

"Shit, it took me five years of therapy just to get the image of that fucker out of my head and two more years to convince me that it was a raccoon. I lost my job, my wife, fauuck...mee!" He drew a deep breath as he scanned his thoughts and the implications of what he had seen on the video. His head swam as he realized that things were changing rapidly. Roger approached him and put his hand on his shoulder.

Roger explained, "The squadron is going to shit, Woody is dead, and everyone was blaming Wickey. We—the real team—had a crisis meeting last weekend at the clubhouse, and we all decided that we had been acting like jackasses over the past few years. The old colonel and the Ottawa guys are all assholes. They don't give a shit about anyone but themselves, and they think we are all idiots. We have been following their lead and leaving our guys out on their own instead of banding together like the crack team that we are. You got screwed, and we didn't really stick up for you or listen to your crazy rantings."

Kitagawa laughed. "Thanks...I guess."

Roger continued, "We are going to go and hunt these fuckers down. Are you up for a hunting trip?"

Kitagawa looked bewildered. "Uh, what are...I don't know, let me think about it for a minute. This is a lot to digest." He sat down at the computer and watched the video again.

Kelly rolled out the topographic map, and the team made plans for their hunting trip. They had assembled their own stores of weapons, which included sniper rifles and some semiautomatic rifles. Alan insisted on large-calibre weapons only; he had seen nine-millimetre rounds bounce off these things. Roger brought night-vision scopes and radios from the lockers at the training camp in Chilliwack.

Troy finally asked Alan the question that they all wanted to. "What happened to Woody?"

"I think it was her." He pointed at the video screen. "Woody was ahead of me on the safety line, and I was following him from the shore when I saw that someone around the corner had grabbed the line and tugged it. Woody came up on the shore thinking it was me. She ripped his throat open and pinned me down so I could watch him go over the falls. I don't know why she hasn't killed me. I know that the male will kill me if he has a chance; he has bitten me twice."

"Poor Woody, we knew that it didn't go down like the RCMP claimed. They blamed you; they said that you tripped him up with the line and he went over the falls."

"Yeah, the RCMP guy is a wanker, and he is still after my ass."

"Did you turn into a werewolf after you were bitten?" The question was only half a joke.

"Don't think magic...think animal. This is a previously unknown species of mammal. Karen is working on the genetics at the lab; it seems they have been around for ages but just recently gotten into our view. I think the hunting in the city thing may be new for them."

Kelly spoke up. "Our people have known of them for many years, but the legends claim that they stayed high in the trees and would only come down to take you if you were old and sick, offering yourself to die. The bones of the elders who were taken by the Stiyaha were cleaned white and placed in the sacred burial caves along with clothes and jewellery. You could go and visit them without fear."

"Is that how your mom died, Kelly?" Troy asked.

"My mom's a retired judge in Ottawa, you idiot, and she's not dead," Kelly replied as Roger whacked Troy Willard across the head.

Kelly put up his hand and gestured to the map on the coffee table. "OK, OK, I vote we start over here at Bear Canyon and work our way up the valley until we pick up traces. We will use our iPhones to pick up their calls and track them down and kill them."

Suddenly Shawn jumped up from the laptop and cheered loudly. "They are real! These things are real; I am not crazy, and I didn't crash that bird! It wasn't my fault." He shouted at the top of his lungs as each of his old comrades hugged him and apologized. He had felt that his most trusted circle had betrayed him by not believing his story.

"Where were the other spots that you heard them?" Kim changed the subject.

Kelly circled three spots on the map and drew a star in the Capilano area. "This area had the most activity. It could be an insertion point. Yet what changed my mind was the activity that Alan and I experienced at the mountaintop over here. We were searching up here for the lost Telus guys, and these things attacked our camp and almost killed Alan. This is where the male guy lives. This one guy and this girl are the ones we are looking for. We need to kill these two, and maybe the rest of them will leave Alan and his family alone. Let's take our individual maps and then add these waypoints into the iPhones and GPSs. We will break into two groups with a sniper/scout team if we need it."

Alan spoke. "This is the spot where you guys get to opt out if you are not into the whole monster hunt thing."

Roger replied, "Wickey, we are all in with you guys. I'm not sure if all of us know what we are getting into, but there are worse ways to spend a weekend than playing soldier with your buddies in the bush." All heads nodded in agreement.

Alan's iPhone buzzed with a text from Karen: *If you are rounding up a hunting pose and running off into the bushes with guns, then you are a fucking loser! These things will kill you.*

Alan texted back: *I was going to tell you. How did you know?*

Kelly looked at the text and laughed. "I told you she was psychic, bro."

The reply from Karen came quickly: *You don't have to be psychic to predict what monkeys do at the zoo.*

The whole group was looking over Alan's shoulder at his phone. Mike laughed. "Holy shit, Wickey, she can shoot, she's hot, and she's psychic—sucks to be you. Total domination, dude."

"Hey, Haddock, your girlfriend has big tits and giggles a lot; what's your excuse?"

Haddock frowned and shook his head. "At least she sucks my dick better than you do, Willard." That produced a few chuckles.

Shawn Kitagawa chimed in dryly. "Yeah, he's right, she does." The whole group burst into laughter as Kitagawa's legendary quick wit returned.

19 Posse

The rainy Saturday morning had just enough grey light for Alan to sluggishly lace his boots. His gear bag was packed and sitting at the door.

Karen stood, hands on her hips at the kitchen door. "I knew it...I knew you were going to do this!"

"I, ah...thought you would understand that we have to go out and kill these creatures that are trying to kill us."

"Yeah, nice little circle of logic, Wickey! Bad monster, me big monster killer, me go out and kill monster. Thought about that for a while, did you?"

Alan sighed. "Karen, we cannot just ignore this. They are watching our house."

She winced with a mix of impatience and disgust. "Didn't you watch the video? These creatures will kick your ass. They are fucking bulletproof, can see in the dark, practically fly, and they are smarter than you." Karen knew how to throw punches in a fight. "Let's just put the house up on the market and move to Victoria or something."

Alan was struggling to keep ahead of the conversation and not just fall into a submissive silence. *Empathy*, he thought, *why is Karen saying this? She is scared of losing me and scared that Teddy is going to lose his dad.* "Look, we probably won't even see these creatures, and I promise that after this trip we won't go out again."

"Alan, what is the first rule of combat?"

Shit, she's using my own words against me now.

"I don't know. Never surrender?"

"Stop being a moron. Its 'He who has the high ground has the upper hand.' Are you planning on leaping from tree to tree?" Karen was furious as she glared at Alan. Alan had no reply.

"You can pack up your shit and live somewhere else if you go."

There it was, the ultimatum; here they were at yet another impasse. Alan drew a deep breath and walked out as Karen began to sob. She turned and went into the bedroom and slammed the door. He paused for a moment as his mind raced through some possible alternatives; nope, no way out of this one. He drove back to the house where the group was waiting.

As he stepped out of the car, the boys looked at his face. "Uh-oh, Karen's pissed, look at that face."

Kelly approached Alan. "Buddy, you don't have to do this. We can handle it. Chances are we are not even going to run into these things. They don't get found unless they want to be found. Go home and make up with Karen. Remember your priorities, Wickey." Kelly was regretting his role in the initiation of this hunting trip; he didn't want to be the cause of a divorce.

"We have to do this, Kelly; these things know where I live. What else do they know? Maybe Teddy's school, Karen's lab? We have to go out and settle this. Don't back down on me now, buddy."

Kelly sighed. "OK, Wickey, let's go find some monkeys."

"We have to be at the parking lot by 0730 hours, hurry up," Haddock shouted.

"You guys got the bird for this?" Alan asked in disbelief.

"Yeah, we're a chopper crew. What good is a chopper crew without a chopper?"

The gravel scattered across the dirt as the big yellow Cormorant settled down onto its weight. The door swung open; the pilot looked over his shoulder, surprised to see Wickey walking towards the aircraft. He said a few words to the co-pilot and nodded his head. The team loaded the weapons and gear into the cargo nets and closed the door.

The headphone crackled with the pilot's voice. "Since when do you need rifles for a survival ex?"

Roger spoke into the headset. "It's survival camp cowboy style, Rodney, don't sweat it." The pilot shrugged his shoulders and pulled the throttles back.

The helicopter's twin engines roared, and the big craft lifted into the stratus clouds and sped off into the dark mountainside. The dense forest rolled past the spotter window as they approached Kelly's landing zone.

"Kitagawa, it's good to see you, buddy. How have you been?"

Shawn grabbed the boom mike on his helmet. "Hey Rodney, I'm doing OK. You're looking good."

"This is Snake 902; we are circling for LZ sierra two, wheels down for five minutes and then returning to fuel at Yankee Victor Romeo."

"Snake 902, you are clear for ops landing. Check in when you arrive at transit altitude twelve thousand feet. Squawk 1108."

"Roger, Squawk 1108." The rotor's spinning disk sank below the trees as the pilot settled down onto the grassy knoll on the hillside. "Gotta keep spinning because this ground is a little soft. So hop out quickly."

The team jumped out and grabbed the expedition gear, then the helicopter pulled up into the skies. Every member began to organise his pack as Kelly and Wickey looked over the map. "Down this ridge and over towards the northwest side of the mountain we will set up camp early and wait till nightfall." Kelly traced the ridgeline with his finger. The troop set off into the dense green fir and pine forest. Huge green ferns swayed in the cool breeze as their boots crunched the salal leaves.

Sartra had tracked the aircraft's approach as it flew directly over her perch in the twelve-story Sitka spruce tree. The craft landed about three miles away. Sartra was very tense these days, and this landing alarmed her. She signalled the alert to wake the sleeping clan. The twisted hammocks of bark and cedar rope crackled as the Salt clan rose. The fema met in the high post and discussed Sartra's plan. She was certain that it was the human man in the aircraft. "The sentries will track the group's every move. They always camp at night, so we will surround them at sunset and see if they are a threat. We will only attack them if they detect us. They may have rifles, so we will have to be cautious." Sartra gave out the individual orders to both the fema and the sentry males.

Shaman was the first to make contact; she paused and watched for a while. Not only was it Wickey, but he had brought out a hunting party and they were looking up into the trees for the Apecs. She signalled to the clan to cease all communications and for the sentries to pull back. Sartra arrived by her side and watched as the troop advanced directly towards them. "They are going to discover our lair shortly, Sartra," Shaman whispered.

"I would love to just kill them all, but I think that another, heavier-armed hunting party will be right behind them. I will draw them down the valley, away from the lair. You get the children and males up to the cave. See if you can quietly break down the camp and clean up. If you hear my warning call, be prepared to come and take them all." Sartra moved quickly through the very tops of the highest, thickest canopy, careful not to jump too far, only fifty or sixty feet at a time to reduce the amount of movement in the treetops. She watched them as they marched in three teams of two. They were chatting and seemed at ease; this was good. Sartra needed to surprise them and then draw them down the valley without getting shot.

The team was only half convinced they were getting into anything worse than wieners and marshmallows. Their rifles were strapped across their backs and the chatting was at a moderate gaggle, topics ranging from movies to hockey games. Kelly and Alan were on point and very uneasy. Kelly watched the iPhone for high-frequency vibrations. The screen flashed red. "Hey, I got something." Kitigawa walked over to have a look. "What are you guys, Cub Scouts? Get back into your wedge formation." The small screen flashed again with a short call.

"Is there any to tell what direction the sounds are coming from?"

"Nope. They will be following us if they have seen us, and I can't imagine that they haven't seen us." Haddock and Willard were walking parallel to Alan in the rustling brush. They had started to flip each other's hats off while exchanging insults. The rain was building up on the pine needles above, and large, occasional drops the size of quarters always seemed to strike Alan just inside his back collar and run down his back. The sky grew darker, and the low clouds covered the treetops.

The doorbell rang, and Karen opened the curtains to see the grey-faced RCMP officer standing on her stoop. Oh shit. He looked up and saw her as she closed the curtains. He pounded on the door. "Karen Wickey! Open this door right now. I am Staff Sergeant Mullens!"

"No…go away!"

"You have to open this door!"

"If you had a warrant, then you'd be in here by now. Fuck off!" *Knock knock knock, knock.* The door shuddered. The knocking continued until Karen opened the door. Mullens pushed his way into the living room of the house.

"You were not invited in; now get out." Mullens strolled around the living room looking into the kitchen and down the hall.

"Where is he, Mrs. Wickey?"

"None of your goddamn business; get out!"

"I am worried about your safety. I think that your husband is dangerous. I think that he is a killer." Mullens' eyes tracked up and down Karen's tall, slim shape, stopping momentarily at her breasts.

Karen's voice calmed. "It's obvious to me that you caught your boss screwing a goat, because there is no way that a man with a brain smaller than an Aplysia squid's could pass the sergeant's exam."

He strolled across the living room. "Look what we have here, a map of the Capilano Park with a spot circled on it. Alan is away for a little hunting trip, is he?"

Karen snatched it from his hands, relieved that he had zeroed in on the wrong location. "Leave now, or I am screaming rape."

"Not a bad concept. Fair enough; I'll be on my way now." Mullens smiled as he touched Karen's shoulder. She recoiled, twisting her shoulder back. He got into his car and picked up his cell phone. "Carl, put together ERT tactical team four, with full bush gear. Yeah, we are going on a manhunt. I think we can catch Wickey in the act. Yeah, I really think he is the shoe killer. No, no warrant necessary."

Two hours later, the black suburban pulled up to the big tactical truck in the Capilano parking lot. The late afternoon rain was washing down the river valley in sheets. The RCMP ERT tac team was unenthusiastic. They didn't like Mullens and did not believe that he had enough evidence to justify a team wandering around in the rainforest. He had placed an X on the topographic map where he believed Alan Wickey was hiding a body. Whose body was not clear; who he had killed was also unclear. One of the guys mentioned that Perry, a well-respected officer, had told Mullens to stick a kazoo up his ass and play a tune upon being asked to join this wild-goose chase.

The troop of eight armed men walked into tree-covered trailhead and up towards the first waypoint. Mullens walked ahead anxiously; he was the kind of guy who didn't fit well into any group. He exuded impatience and anxiety. This very experienced RCMP emergency response team was leaning towards being insubordinate towards him.

The team leader, Corporal McTaggert, was a forty-two-year-old, six-foot-six, dark-haired New Zealander. He strolled easily at the back of the line as they marched up the trail, the rush of the river growing louder as they neared the cliffs. He projected his deep, deliberate voice over the shoulders of his men at the lone skinny figure ahead. "Hey Mullens, if you woke up alone in the woods, half naked, with Vaseline smeared on your ass, would you tell anybody about it?"

Mullens answered sarcastically, "No!"

"Good, glad to hear it," McTaggart answered calmly with a smile, nodding his head slightly at one of his men as the men stifled their laughter.

"Don't be a fucking prick, McTaggart." This was an unfortunate answer that caused McTaggart to crack a broad smile and the entire troop to break out into fits of laughter. Mullens began plotting the reprimand e-mails in his mind. He should have been looking up.

The evening rain was suspended in the treetop mist that had penetrated the sleeping bundles, making Caracin's face wet. The combination of smell and voices startled him. The team of Mounties were marching up the opposite cliffs quietly, but their footsteps were like thunder to Caracin. He was disoriented for a moment as he rolled out of his cot and hung down from the tall cedar. *Where was the sentry; why was there no warning call? How did these guys get so close?* Sentrous was probably correct; this camp was too close to the city. It seemed that hikers were around them every day, and no one could get enough sleep. Yet, this group was different. Caracin moved up into the treetop to see the group. There were many of them, and they were armed, police or maybe soldiers. They did not look like hunters and they were clearly moving at night; this was unheard of. Sentrous dropped down to Caracin's perch and wiped the sleep from his eyes. "Whoa, how did these guys get so close?"

"That's a good question for the sentry. They have short guns, and they are hunting at night. Have you ever seen guns like that?"

"Yes, I have seen pictures on Shaman's television. I think they are soldiers."

"We will have to kill them."

"I don't think that's a good idea. Sartra always—"

Caracin interrupted, "I don't care what your mom would say about it! They are not long guns so even if they hit us, they should not be able to kill us. I say we assemble up the valley and kill them all." Sentrous was quiet. His mind raced through the risks and possible outcomes.

Caracin watched his friend's face closely, looking first for complicity and second for that spark of luminescence that signalled a brilliant plan. Sentrous's values had begun to fade as the first taste of strong clean meat rang through his taste buds. His eyes tracked the dark figures as they filed through the bush. This would be the test. The test to see if humans were really as dangerous as Sartra had claimed for his entire life. Caracin smiled as the anticipated flash of genius lit up in Sentrous's eyes.

Caracin called the clan together. "We must gather to listen to Sentrous's plan. Tonight we will do battle with the human warriors. We shall kill and eat the strongest of the humans and prove our superiority and dominance. We will emerge as the clan who rules both the forest and the human world." The clan cheered and then quieted as Sentrous began to scratch out a drawing on a smooth piece of bark.

More than twenty miles away, Sartra tracked Wickey's hunting party. She had recognized Alan immediately and hoped that she may have an opportunity to kill him, yet she had to stay with her priorities, the first being the safety of the clan. This meant that she couldn't kill the one that she picked. She could only injure in the hopes that the group would retreat with their wounded.

Kelly walked silently as the small screen flashed green. Now the group was calming down a little. "Act like soldiers, you buttheads!" Kelly snapped. Some the men brought their rifles around to the alert posture and scanned through their scopes. A few were still half hearted in their efforts. They didn't believe that there was anything out there but trees and squirrels. Like a down quilt overhead, the fog obscured the treetops over top of the hunting party. The damp, cold air absorbed sound, and the woods were perfectly silent. Sartra could hear every breath and track every step from the cover of the fog. She floated from one spire to another in complete silence, trailing only the *whoosh* of the misty air. Alan looked up into the fog and scanned through his scope. He could hear some faint movement but couldn't see anything.

The gun's sight was pointed directly at Sartra. She chose a human to attack and waited for an opportunity. Sartra hated hunting in the daylight; her eyes burned even on the cloudy days. She hated this trouble that Caracin had brought to her family, the recklessness and the greed of the males. She missed Sentrous, her son, her lost boy. Her eyes narrowed as she slowly crept, inverted, down the tree trunk, her quill colours changing with the bark.

Haddock walked a few paces ahead and turned to lean against a bushy spruce tree. He unzipped his fly and began to urinate on a big leafy fern. There was a strange scratching noise mixed in with the sounds of the urine splashing on the leaves. His back to the tree, he looked up as she reached down and hooked her claws into the tops of his eye sockets, lifting him up with one hand. Willard faced them, frozen with fear. Sartra hoisted the two-hundred-pound man by his orbital bones into the tree. Haddock screamed wildly, clawing at her long arm, but her sharp quills pierced the skin on his palms. Blood poured out of his eye sockets and down his face, spattering outward with his high-pitched wails. By the time Willard had brought his weapon up to bear, Haddock was draped across Sartra's back facing them, begging for help, while steadily ascending into the mist. All of them tracked upwards looking through their scopes. The cross hairs lined up with Haddock's face soaked in blood; the creature was using him a shield while climbing up into the canopy. Kelly was the only one who dared to shoot past Haddock's cheek. The long bullet tore through Sartra's shoulder blade and muscle. She cried out. The ultrasonic squeal hissed at their ears as a sound that wasn't quite a sound.

"Don't hit Haddock!" Roger exclaimed as the spiny assassin and her writhing prey vanished in the rainforest mist.

Willard activated his FLIR scope and scanned the canopy towards Haddock's screams. "I can see him, but the creature doesn't show up on this thing." Instinctively the team fell into formation, running in the firing position and aiming up into the trees. Their pace quickened as Haddock's screams began to fade with the distance.

"Fuck, how does that thing move so fast?"

Sartra moved from treetop to treetop with Haddock now only whimpering. Sartra stopped and flipped him around to drink some of the purple blood bubbling from his eye sockets. The mist cleared momentarily, and Kelly could see the two almost a hundred feet above the forest floor. He exhaled as he pulled the trigger and watched his bullet shred the branches just inches from Sartra's hip. She turned to look down. Kelly could see her disk-like eyes, the black pea-sized pupils fixed on him as he raised the cross hairs to meet her hideous gaze. *Bang! Bang! Bang!* Three shots rang through the damp air. Kelly lost sight of them for a second and scanned across the trees to find them again. The mist had returned. Haddock screamed as he bounced down from limb to limb; his tibia bone snapped, followed by his arm. He plummeted to the forest floor, landing with a thrashing thud.

"Haddock!" The team ran towards the crumpled body in the brush. He groaned.

Wickey arrived and checked his airway, his breathing, and then his carotid pulse. "He's alive!" It was difficult to discern through the dried blood and pine needles if his eyeballs had been pierced or spared by her barbaric claws. "We need to get that helo back now before Haddock goes into shock. Kim, rig me an IV bag, right now!"

"What about his neck? What if it's broken, Wickey?" Roger asked as he scanned the treetops with his night vision.

"We don't have the stretcher for C-spine. I can't feel any spinal deformity or breaks in his neck. We will just have to carry him out to an emergency LZ. Who's got the fucking radio and sat phone?" Alan's mind was racing.

"Haddock," Kim answered.

"Where did his backpack go? Shit, shit. Cell phones anyone?"

Roger and Kelly pulled out their iPhones. "No service." Haddock moaned through his semiconscious state.

"Kelly, you and Willard, go and find the backpack. It has to be back beside that tree."

"On it." Kelly and Willard tracked back towards the original tree, but they had travelled almost a half mile during the attack.

The two were acting like soldiers now; they moved in sequence scanning the treetops for signs of the enemy. They traced their steps back to the original attack spot and found no backpack; it was gone—taken, or hanging from a tree limb in the fog. "Whoa, this fog sucks," Kelly exclaimed as they worked back towards the group.

"Did you find it?"

"Negative, it's gone."

"Would they know enough to take our radios?" Kim asked as he pushed the IV needle into Haddock's flaccid veins.

"They are smart; maybe they do crossword puzzles. I don't know, but backpacks don't evaporate," Alan answered as Haddock moaned. "OK guys, time to set off your PLBs, and that will get the bird over top pretty quick." Kelly nodded to Alan's request and pulled out his yellow personal locator beacon. He switched it to unencrypted, opened the plastic cover, and flicked the red toggle switch.

The tiny light now flashed red as the 403 MHz signal was cast to the heavens. The forty-year-old Russian COSPAS satellite received the signal, and the old rocker switches snapped over to relay the distress signal and the GPS coordinates to a local user terminal in Colorado. The sleepy operator copied the time and coordinates in his logbook and forwarded the text file to the Joint Rescue Coordination Centre in Victoria. The JRCC air coordinator typed the numbers into the SARMaster system, and a red dot appeared on the map.

"Hmm, PLB in the Vancouver/Bowen Island area; looks like it's a strong hit." The air force captain directed his voice towards the marine controller who was watching the hockey game on the big screen.

He answered unenthusiastically, "Oh, yeah."

The other marine coordinator typed the identifier into the database. "What?" The air force officer perked up. "One of our guys, 442 Squadron?"

"Looks like it is. SAR 442 PLB number four is the listing."

"There is nothing going on in that area—no exercises or cases that I know of."

"Get the 902 bird on the horn and find out if she's OK, and ask them if they know who's down there."

"Snake Nine Zero Two, this is JRCC on the line; status please."

"JRCC, Snake 902, we are taking fuel at Yankee Victor Romeo; go ahead."

"Roger, Snake; we have one of your PLBs pinging a position in the Lion's Bay area. Did you happen to drop one out the window?"

"Uh...Roger. We have a few off-duty crew conducting survival training in that area. Maybe one of them set off their PLB by mistake. Before you guys write this up with a number, let me give them a call and check in."

"Snake Nine Zero Two, you have five minutes grace for a chat and then we are lighting this one up, with the whole shooting match."

A few minutes passed as the JRCC coordinators began to organize their response to a potentially serious incident.

"JRCC, this is Snake 902; we called and got no answer."

"Roger, we are tasking you code three along with the Hovercraft Siyhay, Rescue 312, and a land SAR team."

"Roger code three, hammer down. Here are the last known position coordinates and the direction of travel; we have eight souls in the bush. We will send you the names."

"Rescue 902, we copy that; let us know when you are wheels up." With a nod the coordinators pushed the dial buttons on the computer-controlled phone bank and began to activate the search and rescue system.

Back in the woods, Haddock groaned in pain as Wickey tightened the straps on the sticks they were using for splints. The others had fashioned a stretcher out of a sleeping bag and some tree limbs, and they transferred him into the bundle. They could hear the sat phone ringing high up in the distance.

"That's the pack. It sounds like it's up in the trees," Willard said.

"That thing's got it. Wonder if they will answer it for us?" Alan looked up towards the large tree trunks that climbed up through the thick blanket of fog that hung over them.

Kelly spoke in a deep, calming voice. "Let's get to the clearing in the valley over there and set off some smokes. It's about a kilometer away, and we should be able to make it before sunset. I don't want to deal with these creatures in the dark if we don't have to."

The men nodded and began to pack up their gear and get organised. They carried Haddock carefully as he writhed in pain.

The sat phone was now twisted plastic and metal. Shaman's eyes were fixed on the red flashing light that was attached to Kelly's chest as she passed a tiny bone needle through Sartra's flesh. "That flashing device is calling to the other soldiers; we must kill them now and get the device before they bring many more of them."

Sartra knew Shaman was right. "OK, we will attack at the green patch when they move to the far end. We will destroy all of the devices and eat them all." Sartra did not pay any attention to the sinewy thread being pulled through the edges of her wound. The thread was made from the intestines of a homeless man who went missing over a year ago. She called to the clan, and they gathered to listen to their leader's attack plan.

The troop was moving down the slope towards the clearing as the birds went quiet. Kelly was watching the red flashes on his iPhone. He looked around into the dense fog.

"Something's moving above us."

"Yeah, I can hear them too," Alan said.

The other soldiers were very nervous as the movement in the trees was barely perceptible but coming from different directions. They moved into a dense pack of green salal bushes. The fog hung lower here; the wisps were swirling around the soldiers' heads as they moved in a Delta V formation through the thick greenery.

"You smell that?" Kitagawa asked, reacting to the waft of animal scent that drifted below the fog, but all were concentrating on watching their sectors.

Alan spoke up as he took a turn carrying the head of Haddock's stretcher. "I know this area; we did an exercise out here about ten years ago. There is an old mine over there, and the glade is just down the hill over there. I think we should head for some cover."

"I think we are going to need it pretty quick," Kelly replied as he spun towards the sound of whooshing air high up in the fog.

"Let's get moving," Alan said. They all started to move double time into the dense brush, their hopes of being stealthy disappearing as they thrashed through the foliage. Stealth was irrelevant now; it was obvious that the predators knew exactly where they were and where they were going.

"When they strike, cover the stretcher bearer and shoot for the eyes. Don't wait for any fucking orders; just fire away when you have a shot." Kelly's words rolled through the minds of the group of seasoned soldiers, who were now in full combat mode.

Shaman whispered into Sartra's ear. "They are different from any humans we have seen; they are soldiers trained to shoot and kill. Our angles of approach are all covered, and if they hold to their disciplines, then we will lose some of our own."

Sartra's voice was tempered by pain. "My son and Caracin have brought on the time of awakening for us. Things will be different from today on. Now the Salt clan and all the clans will be fighting for their lives. We must either kill this whole team now or pull back and hope that they will retreat and not return."

Shaman knew enough about the humans to realize that Sartra was correct. The chances of them not returning with many more soldiers and aircraft were slim to none. "I am not sure if they have called for help already. We have their big radio, but they have other communication devices, like the flasher."

"We need to attack, kill them all, and pull back into the higher mountains. We will need to get word to the Whiteline clan and the others within the coastal areas. Send one of the males out with a message for a meeting at the Great Tusk." Sartra called the clan to battle; they were all in place and ready to descend.

Kelly looked at his iPhone as it flashed red. "They are talking again, only this time it was short and sweet, kinda like an order. Ready weapons!" The group slowed in the high salal; they focussed up into the fog. Mike Haley had his yellow glasses on to enhance his vision in the fog, but now it was getting dark and he was considering taking them off. A grommet whistled across the forest and struck him in the lens of the glasses. He yelped as he recoiled back; the plastic lens shattered and the tiny stone struck his brow. Two other grommets struck, one on Willard's collarbone and one on Alan's helmet.

"Stay on your sectors! They are just rocks."

"Yeah, rocks that fucking hurt!" Haley said as he picked the plastic shards out of his face. Alan reached across and pulled out his hunting knife and held it tightly as he pulled Haddock's stretcher along with his other hand. Haddock yelped as the tree boughs directly above them opened up, and two males dropped down into the middle of the group on top of the stretcher. The weight of the creature crumpled Haddock's stretcher to the ground. The stricken patient screamed as the creature stood on his chest and lashed at Alan. Alan leapt back; he knew that he had to get clear for the others to fire, but the creature's long arms hit him like a sledgehammer. The hooked claws caught his fatigues, and the creature pulled him closer; its jaws opened as it reached up to pull Alan's head back and sink its teeth into the front of his neck. Bullets peppered past Alan's ears as they impacted the creature's shoulders. The grey-and-black spiked beast lunged forward with teeth extended. Alan thrust the seven-inch serrated blade up into its armpit. Here there were no armoured quills, and he felt the blade penetrate the thick black skin. He pulled it out and sank it in again, fending the creature's mouth off with the other hand. He turned to face to the beast, and as the knife blade sank deeper, Alan saw pain register in the black pupils. Two more of Kelly's bullets cracked past Alan's ear, shattering the beast's teeth and penetrating soft tissue at the back of its throat. Red blood gushed out of its mouth, and it dropped Alan and fell to its knees.

Haley had recovered and was firing into the trees directly above him. The large-calibre rounds were able to punch through the thick quills. The rugged hide of the Apecs was where the quills converged. This convergence, along with the liquid filling of the quills, was very effective at absorbing and dispersing the kinetic energy from the bullets. Any small- to medium-calibre rounds just bounced off the creatures. But this team had all high-velocity ammunition. At close range, these bullets could penetrate their hides and kill them. As the towering male dropped at Alan's feet, the whole Apec attack party paused; this was the first time that they had ever seen a clan member die at the hands of any other creature, especially a human. Two other males stopped their advance when they felt the bullets sink into their flesh. They turned tail and retreated high up into the trees.

"Reload and advance!" The group moved, skittering sideways down the small bank and deeper into the clearing. "Move into the clearing and keep going down to the big rock over there," Kelly yelled. "Alan, you OK?"

"Yeah, I killed that mofo."

"I killed him; you tickled his armpit," Kelly remarked as they walked backwards down the bank into the glaciated rocks.

"Yeah, whatever. It's the first time I've seen one of them die. I was beginning to wonder. I think we need to get out of here." Alan pointed down the slope. "I see the old mine entrance. Let's make a run for it."

"They are going to attack again before we get in there; stay on your sectors," Kelly replied. "Move steady and don't turn your backs." As they reached the other side of the clearing, the clan attacked again, the females leading the charge this time, flashing from tree to tree, back and forth, as they approached in a swirling blur. Haley fired and missed; Casic fired and missed as the two females leapt into the air. Shaman's weight hit Haley, throwing him back as he landed on the forest floor. She ripped out his throat. Blood shot across the group as Kelly pulled the trigger; the bullet ripped into Haley's shoulder blade by mistake. Shaman was holding him up as shield. Sartra dropped from directly above and landed on the stretcher as Alan and Willard jumped back and drew their weapons. Haddock reached up from the stretcher and stuck his knife into her leg. She reached down and thrust her claws into his neck and hoisted him up as a shield from Alan's rounds. She walked slowly towards the group. She was pushing them back, waiting for the other females to drop on them from behind—one more step.

Kelly looked up and behind them and realized it was a trap. "Sidestep, over to the mine. run!" The whole group broke into a run towards Sartra and across as Kelly fired towards the figures behind them in the trees. Both Shaman and Sartra dropped their human shields and leapt up into the trees, flying from trunk to trunk. The air swirled behind the men, and they knew they had only a few seconds to live before the four females and seven males reached out for them. The rest of the clan members had realized that Sartra was right; they were all fighting for their lives. There was no more hesitation, no more contemplation in the clan; this was the first battle of the awakening. They all raced towards the mine entrance. The old wooden door was locked ahead of them.

Kelly lowered his weapon and fired three times at the lock as they reached the door. Both he and Alan raised their legs and kicked. The fifty-year-old plywood door blew apart into splinters as the six men burst into the slippery, wet mine. "Take cover and defend the doorway!" Kelly yelled as they dove to either side of the rocky entrance and took up a crouched firing position.

The cloud cover had thinned, and now the moonlight was shining through the fog and lighting up the doorway. The only sound was the heaving and wheezing of six men who had never run that fast in their entire lives.

"Some camping trip—I thought we were coming up to drink beer!" Roger pulled six cans of beer out of his backpack and tossed them onto the rocky floor. "Anybody want a beer?" he quipped.

"You were running around this whole time with a six pack of beer?" Alan asked with a laugh.

The adrenaline had the team a little giddy. "I quit, I uh…um, not drinking anymore. Kim, you were right. It makes you see things." Roger sighed as Casic half laughed.

"Throw it out there for them, maybe we can get them pissed drunk," Kitagawa suggested.

"I think they are pissed enough," Alan replied with a smile.

"Wickey, this is all you; you pissed them off. Did you see the way that big bitch looked you? She's pissed all right. You should have called, or at least sent her flowers, dude," Casic said.

Kelly picked up a full beer can and threw it out into the door opening. He didn't do it as a joke. They all looked out into the blackness, waiting. They could hear some movement outside as the can sailed back in and hit the ceiling, exploding in foam.

"I guess Wickey is right. They can't be Sasquatches if they don't drink Kokanee." The standoff continued as both sides made plans for their next move.

Many miles away, the squad of RCMP worked its way up the well-worn trail. Their mood was jovial but McTaggert was getting impatient; he had been pulled away from his nine-year-old daughter's piano recital. His mood darkened.

"Mullens, if I had known that we were going on a nature walk, I would have brought my daughter."

"Listen up, you assholes, this Wickey guy is the real thing, a serial killer. If I am right, he is up here with some buddies burying bodies. They are armed and trained by the army to kill clowns like you."

Mullens had turned towards the group, projecting his voice. It travelled across the river. McTaggart walked up through the troop and stopped a few inches from Mullen's face and spoke quietly. "Mullens, there had better be something up here other than bears and raccoons, or my team and I will not be happy."

"Watch your tone, Corporal, and mind your place in this outfit." McTaggart backed up a few inches while maintaining eye contact. *If I hit him it would mean an inquiry and staying a corporal for the next seven years*, he thought to himself.

The raised voices made Caracin stop for a moment and watch them. He wondered what this conversation was about. It looked like a conflict between the tall one and the leader. Conflict within enemy ranks is always a blessing, he thought. The rain began to fall, and a few of the larger drops penetrated to the forest floor. The light mist disappeared with the rain as the troop arrived at the waterfalls. The green river rushed off of the steep cliff and fell two hundred feet straight down into a narrow white column. The beautiful white spire cut into an emerald-green pool surrounded by lush ferns and foliage. The spray and mist churned up from the pool swirled in slow circles up the mossy cliffs. The trail passed by the pool and then followed the cliff base until it turned up into a gruelling vertical series of switchbacks. After a few minutes of gazing at the fantastic falls, Tac Team Four started up the steep trail. This was where most of the tourists and hikers usually turned back. Mullens, impatient with the troop's reluctance, was sure that Alan Wickey and his merry band of murderers were hiding in these hills.

Unknown to the men, the Free clan was set up and waiting to spring their trap. Sentrous had been correct; the humans chose the steep trail rather than the easier one that was farther down the valley. The sun had disappeared, and the dusk was deepening the shadows in the watery valley. Mullens was marching up the narrow rocky dirt trail as it wound up the cliff face. Five huge Sitka spruce trees were perched on the cliff face; the mammoth trunks grew out of the rock face and curved up skyward to a height of over one hundred feet. The trail wound past the spruce trees at varying heights; at some points on the trail, you could reach out and touch the tree trunk at a height of fifty or sixty feet above the tree's base. This was where the clan waited, at the steepest part of the trail. They were in plain sight at the eye level of the prey. Sentrous had told them to be still and with colour. The humans would look right at them but not see them.

McTaggart was not really looking for anything but where to place his next footstep; his men were also focussed on the very tricky footwork required to stay on the trail. The darkness was making the climb treacherous. One of the team stopped for a moment to drink some water and don his night-vision goggles. These helped with the trail and roots. If anyone was to fall at this point, he would surely tumble down the rocky face to meet certain death at the cliff base.

Mullens had his night vision on, but the batteries were close to dead and his vision was spotty as he climbed. He stopped, his chest heaving and his throat wheezing. He was desperately trying to conceal his poor physical condition from the troop, who were all in top condition. Mullens's eyes wandered lazily through the trees until he noticed a slight movement. His gaze fixed on the strange lump hanging from the thick tree limb. He tapped his night vision, and the green display flickered as he thought he saw the shape move. The small screens blacked out again for a moment as he fiddled with the adjustments. The screen flashed back up, but now part of the view was blocked by a shape. The shape's eyes flashed open. Sentrous was only five feet away, and his ghoulish, smiling face filled the night-vision screen. Mullens screamed in a high-pitched, unchivalrous manner as Sentrous pulled the night vision off his head. He pounced on Mullens and pinned him to the rocky face. His claws closed around the shaking human's neck as he tilted his head and leaned in to bite out Mullens's entire cheek. Sentrous loosened his grip to let his prey scream, for this was part of the theatrics of his plan. Sentrous chewed the soft flesh while it was still half attached to his face, swallowing hard before letting Mullens go. Mullens ran directly into the troop, which was struggling to swing their weapons into a firing position. His screaming was wild and unruly as the blood squirted out of his face and onto their black tunics.

The screaming was the to attack, as the other clan hunters swung down from the trees into the melee. McTaggart dropped down the face onto a small ledge and fired his weapon at the moving figures. He couldn't comprehend what was happening, but his extensive combat training engaged a part of his brain that did not require an explanation. One of the young males dropped down and swung through the trees towards him. He aimed his MP5 and landed two shots centre mass and one in the forehead. He had no idea who or what he was firing at, but he watched the shots hit their mark. The creature lurched and dropped down to a lower branch and shook its head. This was when McTaggart met its eyes as it recovered and resumed its attack. He fired again at its face, and it recoiled once more, dropping down the tree limbs into the valley.

The other members of the police ERT team were not as lucky. Caracin paused for a moment as a barrel of a gun was aimed at him, and then he swung quickly out of the sights as the bullets flew. He reached out and snatched the weapon out the policeman's hand. He stopped and perched above the man. Another member fired a burst of three rounds into Caracin's side, but the nine-millimetre rounds did not penetrate his hide. Caracin leapt down onto his prey and tore out his throat. The other members were bounding and tumbling down the trail in the near pitch dark. They were easily overwhelmed by the hunters. A few more bullets were fired, but the remaining members of the troop were butchered, leaving only McTaggart and Mullens alive.

McTaggart had worked his way clear of the trees and over to the side of the waterfall. He took cover behind a rock and watched the tree line through his gun sight. He could hear Mullens's screams as Caracin pinned him down and began to eat some of the choicer body parts. McTaggart decided that he would rather die in the falls than be eaten by one of those fucking things, whatever they were. As two creatures emerged from the shadows and moved towards him, he opened fire. They dodged quickly right and then left as they got closer. He could tell that his bullets were just bouncing off their rugged quill coats. As they lunged, he stood up and stepped back into the waterfall; with arms outstretched he dropped into the mist. Caracin was puzzled by this tall strong one as he watched his body drop with the falls into the deep pool.

Meanwhile, Mullens was now missing his clothes, his scrotum, both cheeks, both ears, and his tongue, but this did not slow him down. He ran somersaulting down the dirt track to the cliff base. He could hear the creatures whooshing all around him as he sprinted in the dark. He sobbed as he reached the green pool and saw McTaggart's body floating facedown in the swirling currents. He kept running down the valley as Sentrous and Caracin watched him.

"Why did you let him go?" Sentrous asked.

"I want the humans to get our message."

"You really are not afraid of the awareness at all, are you?"

"No, I welcome the opportunity to take our place at the top of the food chain in the human cities. This night proves that they are weak and their weapons are useless against us."

One of the males approached. "Caracin, Choppa was hit by one of the bullets in her face. She is badly hurt."

Alan and the team's eyes were adjusting to the darkness of the cave. Casic had his night vision kit on his head, and he could see the rock walls and wood braces with better detail. Roger had finally dug past his of nacho chips and retrieved a flash-bang grenade from the very bottom of his pack. He held it up. "Maybe this could fuck up their senses long enough for us to escape or maybe shoot them."

Kitagawa grunted in disapproval. "Yeah, how fast are we going to run and how long until they catch up? Where are we going to run to?"

Alan was using his NVGs to scan the back of the mine. His light lit up a caged door surrounding an old elevator. It was locked, and the steelworks looked rusted and decayed. "If I remember correctly, this mine divides into two sections. That old rusty elevator shaft drops like a thousand feet down into the shaft where there is an endless network of drill tunnels. Over here is a surface network of natural caves with some underground streams that spread out under the forest floor." Alan flashed his light to illuminate a passageway that led off into the darkness. "I bet that one of these natural caves would pop up in the forest floor somewhere."

Roger spoke up. "So what's the plan? Wait here? Go on a spelunking adventure, or go out and fight?"

220

EMERGENCE

"I am not crazy about doing Custer's last stand out there. My vote is definitely door number two, or stay here and dig in," Kitagawa said.

"Kelly, you're a wise old Indian; what do you think?" Roger asked.

"Well, kemo sabe, I think that we should move out through these tunnels and find a way out of here. The guys will fly in and start a ground search for us at first light. We just have to stay alive until then," Kelly replied.

"OK, sounds like a plan to me. NVGs?" Kitagawa asked.

"It's too dark in here for them to work properly," Roger replied. "We will just have to use our headlamps and flashlights." They all put on their headlamps and started into the natural cave opening. There were signs that other cavers had been there, chalk markings and an old string line. The chalk arrows pointed the way to somewhere, so when they came upon a juncture, they followed the chalk markings. The walls were green and coated with algae; the rounded bottom of the caves was slippery, and the damp air muffled the sounds of the men shuffling through the subterranean maze. The only sounds were the dripping water from the stalactites and the whispering breeze. The narrow beams of light tracked their head movements; one beam illuminated one tiny disc of the cave, and their surroundings were pitch-black. The group worked its way down the rocky corridor as they descended down into the depths. They hesitated as the tunnel dropped steeply. The grade was negotiable; they just hoped it would start to climb back up. They arrived at a junction with three tunnels that led in different directions. They could hear the sound of water echoing through the caves.

One of the tunnels seemed to climb up more than the others, so they followed the wet and narrow passage for another half an hour. Water was flowing along the floor in torrents. They passed a whirling disturbance in the cave floor; water swirled around and dropped down into a man-sized sinkhole. They all carefully stepped over it and continued up against the rushing underground river. Their feet would skid slightly as they placed their footsteps, so they all shortened up their stride. As the tunnel steepened, Mike Haley slipped in the slime; his big frame dropped into the rushing water and he skidded downstream, wiping out Roger as he fell.

The two of them hollered as they tumbled through the icy glacial waters towards the swirling sinkhole. Roger Hamlin reached out and gripped an outcropping to stop his tumble, but Haley kept rolling in the torrent. As he hit the sinkhole, he swirled around once and then dropped into the turbulence. Alan grabbed Roger and helped him up as they worked down towards the hole. The team quickly pulled out their climbing gear.

"Wickey, you anchor up there, and we'll drop a line into the hole and see if he can see it or reach it." Kelly rigged up an empty harness on the end of the line and prepared the coil. They all grabbed the tail end of the line while Kelly fed it down into the swirling pool. Ten feet, twenty feet, thirty feet of line went down into the swirl. The whole group locked eyes as they waited for some sign of life from beneath. Maybe the water had swept him down a thousand-foot tunnel into the abyss, and he was long gone; yet maybe he was holding on just ten feet below them. The line jerked twice. All of them cheered as they set themselves up to hoist up their comrade. Wickey locked his feet and tied the line to his harness. He looked around the tunnel for any obvious belay points but could not see any. The line jerked three times, which meant Haley was in the harness and ready. The whole group started to haul him up. He rose for the first five feet easily and then the weight became greater. They all sang out "Two six!" and pulled hand over hand until the line became stretched and taut. They felt a rapid vibration on the line, which they interpreted as turbulence and water resistance. They called out "Heave!" and the vibrating line began to move again. They hauled together, and suddenly the water swirl expulsed out a form. Haley's headless, armless torso flew up and landed in Roger's lap. He screamed and pushed the torn, fleshy mass off his lap. Reacting to the horror, the team released the line as the remains of Haley slipped back down into the swirl. The line spun between their legs as the water swept the grim figure down into the depths. The line stopped as the men exclaimed their horror.

"What the hell happened to him?" Roger screamed.

"Shit! Did we do that to him by pulling him back up through the tunnel?" Kitagawa asked. The line moved slightly, and then stopped. They all stopped talking and looked down at the line. Wickey stood up in the torrent as the line whipped around and then began to fly down the hole. "Oh shit!" Wickey and Kelly both exclaimed. As Alan clambered for a foothold, the line came tight. Wickey was snatched from his anchor position and careened down the tunnel, sweeping all five men into the swirling tempest. They tumbled down the water tube and dropped into a twenty-foot freefall. They all splashed into the deep pool at the bottom of the huge cavern.

Alan struggled to reach the surface; he had landed on both Casic and Kitagawa as he hit the water. The cavern was pitch-black except for a single light that shone up from the bottom of the pool. It was Haley's flashlight, and it illuminated the bottom of the pool with a green glow. The five men struggled to keep their heads above the water. They swam aggressively towards the pool's edge, weighed down by their gear. The sand was a fine white silicone that stuck to their wet fatigues. The five lay on their backs looking up into the darkness and breathing heavily. Their headlamps did not penetrate to the outer reaches of this large cavern.

The waterfall dropped out from the top of a cliff and into a deep pool about fifty feet across. Kelly and Casic still had their weapons, but Alan and Roger had put them down and subsequently left them in the tunnel above. The men struggled to their feet and took inventory of their gear and their situation. Alan was still in his harness with the line attached to him. The line led into the water down towards the middle of the pool. Alan began to coil the line while pulling it in.

"Was it the current from the waterfall that dragged us down here?" Roger looked at Alan.

"It didn't feel like current. But at least we have some climbing gear and line to get out of here."

"After what happened to Haley, I don't think we are going out that way." Roger pointed to the top of the waterfall. Alan pulled the line through the glowing green water and coiled up the colourful loops. He could see the shadows of small fish swimming around in the light. The climbing rope came easily until he could feel the resistance of something dragging at the end. This would be what was left of Haley, he thought. He was not looking forward to seeing the grisly torso again, but he was obliged to recover it. Haley would be alive if they hadn't taken this little trip.

Casic shook the water out of his night-vision goggles and turned them on. He dropped them down over his eyes and began to scan the cavern for an exit. His head stopped and he drew a deep breath as he adjusted the focus on his goggles. "Shit!" he yelled as the line snapped tight again and Alan flew from the shore into the water. Alan was helpless as he was dragged across the pool to the other side. Casic aimed his rifle and fired two bullets into the darkness. The line went slack as Alan struggled to untie the double figure-eight knot in the water. The line came tight again as Casic fired again, but Alan had the knot undone. The line flew from his hands and recoiled up into the darkness.

Kelly looked through his scope but couldn't see anything but blackness. Alan swam back.

"They're here, and there are at least a few of them. They're hard to see; even with the night scope, they don't show up well. I counted three of them, but they have taken cover; there may be more." Casic scanned the cave as Kelly and Kitagawa pulled Alan out of the water.

"Casic, did you see any way out of here? I doubt those guys came in the same way we did."

"Nope, can't see it, but I can't see much," Casic replied. They could hear movement up on the rocks. Alan watched the water. He noticed tiny swirls at the surface; the water column was moving.

"These guys are going to attack in a second, and I don't like our odds," Casic observed.

Alan shone his flashlight towards the far end of the pool. "Jump in."

"What do mean, jump in?" Kelly asked as the dark shadows moved closer to the group.

"Jump or stand and fight—those are our choices," Alan explained.

Casic looked into his scope and fired a shot into the darkness. "These nine-mills just bounce off them. There are four that I can count, and they are getting ready to jump us—I don't think we have time for a secret ballot!" They all looked at Wickey and jumped into the water. The icy-cold water moved them slowly towards the far end of the cavern, and they could see the figures arrive at the beach and stop.

Wickey shouted out into the blackness, "Yeah, don't like the water much, do you!" The group huddled together, teeth chattering, as they drifted slowly.

"Great, so what now, Wickey? Do we just paddle out here until we get tired and drown?"

"I was hoping that there would be a nice little river that would get us out of here."

"Yeah, like the tunnel of love at the fair, with music and little fairies singing songs," Roger said, shivering.

"Yeah, just like that, little fairies," Alan replied in short breaths as their speed increased.

Casic could see a large swirl ahead at the base of the approaching wall. "You guys aren't going to like this. Maybe we should go back and duke it out with those monkey dudes."

"What, tell me what you see?"

"Shit, get ready to hold your breath," Casic exclaimed as they were sucked into the whirlpool. The water surged around as they all started to circle the giant whirl of water. Once around and then they all screamed as they were pulled into the vortex. The tunnel was about ten feet down, and their passage through it was violent. They were all trained rescue swimmers, and this rough tumble through the rocky passage tested their wits and cold-water skills to the limits. The underwater passage twisted and turned as they rushed along, smashing against the rocks. Wickey popped up in an airspace for a second and took a deep breath before they were pulled down again into the pitch blackness. His lungs were straining and his lower brain was very close to overriding his will and forcing his mouth to open in a terminal gasp, but then he felt cold air hit his face. He opened his mouth and looked forward as the whole group emerged out halfway down a waterfall. They all yelled again as they fell through the air and splashed into the basin. The water pounded them for a moment until they swam clear. Clear of the caves, they climbed up the rocky shore of Klutz Falls, coughing and sputtering. They survived.

"Did I miss the singing fairies?" Casic yelled over the sound of the mist.

"What, you didn't see them? I thought they were lovely," Kelly replied.

"Yeah, we almost sang with angels too," Casic commented as he spat out the icy water. They all laughed as they pulled themselves up.

"Alan, I am never camping with you again—you realize that, don't you?" Roger said as they began their long hike down the valley.

EMERGENCE

20 Academics

The e-mail was from Carl Hail at Duke University: "*Dr. Wickey, Attached is a submission to the journal* Nature. *Jane smells a rat, and we think that this paper is not supported by you. Can you confirm this? There are huge holes in the genetics, and if you can help us out, we can get it stopped before it goes up for review. Jane is flying into Vancouver tonight to discuss this with you.*" Karen's jaw dropped as she read. *Jane as in Jane Goodall? She's flying into Vancouver to meet me? Holy shit!*

Those assholes were trying to publish a paper on these creatures, and they didn't have enough evidence. Karen had met Dr. Goodall in 2006 at a biogenetics conference in Sweden. They shared a bottle of sherry together in the airport lounge. She didn't remember discussing anything but travel destinations and family.

Karen began typing a reply:

Carl,

I didn't think that she would remember me. Of course I will meet her at the airport. I had no knowledge of this paper, but they possess only a tiny bit of the data, and most of their assumptions are wrong. Even their guess on the genus is sketchy. I've run the material and now have a whole gene set, but the assholes are trying to lock me out of my own lab. I have photos and a video of the animals, and I think Jane will be amazed.

She hit send and started to collect her things.

Teddy walked in. "Wassup, mommy dearest? You're smiling."

Karen was bubbling with excitement. "Dr. Jane Goodall is flying in to meet me, yes, me!" She pointed to herself enthusiastically.

227

"You mean the chimp lady on TV is coming to see you? Cool, Mom, you must really be a big wheel." Teddy smiled and touched his mom's shoulder. The MacBook chimed with an e-mail reply.

Ha, jackpot! Jane knew you were being left out of this. She has your picture posted on her Courageous Women in Science website. Didn't you know? She's been watching out for you ever since she met you. She was a big fan of your paper on telomeres and ageing.

"Teddy, you are coming to the airport with me; get your shoes on!" Karen gathered her laptop and backpack.

"Sooo…where is Dad?"

"He's camping with his buddies." Karen had to tell Teddy what was going on, but she couldn't formulate the opening sentence. How did you tell your son that there were monsters dropping from the trees and they had a habit of breaking in to the house? Karen thought about it for a moment.

"Teddy, I think that your dad—of all people—has discovered a previously unknown animal species."

"What kind of species, fish?"

Karen laughed at Teddy's reply. "A hominid."

Teddy knew what she meant. "An ape?" he answered with surprise. "My dad discovered a new species of ape. Are you sure you've got the right—Dad?" His voice pitched with a hint of incredulity.

"Yeah, I know." She chuckled as she shook her head.

Teddy's mind raced at a similar speed to his mother's; he was an extraordinarily bright boy who excelled at anything he attempted, but lately he had lost interest in everything but his Xbox.

"Dangerous?" he asked.

"Very."

"Is Dad hunting it?"

"Yes." She wanted to say more but stopped as Teddy's face dropped.

"This hunting trip wasn't your idea, I take it?" Teddy asked but knew the answer.

"No, it wasn't."

"Is he coming back?"

228

"Teddy, your dad doesn't always make the smartest moves, but he is extremely talented at getting out of tight spots. He has survived situations where he should have died many times. I think he's got nine lives."

"Is he up to nine yet?" Teddy exhaled with anxiety.

"We need to find Dr. Goodall a nice place to stay, so will you start looking for B and Bs in the campus area? Here's my phone." Her motherly distraction techniques worked on men of all ages.

The phone chimed twice with a text. Teddy read it out loud. "It's Dad. He says, 'I'm OK but we lost three guys: Haddock, Haley, and Willard. I'm locked up at the Northshore police station, and all hell is breaking loose!'"

Teddy wrote back: *Dad, it's me. I know about it; Mom told me.*

The phone chimed again. *Teddy, tell Mom I am sorry, and she was right, something else happened to an RCMP team over in the valley. The detachment chief is losing his mind.*

Karen was unimpressed, and her expression showed it.

"He's OK." Teddy sighed.

The first passengers started to walk down the ramp at Vancouver International Airport. Dr. Goodall was easily recognizable as she walked towards the two. Karen stepped up and said hello; she introduced her son, and Jane shook Teddy's hand enthusiastically.

"Let's get you settled into your accommodations, and then we will go for some dinner," Karen suggested.

The detachment inspector's face was flush and his lip was shaking as he barked at the military officer on the phone. "Listen to me, you pencil neck; they were not out there on a DND training mission, so why did they get a helo ride? Just give me their beacon track, and I will decide whether they are suspects or not!"

The e-mail rang in from rescue center, and Inspector Boyd opened the attachment. A dotted red line showed Kelly's personal locator beacon track over the past forty-eight hours. He collected the file and walked into the interview room.

Alan looked across the tiny interrogation room at him; they could hear the ruckus outside as RCMP members tromped up and down the hallway urgently. It had been two hours since they had been intercepted at the helipad. The military police, the RCMP, and the West Vancouver police had all fought over custody, but the Mounties had won, due to jurisdiction.

"I am Inspector Boyd." Alan was surprised to have an inspector as an interrogator. "What were you doing out there, Alan?"

"We were doing a little hunting."

"Hunting. How did three SAR techs end up missing on a hunting trip?"

"We got separated."

"So where are they?"

"I don't know. If I knew that, they wouldn't be missing."

"People around you keep ending up dead, Alan. This makes me very suspicious. Maybe Mullens was right about you; maybe you are a serial killer. In fact, he has a team out looking for you right now. Did you see him out there in the bush?"

Alan looked surprised. "Nope, never saw him."

"His team is missing; they never reported in last night. So how did you get separated from the rest of your team?"

"There was a mudslide and we all fell into the river; we went over a waterfall. Three were missing when we got ourselves reunited in the pool at the bottom."

Boyd shook his head. "That's a bullshit story, Alan. You're not going to be able to show me a slide site when I march your ass out in the bush, are you? You and your guys are in a lot of trouble. We know what really happened, Alan, and the sooner you come clean and tell us your story, the better off it will be for you and your friends."

Alan chuckled. "No, I don't imagine that you have a clue what happened. That's why I am filling in the blanks for you, Inspector."

"Alan, we will keep you in here for as long as we have to. The guys out there like you for these murders. You're a family guy; Karen and Theodore are counting on you, and now you have let them down. What do you think they will say once they learn about what you have done?"

"OK, Boyd, I'm leaving now. It's time to contact my lawyer if we are going around this ridiculous circle."

Boyd shuffled his position as his phone buzzed, and he looked at the text message.

"They have tracked Mullens's cell signal and now there is a team going out to find him. I'm going out to see what he has to say about you, Alan." Boyd watched Alan's reaction to the news. "You're not going anywhere. Take a little time to think about it, and talk to me if you have a change of heart when I get back." Boyd got up to leave.

"Lawyer...lawyer, lawyer, lawyer," Alan replied. "Oh, and say hi to my old buddy Mullens."

Mullens was hiding in a hollowed-out stump; the extreme loss of blood had him confused and lightheaded. The blood that was pouring out of his mouth had slowed; his other wounds had clotted, making his thin, disappearing hair rough and clumpy. He knew that he had to keep moving towards the parking lot. Hopefully the creatures had given up following him. The inside of his cedar stump lit up as his phone rang. The theme song to *Mission Impossible* rang out into the forest, but the little tune did not have to travel far, for Caracin was sitting on top of Mullens's stump.

Caracin had grown bored waiting for Mullens to run, and he took the ringtone as an opportunity to encourage his prey to move along. Mullens flipped open the phone and answered with a muffled grunt. He was missing his tongue, so phone conversation was a challenge. Inspector Boyd asked him, "Mullens, are you OK? What is your exact location?" Mullens realized that he was not going to be able to have a conversation, so he started to text Boyd while Boyd continued to talk on the small speaker. The light dimmed in the twilight, and Mullens looked up towards the stump opening. Caracin's face was hanging upside down in the entrance; he was smiling a horrible, wide grimace laced with yellow, pointed teeth. Mullens howled with horror as he lunged out past Caracin and ran into the woods again. *That's better*, Caracin thought. He tracked the panicky straggler as he stumbled through the bush. Caracin jumped down, landed on his back, and bit into the back of his shoulder. Mullens fell to the ground. Caracin crouched on his back and licked the new bite marks as they oozed blood. He chewed gently on his trapezius muscle and shoulder, tearing off a little piece. This was a playful bite—Caracin's intention was to motivate Mullens to pick up the pace a little. Caracin leapt up into the trees as Mullens sobbed and howled again. He got up on his feet and staggered on; he could see the lights from parking lot through the trees, and he picked up the pace.

Sentrous was surprised that Caracin had not returned with the last human so he went to investigate. He could see the red-and-blue flashing lights in the haze above the parking lot. He watched Mullens break into the clearing and bolt towards the RCMP mobile command van. As Inspector Boyd wheeled the car into the parking lot, his headlights illuminated Mullens's blood-soaked body; he sprinted right past the duty corporal and into the back of the van.

"Holy shit, Mullens, what the fuck happened to you?" Boyd said out loud to himself as he stopped the car and radioed for the ambulance.

The two officers in the van were stunned as Mullens burst in and dropped to the floor. They threw a blanket on him as he began to sob loudly. Boyd stepped in and put his hand on his shoulder. Mullens opened his mouth, and a curdled blood clot dropped over his lip and slid down his chin.

"What happened? Did Wickey do this to you?" Boyd asked.

Mullens groaned and shook his head. The police officers all looked up as the van shuddered from a heavy landing on the roof. The light from the plastic skylight on the vehicle darkened, and Mullens began to scream. Boyd looked up and saw the two white Ping-Pong shaped eyes. The tiny black pupils fixed on Boyd as Caracin tore off the skylight assembly and dropped into the van. The group reeled back as he landed among them with a thud. He looked each man in the eye and then hooked Mullens under his chin with his claws. Mullens rose up, kicking and screaming, back out the skylight. Boyd stood in shock for a few seconds and then grabbed Mullens's feet. They were both lifted up until the rim of the skylight hit Boyd in the face; he dropped back down. The two officers outside were firing their weapons at Caracin as he jumped across to the nearest tree with his prey. He scaled the high fir tree until he could drape Mullens over a bough and collect himself.

"What are you doing?" Sentrous demanded as their eyes met in the treetop.

"I am collecting my dinner," Caracin replied sheepishly.

"You are trying to incite them into attacking us, aren't you?"

"Not really, Sentrous. I just lost track of my meal and went to retrieve him."

"We cannot let them return to the police station and alert the soldiers. We are not ready for that kind of confrontation." Sentrous was furious.

Caracin sighed. "They can't hurt us." Sentrous's eyes glared with anger, and Caracin looked down, as if a little embarrassed at his conduct. "OK, let's go and get them before they escape." *At least it means some more hunting,* Caracin thought.

The five officers had stood in stunned silence as they watched a screaming Mullens disappear up a two-hundred-foot tree into the mist. "Call in the fucking troops!" Boyd shouted as the corporal dove for the radios and the constable opened up the trunk for the shotguns.

The communications constable looked up as he noticed some movement from above. "Oh shit—there are two of them now, and they're coming back!" He drew his weapon and began firing up into the forest. The black shapes darted back and forth and then descended towards the group. Sentrous jumped back and forth, drawing their fire, while Caracin snuck down the back of a tree to pounce at the firing team. The shotgun blast rang out across the valley; the scattered pellets didn't bother Sentrous. The two officers did not see the black shape shoot directly out at them until it was too late. Caracin tore apart one of the officers and took the shotgun, and then he used it to strike the other officer on the top of his head, dropping him to the ground. Sentrous chuckled at the sight; he shouted out from the trees, "Caracin, now that was funny." Sentrous dropped to the truck and jumped in through the skylight; there was a short burst of firing, and then the truck shook violently and Sentrous popped out.

Boyd had made it to his car and was struggling to get his key into the ignition. He looked up at Sentrous, who had spotted him. The whole car shook as Sentrous landed on the roof, denting it. Boyd hammered his foot down on the accelerator; the rear wheels spun, spitting gravel across the lot. He pulled out his weapon and fired through the roof as he drove, speeding down the winding road. Sentrous punched his hand through the windshield and grabbed down and under. He couldn't reach Boyd. Boyd fired, and Sentrous felt a sting as the bullet hit the back of his claw. Boyd was now weaving his car back and forth to shake this creature loose. Caracin was leaping from tree to tree as fast as he could move in order to follow the car. He could tell Sentrous was having fun; what a great ride he was having on top of a car. Sentrous began trying to pound his claw through the roof but was having trouble penetrating the steel. He reached down in front again and grabbed the steering wheel. The car lurched to the side and spun out on the corner. The extreme centrifugal forces threw Sentrous off the roof, and he careened into the trees.

Boyd hit the accelerator again and spun the car around as Caracin landed on the roof and swung his head around to look at Boyd from the passenger window. Boyd swung his gun up, and Caracin pulled his head back up as the bullet shot out the window. Caracin held on as Boyd started weaving again. "Wahoo, this is so fun!" Caracin squealed.

Sentrous was now tracking along in the trees beside the speeding vehicle. "OK, you need to get this guy!" Sentrous called. Boyd was down to his last couple of bullets as he aimed at Caracin's claws. The gun went off, and the bullet impacted on Caracin's knuckles, splitting his skin. Caracin snatched his hand back as Boyd turned hard. Caracin careened off into the bushes.

"He shot me in the knuckle. Wow, that was fun!" Caracin exclaimed.

"You let him get away," Sentrous grumbled.

Alan had been moved to the waiting room. His lawyer showed up and began to demand his release. The desk officer got up and walked out as Boyd drove up in his demolished cruiser. The roof was peeled back, and claw marks decorated the paint and steel across the car. His clothes were in tatters from being grappled. Boyd was shaken and grasping for words as Alan and his lawyer came down the steps. Alan met Boyd's stare; he smiled as he spoke. "I see you met them."

"Wickey, come back here! What...the fuck...are those things?" Boyd yelled.

Alan stopped walking and turned. "Wish I could tell you, Boyd, but there is one thing I do know—they are real bastards."

Teddy pulled the chair back for Dr. Goodall, and she sat down. "What a gracious young man you are, Theodore, thank you." The small talk was kept to a minimum as Karen pulled out her MacBook and played the video footage from the house. Jane was shocked and amazed at the discovery. "They look extremely dangerous. It is as though they have recently started hunting humans," Jane remarked.

"Yes, probably a new routine for them. We would have known about it if they have been at it for a long time."

"Look at her arm and extensive manual dexterity—these are five-digit claws with an opposable thumb. I think this is a branch of cercopithecidae that must have broken off long ago. They are not even close to sapiens."

Karen opened up the gene map file. "I have finished running these genes, and they are remarkable—look at this, the telomere lengths and their open ends. This suggests that they have a very long lifespan. It's hard to determine population size because we have only one genetic individual. But I have a feeling that Alan has some more samples for us."

"You should tell your husband to keep well clear of these animals; they are probably remarkably strong."

"Yeah, he doesn't listen to my advice." Karen's phone buzzed twice. "It's Alan; he's on his way over. Apparently he spent last night in the police station; you can ask him your behavior questions. Maybe you can give me some insights on his behavior as well." Jane laughed at Karen's quip.

"Karen, you need to come and present your findings with me tomorrow in San Diego."

"I am not prepared. The data is a mess, and I can't draw and conclusions; there has been no review—"

Jane interrupted, "Your colleagues were going to present a paper based on one-tenth of the evidence you have here and they were going to walk away with your awards, darling."

Karen was quiet for a moment as her minded rushed through the implications. "OK, I will fly back with you."

Just then, Alan arrived. He sat down at the table, and Dr. Goodall asked him many questions about the appearance and behavior of the animals.

The next morning the news was awash with speculation as to the whereabouts of over the missing RCMP officers and military personnel. As Karen rolled her bags down to the taxi, she glared at Alan. Poking her finger into his chest, she said, "You keep my son clear of this mess; you hear me? You keep him away, and don't you leave him alone for a second, or I will have your balls for breakfast!"

"OK. I will stay with him, I promise."

"What is your plan?" Karen quizzed.

"I, uh, I've got something planned."

"Bullshit! You've got nothing planned. Come up with a plan and text me when you have it figured out. I want Teddy out of here. I swear, you will be a dead man if something happens to that boy." She exclaimed again as she got into the taxi, "Dead man!"

"OK, OK. I promise."

As Karen's taxi drove down the street, Alan dialed Kelly. "Hey, it's me. Yeah, I know. I thought for sure we would both be in jail for weeks. Yeah, I've got to get Teddy out of this horror show or Karen will kill me." Alan listened to Kelly for a moment. "Really, you'd do that for us? Kelly, that would be awesome; thank you."

On the plane, Dr. Wickey and Dr. Goodall worked furiously to prepare the data. The tables and figures all came together to suggest a startling conclusion. Jane called the editors at *Nature* to confirm that Malsner and Atkins were fraudsters, with only a partial theory based on anecdotal evidence.

Jane promised that both she and Karen would publish a fantastic article ready for the next edition due out in three months. Karen was working on the slides and the video as well as some still captures that had been enhanced. By the time they changed planes in San Francisco, Jane had over twenty scientists at Duke University working the findings. Once in San Diego, they sat down for a nice dinner at the conference center.

"I feel underprepared."

"Have you ever felt prepared before a giving a paper?" Jane asked.

"No, I suppose not."

"Situation normal, then." Jane smiled.

Dr. Richard Plank, a well-known geneticist, came across the restaurant floor and sat down at their booth. "Jane, hello, it's good to see you again." He kissed her cheek. "You must be Dr. Karen Wickey. You look like you should be on the cover of a fashion magazine, not starring into microscopes, my dear."

Karen's eyes narrowed as she tried to interpret his remark. "Doctor Plank, it's an honor to meet you."

Dr. Plank continued. "I hear rumors that you intend to announce an exciting new finding?"

Jane answered for Karen. "Yes, Richard, Karen has discovered something extraordinary, and you will get hear all about it in the morning."

Dr. Plank was visibly disappointed at missing out on a secret preview, but he graciously wished them luck and returned to his table. "I have a feeling that we are going to need some press protection because this is going to be very big news," Jane whispered.

Karen was amazed at the fantastic work that the Duke team had done overnight. The highlight was a 3-D model of the creature. All of the data had been checked and verified. She couldn't imagine ever having a research team like that. This was easily the best-looking paper and presentation she had ever seen, let alone presented. The theatre was packed with press; the rumours had obviously been circulating, and now reporters were starting to link this with the chaos that was occurring in Vancouver. CNN and CBC news were reporting that a police team had been attacked by a pack of crazed wolves. Many animal conservation experts were expressing their doubt about this theory. Fox News was speculating that it could be a family of Sasquatch doing the killings.

The large auditorium grew quiet as Dr. Plank spoke into the microphone. "Now for the last-minute addition that everyone has been so excited about, I am pleased introduce Dr. Karen Wickey, a fellow at the University of British Columbia in Vancouver. She had published many remarkable works on ageing and telomerase in cellular reproduction. But today I believe that she has been working with Dr. Goodall on a startling and recent discovery, but I will let her tell you about it." Dr. Plank put his hand out and welcomed Karen across the stage. She was temporarily blinded by the many flashes from the press that filled the aisles.

"Thank you for your gracious invitation to speak here at the GENIT conference. I am both excited and a little terrified at the prospect of showing you data from something so recent and so rough. I hesitate to present it as a formal paper. I ask that you take into account that there has not been enough evidence to truly verify these findings and I have only had time to map out less than a dozen genes in the sample. In any other circumstance, I would not be caught dead up here talking about data analysis that is so premature, but I have been urged by my friends and colleagues that the importance of these findings warrant this hasty and rough introduction. My sincerest apologies, but I do believe that once you see the essence of the evidence that my husband so haphazardly stumbled upon, you will be convinced that this talk is legitimate and warranted. I understand that there will be much scepticism so I have offered up a second animal sample for independent analysis. I would ask that the GEN society and the journal *Nature* strike up an independent review board to decide how to handle this second sample.

"Now for the good stuff. This October, my husband, Alan Wickey, was attacked by an animal in the suburban wilderness area in North Vancouver. He was very nearly killed by this animal and subsequently spent over a month recovering in the hospital from severe bite marks to his throat. The first slide shows pictures of Alan's wounds with the label 'Cougar Attack' and a police file number." There were some gasps in the audience. "He initially contended that this was no cougar but more like a huge monkey or gorilla type of creature that attacked him. This story got him some very good medication and a sympathetic pat on the head from all of us. Yet, from this encounter he produced a hair follicle and tissue sample. This sample was bizarre because it resembled a porcupine quill in some ways and polar bear fur in others. I was curious when I saw the tissue and listened to Alan's report of the account, so I did what any scientist would: I snuck it into my lab and ran a battery of tests on the both the quills and the tissue."

Pictures of the scanning electro-micrograph appeared, and Karen clicked through the different magnifications.

"I ran the key genes 234a and T 312cb first to get an idea of the general layout and genus. At this point, all I had to go on was a curious-looking quill and a husband that might have had too much Scotch one night." The audience laughed.

Karen clicked to the next slide, and it showed the gene sequences compared to Homo sapiens and the rhesus monkey genomes. The common markers were highlighted, and to Karen's surprise the sequences on the big screen suddenly spun around into a neat double helix coil.

"Wow, the guys at the lab have surprised us all with some cool 3-D animation. Let me point out the gene regions that are unique—here and here. Those of you in audience who are familiar with this chromosome will notice that this sequence is all new." The audience reacted with some gasps and whispers. "I don't know the genome well enough to even guess what these genes actually do, but whatever it is the trait seems to be unique to the species. Now let's look at the physiology of this animal from the very little evidence we have gathered."

Karen brought up the video file and played the fuzzy green footage from the home security camera.

"Here we have some interesting footage that shows the creature moving stealthily in a residence. I will pause the file and zoom in to show you this." The video depicted the colour change of the animal's coat; again the audience gasped, and reporters began to make cell phone calls.

"You will notice the arm length and stance. They share common traits with both humans and monkeys but not as much with gorillas and chimps; we have anecdotal evidence that they are tree dwellers and very agile climbers. There is also evidence that they may communicate in ultrasonic frequencies of fifteen to twenty kilohertz, which makes their calls impossible to hear with normal adult human hearing. Children can hear up to about sixteen to seventeen kilohertz, but us old folks cannot detect anything higher than twelve kilohertz."

Karen went on to show the long telomere caps on the genes and discussed some of the other traits to a silent hall. When she finished her presentation, she looked across the auditorium at the speechless crowd. She opened the floor up to questions, and the room erupted into a cacophony. Karen looked out at the sea of hands and picked one.

"Yes, you go ahead."

"What is this species' primary food source? They are carnivorous, aren't they?"

"Yes, it appears so." Karen answered the last question but avoided the first. "And with the yellow shirt, go ahead with your question."

"What's the genus, and where was the split?" the stoic-looking geneticist called out.

"Umm, this is the part where I feel embarrassed to say that we have not determined that with any certainty, but Dr. Goodall feels that it may be as far back as five to six million years ago, along the same lines as the cercopithecidae split. This chromosome shares the most markers in common with the black howler monkey," Karen explained.

"What do they eat?" The reporter's voice echoed across the auditorium.

Karen paused and swallowed hard. "We are not positive but our guess is berries, possibly moss or lichens, and maybe medium to large mammals." Karen tried to sneak in the last phrase, her voice quietening into a mumble, but the audience clearly understood what she meant.

"Humans?"

"We are not sure."

The crowd began to shuffle; the reporters raced back up the aisles and then out into the main hall to make their calls once again.

"Thank you very much," Karen said in closing. She nervously looked around the expansive room. The energy in the room was building; the sea of hands was silent for only a few seconds, and then the crowd heaved up towards the stage. Karen and Dr. Goodall were startled as the security guards moved to hold the stage wings open for them to leave. The flashes blazed, and questions began to fly at them. The two women scurried backstage and down a hallway. The two were not prepared for the vehement reaction of the media, who were demanding materials, photos, and the text for their news stories. They moved into the back parking lot where one of Dr. Goodall's students had arranged for a car. They hopped into the backseat with their satchels.

"That was frightening; are you used to that type of thing?" Karen asked Jane.

"I am a monkey scientist, not a movie star, and I have never had a crowd like that for anything," Jane replied. "Karen, we are going to need some more help on this matter. This whole discovery could get nasty in the next few months—I mean, before your findings are independently verified." Karen nodded in response.

In the meantime, every news team in the western and eastern hemispheres descended upon Vancouver.

21 Awareness

Shaman's claws clenched the jawbone and snapped it. The two pieces fell onto the cabin floor in the midst of her almost-complete human skeleton. The tiny television showed blurry green photos of Sartra in the human home. Shaman was horrified; she could sense that the time of awareness had arrived, but she assumed that Caracin and Sentrous would be the culprits that landed in the news, not the Salt clan leader and her long-time companion. She recognized Alan's photo as it flashed on the screen; he was dressed in a soldier's uniform adorned with medals. She watched and listened, but she could understand only a few of the human words that were spoken. After that news story had finished, she emerged out onto the snowy ridge and flew down into the trees. Her call rang out into the wilderness, and all stopped their actions and headed for an assembly. Sartra was the first one to meet her. Her face dropped with horror when she learned that it was her picture that may have brought about the time of awareness. She was speechless. She was already ashamed that the human hunting team had escaped out from under their grasp in the caves. She had ruled the clan with complete harmony and control for 120 years, and now everything was falling apart.

Shaman spoke to the group; she announced the bad news and tasked the sentries to travel up into the mountains to fetch the leaders of the three surrounding clans for a meeting at the sacred falls the next evening at sunset. The three sentries launched off into the forest heading in separate directions; their voyages were within a hundred miles in the case of the Ridge clan and the Moss clan, but the Whitelines were almost five hundred miles north. They would have to send sentries into the city to kill a few humans and collect some deer and rabbits for the assembly ceremonies at the Great Tusk. This was going to be different because the humans were going to be on alert. No one knew what this would mean. Would they have aircraft looking for them?

Shaman went with the sentry to hunt in the city. She wanted to see for herself if things were different. They flew through the trees and came down into the British properties. This was a very rich district spotted with large lawns, swimming pools, and multimillion dollar homes. They moved over top of the houses, going from tree to tree. They both heard the *wump wump* of rotor blades before the helicopter rushed over them. They descended halfway down the tree and clung to the thick trunk in camouflage. The aircraft did not spot them. They continued down the hill towards Ambleside Park in the hope of finding a suitable human lying on the beach or hiding in the bushes.

They stopped at the ridge above the Park Royal shopping mall and were amazed to see the huge congregation of satellite trucks and emergency vehicles assembled in the parking lot. There were three bright-coloured helicopters along with two dark-green helicopters. The many police cars and army trucks filled the big lot. Huge spotlights lit up the area, and hundreds of people were busy setting up tents and portable buildings. The two looked at each other, both feeling a sense of dread at the huge change in the humans' behaviour. There was no doubt that Sartra had been right—the humans were about to become very dangerous.

They continued on to the park and spotted a couple of men huddled together on a park bench. The young sentry set up in the trees in front of the two while Shaman snuck up behind them. Upon the short signal from Shaman, the sentry threw the grommets and struck the first one in the eye and the second one in the cheek. Neither had a chance to scream for help before Shaman had yanked them back into the bushes and pulled out their throats. The two spent lots of time cleaning up any items or footprints that would alert the humans; the blood would soak into the dirt, hidden deep in the bushes. Many people strolled by while the two worked in silence. When the carcasses were dressed and wrapped, they lifted their prey up into the trees and made their way back up into the mountains. It had been at least forty years since Shaman had hunted; she enjoyed the action but was stricken with a feeling of fear for the events to come.

Wendy's smile flashed again as she looked up at the big-screen TV in the window. The news was running endlessly on the situation in Vancouver. Wendy's slim form was obscured by her short leather jacket and high brown boots. Her straight long brown hair was tied back in a ponytail. The CNN banner read MAN VERSUS BIGFOOT at the bottom of the screen.

Teddy was getting sick of being hounded by the news crews at his house. Wendy had called him when she saw the story and invited him to go down to the mall for a coffee. Karen's face had been shown every two minutes for the past couple of days. "Your mom is pretty. I read her article in Nature. It was really technical but interesting." Teddy couldn't believe that Wendy was interested in his family and even him. "Your dad is some kind of war hero with medals and stuff?" she asked.

"Uh, yeah...he's saved hundreds of people's lives," Teddy said unenthusiastically.

"Cool. He's got the tall, dark, and mysterious thing happening, a bit."

"Yeah, I guess so."

Wendy could tell that he wanted to change the subject. "What's going on with you in math?" she asked.

"What do you mean?"

"You were totally at the top of the class, like Mr. A-plus, 100-percent dude for as long as I can remember. You got a D on the last test, and you were acting like you didn't even care."

"Had a bad day, I guess."

"Bad day, my ass; you also quit the soccer team and the swimming team." She walked along, speaking clearly while pretending to look at the sale rack in front of a girls' clothing store.

"How do you know what I got on the math test?"

"Your student number is the only one with a 115 code. It means you are an honours student, or were an honours student until you decided to go all teen rebel." Wendy smirked while looking up at the top floor.

"Who are you, the vice principal?" Teddy inquired.

"I pay attention." She playfully poked his shoulder, like Teddy's mom would poke his dad. He liked her attention; she seemed to be interested in him. His dad would neither know his grades nor care to ask about them. His mother cared, but often was too swamped with her career or the housework to spend time with him.

"You are totally, all Miss-glee-club-perfect girl."

"Shut up, am not; I can be bad…when I want to."

"Yeah what, put on black lipstick at Halloween?" he replied sarcastically.

She punched his shoulder three times in the same place. At first he just ignored the punches, but the last one hurt.

"Ow," he yelped.

"Don't be mean, Theodore Wickey."

"You're mean."

"Damn right; I'll kick your ass, Wickey boy." She punched him again in the same place.

"Ow!"

"Ow, ow, wittle Wickey boy, what's the matter; are you injured?" she said tauntingly as she backed out the door. The air from the mall rushed past Teddy's cheek out into the parking lot as he leapt out towards her. She howled with laughter as she ran along the walkway. He caught up with her quickly and grabbed her from behind while she laughed again, struggling to wrestle his arms free of her. She grabbed his hands and spun around to meet him face to face. He could smell her breath as she exhaled with exertion. She smelt like watermelon.

Their laughter echoed through empty causeway as Teddy held the young girl, his arms wrapped around her waist. She looked up into his eyes, hoping that he was going to get the hint and kiss her. She glanced over his shoulder at a small bump on the roof line— eyes, there were eyes on the roof. She jumped. "Oh my god, Teddy, there is a racoon or something on the roof over there, it scared me. It was staring at us."

Teddy turned around to see nothing on the roof. The bus pulled up to the shelter. They stepped up into the bus as Shaman and the sentry watched them through the bus windows as the noisy vehicle drive away.

"If I could catch that young boy, then we could lure his father into the forest again and kill him." She did not know that Caracin and Sentrous were working on the same plan.

The sentry frowned. "Yes, the last time we had him in the forest, it did not end well, Shaman." Shaman struck the sentry with her claws, slamming his face down onto the asphalt roof; her claws sank into the quills around his neck. She spoke calmly and quietly. "Sentry, I trust that you will hold your tongue from now on, lest you lose it suddenly."

With his face pushed into the gravel, his reply was muffled. "Yes, Shaman."

A few minutes later, Shaman inhaled and stopped. She turned to look down into the big parking lot. The skinned human body flopped on her back as she swung around and signalled to the sentry. He halted and looked down in the direction of her gaze. "I can smell Sartra's human, or maybe it's his son." Shaman pointed down towards the mall. They moved down to the roof of the structure. Their colours changed in unison, first to black asphalt and then to bronze aluminum.

Kelly stepped onto the dock at Granville Island. The fifty-foot sailboat lifted slightly as his weight left the teak deck. Alan looked along the hull lines of this beautiful vessel. The Italian-made Beneteau had been Kelly's dream since childhood. He had bought the boat last year and had taken it out only a few times. "Are you sure this is OK?" Alan asked for the second time.

"You need to spend some time with your boy, and you need to get out of here for a while, before the cops figure out some way to hold you."

"Yeah, you're right. Karen told me to keep him safe, and I won't be able to do that from a jail cell."

"You taught me how to sail, remember, buddy?" Kelly smiled.

"Yeah, I suppose I did."

"Have you been sailing with Teddy?"

"No, not really."

"Well, here is your chance to fix that glaring omission."

While the bus climbed the hill on Taylor Way, Teddy's cell phone chirped with a text from his father: *Teddy, go home and pack your bags. We are going on a trip.*

Dad, what's going on?

You and I are going on a mission.
A missing school kind of mission? Teddy texted the question.
Yes.
Nice!
Meet you at the apartment.

Wendy's head was resting on Teddy's shoulder as she read the texts from his father. "Where are you going?"

"I don't know."

"You want me to take notes for you in math?"

"Yeah, I guess so." Any other time, Teddy would have jumped for joy at the prospect of missing school, and being with his dad, but right now his arms were wrapped around the most amazing girl he could ever imagine. He hadn't even kissed her yet!

"I don't date D students and athletic dropouts."

"I thought you liked bad boys."

"You're not a bad boy; you're a good boy doing badly." These words stung Teddy a little. She watched his face carefully. "What are you going to do about it, Theodore?"

He reached over and held her cheek. She kissed him. The kiss was light and slow, her lips just barely touching his, and then she added more pressure for a second. Yup, watermelon and strawberries, he thought. She pulled away and put her finger on his lips. "Like I said, I don't date D students." The lights on the bus flickered as it pulled up to her stop. She stood up, facing him.

"I guess you'd better take good notes for me if I'm going to get an A without even being in class."

"If you get an A-plus on the next math exam, there will be a prize in it for you." She turned and walked down the aisle. His eyes tracked her long slim shape as she dropped down and out onto the street. *Wow, what a girl!*

22 The Melinda

Alan looked at his son's sombre face as the white lights reflected off the sailboat's long hull. The graceful *Melinda* glided effortlessly out of her mooring; the engine spat shots of water out of the small exhaust; the lights reflected off of the tiny wake. *What is he so pissed about?* Alan wondered.

"Where are we going?"

"Desolation Sound," Alan answered

"Sounds like a cheery place."

"What's got you so grumpy?"

"Oh, suddenly you give a shit now?" Teddy snapped back. Alan inhaled but then held back his words. Don't *react; do not react.* Alan leant back against the stanchion and gazed at his gangly boy. Teddy had grown at least an inch in the last month. He was over six feet now and judging by his size-fourteen running shoes, soon to be taller than Alan. He had his mother's square smile, green eyes, and fair hair. He had also inherited Karen's wit and clarity of thought. It was frustrating to have an argument with a teenager who could predict your answers.

"Take the wheel, Teddy, I have to go and do some chart work. Keep the green buoy to the starboard side." Teddy took the wheel and perked up; he had never been at the helm of a big boat before. The pre-dawn darkness was peppered with many coloured navigation lights as they slipped beneath the Burrard Street Bridge. The wind was light as the eastern sky began to glow with the rising sun. February winds were chilly but not below freezing, the stars slowly disappeared into the haze of the dawn light. The sea air filled Alan's lungs; this was one of the few places in Canada where the ocean wasn't frozen in the winter. Vancouver winters were mild, dark, and wet. High winds would tear at the coastline from October to March. Hurricane-force winds were a regular occurrence on the rugged outside coast. Alan plotted a course up the inside passage of the five-hundred-mile-long island. Here the weather was sheltered, and the hundreds of islands and bays made it one of world's most beautiful cruising areas. Desolation Sound was halfway up the inside passage, and the trip would take about four days. The great explorer, Captain Vancouver himself, named this area after struggling to get his heavy frigate HMS *Discovery* up the inside passage against the shifting winds and tides. The dark-green cedars topped the sheer granite cliffs. Under the cloudy grey skies, this coastline could certainly look desolate and remote, yet once the sun came out, the place was transformed into a beautiful Shangri-La of emerald-green water and rainforest. Here you could steer the boat up and touch the rocky cliff and still have five hundred feet of water under your keel.

After an hour, Alan came up on deck and lifted up the lazarette hatch, located at the very stern of the boat. He reached in and pulled out a mop-headed, half-stuffed, four-legged doll. The little lamb's body was made out of old fish floats and rope ends. Its cartoon eyes were coloured in permanent marker, and the mop fibres flopped over its little black nose. "Teddy, I would like you to meet Fluffy the lamb."

"Cute—a sailor's girlfriend?"

Alan chuckled at his son's sharp wit. "Don't piss off the little lamb, or she gets upset." Alan bounced the lamb's head up and down and made it talk in a shrill voice. "Hello, Teddy, sometimes I get very depressed being stuck in the locker my whole life, and I just want to end it all."

Teddy's face scrunched up. He looked up towards the mast and then shook his head.

Alan's little shrill voice became a whisper. "Yes, Teddy, I am ending it all. Good-bye." Alan perched little float doll on the rail and then flung it overboard into the sea. The little creature bobbed in the wake of the vessel as they sped away.

"Lamb overboard!" Alan bellowed loud enough to knock the leaves off the trees of nearby islands. Teddy jumped in fright as his dad jumped to his feet and pointed out to the floating fluff ball. "Lamb overboard!" he repeated as Teddy snapped into the realization that he was in the middle of one of his father's legendary surprise drills. Teddy stood up and checked over his shoulder.

"OK, OK, lamb overboard," Teddy replied as he spun the wheel. The vessel swung around in a big circle.

Alan kept yelling, "Fifty feet off the port bow!" He moved up to the bow, his outstretched arm pumping up and down, pointing at the bobbing object. Teddy stood up, one hand on the wheel, as he struggled to locate the tiny object. Then he spotted it.

"OK, Dad, I am going to bring her along the port side—get the boat hook!" Teddy ordered.

"Roger port side, ready," Alan replied, surprised at the many steps Teddy had mysteriously mastered. The boat slowed as Teddy pulled back the throttle, and the little lamb bobbed up to the drop ladder, as if to wait for Alan's outstretched arm. Alan reached out and fished Fluffy out of the sea. Teddy swung the boat around back to the original course. Alan made his way back to the cockpit, wet lamb in his arms. He sat down. Teddy's matter-of-fact expression almost hid his excitement at kicking ass in the man overboard drill.

"Maybe you should give Fluffy some of your Prozac." Alan was too stunned at his son's outstanding demonstration of seamanship to notice the jab.

A few hours later, Alan appeared in the companionway and projected his voice up to his son. "Teddy, slow her down and we'll get the sails up for crossing the straights." Teddy nodded and pulled the throttle back to idle. Alan came up and began to loosen the blue cover and the sail ties. Teddy left the wheel and went up onto the bow to ready the jib sail. Once the sails were loose, Alan went back the helm and nodded to Teddy as he began to haul up the mainsail and then the jib. The huge sails flapped for a moment until Teddy came back to the cockpit and Alan swung the boat away from the wind. The two sails made a thwap as they filled; thousands of pounds of wind pressure pushed the multi-ton Italian thoroughbred over to a heel as she accelerated towards the open straights.

"We will cross overnight while the weather is still friendly." Alan spoke over the sound of the breeze and small waves washing along the hull. "Teddy, where did you learn how to sail so well?"

Teddy shook his head. "I have sailed every summer since I was ten. I have my bronze level four, Dad." Teddy emphasized the last word. "You don't remember because you were off on one of your overseas holidays."

Alan took another deep breath and waited. "Yeah, I guess I was off sun tanning in Kandahar, or skinny dipping in Helmand Province." Although it was a flippant reply to his son's sarcastic comment, he kept his tone neutral.

"Yeah, I bet it was a party." Teddy led with another baiting comment, but Alan did not reply this time. He had missed much of this boy's childhood; Teddy's feelings about it were justified. His anger was tangible, and this was the first time Alan had stopped to listen to more than a sentence. *This may be a long boat ride*, Alan thought. The western sky gave up its evening twilight to the inky darkness. Clouds rolled along, silhouetted in front of a full moon that hung low on the horizon. Alan noticed that the clouds were moving fast. This was in contrast to the light ten-knot surface winds that pushed the *Melinda* across the Salish Sea.

Protected from the Pacific by Vancouver Island, the Straights of Georgia could still offer up heavy seas and high winds. Alan could see the weather coming and realized that they were not going to make the twenty-mile crossing before getting hit by the squall. The big sailboat was built for offshore cruising, and she handled the building seas handsomely. Rising and falling, her wake cut a white foamy diagonal line across the ragged wave tops. The *Melinda* heeled over and sped up to meet the challenge. Teddy was enjoying being at the wheel; his years racing around the yacht club at the helm of a Laser dinghy made handling the big boat second nature. He didn't get nervous when the strong gusts drove the rig lower into the water and the big hull leapt up to meet the face of the next series of waves. Alan looked up at his son. Teddy was smiling and relaxed as he spun the wheel the back and forth to keep the track steady across the long train of seas.

"Two hundred ninety degrees magnetic should get us over to Porlier Pass; you will see the green flashing light once we get a little closer." Alan projected his voice up to Teddy, who replied, "Ok green flash; got it, Dad." The wind built from the southwest and spray began to blow off the tops of the waves. The icy saltwater stung as it hit Teddy's red cheeks. He didn't seem to mind, or was not about to show his father that he was either tired or cold. Alan could tell the winds were approaching thirty knots steady. It was time to reef the mainsail and roll in the jib a little. A big gust of wind pushed the *Melinda* too far over on her beam. The sudden lurch startled both Alan and Teddy. "Dad?" Teddy's voice was a little uneasy as Alan came up on deck to make the adjustments.

"Hey, buddy, you are doing great. I am just going to shorten the sail a little."

As soon as Alan reefed the main, the *Melinda* popped up as if to sigh a breath of relief. Alan made a few more adjustments, and the boat charged along towards the black silhouettes of the Gulf Islands. Alan went below, came back up with a hot chocolate, and sat down.

Teddy was enjoying the challenge of steering the big boat to go fast in the blustery wind. "Teddy, I made you some dinner. It's down there on the settee." He got up after Alan had taken the wheel and went down below to eat. His arms and legs were stiff from the icy wind and spray, and the hot soup tasted especially good. Alan had laid out a basket of fresh buns, and the boy stuffed them in his mouth one after the other. Sitting at the small table, he looked at his dad's chart work. The boat's course was drawn in a narrow triangle to take into account the wind and tide. The course that Alan had given him didn't actually point directly at the entrance to the narrow passage between Galliano and Valdez Islands. The course pointed off to one side, but this would allow the boat to move along almost sideways against the wind and tide.

They were heading directly to the entrance, skittering across the ocean like a crab running across the sand. *This is cool, how does he do that?* he thought. The lines looked like a basic vector triangle, much like the ones he was supposed to be drawing in physics. Lately he had been clowning around in his physics class; his mark had dropped from an A+ to a D. Teddy picked up the navigation book from the bookshelf and scanned through it. *I wonder if there is a YouTube video on this stuff.*

Teddy went up to join his father as the yacht slipped into the lee of the mountains on Valdez Island. This pass was quickly approaching; the jagged rocks rose sharply from the breaking waves. The seas still rolled under the vessel's keel as Alan lined up the navigation lights on the shore to ensure that they would stay in the middle of the channel.

"This is going to be a bit of a ride, because we are going through with a four-knot tide—this means the current will be pushing us along through the pass. We will have to keep up our speed to be able to steer." Alan stood up and tapped the wheel. "You're going to steer us through the dreaded Porlier Pass."

"Uh...Are you sure you want me to drive?" Teddy was nervous.

"Yup, just keep her in the middle of the channel, and I will tell you when to alter to port," Alan replied as the boat was taken into the pass by the shifting current. Alan reached down and increased the throttle.

"Why are you speeding up?" Teddy asked.

"We need to keep our speed up to maintain steering; the water needs to moving past the rudder, or you will lose control."

"Oh, yeah." Teddy's voice came out at a higher pitch. The currents and swirls twisted and pulled at the *Melinda*. Teddy responded instinctually on the wheel as he struggled to keep the bow pointed straight in the passage. The outline of the trees whizzed by them as he concentrated on maintaining his course. His heart pounded from the adrenaline. He looked up at his father. Alan was smiling.

"I can't remember the last time I saw you smile, Dad."

"Neither can I, now that you mention it." The waters calmed as they moved into the islands. Teddy had done well, and he was pleased with himself. He remained on the wheel until the sun perked up over the mountains and the beams of light flashed through the trees.

"How far do we have to go?"

"We don't have to go anywhere, but the place I had in mind is another three days' sail north," Alan answered.

Later that night Teddy woke with the movement of the boat. Alan watched him from the cockpit as his blanket-covered figure stirred on the bunk. He stepped up into the hatchway. "How's it going up here, Dad?"

"It's going OK; it's still pretty windy. Did you sleep?"

"Yeah, how long was I out?"

"A couple of hours."

"Where are we?"

Alan pointed to the red flashing lights high up on the horizon. "That's Winchesley Island; we are back in the open straights now."

"Sounds like a guy could use some coffee."

"You make great coffee; that would be nice, Teddy," After serving his father a coffee, Teddy sat down at the chart table and wrote out the GPS coordinates on a notepad. He placed a small circle on the chart and traced out a course line heading northwest, parallel to the shoreline. The purple-and-pink light began to creep up from the eastern sky. The small screen that sat above the navigation station showed the charted area around the vessel.

"Dad, do you know that we are in the middle of a weapons-testing range?"

"Yeah, it's called area Whiskey Gulf. It's not active today, so we are OK."

"How do you know it's not active?"

"They announce its status on the VHF radio."

Teddy turned the dials on the radio; the speakers barked out static as he returned the squelch control to its proper position. "The wind is picking up again. You can see the stratus clouds forming over to the southwest," Alan said as Teddy turned the radio to the weather channel. The radio spieled the continuous marine broadcast as Teddy wrote down the details.

"Dad, look—old school, with a pen and no iPhone."

Alan laughed. "Yeah, old school. Good work, Teddy."

The marine weather report called for more gale-force winds in the *Melinda*'s path. Teddy reported the weather to his father and then turned the radio back to channel 16. As Teddy reached the channel, the sound of a loud two-tone alarm resonated in the cabin and out to the cockpit.

"Dad, is that a Mayday," Teddy shouted over the noise. Alan nodded.

The message followed the alarm: "Mayday relay, Mayday relay, Mayday relay—this is Comox Coast Guard radio, Mayday; the forty-five-foot sailing vessel *Nelson's Prize* is disabled and drifting towards the rocks on the south side of Yeo Island. Any vessels that may be able to assist the *Nelson's Prize* please contact Comox Coast Guard Radio on this channel."

"Dad, is that near us?"

"Yeah, I think so. Here, take the wheel, Teddy." Teddy came up and took the wheel, and Alan moved to the chart table to measure the distance to the small group of rocky islands ahead of them. Teddy waited anxiously. Alan came up with a cup of coffee and handed it to Teddy and sat down. Now Teddy was almost frantic as he waited. Alan sat quietly with a smile.

"Dad, is it close?"

"Yeah, it's up ahead about four miles."

"Well, are you going to call in? Are we going to rescue them?"

"Not so fast, my little man; let's just listen and see what's going on before we jump into anything." The radio crackled again. "Mayday, Mayday, this is the sailing vessel *Nelson's Prize*; I have struck a reef on Yeo Island, and I require assistance immediately!" The voice was that of an older man with a mild English accent; the urgency in his voice told the story of a man and his vessel in jeopardy.

Teddy tilted his head and glared at Alan. "Dad!"

"OK, OK, that sounds close. I will report in to Comox." Alan returned to the radio. "Mayday…Comox Coast Guard radio, Comox Coast Guard radio; this is the sailing vessel *Melinda*." Alan's voice was cool and practiced. The radio crackled with a reply.

"Sailing vessel *Melinda*, Comox; go ahead please."

"Comox, *Melinda*; we are northbound heading for Yeo Island. Our estimated time of arrival is twenty minutes. Would rescue centre like us to proceed to assist the *Nelson's Prize*?" The radio was silent for a second.

"Sailing vessel *Melinda*, Comox Coast Guard radio…yes; rescue centre would like you to proceed and assist the *Nelson's Prize*."

"Roger, Comox; *Melinda* will proceed, and we will advise you when we arrive on scene."

"Dad, holy cow! We are actually going on a rescue!" Teddy jumped up and down.

"OK, buddy, chill dude. The chances are, the coast guard will get there before us, and they will stand us down." Alan smiled at Teddy's enthusiasm; he recalled his first rescue call and how exciting it had been. "Why don't you go down and check my math for the ETA on the chart while I speed us up a little with the engine?" Teddy jumped down to the chart table and punched the numbers on the calculator.

The *Melinda* dipped her nose through the green spray; the sputtering engine gurgled through the transom as the propeller surged up and down in the choppy seas. Alan handed the wheel to Teddy; he then trimmed in the foresail to bring the racing hull close to its maximum speed. "Drive it like you stole it, Teddy," Alan said. Teddy was handling the big vessel like a racing dinghy, using the helm to keep the wind spiralling across the big white sails. The engine only added a knot or two of speed, but this was a rescue. Teddy's heart was racing as fast as his thoughts. What would the rescue be like? How bad was the *Nelson's Prize*? Was she sinking? He listened as the distress message was repeated on the VHF. Alan came up from down below with a coffee in his hand.

"Nice work, son. We are making ten knots, and we will be able to see her soon; so keep an eye out over there on the port bow." Teddy nodded.

The current pushed them along into the narrow passage and the waves curled, sometimes standing up like haystacks in their path. Alan guided Teddy through the rock piles and thrashing white water.

"Teddy, mind your course while I get the dinghy ready." Teddy took a few deep breaths as the panic passed; he spotted the stricken sailing vessel.

"Dad, that's her! Look, she's sideways to the rocks." The royal-blue hull of the sailing cruiser was being held off the rocks by her anchor line, but she was swinging back and forth in the stiff wind, her stern only feet from the jagged reef. A tall white-haired man was waist deep in the ocean, trying to hold the fifteen-ton sailing yacht from being smashed. He was clearly in trouble and only minutes from being swept up into the surf. Alan stood on the deck with the binoculars and then took the wheel from Teddy.

"Teddy, go forward and drop the sails when I get her up into the wind. You are going to keep us on station in the bay while I row in and pass the *Nelson's Prize* a towline."

"OK, Dad." Teddy dropped the mainsail and rolled in the headsail as they snapped wildly in the wind. He pushed down the throttle to keep some forward momentum on the long hull.

"Teddy, here is the plan—you are going keep the *Melinda* steady here, and I will row in and pass him the towline. Then I will row the line back out, and we will pull him out of there."

"Is your line going to be long enough?" Teddy asked.

"You just worry about your job, and I'll worry about mine." Alan dropped the small inflatable tender over the side and zipped his life jacket. The skipper of the *Nelson's Prize* had watched the *Melinda* sail in and now struggled to find the strength to pull himself back onto his boat. Alan pushed away from the rail, and the towline spooled out behind his little rowboat. Teddy kept the *Melinda's* bow into the wind.

Alan spun the little boat around on the oars and met the old sailor's eyes. "Good day, Captain. I will pass you this line and once you have secured it onto to your bow, I will row out and pass it to the *Melinda;* that is, if that is OK with you. " Alan tossed the line, but the wind caught it and it dropped between his boat and the man's outstretched arms. Alan swore loudly as he sat back down and began to row the boat over to grab the line out of the water, but before he could reach it, the rope was gone.

Alan looked up to see the man's gaze drawn by something going on behind his shoulder. Alan turned to see a huge wave breaking over him. The small dinghy was tipped up onto its side by the curling surf. Alan was nearly thrown over by the violent roll. He was now struggling to keep control of the dinghy and turn it around to face the next big wave. The sea crashed over him, filling the dinghy half full of seawater. Alan reached and began to scoop the water out of the boat. He and the dinghy had been swept away from the stricken sailboat. Alan worked his way back up through the churning white water sideways towards the blue hull. Rowing furiously he pulled the small inflatable boat around for another try. The man was waiting for Alan with his arms outstretched. A coil of white braided line sprung by Alan's shoulder and landed squarely in the hands of the elder man.

Alan turned to see the big stern of the *Melinda* only a few feet from him; she was backed deep into the small bight. The three-bladed propeller was leaping up and down in the shallow surf as Teddy used the throttle and the wheel to keep her transom square to the beach. Once the new towline had been tied firmly by the man, Teddy hit the throttles, and the *Melinda* pushed up through the big curling surf, trailing the new towline behind her. The man smiled as he signalled the thumbs-up to Alan. Alan rowed hastily out to the *Melinda,* where Teddy was trying to steer her and work the long towline at the same time.

"What the hell are you doing?" Alan yelled on approach. His booming voice startled Teddy. Alan secured the dinghy and leapt up onto the deck. "You are acting like an idiot!" His voice rang across the water. Teddy's lip began to quiver as he wrestled with the long line, then his eyes looked back to the blue sailboat. Alan realized that Teddy had successfully gotten the *Nelson's Prize* under tow and he had to snap out of his mood and act fast; this was the most vulnerable time in the of towing another vessel. They had to get the towline into position and bring the two vessels into alignment. Alan grabbed the wheel and hit the throttle as Teddy continued to tie the line off to the winch. Once Teddy finished the knot, Alan pushed the throttle lever down to full speed and the line came taut, springing out of the water. Like a horse jumping up from a fall, the long blue sailboat lurched up out of her stricken pose. The silver-haired captain released his anchor line to allow his boat to be freed from the reef. Alan carefully piloted the two vessels through the narrow pass and into the open water.

Alan's rebuke had shaken Teddy. He tried explain, but the words didn't sound right, and Teddy was just quiet.

Later that afternoon, the *Nelson's Prize* sat at anchor in Schooner Cove. Her captain rowed over to the *Melinda*. The man stood on the deck of the *Melinda* with a wine bottle in the pocket of his life jacket. He grabbed Alan's outstretched hand and gripped it with both of his hands. "Thank you for saving my life, and my fine ship; both of which mean a great deal to me. My name is Gary Greenspan, and I owe you a great debt." Alan thought he recognized the name.

Alan touched his shoulder. "I am Alan Wickey, and this is my son, Teddy. We were glad to be able to help. It was heartbreaking to see such a beautiful boat so near to ruin."

"Yes, I was in a spot of trouble to be sure," Gary replied. He had also recognized Alan.

Gary offered up the bottle of wine, and Alan accepted it. As they sat across the settee from each other, Gary said, "How old are you, Teddy?"

"I am fifteen, sir."

"Well, I must say, my young coxswain, that was some of the finest seamanship and boat handling I have ever witnessed. And I have seen my share of boat driving. Your skill in backing down into that rock pile was astonishing, and I don't offer praise lightly." Teddy shot a glance across at his dad, and Alan looked down while shifting his position. "Alan, we have met before; in fact, you worked for me about twenty years ago in CFB Gander, Newfoundland."

Alan suddenly realized who he was speaking with. "Admiral Greenspan, I am sorry I didn't recognize you, sir."

"It's just Gary now. Alan, it is good to see that you are doing well. I heard that you were wounded in Kandahar."

"Yes, sir. I was hit by an IED."

"Just call me Gary," he said. "Can I offer you a glass of port?"

"I, uh…don't drink anymore." Alan was feeling a little uncomfortable now.

"What about a glass for your young skipper?" Gary asked gingerly, sensing there was some tension between father and son. Teddy looked up at his dad for approval, and Alan thought about it for a moment. "Yes, I suppose one glass would be OK." Gary poured Teddy a glass of the deep-red tawny.

"Port is the original drink of sailors, long before anyone brought a cask of rum to sea." Gary spoke for a while; he explained that he had retired from the navy after thirty-five years of service retiring as the admiral of the Atlantic fleet. He had lost his wife to cancer just a few months earlier and was on a two-month solo sailing expedition up the inside passage of Vancouver Island. Trouble had begun when he wrapped a crab-trap line in his propeller. The *Nelson's Prize* had been unable to manoeuvre, and the wind pushed her into the bay and up on the shoreline. He had jumped into the shallow water to pull the trap line free and to attempt to keep his boat from the rocks.

"I fear that I was only moments away from real trouble—both my boat and my bones were in danger of being broken."

After a while, Teddy announced that he was taking the dinghy ashore for a walk on the beach. Alan could tell that his son was still upset as Teddy left for his walk.

"You all right, Alan?" Gary searched Alan's eyes.

"I was a little too hard on Teddy today."

"Yes, taking matters into his own hands, making command decisions on the fly. It sounds like you, actually. I can't recall your exact words to me when I busted you for similar actions. Do remember what you said?"

Alan replied sheepishly, "Something like, it's only wrong if you can't pull it off."

"Yes, if I remember correctly, that little quote spread out as a favourite on the lips all the new cocky A-school grads." Alan smiled and nodded.

"That boy is your gift. You only get a couple of chances, Alan, and then it's too late. I know all about being too late." Alan acknowledged him with a nod. "I have to haul out the *Nelson's Prize* tomorrow in order to inspect the propeller shaft and rudder for damage. May I borrow your son as a deckhand tomorrow? I'm still a little shaken up and I might need a hand getting my boat into the shipyard cradle for the inspection."

The next morning, the *Nelson's Prize* slipped through the water; Gary was at the wheel while Teddy worked up on the bow getting the anchor stowed and the bowlines ready for securing to the haul-out cradle. The trip to the shipyards was about an hour's sail south to Nanaimo. Unlike the previous day, the straights were calm. The sun peaked through the nimbus clouds. Alan had the *Melinda* under sail about a quarter of a mile behind them. He was still kicking himself for being so hard on Teddy. He would have done the exact same thing in Teddy's situation. The admiral was right; he choose not to follow orders many times in his career. Sometimes this was a good move and sometimes not.

"Gary, what was my dad like back in the olden days?"

Gary smiled. "He was a legend, and a legendary pain in the ass. I was his base commander so I wasn't his buddy or anything. You have to understand that your dad has been through hell on a few round trips. Even one of these traumatic incidents could have turned an ordinary man into an emotional pretzel; your dad has survived a half dozen of these situations."

"Why was he a legend?"

Gary paused for a moment to arrange his recollections. "In 1993, the *Silver Purveyor* transmitted a Mayday after being struck by a ten-story wave, four hundred fifty miles north east of St. John's, Newfoundland. She was a one-hundred-twenty-thousand ton bulker out of Antwerp, loaded with iron ore. This ship was in a bad way. The twenty-seven crew sat paralyzed with fear as they watched the midship cargo hatch lift off the ship like an orange peel. The fifty-five-ton hatch was gone, and the sea plunged in the cargo hold. The next wave rolled across the huge ship from stem to houseworks, and the sea began to twist the ship's bones to the breaking point.

"'Mayday, Mayday, this is the *Silver Purveyor,* we are going down!' I could hear the first mate plead with St. John's Coast Guard Radio. You see, Teddy, there was a vicious fifty-knot icy spray that was freezing and building on the ship's decks with every wave. The Newfoundland storms were notoriously dangerous because the ice spray would rapidly form on the vessel's decks, adding many tons of weight. My phone rang at three a.m. to let me know that Rescue 318 had taken off for the *Silver Purveyor*'s last reported position. Rescue 318 was a fixed-wing C-130 airplane with two SAR techs on board; your dad was one of them."

Teddy was transfixed as Gary spoke.

"On the first pass, the flight crew could not believe their eyes—the ship was breaking in half as they watched. All of the forward cargo section—more than three-quarters of the ship—was separated from the stern. The crew were trapped in the back piece that held the houseworks and bridge. This piece was now floating away from the other section. The stern was now facing straight up at the sky, and the crew were hanging from the walls inside the bridge. If I had been able to see this, I would have never let the SAR techs jump, but this was not my call. There were twenty-seven ship's crew who were about to be lost, as the plane watched. The coast guard ship *Teleos* was on the way with an estimated time of arrival of about three hours. This was what motivated the SAR techs to parachute onto the broken stern piece. The pilot did a few practice runs to make sure the jumpers would not miss their target. Scott Denton jumped first, and your dad paused for a second or two before he jumped. After your dad's chute opened, he was vectoring in for his landing and a huge wave hit the stern section! The whole thing rolled over onto its side, right underneath your dad's feet. He landed on the side of the hull and had to clamber up to the rail, as the hull rolled. He had no idea if the crew were still alive or not."

Gary used his hands to show how the ship's stern wallowed in the huge waves. Teddy was quiet and intently listening.

"Were they alive?" he asked.

"I'll get to that." Gary continued, "Alan got to the bridge to find that some of the crew had already jumped into the sea in their life jackets, but nine men were left clinging to the rails. Your dad could hear 318 repeatedly calling SAR Tech Denton for a SITREP, but he wasn't answering. Alan could see that the stern section was sinking and could roll over at any time. They had to get off the ship quickly.

He moved the men down to the boat deck and wrestled the raft capsule free of the sideways rack. He pulled the pull cord out to the end; the last yank trigged the compressed air canister and the fibreglass capsule split open and the rubber raft crawled free of its cocoon. The bright-orange tented shape inflated in front of the crew. But it was still at least twenty feet from the water. Your dad tried to wrestle it down to the water, but the wind crept underneath it. The whole four-hundred-pound raft leapt up into the air and began buck and lurch like a wild horse. The ballast flaps that collected water and weighted it down to the sea's surface did not have enough chance to fill. Before they could get in, the raft blew up with Alan hanging on to the tie lines; he would not let go as he was pulled over the rail and out into the sea. The raft dragged Alan as it tumbled like a beach ball across the waves. He had no choice—this raft was going to drag him away from the ship. He let go of the raft and began the frantic swim back to the ship; the icy swim almost killed him as he struggled to make it back to the sinking ship. His snorkel was high enough above the frozen sea foam that he could breathe. He had to pop his head way up to see the ship and then he would duck down and plow through the torrents with his strong stroke. He pulled himself back onto the ship, over the rail, and lay down gasping on the sideways deck.

"Discouraged, some the crew had decided to jump into the sea, so they made their way down to the boat deck, but Alan raised his hand to stop them, and with every ounce of strength left in his body, he pulled himself to his feet. He knew they wouldn't survive the icy North Atlantic. Alan worked his little line of scared ducklings up a deck to the only remaining lifeboat. The big red enclosed boat was lying sideways. Alan wasn't sure if she would launch properly at this angle, but this was their only chance. He worked the tiedowns loose and pulled the break; the lifeboat wallowed and rolled sideways out over the rail. It bumped and dragged itself to the water's edge. The orange floating capsule was lying on its side, but the crew managed to crawl inside and strap in. Alan broke the glass cover and pulled the onload hook release, and the lifeboat tumbled down the side of the hull and hung, tangled, upside down across the stern of the ship. They were about ten feet from the water; all the passengers screamed and panicked as they hung precariously. Alan waited. A huge wave the size of an apartment building swept over the whole ship. They tumbled into the sea upside down. These enclosed lifeboats are designed for this, so it self-righted and drifted away from the ship. The *Silver Purveyor* rolled over and sank right in front of them; her propellers were still turning as she dropped into the sea. The churning sea was lit up by the lights on the ship as it descended into the depths. They were rescued by the coast guard ship *Teleos* two hours later."

"What about the other guy?"

"Denton was never found—there was no personal locator beacon signal, no light or radio transmission. He had just disappeared into the storm."

Teddy was dumbfounded; he had never heard this story. He had only ever heard a few of his dad's stories. Gary spoke again. "You should give your dad a break. As I said I didn't know him really well, but one thing that I remember about him is that he never gives up, at anything."

"I don't know about that," Teddy grumbled. Gary chuckled and pushed on Teddy's shoulder. "Life's long, kid; don't get too worked up about any one minute in it."

"Hmm." Teddy sat and thought for a moment.

A few hours later, the *Nelson's Prize* sat up in the giant lift as the three walked around the hull looking for damage. The propeller shaft was a little bent.

"Wow, she looks pretty clean, considering," Alan said.

"Yes, I am a lucky man. Maybe some of that lucky Wickey magic is wearing off on me." Gary smiled. "Oh, I told your boy about the *Purveyor* incident. I thought that he needed to hear it."

Alan's face dropped with a little sadness. "Oh…OK, sure; did you tell him about Scotty?"

"Yes."

"OK…yeah, sure," Alan repeated quietly.

With a handshake and backslap, they parted ways. Alan and Teddy sailed north, and Gary stayed with his boat at the shipyard. Gary envied Alan; what a fine boy he had.

The *Melinda* sailed herself on a beam reach. When a hand pulled on the wheel carelessly, she would recoil with an indignant pull to windward, like a cat swatting at your hand. Teddy had a better feel for her than Alan. All those years of dinghy sailing paid off, he thought as he watched Teddy handle the boat up to windward for a tack.

"Helm's a lee, Dad!" he hollered as the big form swung the eye of the wind, the sails flapping while they waited for Alan to trim them in. "Come on, Dad; don't be so slow, old man!" She settled into the next tack and accelerated.

"Did you know Kelly's wife, Melinda?" Teddy inquired

"Oh yeah, sure, we were all very close. She loved to take care of you when you were a baby."

"How did she die?"

"Overdose."

"Oh, I didn't know that."

"Yeah, none of us talk about it much."

"Why?"

"Why don't we talk about it, or why did she do it?"

"Why did she do it?"

"Who knows, she was just a really sad person. They tried to have kids and they couldn't; that's why she liked to babysit you so much. She got more depressed as time went by; Kelly was either in Afghanistan or up north with the Rangers. She was lonely, I guess."

"Did Kelly ever get over it?"

"You don't get over something like that. You just push on." Alan tapped the top of the winch with his hand. "Melinda had always wanted a boat, so Kelly cashed out his military pension and bought this beauty in her honour."

"Does he sail much?"

"Not much. I think he gets sad when he is out here by himself without his wife."

"That's kind of sad."

"Yeah, it is…whew, let's listen to some music. Why don't you put on some of that crazy music in your iPod?"

"Sure, I'll put it on." Teddy dropped down and plugged his iPod into the stereo. "I don't have any old man music; sorry. You're just going to have to put up with the good stuff." The *Melinda* sailed along the waves, the lapping on her hull in time to the beat of the music. The little ship worked her way up the coast, past Quadra Island and then across to Desolation Sound. Two days later they arrived at a magical place.

"OK, Teddy, we approaching Teakern Arm. There's a trick to this place; we anchor off the bow and then we run two stern lines across to iron rings in the cliff. You can row across in the dinghy or you can swim them over; it's up to you."

Teddy looked ahead; he couldn't believe how cool this place was. Two high cliffs surrounded a deep inlet with a huge waterfall. The falls shot out of the rocks like a fire hose, and the water landed directly in the deep green sea. The rocky cliff dropped straight down into the depths. It looked as if you could push the bow of the boat right up into the falls and still be in hundreds of feet of water. Alan readied the anchor and the two stern lines as Teddy steered her into the narrow gulch. The mist from the falls swirled around the boat as Alan stood on the bow giving Teddy hand directions. Deeper and deeper they went towards the falls. Alan knew that the only shallow water for anchoring was almost directly below the falls. He waved Teddy in, but Teddy was hesitant; it looked like the falls were going to crash right on the bow. When the bow was only a few feet away from the crashing water, Alan let the anchor go; the chain rolled out fifty, then seventy-five feet, then hit the rocky bottom. Alan signalled to start backing down on the anchor, but Teddy was already on this.

He pulled the throttle in reverse, and the big boat pulled back until the anchor held fast on the rocks below. The *Melinda* pulled to a stop.

"OK, buddy, now it's time for a race if you're up for it. You and I are going to pull these stern lines to those cliffs and tie up to those rings in the cliff face. Let's get changed into our swim shorts, and we will…" There was a splash, and Alan turned around to see that Teddy had jumped into the cold water with his clothes on. He gasped for a moment and then, with the rope over his shoulder, he started for the cliff. Alan laughed as he plunged over the side in his clothes; his competitive nature forced him to swim hard. His strong strokes pulled through the water as he accelerated to the cliff face. The heavy line made the swimming hard, but he made it to the edge and then began to climb up the ten feet to the ring. He threw the line through the old rusty loop and tied the bowline tight. He looked across, expecting to have to swim over and help his son. The other line was tied onto the ring, and Teddy was gone. Alan climbed up higher to see the water on the other side; maybe Teddy was swimming back to the boat.

"Dad!" The teenage voice echoed back and forth across the small gorge. Alan looked up. Teddy had not only beaten his father but had also scaled the fifty-foot cliff to the top. To Alan's horror he was waving from the top.

"Come on up! You're the big rescue guy; why are you so slow?"

Alan suppressed his urge to yell at his son for climbing the dangerous, sheer cliff. He took a deep breath, swam over to Teddy's side, and clambered up the cliff. As he reached the top, he panted. He looked at his young son who was teaming with enthusiasm and energy.

"Let's jump from that ledge down over there," Teddy said.

"Yeah, that's probably not a good—" Alan stopped in mid-sentence as Teddy clambered down to the ledge and jumped off. Teddy's legs bicycled as he dropped into the bright-green water. Alan looked over the cliff and shook his head. *Crazy kid.* He jumped. As he surfaced he could see Teddy splashing him.

"This place is awesome!" Teddy exclaimed.

Alan splashed him back. This was the first time he had fun with his boy in many years. The cold water swirled around their bodies, washing away the stress and conflict. Alan felt the toxic thoughts leave his mind; he felt the misery wash out of his chest. Here was a smiling son.

The lantern flickered, lighting up the cockpit as father and son talked. "Dad, why did you leave us last year—was it because you and mom were fighting too much?"

Alan took a breath and thought about his answer. This was a huge issue for Teddy and the source of a lot of his acting out and anger over the past year. "No, it wasn't your mom or even the fighting. It was me. I let the pain get a hold of me." Teddy looked confused as Alan paused. "When I got hit in Afghanistan, my head got scrambled. The nerves in my neck gave me shooting pains throughout my skull, and I couldn't handle any noise or activity at all. Driving was hard, going to a hockey game was murder, the mall, downtown streets—they all drove me crazy. I couldn't really tell anyone, not even your mom, but she figured it out. I started on the pain medications: first codeine, then Tramadol, Lyrica, a whole bunch of stuff. The drugs made the pain less acute, but they dimmed my thoughts. Then along came OxyContin; that's the pill that took me down. Oxy made me feel bulletproof for a while, then awful. I needed it more and more until the pills started to run the show. That's when things got ugly between your Mom and me. She knew what I had to do, but I couldn't rustle up the courage to do it. I tried a few times, but the pain would creep in and put me down. You and Mom were the most important things in my heart, but my head would keep pulling back onto the booze and Oxy."

Teddy just listened intently. His dad was speaking to him as if he were a friend or confidant. Alan started again. "It wasn't until I was attacked by that thing that I realized that I was only halfway up the pain ladder and it could get a lot worse. It did get worse for a while—the doctors pulled me off all pain meds, and that was really difficult. After I got attacked again in the park, I realized that these creatures fed off the sick and indigent. If they were after me, then that meant I was sick and indigent. That's when I knew that I had to make a choice to live or die, be a dad or a psycho homeless guy. Some of those guys lying in the bushes in the park had kids and houses, careers and nice cars. It's not that hard to get there—you can land yourself homeless and out of options in a matter of weeks. I didn't want to be homeless, and I didn't want to get eaten."

"Why did they pick you?"

"I don't really know; wrong time, wrong place, I guess, but once I escaped, I think I became a major problem for this one guy. I don't think they are in the habit of leaving witnesses." Alan was surprised at how Teddy seemed to accept his answers. He couldn't see ever forgiving himself for his conduct in the past year, yet his son seemed to accept his explanation. "I am sorry, Teddy."

"It's OK, Dad. It's OK."

Over the next few days, the *Melinda* made her way down the coastline back to Vancouver. Alan felt a huge sense of relief and even a few moments of happiness. That was a word that did not follow war veterans around very often. As they tied up to the dock, Alan checked his phone. Karen had texted him that she was to return in a couple of days.

Kelly met them at the slip with a smile. "Wickey and little Wickey, both with smiles on their faces. Did the wind blow away your troubles?"

Alan smiled. "Yeah, something like that."

"Well, since you have been gone, all hell has broken loose. The cops have been at my place about five times, and the army has arrived and set up at Park Royal Mall. They really want to speak to you." Kelly grinned. "You just can't live the quiet life, can you? I swear that if aliens invaded the Earth, they would land on your roof."

Alan laughed. "I know; what's with that?"

"Teddy, please take my advice—don't be like your dad; when you see trouble coming your way, just turn and walk the other way." Teddy just smiled as he went about tidying up the deck. "Look at your boy; he is cleaning up and everything."

23 The Dancing White Stripes

Calmon sailed from tree to tree as he struggled to find the markers. He had covered about a hundred miles but could see trouble ahead. He stopped in a Douglas fir that stood high above the forest floor. He looked down at the dirt road and then ahead to the clear-cut wasteland that the logging companies had left behind. The markers were left by clans for long-distance navigation, but there were no markers because there was no forest. Calmon had never seen a whole forest missing. The cut seemed to stretch for as far as he could see. He had a choice of going to ground or going around the cut and then trying to pick up the markers after.

He decided to wait until darkness and go directly across. As he sat quietly, his hatred for humans seethed. He could not understand why any creature would kill a forest. Their machines, their greed, their blood thirst for all creatures, it all was despicable. Maybe Caracin and Sentrous were right; maybe all the humans should be killed and eaten.

As the sun began to set, a white pickup truck drove up to the base of Calmon's tree. Two foresters got out and looked right up at him. His colours were on and they should not be able to see him, yet they continued to point directly at him and then write things down on a clipboard. Calmon sat deadly still but became panicked. One of the humans pulled out a sight scope and looked up into the trees; the reflecting glass lens swung towards him. He closed his eyes.

"Yeah, it was a hell of game. The Canucks did their standard old thing—kicked ass for the first period and then went for coffee."

"What is that?" The shorter man dropped his scope and pointed towards the tree beside him.

"It's a loge-pole pine. Yeah, they are not common, but I have seen them up here before."

"Oh yeah, it's a pine." The forester dropped his scope and reached into his pocket for his camera. He walked up towards the tree in front of Calmon and raised the camera. Calmon's heart raced as he looked into the man's eyes as he approached. He had to act. The forester looked through the lens; the auto focus whirred as the lens tried to track the dark figure that dropped towards it. The picture was clear for a tenth of a second, then *ooof*!

The other forester had returned to the truck and was digging through his pack in the cab when the strange *whumph* sound made him look up. He looked across the cab and through the side window to see the black-and-greyish figure pulling his friend's head apart. Then the creature's eyes met his.

"Holy shhhhh—" he gasped as he jumped into the truck and started it up. The engine revved, and Calmon leapt towards the vehicle. The back wheels spun, spraying rocks and woodchips. The truck accelerated along the rough logging road. Calmon landed in the bed of the weaving vehicle. He looked around at the speeding scenery. The human swerved the truck wildly, and Calmon gripped the cab roof. His claws penetrated the steel as he held on tight. His fear yielded to curiosity as he watched his prey operate the truck. Calmon leant down and peered through the back window; he stared at the controls and how the man was using them. The forester reached for his phone and tried to dial with his free hand. The glass shattered as Calmon snatched the phone out of the driver's hand. Calmon crushed the phone and knelt down to peer into the cab. The driver screamed and swerved the truck through a series of violent skids in a desperate attempt to shake the creature off, but Calmon was enjoying the ride.

He had never moved across the ground so quickly, and he was even travelling in the right direction. He could see the forest wall in the distance as the truck hurtled along at speeds topping seventy miles per hour. Calmon realized that he had left a body behind, which was strictly prohibited. He decided that he would return to clean up on the way back from his messenger's journey.

The forester was panicking; he reached for the rifle lying behind the seat. The truck rumbled and skidded along the piles of gravel on the shoulder of the wavy dirt road. Calmon yelped with delight when the truck lurched and swayed. He bobbed his body up and down like an excited child on a kiddie ride. He saw the long barrel of the rifle swing out from behind the seat of the truck. He reached down and snatched it from the driver's hands and tossed it into the truck bed. The forester then found his hunting knife and held it up towards Calmon, who was annoyed as the truck slowed down. He thrust the blade at Calmon, who grabbed it in his claws and pulled it out of the man's grip. Calmon flipped the blade around and plunged it into the top of the forester's shoulder at the base of his neck. The man screamed in agony. The blood pumped out past the blade and ran down his chest.

Calmon slapped the top of the forester's head and made gestures to keep driving faster. The forester realized that he was about to die. He sped the truck up and spun the wheel; the truck slid sideways with a huge plume of dust and then drifted off the road. As the truck's chassis hit the logs and stumps, the truck rolled violently many times, ending with a wild spinning cartwheel. Calmon flew from his perch, tucked and rolled once, and then landed back on his feet. He brushed the twigs and dust from his thorny coat and shook his legs and shoulders, like an athlete warming up for a run. The forester, badly injured, crawled from the twisted and bent metal. His broken bone ends grinding together, he slowly pulled himself up. The forester looked up to see Calmon squatting on top of the truck, only a few feet away.

Dragging his shattered leg, the forester whimpered as he broke into a limping trot. Calmon was disappointed at the pitiful pace of his soon-to-be-meal, but the savoury aroma of the man's toxin-free flesh was almost irresistible. Calmon jumped up close and inhaled the human's breath and then he let the man run for a little longer. After a few minutes of this, Calmon became bored; he reached out and grabbed the man by the back of his skull and pushed his claws into the base of his neck just deep enough to hook the ridge of occipital bone. While the man screamed, Calmon dragged him backwards towards the wrecked truck. He dropped the human and pushed and pulled the overturned truck until it flipped back onto its wheels. Calmon gestured to his prey to get in and drive, but the forester was close to losing consciousness. Calmon climbed into the cab; he had to bring his knees up to his face to fit into the small space. He grabbed the wheel and pushed the pedals, but the engine was no longer running. Extracting himself from the cab, he walked over to his prey. He looked the forester in the eyes and then sank his long fangs into the man's neck. Calmon drank the blood until it stopped flowing; he then ate the choicest meat strips and finally dressed the carcass. This had been the best meal of his life. He was killing and eating the killer of the forests.

Calmon's thoughts turned to the reaction of the Whiteline clan to the news of the awareness. The Whiteline clan was rumoured to be cannibals—maybe they would just kill and eat him before he could blurt out his message?

Calmon dragged the carcass into the tree line and climbed to the top of a first-growth cedar. He finished dressing the forester's corpse. He was feeling guilty, but not about killing the clean one—he felt guilt over the sheer carnage behind him. He had broken about a half-dozen of the sacred rules. His chest rose and fell with a forbidden giddiness; maybe it was the taste of the clean human blood on his tongue. One body left for the vultures and a blood-soaked white truck twisted into a steel Tootsie Roll; this was carnage. Sartra would kill him on the spot.

Or maybe the Whitelines would kill him and eat him first; at least that's what the legends said. At least he would die in glory. He began to move north again, his leaps shorter due to the backpack full of meat. He began to feel the eyes on him from above; maybe it was ravens. The ravens were one of the few animals that were able to keep ahead of the Apecs. They were extraordinarily hard to catch; only Shaman could catch them. He stopped to catch his breath. *Whump.* He was hit simultaneously by two big males, one from above and then the other, who flew a good forty feet across the forest to pile onto him. His arms were wrenched as they strung him up. When they were finished arranging his hanging rig, they assembled in front to have a good look at him.

"Salt clan or a Traveller?" Fonzo fired the question.

"Oh, he is a Salt guy; look at his quills," Moody said.

"As if you know what a Salt guy looks like."

"I know lots of stuff. Look at his quill colour—see the speckles?"

EMERGENCE

"You don't know anything…speckles, my ass." Fonzo slapped Moody on the back of his head. Calmon watched these two as he hung upside down. They had strong accents, but he could make out what they were saying. These were Whiteline sentries. Their colours were fantastic; white and grey lines shimmered across their quills like a billboard at a football game. As they spoke their quills changed colour as if to emphasize their words.

"Are you cannibals? Do you intend to eat me?"

Fonzo's face lit up with delight. "Cannibals…uh, yes, we are cannibals, and we *really* like the taste of the Salt clan…the salty clan we call them." Fonzo looked sideways at Moody.

Moody joined in. "Yes, the Saltys; the old Saltys, we call them…numm, numm!" Moody licked his lips.

"Salty eyes, yes, my favorite—big salty eyeballs, taste better than blueberries!" Fonzo added.

"Salty eye berries, yes. We will have to eat him right away," Moody proclaimed.

"How did you know I was Salt clan?" Calmon asked as he tried to shift his feet out of the tight bindings.

Moody's arms flew up above his head, and he began to swing his hips. "Oh yeeeah, yes, yes, he is sooo Salt clan, Ieeee knew it, called it, called it from miles back there, yup, yup. You—you were saying, maybe he's Traveller, maybe he's just a loner guy who hates tree cutters." Moody used a mocking voice to imitate Fonzo.

Fonzo replied, "Was not—I knew he was a Salty!"

"Shall we eat him?"

"Yeah, let's eat him. Let's eat his balls first," Fonzo chimed in.

Calmon blurted out desperately, "I must get a message to your chief, a message from the chief of the Salt clan. This message is of the utmost importance. Many Apec lives count on it!"

Fonzo and Moody looked at each other. Their eyes rolled. "Nope, no message."

"We will have to eat you first, then you can give your message," Moody added.

Fonzo whispered to Moody, "That doesn't make sense." Fonzo spoke up.

"Your salty eyes and your balls, then message," Moody added.

"Salty balls," Fonzo said melodically.

"Yeah, your big googly eyes, and we even eat your thighs!"

Moody looked at Fonzo as the music halted. "Thighs, really? That's a little weird."

"What? Thighs…It rhymed with eyes."

"You eat his thighs."

"You always ruin it; whenever we get going, you always…You were the one talking about eating his balls. That's weird; I'd eat his thighs before his balls. You eat his balls." Moody looked up at Calmon and pointed at Fonzo. "You ruined the mood." They both suddenly looked up into the trees. "Oh no…It's Samsa."

The tall fema landed with a thud on the big tree limb between the two and Calmon. Samsa looked Calmon over. "Salt clan sentry." She spoke as she ran her hands up and down Calmon's quills. "Let him go, you morons. He is one of Sartra's sentries."

"Yes, ma'am." Calmon was quickly released, and he swung around to meet Samsa's steely gaze.

"You're not going to eat me?" Calmon asked.

"Eat you? Do you think we are cannibals?" Samsa turned back to look at her two sentries. Moody and Fonzo looked away.

"Hah, cannibals. That's disgusting," Moody chimed in.

Calmon spoke up. "I have a message from Sartra." She nodded, and he recited from memory:

> Samsa,
>
> I fear that the time of awareness may be near. Sentrous has broken away to join Caracin in his male-led clan. They are hunting the humans in the city without regard. The humans have come for us in hunting packs, and there have been witnesses that have escaped. I apologize, for this is my fault; I could not stop my son, and now the humans are aware of our presence. We will hunt the breakaway clan and kill them, but if the humans bring their big weapons, we may be killed in the battle. Please get the word to the northern clans and be cautious because I am

afraid the humans may communicate and organize across the lands to hunt us down and kill us.

Samsa was quiet. She looked down into the forest below for a thoughtful moment. "Sartra's own son," she said, speaking to herself. "Get this boy over to the lair and get him some food."

The lair was made from trees topped with huts and line swings. Calmon was amazed at the engineering and workmanship that had gone into the huts and the tree gantries. He greeted by the young ones who followed him in, touching his quills and chattering.

The whispers were faint, but he could make out some of the words. "He is from the Salt clan near the city; he hunted and killed a tree cutter in the middle of the cut."

Calmon could hear Moody's voice. "He grabbed the tree cutter and began to drive his vehicle. Then he hit the human on the head with his gun and killed him. Here is the human meat; it is in this pack." Moody held up the pack; the story was greeted by oohs and aahs.

Fonzo came by. "Hey, human eater, we were just kidding about eating your balls and all."

Calmon smiled. "You guys had me going for a bit, but I figured it out."

"How do you guys change your colours together like that?"

"Oh that, yeah; it's a Whiteline thing, but me and Moody are the best at it. We can shimmer and make shapes that mean things, even send secret messages without calling."

"That's cool," Calmon said.

"You're cool—you are like the coolest guy ever! We watched you from the tree line. Killing the tree cutter guy like that; it was awesome!"

"Yeah, I broke a few rules on that guy, but he is really tasty. Did you want some?" Calmon reached for his pack as Samsa looked over and shook her head in disapproval.

"Would love to try it, but we would catch it from the chief," Fonzo replied.

Moody reached over and whispered, "Yeah, I stole a bite when we hung you up. It's really tasty."

Samsa was watching the trio carefully. She was worried that Calmon could have a dangerous influence on the sentries. She struggled with the urge to send Calmon back on his own, but her old friend needed help; she would send Fonzo and Moody to accompany Calmon back to the city. She didn't want to expose her clan to this new city culture, trending against Kamptra. Sartra was certainly paying the price of awareness with the blood of her own son. No clan needed these problems.

The sun came up, and they all headed up to sleep. Samsa said to Calmon, "In the evening we will wake up and make a plan for the Salts." Calmon slept soundly.

Calmon stopped at the tree line where he had dropped down upon the foresters a few days before. The body was still lying there, covered in maggots. The three discussed what they would do with the remains. They decided to bury them inside the tree line and cover the grave with leaves and branches. Apecs were excellent trackers, and they knew how to disguise the ground perfectly. They dug up the blood-soaked dirt from under the remains and scattered the dirt. Their muscles were tired from dragging the twisted truck from the other site a few hours earlier. They'd wrestled it over to the trees and then covered it with branches and leaves.

Fonzo and Moody had never travelled outside of the territory, and they were enjoying the sights of far-off lands. The climate changed as they approached the southwest coast of British Columbia. The trees were higher, and the air was damp.

24 Snatched

Caracin and a couple more hunters sat on the expansive rooftop of the Drake Hotel. This nineteenth-century building had a mottled grey façade. The Italian marble was once glamorous in the hotel's heyday. Now the dilapidated downtown edifice stood guarding the entrance to the Vancouver skids. The Free clan was almost exclusively hunting in the city; they were sailing across the rooftops of the very same hotels where the news teams were sleeping. They hunted throughout the back alleys and walkways, not just taking the rotten ones. The Drake rooftop was a stash for the bones of city workers, night-shift employees, and even an off-duty city police officer. They ate until their bellies bulged. This recklessness was sheer anarchy, and the Free clan was revelling in it.

The males had changed the basic strategy of the clan from defensive/elusive to offensive and aggressive. There were very few sentries, and the males did all of the hunting; they also insisted on muddling through the logistics. While Caracin and boys were gallivanting, most of the females were pregnant and restricted to the refuge lair. The plentiful meat was going bad and animals were infesting the food stores; rats and critters became a problem at the refuge lair. The females were growing tired with the new order of things; for thousands of years, the fema had dominated and led the clans, but now they just sat together and waited for the males to provide for them. The alternative lifestyle was not what they had expected; they expected the males to do a better job, be organized, and take care of the clan's needs. That wasn't how it was working out. Many things were troubling Sentrous, but Caracin could only identify the obvious thing.

"We need to get the human." Caracin spoke through a mouthful of muscle and scanned Sentrous's face for his reaction.

"Yes, he has earned his death," Sentrous replied.

"I have been thinking about him." Caracin spoke with his mouth half full, waving the meaty humorous bone and pointing it at his friend. "I have a plan that will bring the man into the forest right to our refuge layer, right into our trap."

Sentrous looked up. "What's this plan of yours?"

Caracin smiled.

Alan's apartment was small for the whole family. The move out of the house had been hurried, and Karen despised the chaos. Karen had been busy for the past weeks working with three different scientific teams around the world to analyze the new DNA. Dr. Goodall had managed to protect Karen from the "old boys" network. A group of scientists led by her previous colleagues from UBC were trying their best to get control of the project. They had solicited the American and Canadian military in an expedition to locate some new samples. The military expedition was composed of twelve scientists, forty or so soldiers, three helicopters, and a mobile command post.

The troops wandered around in the forest for a week and ended up with only a bag full of bear fur and some raccoon skins to show for it. The media frenzy began to die down with the lack of new information. Alan had been followed by CNN, CBC, and FOX News and hounded to tell his story. He was a master at playing ignorant, though, and the news crews soon tired of his shrugged shoulders and goofy, vacant grin.

At 7:00 a.m. Alan looked at the alarm clock. Finally, a few hours of slumber, he thought. Teddy had already gotten up and gone to swim practice. He had decided to re-join the swimming team, mainly on Wendy's insistence.

The apartment couch was vibrating. Alan walked over and lifted the pillow up to see Wendy's pink phone buzzing. She must have left it here last night, he thought. He looked at the text; it was from Teddy. It read, Let's meet at the coffee shop and study math after school, K? The next text read, Here is my smile just for you. A picture was attached. Alan looked at the picture and smiled for a moment at Teddy's square smile. His smile faded when he noticed a dark smudge in the background. "What is that?" he said to himself as he transferred the photo over to his computer screen. He zoomed in on the back of the classroom, and at the top corner of the skylight was a small, dark figure looking down into the classroom from the roof. Alan zoomed in closer to the figure; it was the round shape of a head looking into the classroom. The pixelated form was hard to make sense of unless you knew exactly what you were looking for. The blurry face was a familiar one—it was Sentrous.

Alan's heart leapt as he jumped up from the couch. The closet hangers swung when he slammed the door. Alan jumped across the hood of his truck and drove down the driveway at flank speed. Karen came out of the front door to investigate the commotion. Her stomach fell as she saw Alan speed away. Alarmed, she looked at the laptop screen.

Alan arrived at the schoolyard in a swirl of tire smoke and gravel. The school was chaotic; kids were running in panic as the teachers tried to calm them. The vice principal was trying to clear parents' vehicles from the parking lot to make room for the soon-to-be-arriving police and fire departments. He recognized Alan as he approached, and his expression told Alan that all of his worst fears were true. "Teddy?" Alan exclaimed.

The vice principal stuttered, struggling for words. "Those things…they took him."

Alan shook his head. "No, no…they…are you sure?" There was a pause. Alan felt a wave of vomit punch up from his stomach, but he held it fast.

He spoke in short bursts. "It was the creatures—they smashed the glass and dropped in from the roof; they killed kids, right in the hall. One of them dragged Teddy up and through the broken skylight."

Alan struggled to keep his mind clear. "How long ago? Where did they go? In what direction did they leave?"

"About twenty minutes ago. One of the students pulled the alarm, and we evacuated the school. I don't know what direction."

The school doors burst open; three teachers carried out a young girl drenched in blood. It was Wendy. They placed her down on the steps. She was sobbing as a teacher tried to control the blood that was pouring from the gash in her arm. Her clothing was shredded and her skin was pale from the blood loss. Alan jumped to her side and pulled out the trauma packs from the school's little first aid pack. He fastened a tourniquet on her upper arm and wrenched it tight; she groaned with pain, but the bleeding stopped.

"I am so sorry, Mr. Wickey. I tried to stop them; I tried to hold on to him, but they were so strong." She cried as she spoke. The ambulance had pulled up behind them, and the paramedics pushed past Alan and started to work on her. Alan barked out orders to the paramedics. "She needs some fluids; somebody get a line in her quickly because she is in shock. Wendy, I know you did your best, honey. I will find him," Alan reassured her as she was loaded into the ambulance. She kept apologizing as she drifted in and out of consciousness.

As Alan walked back to his truck, Kelly's truck drove up and stopped. Karen stepped out and walked around the front of the vehicle towards Alan. The tears rolled down Alan's cheeks as he met her.

She looked into his eyes, and she knew immediately that her son was gone. "Is he alive, Alan?" She spoke deliberately.

"I don't know. They took him from the top floor of the school," Alan stuttered, his lips quivering.

Karen's pupils were wide and ratcheted back and forth, yet her voice had an even and calculated tone. "Alan, stop crying right now and listen to me. You need to gather all of your guts and mojo and whatever else makes you get up and move. You need to go out and get my son back." Her voice broke slightly and then began again into a steady crescendo. "The world has stopped, Alan! The...the world has stopped. You...need to go and get my boy, and bring him back." Now her tone rose shrilly. "Do you understand me? Do not come back without him!" Now her lip was quivering. He stood silently, tears still rolling down his cheeks.

"OK, I will."

"Stop crying. As of now...You need to become a big boy, Alan—no selfishness, no...no fucking whining, no self-doubt, not even a thought about yourself, not even a fucking thought!" Her voice broke again and then filled out. "Not even a thought, or a word, about yourself, until you get my son back." Alan just managed to nod.

Teddy opened his eyes to an upside-down world. He remembered the glass flying through the hall and being snatched up into the air by hooked claws. He remembered the searing pain of his ripping flesh mixed with the sound of Wendy's voice and her screams...yes, the sound of her screams. Was she OK? Did these bastards kill her? He twisted and writhed with anger; he yelled, but the deep green canopy swallowed up the sound. He had to tilt his head back to see the forest floor two hundred feet below. "Shit, that's a long way down!" The sight of the vast expanse made him gasp with fear. He wiggled and twisted again. The ropes that suspended him were rough and cut into his ankles.

His hands were free so he folded up and grabbed at his bound feet. Twisting, he looked up and was startled by Sentrous's stare. Sentrous was only a few feet away, studying his prey. Teddy froze; the face of his captor was terrifying: the quills, the yellow pointed teeth, and the white round eyes. Teddy let out a cry for help. Sentrous tilted his head curiously; black pinpoint pupils darted back and forth until they fixed on his own. Teddy was spinning around slowly, and Sentrous was now a fixed part of his circular, upside-down landscape. For the next hour Teddy was silent. He looked at Sentrous, and Sentrous looked at him. Teddy tried many times to loosen his bindings. Sentrous did not react at all. He just sat and watched calmly.

Caracin arrived and took a perch beside Sentrous. "You shouldn't play with your food," Caracin said, his eyes flashing to Sentrous.

"As if you should talk," Sentrous replied.

"This whole plan would work just fine with him in our bellies. Why are you keeping him alive?"

"Shut up," Sentrous snapped, slapping his friend on the shoulder.

"No, really; he is a problem, not an asset. He is screaming and making noise. His father will come regardless if he is dead or alive."

"I am not so sure. If his father has no proof, then he may not come. My mother would not come."

Caracin's eyes rolled. "Your mother is heartless bitch who is trying to kill you!" Sentrous's lips began to tremble, then rolled up into a curl; he turned and struck out fiercely, the backs of his claws careening across Caracin's face. Caracin, caught by surprise, reeled back and swung out to another branch.

"Whoa. OK, OK, no mom comments, I get it."

Sentrous's angry eyes met Teddy's again. Teddy was watching the silent conversation.

Sentrous thought, *Maybe I should just kill and eat him. I hate him; look at his big deer eyes, and weak little arms, his pink and shiny skin.* He didn't notice that Caracin had moved to the other tree, and before he could move to intervene, Caracin cut the rope. Sentrous jumped to grab it, but it slipped through his fingers as Teddy spiraled down into the foliage. Teddy grappled for a grip, finally grabbing a green bough. It flipped him around, slowing his descent, but the needles shredded through his hands, and he began to fall again. He snatched another branch, and it bent under his weight but did not give way. He swung into the tree and held onto the trunk for a moment, panting. He stood up on the thick branch and swung around the tree. Sentrous was waiting on the other side of the tree. They met face to face. Sentrous did not move; just studying Teddy, he sat to look at him as Teddy swung back to the other side of the tree and hid himself from view. The bindings around his feet had loosened with the slack and movement. Teddy flipped the choker knot free from his feet and pushed his back up against the tree trunk. After catching his breath, he peeked around the tree at Sentrous. Only a few feet away, Sentrous waved. Teddy snapped his head back and took a deep breath. His mind raced; he looked down to see the forest floor. He was still at least seventy feet from the ground. He looked to the branches above him to see Caracin, who also waved.

He looked over to the next tree, at least ten feet across. With a yelp he dove across the void, grappling for a branch from the far tree as he dropped. The thick branches bowed over to let him drop down another twenty feet, and he landed with a thud on a thick trunk. Teddy was close to the ground—one more jump, and he could make a run for it. Sentrous lunged forward and grabbed Teddy's foot, spinning him upside down. Up and up they went, right up to the very pinnacle of the huge red cedar. Sentrous draped him across a branch, and he clung to it helplessly. He hyperventilated; he couldn't even see the forest floor from here, the branches were thin and barely held his weight. He was terrified to move, for he would surely plunge to his death.

Sentrous pointed to the boy as he spoke to Caracin. "He's pretty good for a useless human; he stopped his fall. When was the last time you saw a human do that?"

Caracin looked at Sentrous in disgust and shook his head. "He should be dinner, not entertainment." He dropped away, leaving Sentrous and Teddy alone. Teddy looked around; they were in a tree that stood higher than the rest of the forest, a perch tree. He looked out over the misty valley. The clouds swirled in and through the treetops. He could hear the faint rush of a river somewhere below. It was close by, maybe a half mile. There was no escape from this perch; in fact, if he fell asleep, he would surely fall to his death a full three hundred feet below. He looked across. Sentrous cocked his head a little. For a moment he looked friendly. *Yeah, friendly for a killer*, he thought.

Not far away, Calmon and the two Whitelines had gotten lost in the fog and missed a marker.

"What, you don't know where you live, salty boy?" Fonzo quipped.

"Yeah, I know where we are; I just got a little off track, but this is the way." Calmon pointed to the north. Moody was a few trees over when his quills shimmered and flashed. Fonzo turned to Calmon and raised his finger to his mouth. "Shh." All three froze, and their colours flashed to match the surrounding trees. Moody's coat flashed again, and Fonzo whispered, "That guy over there, is he one of your sentries?"

Calmon tilted his head and squinted in order to see the lone sentry that sat perched in a treetop about a half mile away. He was surprised to see Aelan. "He's part of the breakaway clan. He used to be one of us."

"Shall we kill him?"

Calmon thought about it. "Better not. We don't know where the rest of them are. We should keep heading to the Salt lair and report their position to Sartra.

"Let's go." Calmon waved, and they moved off to the north.

After a day, Teddy was losing his strength. The Capilano River twisted and turned down the valley, and this was where Teddy was trapped. He was left alone for a few hours at a time, but he had the feeling that one of them was always close by. He tried to descend to some of the branches below, but they were too thin and he felt as if he would plunge with any movement. He would doze off and catch himself slipping and then wake up. If something did not change, it would not be long until he woke up falling to his death. He tore a strip off his pants and tied his hands around a branch that hung close above him. This gave him a little stability; now he could steal short naps.

Sentrous watched him. Teddy felt better when Sentrous was there, because if he fell from the branch, then at least he had a chance that Sentrous would catch him before he fell all of the way. He noticed his captors were scarce during the daylight hours. Hanging from his homemade strap on the bough, he began to work on a plan. Teddy waited until the afternoon. Sentrous was gone, and he had seen Caracin move off to the south. Now was the best time to act. He had picked out a path, choosing various branches that he thought would hold his weight. He planned out his jumps like a gymnast choreographing a routine. This routine had to be perfect the first time; one slip, and he would fall. He slipped off his homemade bindings and arranged his posture to face the target branch below. This first jump was going to be the hardest and riskiest. The limbs were so thin at the tops of the trees that he feared they would sheer under his weight. He swung around, hanging for a moment under his perch. He heart raced with fear as the breeze from the river wet his lips. He dropped.

Sentrous was sitting a few trees away, trying to insert the battery back into Teddy's cell phone, but he couldn't wiggle the little square into the casing. The thrashing branches announced Teddy's movement: *whoosh, crack, whoosh*! Teddy had dropped to the first branch but lost his balance and fell down to the next group of branches where he grappled for control of his descent. The big bough dipped down as Teddy held on to it desperately, hanging upside down. This was not part of his gymnastics routine. He reached below to grasp the larger branch and dropped onto it with a thud. He could hear Sentrous moving around above him. He looked across and saw a large limb from another tree and jumped for it. This limb swayed but held fast as he moved along it to the next trunk. Here he saw the top of a smaller fir tree, and he leapt out again. Landing in the apex of the fir, the whole tree bent under

Teddy's weight and transported him across to another group of big cedars. Now he was only about fifty feet from the ground.

Sentrous was delighted at this kid's ability in the trees, yet now he realized that his prisoner may actually make it to the ground. Teddy was exhausted; his arms burned with lactic acid and his chest rose and fell as he gasped for air. He leapt again to a larger branch below in the cluster of giants. Now he spotted his elevator ride to the forest floor, a long cedar bough that hung about ten feet below him. He dropped down onto it, grasping for a handhold. The green bushy limb dropped him down where he hung about twenty feet from the forest floor. *Thump!* He landed flat on his back into the soft moss and salal. Teddy's gaze fixed on the dark figure dancing across the trees above him. How could he escape a creature that moved like that? *Get out of the trees, that's how!* He leapt up and began to sprint through the forest; he knew exactly where he was going.

Sentrous now realized Teddy's plan—the river. If Teddy made it into the river, then he had a real chance of escape. Sentrous had been trying to teach himself how to swim, but he was not up for swimming in the rapids at the bottom of the canyon. Teddy found a narrow pathway and took it to speed up his pace. He was now sure that Sentrous was close behind, but he could see the long suspension bridge that spanned the canyon. That bridge would be his salvation. Breathing furiously his arms chugged at his sides as his stride opened up to a full sprint. Sentrous was catching up but not fast enough to intercept him. Teddy had entered the clearing at the bridge when his jacket was caught by Caracin's claws. He was flung violently back into the trees and landed with a thud. Caracin straddled Teddy. Teddy could see by the look on Caracin's face that Caracin wanted to kill him.

25 Command and Control

The house had been transformed into a command post. Temporary floodlights were pointed out towards the forest. The driveway was full, and the street parking was lined with trucks and cars. The doorbell rang, and Alan answered it. It was Inspector Boyd, Constable Perry, and the conservation officer Ryder. The three were not in uniform and laden with gear bags.

"What are you guys doing here?" Alan asked.

Boyd answered. "We came to help you find your boy."

Alan was shocked.

Boyd continued, "The RCMP is not officially helping you, just us guys."

"Why aren't you out on the official monster hunt?" Alan asked.

"The pinheads from Ottawa got off the plane and threw my detachment into a state of chaos and confusion. They—the pinheads—are not sure whether I am a lunatic or there is really something out there. After a week of debate, they called in the Yukon tracking team. Those jerkoffs took over the search and then had the nerve to tell me to go back to my desk and do paperwork. I told them to go and fuck themselves and took some stress leave."

"Thank you," Alan said.

Both friends and acquaintances had been out searching the forest for days now. Allan and Kelly had traipsed day and night through all the areas they knew to be active with the ultrasonic calls, yet the woods were silent.

Karen maintained a calm but uneasy intensity. She was busy assisting with the search teams and helping with the logistics of keeping dozens of people provisioned and on task. Charts and maps covered the walls, radios crackled. The federal and provincial authorities were neither helping nor hindering the search for Teddy. The local team that called the Wickey home base camp included top experts in survival, combat, counterinsurgency, and search and rescue, yet there was not one uniform. The phone rang, and Alan picked it up. "Hello?"

"Captain Wickey, is this you?"

"Colonel Harris?"

"Carl, call me Carl. We are in a cab on the way over, Kit and I and a couple of other guys from our team in San Diego. Is that big Indian around?"

"Yes sir, he is here. Thank you very much for coming up to help; I can't say how much—"

"Yeah, yeah, let's just get your boy back."

Karen moved from task to task with the efficiency of a machine; every movement, every stroke of her pencil, was a carefully choreographed action. Her smiles and quiet manner broadcast the tension throughout the teams like a metronome keeping everyone up to tempo. This tempo was steadily increasing as more time passed without any sign of her son. She was bent over the topographic maps, hatching off each forested region that had been searched with different coloured pencil crayons. Each colour was assigned to a team, and these teams had to report to their progress directly to Karen by radio. One of the younger crewmembers sitting on the couch, oblivious to the emotions in the room, pulled out a six-pack of beer. When a beer can stopped in front of Alan, Karen's pupils flashed wide for a moment; her gaze fixed on the group of men. Had Alan been paying attention, he would have recognised the look, but he had missed it. She walked slowly over towards the doorway as one of the beer cans cracked and hissed. She stopped at the stack of gear bags, unzipped one, and pulled out a rifle.

"Winchester 1884 lever action carbine. Whose is this?" Karen asked as she opened the breach and looked down the barrel.

"It's mine!" Ryder replied.

"Does it shoot straight?"

"Straight as an arrow. I just had it out on the range on Sunday."

Kelly was sitting on the armchair with his unopened beer in hand, hanging over the side of the armrest. He was looking down when the breach snapped shut with the lever action. He noticed the barrel of the gun swinging towards him. "Karen!" he shouted as the beer can exploded out of his hand into a plume of spray that shot across the room and across Kelly's face. The lever snapped again, and the barrel of the gun swung over to Ryder, who tossed his beer over to his left. *Bang!* The can exploded in the air and the shower of beer covered the living, but now all of the men were down on the floor and hiding behind the couches, even Alan.

"Sweetie, put down the gun." Alan projected his voice over the pillows of the couch.

"Don't call me sweetie. You fellows put down the beer please. You may drink beer after you find my son." Her voice was calm. A beer can popped up from behind the table. The bullet sent the can spinning wildly and shooting liquid out like a rotating sprinkler. The other two cans were placed gently on the table by hands. Alan popped up to see the barrel pointed directly at his head.

One of the SAR guys whispered to Perry and Ryder, "You guys should arrest that crazy chick. She could have killed us."

Perry, Ryder, and Boyd all looked at each other for a moment. Perry reached into his gear bag and handed the SAR guy his handcuffs. "You arrest her; we'll see how that works out for you."

"Is that all of the beer?" Karen projected her voice.

"Yes, that's all of it, Karen," Alan replied.

She spoke calmly with an exhale. "Well then, who would like some hot cocoa or lemon tea?"

Boyd spoke up. "Yes ma'am, hot cocoa would be nice." Karen returned the gun to its case and walked over to the kitchen, while the troops all got up and wiped themselves off. The smell of spilled beer and gunpowder changed the atmosphere. Both Alan and Karen were hanging just on the edge of insanity.

Caracin was seething; Sentrous had given him a thorough ass-kicking over the boy. Sentrous wanted to keep the boy alive until the man came to get him. Teddy was getting on Caracin's nerves and when he had made a dash for the cliff above the river, he thought he would take advantage of the situation and kill the kid. Sentrous was too quick, though, and had pulled him off of Teddy. A vicious fight had ensued. Teddy had lain on the ground directly below the two titans as they grappled and struck each other. Teddy realized that he would never win a fight with these creatures. He had a better chance of fighting off an attacking great white shark than going up against these guys; yet escape was definitely possible, if he could get the right opportunity. He would have to survive the long fall into the river, but dying in the river would be better than being ripped apart and eaten. He would have made a run for it during the fight, but they stayed close to him as they fought. Sentrous subdued Caracin with a great blow to the side of his head. Teddy noticed something silver drop out of Sentrous's backpack as he struggled to gain control of Caracin. Teddy rolled over and snatched his silver phone from the moss. He flipped it over and noticed that the battery pack was missing. *How did these guys know anything about batteries? Not your average primates, that's for sure.* Sentrous carried Teddy back up into the tree but placed him on a larger branch this time.

The sun had just set, and Teddy and Sentrous sat across from each other in total silence. Sentrous studied his young captive; he had noticed that the cell phone was missing from his bag. He could see the outline of it in the ragged pockets of Teddy's clothing. He reached into his pack and pulled out the battery for the phone. Teddy's eyes went wide as Sentrous waved the battery. He tossed the little battery up into the air and caught it; his eyes fixed on Teddy's, he tossed it again; it tumbled out of his fingers, the battery dropped down, spinning in the evening air until it hit the leaves on the forest floor with a whooshing thump. Teddy almost jumped into the air to catch it, but he would have been too late. Sentrous was sitting still; he looked down and then across at Teddy. Sentrous shrugged his shoulders as if to say *whoops.*

What is this guy up to? Teddy thought.

Sentrous left into the darkness while Teddy stood on the branch and looked down at where he thought the battery was. *They obviously want me alive for some reason; maybe they want to eat me at a feast, cooked over a fire or something. Yeah, well, whatever their plan is, it certainly won't be enjoyable. What do I have to lose?*

Teddy dropped down to the next branch and then the next; he swung over to the neighbouring tree and followed the route that he had been planning in his mind since his last escape attempt. He made it to the ground and stopped to listen for the sound of the creatures moving in to get him, yet it was silent. He walked over to the area where the battery had fallen and dropped to his knees. The twilight had given way to the dark-blue forested pitch. The cold air smelled of dirt and leaves as he swept his hands out in a circular motion looking for the tiny piece of metal and plastic. As he shuffled forward, he felt a hard piece under his knee, and he looked down. This was it; after a quick wipe with his shirt, he inserted it into his phone, and the small screen lit up.

Searching...Searching...Searching...No signal. Teddy began to walk towards the cliff, holding the phone up in the air. *Beep, beep.* Teddy looked at the signal indicator—one bar. He pressed his father's phone number and hit send, but the screen dimmed and went dark. "Shit, no!" He shook it and then pulled the battery out as he ducked behind a tree. He wiped it again and then inserted it, but it was dead. He had been in the forest for days, so this was no surprise. Sentrous's claws reached down and snatched Teddy up by his hair. He screamed in pain.

Wendy's wounds were healing; the cuts on her arm were dressed in waterproof bandages. Her father had been adamant that she stay in bed and follow her doctor's orders. Wendy was stubborn, and after she'd sneaked out a few times, her father finally gave in and let her help search for Teddy. At least this way he could keep an eye on her while they both looked for the lost boy.

Wendy twisted the throttle, and the Jet Ski leapt up out of the water. She gunned it back to the boat ramp. It was getting too dark to see the shoreline, and this would make searching impossible. The girl had been searching the river and lake chain for the entire day, looking for any sign of Teddy. Wendy's father backed the truck and trailer down the ramp. Wendy popped the Jet Ski up onto the trailer chalks. Her father did not know what to think of the crazy monster stories, but after four days of hysterical tears, he was happy to convert her energy and focus onto searching the shoreline. Eight days, and there was no sign of the lost boy. The RCMP and the military were searching higher up the valley, and the Northshore SAR crews were searching closer to the city. But Teddy had disappeared into the mist, and any hope of finding him alive was dwindling..

26 Canyon Bridge

A line of sentries advanced quickly, from treetop to treetop. Shaman and Sartra stopped for a moment, their eyes sore from the morning light.

"Are you ready?" Sartra asked.

"Yes, of course. The question is, are you ready?"

Sartra's face darkened. "There is no other way to fix this tangle."

"I can kill him for you if you wish; it will be easier for me."

"No...no, I will do it; he is my son. I will kill him as quickly as I can." She swallowed and took a breath.

The assaulting forces were from many clans. Moody had trained some of the Salt clan on how to display symbols on their back with their quills. This allowed the whole troop to move in silence and still communicate. The plan was simple: ambush the Free clan and kill all of the males. The females were to be taken prisoner and possibly convinced to come back to the original clan. They were all staying high in the red cedars and Sitka spruce. An attack from above had a much higher chance of surprise. They outnumbered the Free clan, but Sentrous and Caracin were very powerful enemies, not to be underestimated. Shaman leapt out into the sky, the orange glow reflecting from her quills; the fantastic canopy rushed below her as she landed in the top of a huge three-hundred-foot-high red cedar. She was still getting used to creating the new signals, and sometimes her back would flutter in confusion as she concentrated on the shape she was supposed to make. Most of the signals were just a series of flashes, but some of the symbols indicated directions or special commands.

As the sun disappeared, they arrived and slowly positioned themselves around the Free clan. Over the next few hours, they would settle into reconnaissance posts. They would attack at sunrise and crush them quickly.

The humans would be a surprise for the attacking clans, but not for the Free clan. Sentrous was waiting for him.

Alan and his troop, a mix of police and off-duty Canadian and American special forces, also converged on the valley and then worked their way down the mountainside where he suspected the clan was living. This canyon was only a few miles from where he'd escaped through the caves a few weeks earlier.

Karen walked with a sniper rifle slung across her back. Carl Harris spoke to her. "I haven't seen you guys since the award ceremony in 2007; how's Alan been coping?"

Karen signed. "He's coping OK, I guess; it's up and down. He feels responsible for the two who were killed on the mountainside that day, and he doesn't think he deserves the medal. He thinks he called in the ordinance directly onto the firebase by mistake."

Colonel Harris furrowed his brow. "What, that's crazy. He and I drove that LAV across a minefield and through a barrage of heavy fire and straight up a cliff. He saved all of them from being shredded." He paused for a moment and thought. "Wait a minute, I remember an after-action report that crossed my desk about six months after that." Harris put his cell phone to his ear. "Andy, it's Carl, yeah, it's going OK in Vancouver. Haven't found anything yet…no. That's not why I called you—do you remember an after-action report from the Karingal in 2006? Remember the day that Alan Wickey and I drove up the cliff to fetch our boys? There was something in there about the WAAS Datum being off. Yeah, yeah, can you pull that report for me and send it to my phone? Thanks, Andy; yeah, I will." He looked up at Karen and smiled. "I think I might be able to help." They all sat down for a rest on a group of logs, and Carl's phone chimed. He looked at the screen and then up at Alan. "Alan, have a look at this e-mail." He handed the phone to Alan, and he read the text:

AA103rd AFG 2007071020-2230

Targeting SAT feed WAAS report: Number 4566

Text: *Digital Differential Satellite correction signal was out of phase (error 0.3123 KM) for twelve hours. All targets in areas 40-62 not lit locally were guided in*

*approximately 300 meters to the NW off requested
coordinates. This may be a factor in US casualties KIAs
and two Canadians in Areas 48 and 52 during the period.
Error was detected at 2120 and corrected at 2230hrs.*

Alan read this over and over in silence and finally looked
up at the colonel. "You mean my coordinates were correct? The
satellite was wrong?"

"Well, it was a local-user terminal that sent out the wrong
correction, and pretty much all of the ordinance that fell that day
was dropping in three hundred metres off target. Group four
NATCOM just forgot to mention it, and I didn't even know myself
until we were back stateside."

Alan swallowed hard as the small group all looked at him.
"I didn't kill those guys?"

"You didn't kill those guys, Alan. I told you that you didn't
drop the bombs or shoot the guys. You saved all the others that
were in the firebase—that's why I recommended the medal. Your
action was heroic and outstanding."

Alan sat quietly and looked at the e-mail for a minute. He
shook his head in disbelief. "Fucking satellite!" Harris cracked a
smile and patted his shoulder.

"Yes, fucking satellite," Harris repeated.

They worked their way down to the parking lot. After a
long day hiking, they were looking forward to a little rest. The
group was divided into three squads of ten: Kelly was leading one
of the squads, the SAR guys and the police volunteers were led by
Perry, and Alan and Karen were in the third. They had covered an
extraordinary amount of forest in the past three days and were
planning to converge in the parking lot and head back to the house.

Boyd's cell phone rang. "Boyd," he barked and then held
his finger up listened for a moment. "Yeah, when was the hit? OK,
OK, text me the coordinates and get the moron to send the squads
over to help us. We will be there in about twenty minutes." Boyd
looked up into Karen's eyes. "Teddy's cell powered up early this
morning for a few seconds. It was hidden in the inbox of some
TELUS weenie until one of my guys checked in with them. The
position is close to the Capilano suspension bridge."

The whole team gathered and looked at the map on the
tailgate of Kelly's truck. A three-pronged attack was plotted with

Alan, Perry, and Ryder going across the bridge first to secure the other side, and then the second group would come up the valley and sweep the lower hillside. Kelly and Karen would set up on a bluff above the bridge and give sniper support. During the drive Boyd was having trouble getting the RCMP to divert resources, but apparently they said they would send the helo over with a spotter to help out.

Alan jumped out of his vehicle and checked his weapon. Kelly and Karen were stuffing their bags full of gear. The other vehicles sped into the parking lot, kicking up the brown dust. Kelly noticed Alan's expression change as the dust hit his nose—the dry, swirling dust. Alan's eyes began to dart as his heart raced in sheer war-torn panic. He clasped his chest and sat down on a rock, hyperventilating. Kelly walked over to him. "Alan, hey buddy, it's just Canadian dust, it's not Kandahar. Take a deep breath and keep your focus, soldier."

Alan brought his breathing back into control, and his eyes came back to meet Karen's. "OK, I'm OK. Let's go do this." His chest still rose and fell as he did his best to recover from his incapacitating flash of panic and fear. Alan and the two woodsmen walked across the bridge. High up on the cliff bluff, Kelly's iPhone began to flash with the ultrasonic calls. Kelly nodded to Karen and squeezed his microphone. "Getting some calls detected on the app. I think they know we are here."

Teddy could see the clan members scramble to get themselves into their positions. It wasn't until now that he realized that he was bait for the trap set to kill his father. He looked across the trees and saw the whole clan moving in coordination. Sentrous posted a watch on Teddy to make sure he would not escape during the slaughter. Caracin had told all the clan members that he was saving Teddy's sweet flesh for himself while Sentrous would devour his father during the great feast. This would be a wondrous victory and maybe once they had butchered their attackers, they would prove the feebleness of the humans and demonstrate how the practices of Kamptra were archaic. Teddy knew that this new sentry didn't know about his newfound talent in escape. He assured himself that this was indeed his father attempting to rescue him. His only chance of survival was to make an escape while the creatures were otherwise engaged.

EMERGENCE

Higher up the valley, the Salt clan closed in. Shaman landed beside Sartra and announced the arrival of the human man and some soldiers with guns. Sartra had already caught the scent of the team of men as they walked down the far cliff top. Her mind was racing as the situation became infinitely more complex. Shaman waited patiently for Sartra to formulate a modified attack plan.

"The humans are not here for us. They are here for Caracin and the others. I think we will wait till the battle begins; if Caracin and Sentrous decide to retreat, then we will be waiting for them down the valley." Shaman nodded and then went to tell the others of the plan.

The sun was low on the mountain and settling behind the trees to west. Alan and the two officers reached the halfway point on the swaying bridge. He pulled out his binoculars and looked into the trees. He could see nothing yet, so they kept going across.

Alan reached the other side and crouched behind the broom and trees on the side of the trail. The other two took positions across the other side of the path. Alan looked up into the trees through the green salal leaves; they were wet with mist from the roaring river. Karen looked through her scope at Alan and then up into the trees. Alan could not see any sign of them, but he knew they were there, waiting to pounce. This was clearly a trap for him, but he could not see any other way to get his son back.

The rest of the team had crossed upriver and were moving up the cliff side towards them. They were still about a hundred metres away when a creature leapt from the trees and grabbed Ryder. Ryder reached around and grabbed his knife, but the iron claws tore at his chest muscles and then the beast reeled Ryder's ragdoll body over the cliff face, and he fell down into the rock face below. Alan aimed and fired once; the bullet impacted the creature, and its face was peeled back by the large-calibre projectile. The huge form dropped. Alan swung his weapon around and scanned the trees, but he could not see any movement. Caracin was above him, shocked to see one of his precious clan slaughtered so easily. He looked up to check on Teddy and then set his sights on Alan.

Sentrous was hanging on the cliff face waiting for the group to pass over him. The American and Canadian soldiers worked slowly up the cliff line. Troops were taught to keep close to cover and out of the open, but in this case they needed to keep clear from the trees so they stayed close to the cliff. Sentrous was counting on this. As they passed close, Sentrous leapt up and lunged at Kit, who levelled his weapon and fired twice into Sentrous' chest. Sentrous did not flinch as he snatched the weapon away with his long reach and then grabbed Kit. He turned Kit around to face his friends; they held their fire for a moment as Sentrous pulled the soldier's head back and ripped out a huge piece of his neck with his teeth. Kit erupted in a geyser of blood as Sentrous pulled him over the cliff face. He tossed the limp body down into the river below as he swung along the rocks and then up over the group and into the trees. A hail of bullets followed him.

Karen scanned the trees until she caught a glimpse of blue cloth high in the canopy. It was her son; she could just barely make out his cotton shirt. He moved; he was alive!

She squeezed the transmit button on her radio. "Alan, he is alive; he is standing in one of the highest cedars about one hundred feet in the forest from the bridge."

Alan focussed his binoculars up into the canopy but couldn't see his son. "Roger, I am heading that way." Karen focussed the scope on the tree and then saw Teddy's guard. He was exactly the same colour as the tree's foliage, but his sunglasses were clearly visible. "Kelly, I've got one of those things in the scope right beside Teddy."

Kelly dialed the sight in focus and saw the creature. "It's close, but I can get him."

"No, please call the shot for me. I will get him." Karen steadied herself with her elbows.

"OK." Kelly put down his gun, pulled out the scope, and shot the laser. "Seven hundred fifty metres with a three-knot southerly wind."

"Thank you." Karen dialled in her scope and slowly squeezed the trigger, and the shot rang out as the bullet whizzed past the far side of the creature. She was favouring the side away from Teddy too much. The creature turned its head at the noise but stayed still.

Kelly spoke. "Missed to the left. Karen, you need to aim two points to the right, basically right at Teddy. I'll watch the wind for you."

Karen lined the cross hairs directly onto Teddy and swallowed. "Are you sure?"

"As long as the wind is the same and you haven't adjusted anything, then yes. The wind has increased, so take your shot."

Karen heart's was racing; was she going to kill her son? She had to trust Kelly. He was an expert. He would never hurt Teddy. She exhaled and in the pause between breaths squeezed the trigger. The bullet whistled across the river canyon for a full second. She could see the wind take it sideways. As the bullet tore into the throat of the creature, it reached up to clasp at its mouth, then fell.

"Go, Teddy! Go!" Karen yelled and shook her fist as Teddy leapt across the branches like an Olympic gymnast, moving from tree to tree. In minutes he was on the ground. He could hear the movement of the clan above him, but he had a good head start.

Kelly called into the radio. "Alan, he's down from the tree, and he's heading your way." Now it was Kelly's turn to do some shooting. "I know this was a trap, but I don't think they considered two snipers in their plans." Kelly pulled the trigger, and the round cracked across the valley, narrowly missing Sentrous. Sentrous was about twenty paces behind Teddy and gaining fast. Alan stepped out in front of his son with his rifle raised up on his shoulder. "Teddy, down!" Teddy dropped as Alan fired, but Sentrous was gone before the bullet arrived. Alan grabbed Teddy and hugged him. "Thank god you are alive!"

The bullets ripped through the air around them to meet the attackers that were dropping from the trees. Alan turned and ran with Teddy to the bridge. They made it to the swinging span and ran out on it at full speed. Both Sentrous and Caracin flew out into the valley air and swung under the bridge to protect themselves from the gunfire. They flew along underneath the rope span, pacing Alan and Teddy. Sentrous raced ahead, and Caracin stayed behind them.

Karen looked up from her scope. Her sightline was straight down the bridge deck. "Shit! We are going to need to get a better angle." She leapt up and began to run along the cliff face. Kelly was surprised, but he got up and collected the kit and followed her. He was bound by his promise to Alan to stay close to his wife and protect her. She accelerated and leapt, her long legs striding across a chasm that dropped hundreds of feet below her. Her shoes crunched in the damp moss on the jagged rocks. Kelly looked down at the gap and stopped at the edge. "Shit, how did she make that?" He looked across and saw movement in trees high above the cliff top where Karen was heading. "Fuck!" He backed up twenty feet, started running, and sailed across the gap with a holler: "Holy shiiiit!" He landed on the other side and kept running to catch up. Karen had found a spot to set up her rifle. She was focussed on the bridge deck and not the trees above.

Both Caracin and Sentrous flipped up onto the bridge deck ahead and behind Alan and Teddy. All halted; their eyes locked. Alan wheeled up his rifle, but Sentrous grabbed the barrel and bent it. Alan pulled it back and then hit Sentrous on the face with the butt of the rifle, but Sentrous was not fazed. As far as he was concerned, humans without their guns were as powerless as deer. Alan leapt back and made contact with Teddy. They were standing back to back in the middle of bridge, each facing their opponents. Alan pulled out his sidearm and aimed at Sentrous's eyes and fired repeatedly. Sentrous turned and moved side to side as the small bullets bounced off the densely packed quills around his neck. *These things move incredibly fast*, Alan thought as he fired again.

"Teddy, grab my knife!"

Teddy reached round and grabbed his dad's knife from his belt and held it up in front of Caracin, who smiled, exposing his grisly yellow and red-soaked teeth. Teddy lunged to strike at Caracin, who stepped forward to catch the blade in his hand and twist the knife out of Teddy's grip. He backed up a step and tossed the weapon over the cable rail. Caracin raised his claws for the fatal blow, yet his bullet was already on its way, travelling ahead of its own sound wave. The large-calibre sniper round entered Caracin's ear and lodged firmly into the middle of his brain. He shook for a moment, blood pouring from his ears and mouth, then he dropped, tumbling over the rail and down into the rushing water. Karen's aim had been perfect. Sentrous paused for a second to see his companion fall. This shocked him; how could this be?

Alan was running out of ammunition; he aimed carefully, putting a bullet into Sentrous' mouth. The bullet shattered some of his teeth and opened up his cheek. Sentrous howled with pain. Now he attacked.

Through the scope Karen had watched her shot hit Caracin squarely. Now she turned her aim on Sentrous. Her attention fully into the scope glass, she did not notice the spiky female figure standing over her. Sartra's claw gripped Karen's backpack and lifted her from the ground. She twisted around to face Sartra as her teeth extended towards Karen's neck. Karen recognised Sartra immediately as she began to kick and punch. Kelly's bullet tore across the top of Sartra's head, ripping away quills and some black and greenish flesh. Sartra reeled and dropped Karen as Kelly fired again into her shoulder. Staggering for a moment, she leapt up, but another bullet penetrated her shoulder blade. She rolled, disappearing over the cliff side.

Alan and Sentrous were locked in a grapple. As Karen's bullet passed between their faces, Alan looked up the valley at Karen's position as if to say, *Hey, not that close.* Alan yelled, "Teddy, run back to other side!"

"No way!" Teddy leapt across and jumped on Sentrous, the spikes digging into his clothes. The three grappled; Sentrous reeled and Teddy tumbled over the cable rail, clinging to the ropes stays as he hung. Alan jumped to grab his son, and Sentrous struck Alan, digging his claws into his back. Alan dropped to the bridge deck. Sentrous reached down to grab Teddy's wrist as another of Karen's bullets hit Sentrous in his side. He lurched over the rope and began to roll with Teddy flailing below. Alan leapt to grab hold of Sentrous, and all three of them tumbled over into the misty canyon.

Karen screamed as she saw her whole life drop from the suspended bridge into the swirling mist. Sartra hung to a large branch on the face of the cliff about ten feet down; she could use only one arm, but that was all she needed in order to finish this kill. She swung up to another branch close to the cliff top and then looked up. She was face to face with the barrel of Karen's rifle. The muzzle flash blazed with fire and exhaust swirling from the short trip of the bullet. Sartra's body landed on the rocks below.

Both the Salt clan and the Whitelines descended on Kelly and Karen. They had killed the chief of the clan. Kelly fired again and again with Apecs dropping from the tress all around them. Karen fired into the trees above, killing a male sentry. As the creatures rolled down the branches, Karen thought that she would be killed soon. She planned to jump over the cliff before they took her. She noticed the air around her was thumping and swirling. The rotors of the helicopter lifted above the cliff face with the machine guns pointed into the trees. The rolling Gatling gun barrels blazed into the foliage, ripping up both trees and flesh. Karen dove facedown into moss as a storm of lead careened above her. She looked up at the helicopter and noticed the sniper in the helicopter was firing over to the side. She looked over to Kelly to see that a creature was on top of him. Karen swung her rifle around and shot the creature in the side of the neck. It jumped up and leapt towards the trees, but then tumbled, crumpling to the rock and finally rolling onto its back. Kelly's seven-inch hunting knife was sticking straight up out of its sternum. Kelly was lying still as Karen ran over to him. Both his neck and his chest were gashed and gushing blood. He held Karen's hand and pulled her down. "The note is in your pack." His words were weak and garbled with the blood.

Karen rifled through her pack, pulling out the trauma dressings. She pushed the soaker pad deep into Kelly's neck. "Come on, Kelly, don't die on me; I need you…Kelly!" she called out as she squeezed the dressing, but it was too late. Karen wept over Kelly's chest; she had lost everything and everyone.

27 River Lavage

Sentrous popped up in the turmoil of air and water as the three rushed along the river. He swam towards Alan. He grabbed Alan, who spun around. "Oh, it's you!" Alan pulled Sentrous under the water. Sentrous swung at Alan and struck him hard. They struggled, rolling over and over in turbulent rapids. Sentrous slashed and bit, but Alan's vice grip did not relent. Sentrous was running out of air. The icy water poured into his throat, and with a gasp, he fell silent and drifted away as they both swirled towards a plunging drop.

"Dad!" Teddy called out. Alan swam towards him and grabbed him from behind to support him in the rapids. His years of rescue swimming training allowed Alan to keep the two of them stable and steady through the turbulence.

"Teddy, are you all right?"

"Yeah, I'm OK. Are you?"

"Yeah, sure," Alan answered, but he could feel that something was wrong. His chest felt tight and it burned. Unbeknownst to him, Sentrous's claw had penetrated his chest cavity through his back. A small hole, the size of a penny, was letting water and air seep into Alan's pleural space. The hole was letting water seep in, but not escape out, and it flowed slowly into the space between the inside of his chest wall and the membrane that covered his lungs. Alan held his son tightly as they dropped down another set of rapids together. He would not let Teddy go, never again, not for a second.

"Did you get him?" Teddy asked.

"Yeah, he couldn't swim too well," Alan replied.

"Shouldn't we swim for the shore?"

"Not much use right now. We might as well enjoy the ride till we get to the big pool, and then we can get out at the dock."

"Oh yeah, that's a good idea."

"Are you cold?" Alan asked.

"Yeah, a little, but I'm OK. Thanks for coming to get me."

"Of course I was coming to get you."

"This kind of stuff is easy for you, huh?" Teddy asked.

"Easy? No, not easy." Alan coughed some blood as his body tried to compensate for the increasing pressure on his lungs.

Teddy was feeling more relaxed. "Dad?"

"Yeah, Teddy." Alan tried to sound calm.

"Tell me about the time you got the medal."

"Yeah, OK, son." Alan suddenly felt ashamed that he had never found the courage to open up to his son before about this, and now it seemed so easy, so irrelevant. He told Teddy the whole story, from the attack to the bombs falling in the wrong place to the rescue. Teddy listened intently.

"So it wasn't your fault at all—the computer error made the bombs fall in the wrong spot?"

"Yeah, apparently," Alan answered.

"Dad, what was the most amazing thing that you have ever seen or done? I mean, you have been to so many countries and saved hundreds of people. What was the best thing in your life?"

Tears started to flow down Alan's cheeks; they mixed with the green water. "That's easy. I had a little boy, an...and...I got to watch you being born. All the other stuff was a lousy distraction from the real important thing. The search and rescue, the damn war, the monsters, it was all a shitty trick to keep my eyes off the real target. I'm sorry it took me so long to figure it out, Teddy."

Teddy was quiet for a minute as they drifted along. "I love you, Dad." They dropped down the last rapids and into the big pool, but Alan had let Teddy go.

"Dad, where are you?"

Slim pink fingers reached down and grabbed Teddy. The small-framed young lady struggled to haul him up onto the side of a Jet Ski. It was Wendy.

"He was right there a minute ago." Wendy held Teddy as he tried to sit up, but he could barely move. His muscles were stricken with cold. "Go get my dad, please."

Rescue boats searched the river for hours, but Alan was on his way back out to the sea.

28 Beautiful Corona

In big capital letters; *MSRA precautions activated* written in red dry erase marker on the whiteboard. The blue ribbed intubation hose was taped to the side of Kim's mouth, he was heavily sedated because of the chest tube and the pain. The wounds inflicted by the creature were dwarfed by the invading infection that covered his arms and legs. The dressings were covering the massive sores that had grown rapidly in he few days since the battle. Most of the skin on his arms had just melted away.

"The medical team was fully clad in masks and thick rubber gloves when they entered his room.

"Any luck with the cultures?" The doctor asked his colleague.

"MSRA came back negative, maybe its gangrene?" The internist replied.

"Its not gangrene, its gotta be some kind of staff infection."

"What ever it is its killing him." The doctor asked the lab tech for another battery of tests.

One note from Kelly, one from Alan, and a set of small keys. The inventory of envelope was simple, but reading the contents was unbearable. Karen sat in the hospital waiting room and stared at it. Teddy was recovering well and would be released soon. Wendy was at his bedside, holding his hand. Out of their party of fifteen, seven were killed. Kelly's note was short:

> *Alan, Karen, and Teddy, you are my family. I hope that I can help you find peace in the future. Please take care of my boat the Melinda for me. Keep her in good shape.*

Karen read it and bit her lip for a moment. When the swell of emotions had passed, she folded the note and put it back into the envelope. She was not ready to read Alan's yet. She was focussed on getting her boy out of the hospital and safe at home. She had been by to visit Kim Casic's room but he was in isolation for some reason. She had noticed that he was now on a respirator. This seemed odd because his wounds were minor. She though he would have walked out by now.

She stopped one of the doctors "What is Mr. Casic's status?"

"I am sorry but I can't tell you unless you are immediate family, but he is very sick."

Karen noticed the language "Is he sick or injured?" She asked as the doctor realized he had revealed too much.

"I suggested that you ask his mother in the waiting area, she can decide if she wants to share the details with you." The doctor walked away. Karen was surprised, sick meant disease not injuries. She walked by the whiteboard and noticed the message. *MSRA infection* her eyes narrowed. *What the hell?*

Karen strolled by Kim's room again to see two fully gowned nurses changing his dressings. His arms looked as though they had the skin burned away. She looked behind her and then around the corner before she snatched two tissue biopsies from the lab tray outside his room. Kim died that night of septic shock.

Later that day, Karen drove down to her lab. She had a number of APEC tissue specimens from the one body that the army recovered from the scene. The Clan had been quick to collect their dead and disappear. She also had Kim's samples in the portable cooler as she walked into the lab. She began to prepare the first set of samples from the creatures for the long months of DNA sequencing she had planned. Her thoughts kept coming back to Kim Casic's sample. His sores did not look like MRSA infections. What really killed him?

After preparing the slides, she slid it into the scanner. She isolated the coloured circle and stained it. As the magnification increased the star shaped form came into view. "Shit, shit! I should have known; what an idiot I am. This isn't a staff infection, it's not even bacterial!" The tiny dots when magnified under the scanning micrograph revealed their true nature. It was a tiny critter. Light enough to fly across the room if coughed out, and tough enough to stay intact on a bathroom sink for days. It's characteristic star shaped proteins suggested that it may be a retrovirus, but there was no doubt that is was a brand new killer. Karen knew just by the shape of it what she was dealing with. The beautiful little round stars were ordained with purple crowns that twinkled on the big screen.

She ran a sample of Teddy's blood from the hospital, but the spots were not there. She would run an antibody test once she identified the unknown critter.

Sheila, Karen's lab tech, came in and looked at the shape. "I didn't know you were working on the cold virus."

"I'm not." Karen looked up momentarily to see the reaction.

"Oh…uh, well then, what's that….SARS?" she asked.

Karen took the sample and bundled it up. "That's your bad luck. You walked in at the wrong time, girl! Now go and get your bio-suit on and then get your ass down to the secure lab." Karen pushed the red alarm button, and sirens began to wail throughout the building. She picked up the phone. "Quarantine level three. Get the team dressed and clean out my lab immediately. Sheila and I will be in the sanitation facility. I have a priority sample for rush shipment to Aileen Cummings at the ICID lab in Winnipeg."

After twenty-four hours of quarantine and blood tests, a large team had flown in from Winnipeg. They had taken control of all the labs on the floor and set-up a network of showers and sanitation chambers in the halls. The hospital was also quarantined because a nurse and another patient had come down with the deadly virus. Karen and Sheila had been tested and cleared. The bug was a brand new rugged little killer, a retrovirus as deadly as they come. The initial disease comes on like a flesh eating bacterial infection but it is no bacteria, not at first anyways. This bug travels down the neural pathways and explodes into the tissues at the nerve endings. The pain is indescribable; skin and muscle tissues disintegrate causing massive sores opening fissures right down to the bone. The huge festering sores are open invitations for bacteria and the combination of the ravaging viral infection and the bacterial infections makes survival very difficult.

If the patient fights off the bacterial infections without dying of septic shock, then the viral infections suddenly stop and the virus goes dormant hidden deep in the DNA library of the nerves cells. The horrible thing about a retro-virus is that years later, without warning, the nerves cells can express the virus and the disease attacks again.

The experts had control now. Karen went home. She told Teddy to pack his bags and tell his girlfriend that he was going away for a while. Teddy protested vehemently but did as his mother asked. The house sold quickly, and the money was loaded into a suitcase full of US dollars.

The helicopter had stopped the slaughter of the humans. The heavy machine guns had killed three of the Salt clan before they retreated back into the forest. Over the next few nights, the Salt clan had managed to track down and kill most of the Free Clan, but there was no sign of Sentrous. Shaman was now chief, and she called upon all of the clans to retreat far back into the forest and into the subterranean caves. They had had enough of humankind for now.

The mayor of Vancouver called for a mass logging of all the trees on the city perimeter and Stanley Park. The famous wooded park was clear-cut and re-planted with fruit trees and shrubs. The logging companies were offering to clear the whole province of trees, especially the high old-growth forest. This was a heated debate in the legislature.

The *Melinda* cut through the waves as they headed out to Cape Flattery into the stiff south-westerly breeze. Teddy and Karen had provisioned her for at least a couple of months. The winds were cold but steady, and the sea was waiting for them.

THE AUTHOR

Born in Vancouver, Tyler started off at sea in 1986, sailing as a young bosun's mate on a 130' gaff-rigged schooner. After finishing a Neuro-Science degree he returned to the sea. Sailing for more than twenty years in the Canadian Coast Guard as a rescue specialist ship's officer. He lives in Canada with his family and writes during the quiet times when not out on the water.

Made in the USA
San Bernardino, CA
14 May 2016